Foreword

There's a beautiful place in Catalonia called Yapanc.
It has beautiful people bathed in a beautiful light reflected from the beautiful sea and is tranquilo – quiet, fresh and alive.

The local Health Service actually works, the good schools are free to all and there's very little traffic so it is easy to park in the centre of the sleepy neighbouring town called Palafrio. When you shop, you go to Palafrio's markets for your locally caught fresh fish and other produce. Simple, loose and unpackaged food that you carry around in your hand-woven basket feeling relaxed, having spent time talking to your friends and eating breakfast together sitting outside one of the little cafes in the pretty square.

Then you go home refreshed and happy, feeling at one with a simple life built around real genuine people who share that simplicity.

When the sun goes down you can stand on the hill above Yapanc by El Far – The Lighthouse and watch the sun set behind the hills to the west of Palafrio that is spread far below you, feeling at one with the real world.

In my 'home' of Yapanc I have 'Real Life' where less is truly more.

★ ★ ★

There's a place I originally thought was beautiful in Cheshire called Tettenhill.

My friends were the beautiful people but are now forgotten acquaintances, which in fact they always were.

It constantly seemed to be grey and rainy but as I was always working away from 'home', I can't be totally sure, so maybe it was just dismal in my heart and mind.

You would wait days for a doctor's appointment and then see a locum; pay twelve thousand pounds a year for your child to be in the right school for the right 'friends' and always queue in traffic on the A51 at any time of the day. These queues stretched right into the Sainsbury's car park, even when we went in early or late to miss the stampede for processed and over-packaged food, taken away in a host of plastic bags.

It was a frustrating place. Overheating with people who were preoccupied with possessions like cars and TVs. There were always things to do and so it developed into a meaningless drive to nothingness for many individuals and not just me.

So this was not 'Real Life' and therefore many people were not truly happy.

There is also a hill above Tettenhill as in Yapanc. This is reached via a stunningly beautiful footpath through a valley called Dingle Dell where the trees form a natural tunnel as they lean into the sun. If you walked up this trail you reached a window on the west where you could turn and contemplate the same sunset as in Catalonia but behind the distant Welsh Hills. You could feel at one with the world and be a Sun sharer with a loved one in Yapanc – but of course it's England and there's no time to take spiritually uplifting strolls like that.

★   ★   ★

The places in this story don't matter but the people do.

Because people make life, not places, not possessions, not things.

There is no way you can avoid the highs and lows of life but you will see that 'Real Life' needs those lows to make the highs that much higher.

It's all about what you say and do and not what you think or propose to do.

Doing changes mundane and meaningless to a reality that is exciting and important.

You have to remember that it is down to you only and therefore you cannot blame anyone else for the life that you lead.

Someone said to me at work.

"Jack, why are you going to live in Yapanc?"

This was a question said with an incredulous voice and reinforced by a quizzical look, as if Yapanc was at the end of the world.

"Because, I can," and I left it at that.

Acknowledgements

To the real Joseph, this book is dedicated to you. You can now understand that I meant what I said and I did exactly what I told you I would do. I had to leave Mummy and I had to go and write my trilogy in Spain.

I'm so sorry that you temporarily lost your Daddy at nine years old.

I vividly remember sitting on an aeroplane rushing back from Hong Kong to see your Mum in hospital and I was terribly worried about you surviving if born eight weeks too early. Whilst looking out of the scratched plastic window and staring intently at the failing sun, I talked directly to you.

I told you about life and I wished it for you and I told you how you must fight.

So it is no surprise that you have proved yourself over the last two years. How you have showed me that you are spiritually strong and that you are aware of the deeper more important things in life.

Now you will realise that we can go on together far better than before with the past fading to nothing as we have forty-six more years ahead of us.

I will always be there for you and so will Nim because I know he is inside of you waiting to be played out to a greater audience.

Love from Dad, seven times as always. x x x x x x x.

Thank you to my trial readers who gave me encouragement to change the many drafts and the confidence to carry on when all seemed impossible. You were great.

Thank you John, Neal, Lulu, Elizabeth, Kate and especially Franny who never lost faith, when others judged us wrongly from a base of their own immorality.

Jack

Written by
Jack George Edmunson.
March 2008.

Exactly fifty-four years after the day I was born in 1954. Everything I do and say is preparing for my death and rebirth into the Collective in 2054. That is my fate and true path and therefore it cannot be changed.

1

Tettenhill
The beginning of the end

Each day when eight-year-old Jack arrived home from school he would squat in the window ledge of the modern semi-detached's lounge to be as far away as possible from the foot of the stairs and the ghost that haunted his imagination from somewhere above.

He would squint at any remaining sunlight, desperate to see his Mother returning from work as she strode expectantly up the road, anxious to receive a hug from her handsome little boy.

He was too young to be 'a latch key' kid living near Bewdley in Worcestershire but because of his youthful innocence he noticed things in his loneliness that adults would miss, but accepted his thoughts were never to be shared.

Sometimes, he would gather up all of his courage and quickly stamp up those seven stairs, counting upwards from zero until he leapt onto the top landing where he yelled in a panic stricken and tearful voice.

"Go away! Leave me alone whoever you are; you have no right to be in my Mummy's house!"

Was it a fantasy created by the fear of an imaginative little boy or was it the dawning of his awareness that he had a psychic gift? The fear as he felt unloved and alone needing his Mother to praise him about the events of his day at school. The unknown gift pushed to one side like the child who needed the love.

But Nim was always there acting as his spirit guide; trying to protect him at that tender age and of course Nim never went away.

So an invisible Nim listened quietly, no matter how often a trembling Jack screamed whilst facing the closed bedroom doors, terrified in case one should open.

Then Nim would smile as he watched the mature child with the brown hair scramble back down the stairs, jumping the last few to resume his safe window perch and listen to his thumping heart.

Jack had been a sensitive and lonely child troubled by the spirit World and would experience those same feelings of insecurity when he became a man living in Catalonia and searching for his true path.

Only then would he understand the reality that knocked on his door just like his beloved Mother.

Inevitably, forty-one years later Jack George Edmunson was still watched by Nim as he pulled his silver Mercedes into the gravel drive of his home in Tettenhill.

It was a 'Cheshire Brick' cottage with a dark blue front door centralised between windows to create a smiling and symmetrical face that stared at the sun warming its south facing walls. Jack adored the mirrored smile when it regarded the summer across the most colourful cottage garden, complete with a living pond that was an inherent part of the beautiful spot.

But on a Friday evening in the winter, and after a gruelling weekly commute home, he was only watched by Nim who remained silent in Jack's mind, repulsed by those original childhood defences.

Jack stared intently to see if his six-year-old son Joseph was waiting for him, sitting in the front bedroom window, but turned away disappointed as he saw the curtains were drawn.

Jack, listen to me again and start to believe in me.
I still feel those same fears I sensed in 'little' Jack when
I watched over you and they will never disappear
until you find and follow your true path.
It doesn't matter what you look like Centurion.
I know your Karma and will always find you after
every reincarnation.
You don't remember yet but your time has come again
and this will be your last opportunity for eternity.

Jack opened the heavy car door and stood motionless, feeling the light westerly wind on his face carrying a distant voice that he struggled to hear. He wiped his two hands across his nearly bald pate but with his dreamy green eyes he was still handsome as he stretched his arms above him and ignored the voice of his spirit guide.

He looked and thought like a successful businessman.

A small man in a small World who didn't realise that in this Karma he was meant to be a big man in a big World.

Nim was above Jack as he strode purposefully towards the rear entrance of his home, leaving his briefcase, laptop and suitcase in the car boot in his excitement to see his son Jojo. A smiling moon shone above, closely caressed by a few bright white stars.

I know this man who doesn't understand either his
history or his destiny.
Listen to me again Jack; it's been a long time since we
spoke together.
You were born in Catalonia sixteen hundred years
ago and became a proud Roman Legionnaire who
nobly died for his Sun Sharer.
Now you must seek her out again to serve your future
and become my instrument in delivering the
'fifth World'.

Jack stepped into the warm cosy kitchen and looked around for his boy.

The only person he could see was his wife Melanie setting out dinner plates on the cherry table of the conservatory. With her short square body, flat head and highlighted blonde hair she was bustling around the table in brown clothes bought that morning in the DKNY shop in Chester. She didn't even turn to face him as she summarily greeted her husband after his week working away from home.

"You're late! If you are going to shower and change you need to hurry up. Everyone is due in a quarter of an hour. Put the new Prada things on that I've left out on the bed." Jack was confused.

"Hello lovely, don't I get a kiss and a cuddle then?" He walked around the large table and received a quick peck on his left cheek as she brushed past on her way back to the cutlery drawer. He smelt the familiar 'White Linen' perfume that instantly turned on his desire but he was dismissed before he could grab and kiss her lips.

"I can't stop now; I need to get on Jack." He could only plaintively ask about his second emotional thought.

"So where's Joseph?"

"I sent him to bed early so that he didn't get overexcited by the dinner party preparations. I didn't want him late to bed."

"And what about me? What about the importance of seeing his Dad for the first time since last Sunday?"

"Precisely, he would have been overexcited by that as well. You'll see him tomorrow so he won't miss you."

"That's very convenient Melanie. Bundle your son into bed early so that it is easier to prepare things to impress your friends." Jack resented the bad welcome from his wife but more especially no loving hugs from his son.

However she didn't reply and he had no time to dwell on his emotions or argue with her, so he went outside to fetch his bags from the car before getting ready for the dinner party.

Now I understand your circumstances Jack so all you have to do is listen to my story and follow me to relive your past and create your future in Catalonia.

The wind had risen as he opened the car boot and made him shiver through his thin white shirt as he listened to the rustling leaves left on his neighbour's tall beech tree.

He looked up at the myriad of stars in the clear winter sky and then sadly across to his son's bedroom window.

"Night night Jojo, love you lots." Turning back to the cottage with shoulders bent he crunched his way laden with his heavy load that was more emotional than physical.

That Friday evening six friends arrived at the Edmunson cottage expecting the usual convivial dinner.

Including the hosts there were Peter and Bridget Edam, Jean and Martin Shilling and Matt Diamond with his wife Harriet. They were all long-term acquaintances who lived locally and had been collected by Melanie over the previous ten years through meeting the wives at pre-school events.

Melanie had been planning for days to ensure her 'fab' signature dish of vegetarian lasagne was perfect, but no real time had been wasted out of her busy social schedule as the ingredients had arrived via Ocado's home delivery service.

Jack was slightly tipsy when the guests arrived politely late. The need for a drunken stupor was brought on early by another nagging session shortly after the cool welcome home. This time it was about the choice of clothes he wanted to wear after his power shower in the Matki designer cubicle. Always brand names had to be used in the Cheshire set with a cheap Mira never good enough.

"You can't possibly wear that brown belt with those trousers Jack." Melanie expressed her disgust in a very clipped and exacting voice, clicking the 'ack' part of Jack off the top of her palate to emphasise he was doing wrong. Her husband was perplexed; half his clothes weren't even stored in their bedroom so as to make way for all of hers and so he was still choosing.

"Well, I thought my Mulberry shirt, Church boots and Louis Feraud jacket would look nice with this belt?" She stood with her hands on her expensively clothed hips.

"For God's sake man. Are you colour blind? Even Joseph would do better than that."

Her tired partner chipped back. "Okay Melanie, I'd go and ask him but he's asleep."

"Look," she said, "wear a black belt and the Hugo Boss boots with the Prada jacket and you'll look 'fab'."

Jack slunk away to change into exactly as instructed, thinking it was like being dressed as her Barbie Doll but not wanting another fight. They were just clothes after all. He was hoping to keep the peace until bed time to see if he could persuade her to have a quick shag before his bollocks burst with all the pent up semen in them. He quietly went downstairs, to avoid waking Joseph, defeated by his wife for the second time in half an hour. He remembered their first few months together when she was kind and sensitive as he battled with the depression caused by his first wife leaving him for his best friend. Number one had told him on Valentine's night and left him on Good Friday with his two young children waving goodbye through the back window of her car. So Melanie was convenient. Young, slim and willing to have sex many times a day. A shoulder to cry on and a friend for socialising to avoid the loneliness, but he knew it was wrong even then. However, convenience is what most people are happy to accept in a relationship and his lack of courage and her intense desire to snare a rich husband had kept them together.

The new kitchen area looked resplendent with its oak beams and blue painted island unit. The Emma Bridgewater china at twenty-seven pounds a plate sat ready on the exorbitantly priced granite, specially selected and cut in front of Melanie somewhere in the depths of Birmingham. A small sample would never have been good enough for her to choose from and a trip to Italy would have been preferred but Jack could put his foot down in extreme cases. The stone was black but if you looked closely at the right angle you could see random blue eyes stare back at you.

The lump had changed to match her husband's attire and

appeared dressed in black to make her look thinner. She always wore trousers since their marriage although a miniskirt would have looked grotesque.

"I see you have got yourself a beer then. Did you even think about getting a drink for me?"

Jack was admonished for the third time since arriving home and silently hurried to open a bottle of Cloudy Bay Sauvignon Blanc as the door bell chimed.

The first arrivals were Jean and Martin.

"Mister Edmunson!" Jean stepped into the kitchen from the porch and kissed him lightly on the lips whilst staring into his eyes as a deliberate tease. Jean could be summed up in three ways. Wild hair, wild thoughts and wild clothes courtesy of the expensive Morgan shop in Chester.

Just three of Melanie's friends addressed Jack formally. He often wondered why and had vainly concluded that it was to reinforce the physical boundaries whilst giving a sexual tease. 'You are married keep your cock in your pants', but each one of them would always kiss him sexily on the lips or hug him close, pushing their breasts or groin into him as a temptation, a flirt without possibilities but this was only when their husbands couldn't see. This discreet sexual behaviour was used to reinforce their closeted need to feel sexy that is a basic 'Britishness' never shared by those from the Mediterranean countries, who always lived their sexuality rather than hiding it away.

However, one of the friends who called him Mister was Bridget and she was different in Jack's mind. The hug always lingered when she manoeuvred to get ahead or behind her husband on arrival. It was a sensitive touch and was charged with electricity that made them both breathless. Then she would excitedly smile into his eyes reinforcing that theirs was more than a friendship.

Jean pulled away from him with a squeeze to his hip and an outstretched thumb resting lightly on his groin to reveal her husband Martin. He had always hidden behind his wild wife in every way since they were married. He was a typical tax inspector, boring, never leaving the telly in his spare time and never missing a game of televised football especially if it was Man United. Martin and Jean had been introduced to them by Bridget who was a close friend of Jean since their children went to a privileged school together at the Grange. They had always accompanied each other at school functions as they represented the face of poverty in the parents at the expensive school. It was 'the' school where you sent bright children and the not so clever were always found an alternative but with a plausible excuse from their parents. Sometimes it was the child's dyslexic behaviour or their love of rugby or in fact any excuse implying that the school wasn't suitable for their 'thick' child. So the bright Shillings and Edams went to the Grange and their relatively poor parents spent their money on education and did without the rest of the pretentiousness like the Rolexes and Lexus four-wheel drives. The latter were inevitably driven by the non-working mothers, were powder blue in colour and specifically bought for the half mile of 'off-road' lane that reached to their husband's large mortgage with its ten acres and a pony.

As Jean stepped further into the kitchen to be greeted by Melanie, Jack watched her pert bottom swaying to entice him and secretly envied his best friend Peter, assuming he was having a hidden affair with Jean because of their constant and overt flirting, but as Peter constantly quoted, "A secret is only a secret if you tell it nobody." Jack took that as an affront because it even applied to sharing things with his supposed best male friend. He stopped his pondering and took Martin's proffered woollen overcoat.

"Hi Martin, what sort of a week have you had?"

"Oh you know, so so, not bad, you know." The non-assertive answer came back to kill any potential conversation but that was Martin's character. Bland and boring, a typical taxman who was excited by his figures and ecstatic at every budget.

The tall blonde figure of the beautiful Bridget suddenly appeared behind Martin and so Jack quickly pushed the quiet man towards Melanie to concentrate on the lovely Bridget. But he was too late as her husband Peter ran in through the half open door behind them. The rough diamond pushed past his demure wife and asked coarsely.

"Hey Edmunson, how's it hanging mate?"

"Frankly pal, it was great until you turned up." Jack was sincere in his response as he'd only managed a quick cheek to cheek kiss with Bridget before he took all of their coats upstairs to lay them on his much sought after brand name bed from The White Company.

Doctor Matt Diamond and his wife Harriet arrived half an hour later.

He had been called into surgery at the Crewe General Hospital after yet another car smash on the A51.

Short and stocky with thick horn-rimmed glasses, you would place him as boring but Jack got on well with him, sharing his love of sports, fine wines, fast cars and hi-tech gadgets. Jack shook hands warmly.

"How are you Matt?" The consultant smiled and was happy to see his friend again.

"All the better for a glass of red, old chap, and if you want to crack open this fifteen-year-old claret we can relax into some luxury. You know I've had this lying offshore for so many years I thought it had gone into tax exile! Bloody good idea hey Martin?" Matt went over to shake hands with Mister Boring.

"Oh yes, you know, not bad I suppose. Less tax is good yes." Martin sat on the fence with his reply as always. All of the three men laughed together as Matt then moved on to kiss Melanie.

Matt's better half or in fact better eighty per cent had quietly lagged behind her husband as usual.

"Well Soul Shiner, have you had a good week too?" Jack was entranced as he greeted Harriet. She had an air about her that was soulful, and living on a higher plane compared to everyone else in their circle of friends.

"I'm fantastic Jack my poppet but did you see the news about the Pakistani earthquake – wasn't it horrible?" She gave him a wholesome and genuine hug. "And how are you poppet?" She stroked his right arm with her left hand lying gently on his right shoulder.

"I'm always fantastic too," replied Jack "it's just everyone else that's not." She laughed and looked with concern into his dark green eyes to read behind the bravado. She had always considered how hard it must be working away from home and the lack of reality in a hotel without his family to relax with each evening.

"Jack, I bought this fantastic print yesterday by Ray Woodard Fairchild. Have you heard of him? I can only say that the picture looks fantastic in our lounge, it's called Santa Maria Della Salute and is a picture of a church in Venice linked with stories about the Holy Grail. It's so fantastic! You must come down to the house tomorrow and see it poppet."

You never knew how to reply to Harriet, whether it was the painting, the potential visit or the use of her constant and embarrassing endearment towards him but by the time Jack had floated by on her wave of soulfulness, she had moved on to Melanie and was into something else fantastic which became 'fab' in each of Melanie's replies. Harriet herself was fantastic which is why he called her Soul Shiner.

She was a red-headed beauty with streaks of grey hair at forty one. Short to match her husband, she was always happy between bouts of extreme caring. Nothing meant more to her than art and the events in the World. If she saw a tragedy like the tsunami as on the previous Boxing Day, she lived and breathed it through the souls of the victims as if she were there in spirit. That was why everyone loved and respected her because she was genuine and never changed her approach with anyone no matter how badly they treated her.

The smoked salmon starters were consumed with a glass of Moet et Chandon to many 'fantastics', 'fabs', 'so so' and 'not too bads' and the generalities of children, schools and work. These day to day issues were always essential to digest before the main course when polite niceties could give way to more relaxed fun. Melanie's vegetarian lasagne was hefted to the table in its giant Bridgewater dish full of enough pasta to feed the party twice over. The very concept of a signature dish which was renowned far and wide in Cheshire worried Jack. It was a delight but he always asked himself why you can't enjoy your friends for friendship and eat normally rather than trying to out do or in this case out 'sign' everyone invited?

Even the new kitchen looked perfect with no sign of any cooking remaining.

The boys were feeling argumentative after a few glasses of claret and as always the girls seemed happy to drive home, although Peter and Bridget only needed to stagger around the corner.

The first personal salvo came from Melanie and continued the cold welcome home. She felt that she had cleaned up behind Jack since his arrival in 'her house' where he was disturbing her routine.

"Bridget. I don't know about you but sometimes I wonder whether it's just Jack or is it all men? They seem incapable of putting the toilet seat down, don't they?"

"Yeah yeah yeah," Jack intoned. She carried on remorselessly as Bridget remained politely quiet.

"Bridget, is it all men who in the dead of every single night seem to miss the toilet completely and pee on the tiled floor?" Melanie was smiling sadistically but Jack couldn't let that one go.

"Well who put white tiles on the new ensuite floor for goodness sake? It's asking for trouble. At least the carpet used to soak it all up before. Anyway, I'm usually so drunk I have to stagger in and sit on the sodding toilet before I fall over and so it must be your fault for standing on the seat and pretending to be a man." The other boys laughed seeing Melanie as a touch manly in her aggressive ways.

"You must find going to the bog a bit wearing Edmunson," chimed in Peter. "Let's face it at your age you are so incontinent you must go ten times a night." Jack smirked.

"That's not incontinence mate that's cystitis from having too much sex."

"In your 'effing' dreams," said Melanie laughing with her girl friends. Jack tantalised her.

"Well, just think, at least you don't have to put up with me much longer Melanie. Do you realise that statistically speaking I only have sixteen years left to live and you have got thirty-two? That means sixteen more years of hard graft for me and one hundred and ninety two shags." Peter, his straight man, dived in.

"If you are lucky wanker." It didn't matter whether it was him or Jack who used the expletive as they just alternated it randomly with 'tosser' as a friendly greeting. Jack continued drunkenly.

"That means just five more shags when I'm on top. That's sad hey boys! If I'm lucky, Melanie will die first so I can be buried last and have the pleasure of sharing her grave but at least I would be on top forever."

Melanie wasn't laughing as she responded but everyone else thought it was funny.

"Well, Jack I need to change my will and make sure I am cremated then."

The girl boy verbal tennis had barely started. It was the pattern of most nights when they all sat with excess food, booze and the same friends in the dining conservatory next to the new kitchen.

"All men need is a hole to fill," said Jean as an aside to Bridget. Jack overheard and looked over at Bridget and questioned whether she was his Soul Mate, his true love out of the two point eight billion women on the Earth. He couldn't resist Jean's jibe and had to respond.

"Some men have got in touch with their feminine side and are not as insensitive as you make out Jean. Men might need a hole to put their dick into but what they really need is a woman who will pretend that they love their man and appreciate their dick rather than pour scorn on it. A man needs to feel wanted occasionally whereas women need true love all of the time. They want pink clouds and they have a need that only other women can interpret.

That's the emotional difference. But of course I am extremely well in touch with my feminine side."

She leaned back in amazement at his tirade before commenting. "Well that's nice to know Jack. I am almost impressed but why do you feel you are so in touch with it?"

"Well, when I am reincarnated I have told God that I want to come back to Earth as a woman."

"Really?" Jean was amazed and gullible at the same time.

"Yes Jean and then I can spend all day feeling my tits." Jean smiled thinly and put him in his place.

"Trust me that is just your age Jack."

"Oh God Edmunson," Peter slapped the wooden table top "that is so bad but of course you also know there is another symptom of getting old."

"Is that right tosser, what's that then?" Jack was also a good straight man.

"It's when your sperms lose their wiggles wanker."

"Is that right mate? So how do you know that?"

"Well Jack, I tend to find that it makes her less likely to throw up."

A leftover piece of ciabbatta flew from Bridget's hand towards her husband's head as she tossed a comment to go with it.

"That day will never come in our house!" Peter skilfully ducked the flying bread before replying.

"Well, perhaps I will have to make do with anal sex whilst you're asleep then Bridget." She wagged her third finger to admonish him.

"In that case I will start to sleep on my back!"

Jack's flippancy couldn't be stopped by the spectre of Melanie bringing in some original Cartmel sticky toffee pudding brought from Bridget's farm shop earlier that day. As she placed it on the table he said, "Well, you know me boys. I don't want to be controversial, but girls are completely useless at sex without one hundred per cent emotional involvement. On top of that, they are so physically driven by their hormones that all blokes may as well understand the facts of the matter right now."

The boys stared expectantly at Jack as he continued and then glanced uncomfortably at their partners.

"They take one week of their cycle building up to their period, one week building down from the period, one week on the period and that leaves just one week where they are interested in sex. In that one week that they are interested, you have to catch them on that one day that they are voracious and demanding, avoiding the two days that they have a headache and leaving five days you can't have sex because they are 'tired'. Are you with me boys?"

"No Jack," they all responded except Martin who corrected him.

"Four days not five, I think, you know, possibly."

"Right Martin," he carried on "remember in those four days," he glanced at Martin and got a nod back "when they are 'tired', you are bound to be away on business one night and she's bound to be out with the girls on another. That leaves just two days left. On one of them, you have gotten up at five in the morning to go to a systems meeting in Glasgow and then driven a further five hours to get back at eight in the evening and are therefore so knackered you can barely blow your nose never mind blow your woman!"

The boys were all choking back their laughter by now as it was so true in their own lives but behind closed doors and never discussed even with their mates.

"That means you only have one day a month when you can have average sex and one day when it's excellent, that's provided the kids aren't ill!"

"Hah bloody hah!" Melanie wasn't impressed as she spooned out the ice cream and attacked the weakest member of the group.

"It's a bit like your financial periods then Martin isn't it? All action over just two days and pure drudgery in between. You know we could use your expertise to save us some money at the moment. Jack and I have a joint account you know, he puts it in and I take it out."

Thirty all in the verbal tennis match. The spin on the serve was increased by her next comment.

"Or looking at it another way, what is mine is my own and what is his, is mine as well."

Forty thirty to the girls. Jack vainly tried to mitigate the attack.

"I agree wholeheartedly that if I put it in, you keep taking it out and that applies to my dick as well as my money."

Martin always perked up when listening in to any conversation about sex because he only had intercourse three times a year at most.

"I seriously believe you know, that girls dress up for each other and not for other blokes. It's just a competition to keep their man and prove to the other girls at any function that they can retain their hunter gatherer. Just basic animal instincts dressed up to woo and kill. Man is the hunter gatherer and is out there obtaining the money, riding round looking at the other hunters and comparing weapons whilst the woman looks after the cave. Metaphorically, that means we chaps look around at the size and type of our opponent's car. So for example, a sharp dagger is a Golf GTI and a sword is a Jaguar XK."

Matt interrupted. "Well that explains why women drive GTI's and why they keep running into the back of my 'Jag'."

Deuce. As the night passed towards midnight and the 'Taylors' thirty-year-old port was handed around the table the conversation became more extreme, provoked by the host.

"I don't want to be controversial but! I have a theory called 'why men can't listen and why women can't read maps' that's by me of course." Jack slurred as he spoke. "Or men are from Mars and women are from Venus by John Gray, that's not by me, that's by a woman calling himself a man. What the hell did his Mother do to him to make him demean men so much?" The boys nodded sagely without comment as they were confused by the genders thrown at them by the drunk who slurred on. "Quite frankly, we don't need a guide to relationships and communicating with the different species called women, you just get a Cray computer and some coloured lights like in the film 'Close Encounters of the Third Kind'. If you can successfully talk to aliens well then you might have a chance with women. Men and women are different and will always abuse each other through these differences no matter how many women read that frigging book. Women seem to accept it as a comic, joking at their man's expense. If we all buy crap like that and think the book is logical and sane then you would have to conclude that Osama Bin Laden is a great leader of men."

"Maybe he is Jack," suggested Matt, "but believe everything and believe nothing about him when reading a newspaper. They can't even find him now, never mind know what he is thinking. It's all a pile of made up crap regurgitated from one paper to another but usually slipped a couple of days forward. Absolute, unbelievable crap." Matt believed there was a Government conspiracy theory on all major events and that 'the people' never got more than five per cent of the truth, especially from the *Daily Mail* that sold exceedingly well to the ladies of the Cheshire set sat around the table. Morose Matt emptied the fourth bottle of red wine and quietly pondered his supposed truths about 'Al Qaeda' which he read in his daily *Times*.

Martin filled in the gap in the conversation. He had a friend at work, just the one, who sometimes helped him back into 'Real Life' from his constant taxing misery by sharing an odd joke. He butted in whilst staring at Soul Shiner to obtain her reaction.

"Did you see the news yesterday about that dreadful earthquake in Pakistan?" Soul Shiner looked horrified.

"Yes Martin, wasn't it terrible?"

"Awful, Harriet," Martin said in mock revulsion and horror. "You know despite all of that devastation, I hear that IKEA are opening a new store in Islamabad shortly."

"Really? That doesn't seem right," she said innocently.

"Yes, it specialises in flat pak furniture."

All the boys and the boys alone laughed at the racist joke as they belonged to the white county of Cheshire where it was deemed acceptable. Martin was happy with his single borrowed and rehearsed joke and the kudos would satisfy his non-assuming character for the rest of the year. More importantly he had gained 'street cred' from the boys by standing up to the girls but none of them raised any concerns about racism which was endemic in the Cheshire set. Matt was determined to be the funniest though.

"Melanie, I walked into a pet shop in Knutsford the other day and saw a 'fab' parrot with no feet or legs. I said, Jesus what ever happened to you? 'I was born this way, I'm a defective parrot'.

What? You understood me?

'Yes and before you ask I use Mister Wiggly to hang onto the perch'.

Wow, you would be good fun to have as a bit of one-upmanship at dinner parties.

'But sir, I can also speak Spanish and English, am an expert in philosophy, politics and the premier league and would be a great companion rather than an object to show off to your friends.'

Too true parrot and with that I bought him. You know Melanie, I spent weeks talking to that bird until one day when I got home it said to me in its squawky voice.

'I don't know whether I should tell you this but it's about your wife Harriet and the Ocado delivery man.'

What are you talking about parrot? Needless to say, I was shocked Melanie!

'When the delivery man came today your wife greeted him at the door in a sheer black nightie.'"

Matt hesitated and Melanie couldn't resist the stupid question.

"What happened then?"

He continued in a parrot squawk, almost a parrot phrase.

"'Well, the delivery man came into the hall and lifted her nightie and started sucking her nipples.'

Oh no parrot what happened then?

'I've got no idea,' said the parrot 'I got a hard on and fell off the perch.'"

Game set and match to the boys.

"Yes!" Jack and Peter shouted raising their arms in unison. "That was fucking hilarious."

"We need to go I'm afraid Melanie my love." Bridget apologised as they hit one in the morning.

"My Mother is house sitting to make sure the girls don't trash the place in our absence."

Jack asked Peter how he got on with his mother-in-law who lived close and was in their home ten times a day.

"You know Jack, I can't keep her out but I think it causes Bridget more problems than me."

Jack consoled him. "Peter, your mother-in-law in comparison to mine is a positive angel mate."

"You are joking?" Peter looked surprised.

"Of course not. Yours is an angel but I'm not so lucky because my mine is still alive."

Not quite the thing to say at the end of an evening as he knew he would face the wrath of her daughter later.

"Who cares," he thought.

As the dinner party died a natural death, they all felt vindicated in their positions. The girls never took any of it seriously, the boys got seriously drunk and it was only Jack who took everything in and analysed what was said between the different couples.

As they milled around the kitchen he demanded an answer but was ignored because of the impending departures.

"The most important thing in life is to feel emotional about something and not to go through life and avoid any commitment. It doesn't matter about the subject. It can be your wife, following your football team or stuff you might see as boring like stamp collecting. You should never judge people based on your own values, ideals and interests it's just not fair." Jack was on his pet subject, maybe on a high horse, maybe it was the truth. He repeated Peter's often used refrain in a sad drunken tone. "Life's a bitch and then you die or maybe you just marry one."

The odd assembly quickly dispersed to return to their own private battlegrounds whilst Jack's was spilling out into every successive dinner party.

The friends never told their friends the whole truth, leaving drunken Jack to contemplate his own pile of shit over a final glass of red.

★　★　★

Melanie was waiting for him upstairs as the unwitting fly staggered into her trap.

Sitting patiently on the side of the bed, she was still wearing her new DKNY clothes and had not started taking her makeup off. She stood and walked across to him as he entered the creamy coloured satin bedroom.

"Do you fancy a cuddle then?"

It wasn't subtle but as she started to kiss him and undo the buttons on his grey Mulberry shirt his cock became instantly erect. Apart from one guilty and unsatisfying wank he had not had sex for over a week. He didn't fancy her but as Jean had said earlier, men just need a hole to fill. Jack pulled her blouse over her head and fumbled with her bra.

"Let me do that." She took over and her small droopy tits dropped onto her chest.

As he leant forward and started to suck them, he thought the only good thing about them were the large brown nipples which were now erect and requiring delicate licking. He quickly shoved his hand into the crotch of her black trousers and moved it around before sliding it upwards and fumbling for the belt.

"Let me do that." Again she took control and slid her trousers down her chunky muscled legs.

Jack shoved his hand under the lace panties and felt her wet cunt, sliding two fingers deep inside and using his thumb to rub her proud clitoris. Melanie moaned slightly.

"Do you want to do this as well Melanie or should I just carry on my way?"

"God that's 'fab'" and she dragged his face up to hers to shove her tongue into his mouth.

As she swirled her hot tongue around his, she undid his flies and put both hands on his dick. Manipulating it with her left hand by pulling the foreskin gently up and down she used the other to fondle his bollocks. She turned him towards the bed and pushed him back. Pulling down his trousers together with his pants she fed them over his ankles and dropped them on the best Berber before placing both hands on his strong thighs and starting to suck his hot red cock, holding it upright and away from his body to increase his pleasure.

"Jesus." Jack exclaimed in frustration.

It was too long to go without; he needed sex every day now and felt his sexual appetite was as great as in his late teens and early twenties. Melanie stopped sucking as she tasted a tiny leak of spunk. There was no way she would or had ever sucked him off and taken his spunk into her mouth as he came. Jack momentarily thought about that rejection as she pulled off her own pants and sat astride him using her fingers to locate and then shove his cock up her.

"Back off a bit Melanie, I'm nearly coming. It's too risky hey?" Jack worried about babies.

"Does it matter?" she said disingenuously as she started to ride him.

"Of course it does!" Jack panted as he thrust upwards and pulled her arse towards him to feel his prick bump into the top of her vagina and his heavy balls hit the cheeks of her arse as they slapped in a fast rhythm. Melanie was breathing quickly as she reached over to the side table and took out a Durex in an orange packet.

"Put this on, I just need the loo." She dropped the packet on his chest and heaved herself off him to thump away across the floor.

"Fuck," he thought, "every fucking time we make love she has to go to the fucking toilet."

By the time she came back into the bedroom from the white tiled ensuite, he was leaning against the pillows mounted against the headboard but his prick was limp. She started to suck and manipulate him again and it took Jack another five minutes to get his cock erect. He rolled the Durex on whilst she glanced at the alarm clock impatient to go to sleep. Her demeanour reduced some of his stiffness as did putting the 'johnny' on. It didn't boost his manliness as she sat on top of him again and started to move quickly rubbing hard with her pubic hair and clitoris against the base of his dick.

"Hold my arse," she moaned. "Oh God that's 'fab'," and thrust again and again until she shuddered with her orgasm.

Smiling she rolled off him and lay on her back, opening her legs and manipulating his body and mind.

"Come on, your turn now."

Jack pulled himself on top of her and pushed his hard prick inside. She closed her legs and thighs together as he started to thrust up and down and tucked his head into her neck. Bringing his face to hers he stuck his tongue in her mouth and moved it in and out to the rhythm of his cock. Every time they made love now he kept his eyes closed and thought he was kissing Bridget. That's why the orgasm was delayed despite his desperate need to come quickly. It was pure guilt but he climaxed eventually and shuddered, arching his back by pushing both arms straight either side of her head on the pillow. His eyes remained closed and carefully watched by the predatory spider he rolled off and took his prick out. They had long gone past multiple orgasms and keeping his prick inside her to make her feel loved. The animal in both of them was satisfied even if their spirits weren't and so Jack rolled off the bed and went into the ensuite to dump the Durex down the toilet and quickly wash his balls, which were smarting from her acidic juices. Looking into the mirror above the washbasin he stared at himself and felt dirty and used. He washed the outside of his mouth and chin with soap and boiling water as hot as he could bear to avoid little white spots around his mouth in the morning.

The bedside lamps were both already darkened when he closed the ensuite door, flicking the light off with the external switch but still leaving him naked and vulnerable.

He felt his way to his side of the bed in the absolute darkness and jumping in he immediately turned his back to her as they both welcomed their mattress edges as far apart as they could possibly be.

No goodnights were lovingly spoken nor were any gentle kisses exchanged and so they both drifted off to sleep with their personal and unshared thoughts.

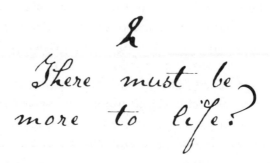

2
There must be more to life?

J ack Edmunson had been a bubbly boy at eight years old who radiated tremendous warmth through his personality and lived every day with an open and enquiring honesty that people loved.

At night in his bed he had two reasons to hide his head under the thin flannelette covers. The most practical was to avoid the biting cold, as few homes had central heating in those days. The second reason, which was much worse than the physical cold, was the dread but freezing fear of someone imagined at the bottom of the bed, waiting to pounce on him.

He always pictured a blue 'U' on his forehead shaped like a horseshoe to protect him from the Evil that threatened to come into his bedroom. He was positive that this would work as his Dad had explained graphically how Dennis Wheatley's heroes had used the symbol in the book 'When the Devil Rides Out' and he trusted his Dad without question.

In the last few minutes before slipping into sleep he would peek out from under the quilted sheets. On the ceiling he could see his Crusader's sword which was also in a safe spiritual blue and created by the outside light slanting in through the gap in the blue curtains. Protected by a magical sword and the power of the 'U' he would keep his head above the covers and in a last sleepy moment he knew he would pass the night without harm, accepting

Nim who stood at the bottom of the bed because that's what eight-year-olds can do.

Now forty-nine years old he remembered those nights as he woke early on the Saturday morning after the party.

He blinked his hangover at the sword on the ceiling, caused by the slight chink of light working its way between the curtains of the cottage in Tettenhill. The village was in a pretty part of Cheshire with his local pub The Pheasant Inn just behind his rear garden and all nestling at the foot of the secret valley called Dingle Dell. It was only six am and he was already alert and unable to relax in the matrimonial bed. A dark mass stirred beside him and settled on her back, emitting a stinking fart at the same time. His wife started to snore loudly through her wide open mouth, irritating him to the core.

"What the fuck am I doing here?" he said inwardly as he slid out of bed and grabbed his dressing gown to go downstairs. As he quietly closed their bedroom door he met Joseph on the landing at the top of the stairs. His blond son, tall for his six years, was standing still and looking guiltily at his Dad for getting up earlier than commanded by the lump. Jack signed for him to remain silent with a single forefinger in front of his lips and the pair crept downstairs to happily and secretly share the early morning alone.

So on that Saturday morning there was a regulation family of three, part of the Cheshire set, living not too far from Tarporley, that is pronounced as 'Tar poor lee' when one moves in the right circles of middle class Cheshire.

After a quick hug and a whispered good morning Joseph sped off to watch TV in the day room, but as always Jack paused by the lounge door in trepidation. He felt someone or something was lurking inside whenever he was at home and when the door had been closed for the night he could always see in his mind an old man sitting on the sofa at the far end of the room.

"Don't be stupid." Jack talked to himself a lot these days, "just go in. Nothing can hurt you."

He fearfully pushed open the door and forced himself to look at the empty sofa. There was never anyone there but as he walked towards it he felt the cold in the centrally heated room and assumed it was because of the large inglenook chimney letting the warm air escape. Quickly, he turned to walk out but he shivered, feeling someone looking at his back as he quickly closed the panelled pine door.

Good morning Jack.
You can see and talk to me if you try.
You have the power and the knowledge but need to
lose your fear of the unknown and embrace your past.
It is your time once again and you know you cannot
deny me.

It was only the previous weekend he had sat with his Mother on the same sofa talking about spiritualism after a family lunch. He couldn't remember why she had brought the subject up but she had been in that very spot. The cottage had been spiritually health checked by dowsing when they had moved in by their new 'friend' from down the road, who successfully practised expensive dowsing, acupuncture and herbal remedies on the rich of the area. The exact place where the imagined man supposedly sat showed a deep trough in the Earth's magnetic field due to the opposing forces of two local ley lines. No matter what magical magnetometer machines were plugged in and left in that place they would not budge the negative energy field, and so it remained, a black stream caused by the rocks deep beneath the cottage or juxtaposition in the invisible magnetic field. The theories about ley lines were endless and all unproven. They reputedly followed straight paths and many cultures around the world also presumed that spirits or ghosts could only travel in a straight direction. This place on the sofa was predicted to affect one's health if sat in for long periods and was therefore studiously avoided by Jack and actively disbelieved by Melanie, although Jet the black cat seemed to lie there all the time.

"Your Grandma George was a spiritualist Jack," Mother shakily got the words out of her mouth. She seemed more fragile every time they saw her and always more forgetful about recent events. Gone were the days of the strong beautiful woman who managed two jobs, the house, her two sons and Dad.

"She used to have a giant poster of a Navajo Indian Chief above her bed and called him her spirit guide."

"A Navajo Indian Man or Nim for short then Mum," replied Jack with an uncomfortable laugh.

He ignorantly believed in spirits, spooks and the afterlife but knew nothing about any of it and until recently had avoided anything to do with it. He felt so worried about the unknown that he could never face watching films about black magic or Evil in case he became possessed. He knew it was stupid believing in Good versus Bad spirits at nearly fifty years old but his mind had started to gravitate towards learning more about this grey area over the last few weeks, as if pushed by an unknown mentor.

Saturday was the in-between day.

In between Friday night when Joseph usually welcomed him home from his working week away and Sunday afternoon by which time Jack felt at home, loved and wanted by his family again; that is until the evening when mentally and physically he prepared for his next week away in a hotel.

Joseph sat on his Dad's lap in a pretty flower-patterned armchair with Jack's arms clutched around him. As Joseph watched a repeat of Blue Peter on the television Jack went through his mental list voiced by Melanie the evening before.

"The kitchen tap won't stop dripping, the seeds I bought need planting, my car needs cleaning, can you go and buy yourself some meat as I don't eat meat and anyway I haven't got time as I have to prepare our food."

The list was never-ending and the tone always relentless.

There was never a please or a thank you. Never a warm cuddle or a light touch to share and dissolve the stress from the week's work. Just a constant me on me deluge of jobs driven by his wife Melanie's agenda. On most weekends he felt like a stranger walking into his own house, the house he paid for and maintained with his hard work. The expected love not being given anymore as she lived life in La La land with her Cheshire set friends doing lunch, coffee, gym, shopping or any equally unproductive thing that cost money whilst putting less effort into any form of work but worse still into maintaining their married life.

She pretended that her values had changed and that their shared marital ethics as a couple who 'worked hard and played hard' were not vital anymore, but she had just got lazy and too comfortable in the one sided relationship and togetherness was now a forgotten trait. Whenever Jack dared to broach this subject of changed values and her lack of action, there was always a reason why something had not been done and the reason was always somebody else's fault.

"Yes, well I know I didn't take that cheque to the bank but your Mother called and the school car park was a nightmare so I lost a lot of time on the way to the gym. Anyway, what does a week matter?"

"It matters a lot Melanie. A five thousand pound cheque matters when it stops our joint account going into the red. It matters that I asked you to do one thing this week whilst I was away and you couldn't be bothered in the five days you had to do it."

Jack always seemed to be pissed off with her and this was increasing every week he returned to Tettenhill as he felt homeless and less loved.

"Well, I may be able take it to the bank on Monday and put myself out for you. It's not my fault that things happen." A lame reply and a symptom of the lack of respect she exhibited more and more when their paths crossed at the weekends. Even these two brief days she deemed hers after her 'hard week' and so Jack was given all the responsibilities for their son so that she could relax. He happily took on the task but didn't enjoy everything to her agenda as he was made to fit into her life as a temporary visitor to be tolerated.

She was losing the respect that he knew was essential to maintain in a good marriage, no matter how difficult it becomes.

Joseph squirmed on his lap and he hugged him tighter. His boy was sensitive and caring with a warm personality that immediately attracted friends in his peers and praise from adults. However, he had part of his personality, a deep place that Jack knew his boy never shared, that aligned him with his father and that worried his Dad because of the strange and consistent pressures that were building inside of him.

Jack's prick got hard thinking about his lack of sex and the poor attempt made the night before and so to cover his embarrassment from his boy he got up to make coffee from his automatic Miele machine. Another waste of money and a further complication in his life but 'names, names, names', always expensive and fashionable brand names ruled their lives. The Miele coffee machine whirred to grind the fresh beans until an error message came up: 'Please clean the main filter.'

"For fuck's sake," he said under his breath so Joseph couldn't hear. "You've had your stupid friends round to talk about curtain fabrics or paint colours, drunk your cappuccinos and can't even be bothered to clean up after yourself, you lazy fucking cow."

Every little thing seemed hard work today, partly because of the Friday night wine but also because of the release of tension after his work. He had spent all week grafting on a big IT project in Rosset, Bedfordshire for putting together a new system for the buyers and he felt good about what he had achieved. He knew he would be contracting there for a year or two and had settled into the routine of being away from home all week and commuting down to Rosset at five in the morning on Mondays and then returning by eight on a Friday evening. Plans had moved on and people were responding to him and so he felt confident in himself.

That was Jack, always responsible and motivated by his achievements.

He took a swig of cool coffee to stir his mind as the machine never made it hot. He sighed as he stared out of the kitchen window at his beloved garden and yearned for the spring.

"I don't know," he sighed loudly again, "am I happy with all of this? Ask a sane man and you may get a realistic and positive response. Ask a fifty-year-old going on forty the same question and you would end up writing a book. Maybe that's what I should do."

"'Fifty is the new forty: bollocks' – the working title of a novel by Jack George Edmunson."

He went into his study and turned on the PC. With a wry smile, he entered into the Google search engine 'Navajo Indians' as he thought he might find out about the non-existent Nim who was watching him from above.

"If Grandma George had Nim as a spirit guide maybe the same one can help me too. Unless he's dead of course!" He laughed at his little joke and so did Nim, who was happy that another step was being taken towards their meeting.

Google always worked but it took ten minutes to get what he needed. He likened it to wanting a drink of water and holding a glass under Niagara Falls. You always got too much and don't have the capacity to handle it. The screen blinked and settled.

'Native Americans believed in the fifth World but we currently inhabit the fourth World which will end at the winter solstice in 2012. The fifth World will arrive following a cycle in nature which affects our Solar system. Our Earth will bear an egg which then moves up within our space to reach its crowning place. Earth will then be raised to its perfected eternal form. This is the point of purification when time actually changes and we must choose between natural time i.e. that we have now on Earth with its opportunity to reach the fifth World and unnatural time which takes us away from nature. You have to choose. The fifth World on our Earth or the oblivion of the alternative removing us from this planet. But ultimately this path to the fifth World will frighten most people as it is the end of now and holds the terror of the unknown.'

You will understand and create the fifth World in your
new life in Catalonia when all will become clear.

"Like my contract job," he thought whilst dismissing words he couldn't quite hear from the TV. "Change is too hard to contemplate for most people at work but even more so at home. Hence the convenience of marriage. You never meet your Soul Mate; you just shack up with someone from the office or a girl you met at school. I suppose that most marriages are convenient and not true love. We are just weak human beings. Animals most of the time, dog eat dog. We want a structure to feel wanted and needed, believing we have a daily part to play as the bigger picture is too scary."

Melanie walked past the door. "Are you on that computer again? You are always on it for hours."

Jack grimaced. "Just doing my accounts lovely. It's my job and makes us money remember; I won't be too long."

He immediately switched to Liverpool Football Club's website until she went back upstairs to flop heavily onto the matrimonial bed, with a thump that reverberated down to the study below.

"So where are you from Nim?" Nim talked back through his Google search on the flickering screen.

We were created in Dinetah when a holy supreme
wind swirled the mists of light into the darkness.
These gave purpose to my holy people who are
supernatural and sacred in the three different lower
Worlds of air, water and Earth.
We lay inside creation and although we can take on
human forms we prefer to reside inside natural forces
creating nature itself.
We were proud to live with each other and we fought

for supremacy until God told us to leave and live in
the fourth World.
The first Man and Woman were formed from the
ears of yellow and white maize and lived separately
not understanding each other's contributions to life
and this allowed monsters to develop that will start
to kill people off through the length and breadth of
the next World.
Eventually man and woman shared their attributes
by joining in physical love and creating new life.
Two hero twins are our saviours, Monster Slayer and
the Child of the Waters and they protect us here in the
fourth World.

Jack was intrigued but scared by a disembodied spirit that didn't exist telling him so much about something he had never heard of and so he wondered if it could be a hidden memory given to him by his Grandmother.

"Tell me more Nim."

We believe in iinaa ji the life or beauty way.

"Almost the same word as energy Nim?" enquired Jack politely.

Yes but this means to live a long life through
happiness and so energy must help this.
It is family orientated, shaping a person for life and a
way of keeping creation and destruction balanced and
in harmony.

"That's why marriage is a convenient structure then. What is your Navajo name Nim?"

Johonaa ei or the sun bearer.
I carry the sun across the sky on my back and store it
in the west every night.

*My power animates principle and purpose that resides
in the sun and gives life to all creation on the Earth.*

"So if you exist where do you live Nim?"

*I live in a Hogan with four posts representing the four
sacred mountains.
The floor is Mother Earth; the dome-like roof is
Father Sky.
We have four sacred objects and four sacred colours
representing your four cardinal directions.
To the east is the white morning sky symbolised by a
white shell.
To the south is blue and turquoise.
To the west is yellow symbolised by Abalone and to the
north is black and the stone you call Jet.
There is a place in the World in which you will soon
live and there are four sacred mountains.
This place you have already seen and you will be
drawn back very shortly.*

"What?" Jack hadn't read that bit. He glanced around him
searching for the voice that seemed to invade his space more often
recently. "What does Navajo mean Nim?"

*It comes from the phrase Tewa Navahu meaning
highly cultivated lands.
We are not an old people on your Earth but we belong
here from the start of creation and lived in many
places in your World.
When the Almighty created this World he was a
formless existence seen as powerful through the sun.
This World is infinite and when you die you will have
a new existence in another part of the Almighty's
Universe, so do not be afraid of life or death Jack as
you have been chosen.*

*Just live every day as if it is the only day and your
best day.*

Jack clicked the shut down button on the screen. He was interested in what he had read, but scared about what he thought he had heard from the fictitious Nim, but decided that the previous night's claret was clouding his brain.

Slumped in a chair next to Joseph, who remained entranced by the TV, he rang his daughter Edima.

She lived near Meaux, east of Paris which was growing into an expensive commuter area for the capital now that the new rail links, including the one to Euro Disney, were up and running. She had always been a handful for Jack but at thirty she seemed to have settled down. The marriage break up to wife number one had affected her more than his eldest son Rodney. A tall slim blonde with eleven GCSEs, she had walked out of her A levels somewhat diverted by her circle of friends and had followed her Dad down to London to train as a physiotherapist. He could never understand and was never close enough to know why this bright slim girl managed to start lap dancing, take cocaine and borrow money from loan sharks to feed the habit. As her Dad left her to move to Manchester on a new contract, she proceeded to fail at her second year exams, lose the plot completely by working in pubs to provide free booze and quickly put on eight stones in weight. Eventually in a mess she had reverted back to her Auntie's home to seek some sanity in her life.

But that was Jack's problem, he was too far away and too detached from his only daughter and always felt guilty about it, using the excuse of being too busy to see or talk to her. The reality was they had drifted apart after the divorce to number one because Jack as usual had thrown himself at his work to be perpetually busy.

Always busy and always trying to be successful to offset the failure of his first marriage and now he was doing the same in his second. When he was busy he didn't think, as thinking was too hard as his memories stretched into a past that he wasn't prepared to discover.

"This wedding, Edima. Are we having roast potatoes on the menu or not? All blokes care about is the food. Not the place, not the hotel reception room or colour of the bridesmaids' dresses or even the music to be played by the DJ. Just the food lovely."

"Dad, stop joking with me," his daughter was smiling at the other end of the line. "Do you really want roasties then?"

"Anything you want lovely" Jack smiled back. "Anything to make it your special day. But I am definitely interested in the seating arrangements, so as to avoid wife number one or wife number one's husband and my ex best friend!" Edima laughed.

"Don't worry, all that mess was years ago, just relax and chill Dad."

"I am always chilled Edima, it's everybody else who isn't. For example, have I ever complained that you are marrying a Frenchman who wears green and pink stripy shirts, eats snails and has a better national football team than England?"

"Dad! You get worse you know. Is it anything to do with your age or is it the battleaxe?"

The wedding was planned to take place in Meaux about two weeks after Jack's fiftieth birthday and although he was dreading it because of a retreat into his old life, he also wanted to be there for his beloved daughter.

"Is that Edima?" Melanie the battleaxe appeared on cue in her misshapen dressing gown hiding a body built of walnuts and ready to split the pink material in half like the Hulk. She always interrupted every telephone conversation and put the handset on loudspeaker or listened in on a spare one. Edima whispered down the telephone avoiding the controlling female at Jack's end.

"Good timing hey but I know it's both. Poor you Dad, fifty and married to that woman." His daughter spat out the word 'that' as Melanie interrupted again.

"Ask her if she can reserve us a 'fab' suite in the hotel for the wedding and get it confirmed in writing and then she can fax it to you at work. Tell her we want a separate but adjoining bedroom for Joseph and not close to the disco so that we can get some sleep. Have you told her that?" Everyone was expected to run after Melanie and cost didn't come into any of her decisions. She was a good organiser and had grown into this demanding style over the last twenty years but not everyone liked the approach, especially Jack who felt like he was six years old rather than fifty on the next weekend.

Melanie shrieked from a few feet behind Jack's ear causing him to wince. "Did you get that Edima?" Jack and Edima sighed together.

"Yes, Dad just say yes to her. Speak soon, love you lots, bye!" A slightly deaf husband turned to face the blancmange oozing into his sacred study.

"Melanie, I'm going for a quick jog, okay?" Jack was preparing to slide past her to sprint up the stairs and put his kit on.

"You need to pop into Chester for me first," came the reply. "I need some food from M and S for tonight."

"What? Why didn't you get it yesterday when you shopped there?"

Jack was annoyed but Melanie remonstrated. "I can't think of everything and anyway it will be fresher today. Whilst you are there you may as well get some nice bread rolls and I also think we have run out of toilet paper." Melanie's list continued without a please or thank you as Jack quickly grabbed his wallet and car keys before peering around the day room corner at his son.

"Joseph, when I get home do you fancy a game of soccer in the garden mate?" Joseph rolled off his bean bag and briefly took his eyes away from the television.

"Please Dad!" He returned his gaze to the TV.

"Okay, so go upstairs, get dressed and read a book and then when I get back in an hour we can play. Okay?" Jack reinforced it by pulling Joseph off the bean bag, turning him over and tickling him before turning the TV off.

"See you soon mate, be ready!" Jack briefly stared at his son who was still slumped on the best Wilton and pledged to spend more time with him before it was too late. Joseph was putting on too much weight, allowed by his Mum to chill rather than play in the garden with his Dad or friends. Jack ruffled his boy's hair and rushed off, leaving Joseph to contemplate whether to turn the TV back on or do as requested. Melanie's strident voice cut short his simplistic childhood thoughts.

"Joseph, get upstairs now! I've told you twice to go for a wash and you also need to tidy your room today as it is Saturday. When your Dad gets back he can do your homework with you," and Melanie carried on ordering the household around.

Joseph was tall for his age with a short Cromwell-style haircut, a mere fifteen pounds a time at Jacob's Finesse, his Mum's hairdresser in Chester. He was an intelligent child and because he understood the game of Mum all week and Dad at weekends he had decided at this early age to push them both to their limits at all times.

"Can I just watch TV a bit longer Mum as Dad said so; it's halfway through the programme about blind dogs?"

"Guide dogs Joseph, for the blind, and the answer is upstairs now!" Melanie growled at her son who slowly raised his body but consoled himself by pressing Sky record for later viewing and the fact that soccer was a good substitute if his Dad got his way. He knew when to acquiesce to his Mum and wandered slowly upstairs.

"Brainless boys Joseph," shrieked Melanie. "Girls are so much easier to handle. My friend Bridget never has these problems and she has four of them."

Brainless boys and clever girls.

You can see it at a very early age and the boys carry on being brainless even as they become men and then old men when they revert to being boys again.

★ ★ ★

35

A rugged face at the front door peered through the glass panels at a still unwashed Joseph, now dressed in his favourite Man United kit and sliding on his bottom down the steep central staircase.

"Nice kit mate. Far better than that rubbish team of your Dad's." Joseph smiled back before shouting towards the kitchen and then turned and ascended the stairs. "It's Peter, Mum."

Peter Edam kicked his muddy boots off at the back door and walked into the pristine blue and oak coloured kitchen. He was everything but pristine but vaguely had the same colour scheme in his clothes. He was always dirty, with his jeans torn on one knee and the top of his three layers looking as if they had been dragged through a field. Even travelling in his old grey diesel car was like sitting on the ground.

He was part-owner of a small family business, the local Edams Garden Centre on the main A51 Chester road. His brother and his wife Bridget ran the farm shop and the retail side of the Garden Centre whilst he concentrated on the production of their plants. Every time he passed the Edmunson cottage at the weekends he would call in for tea or coffee and any spare cake, biscuits or lunch as and when available.

As Jack's best mate he was the person to go for a few beers with at The Pheasant Inn, which was handy for Peter's large cottage adjacent to the Edam greenhouses where Dingle Dell met the River Dee plain.

"Is Edmunson around gorgeous?" Peter was always happy in his life no matter what was thrown at him and beamed her a wide smile.

"He will be shortly," replied Melanie. "I sent him off to do my errands."

"Nothing new there then!" Peter grinned more widely. "Is the kettle on or can I have one of those fancy coffees?" He calculated the time that Jack would be away from home whilst slipping his hand down her back to rest on her bottom which he squeezed enticingly.

"No Peter, we haven't got that amount of time you terrible man and anyway Joseph could walk in." She quickly pecked him on the lips leaving her hand on his strong chest to avoid an inevitable response.

"We can always go into the downstairs loo if you want to and lock the door. You know it's only you who makes a noise Mel."

"I said no! Playing around is okay but playing for keeps is a different matter."

The thought of a marriage break up cooled his ardour and so he chatted to her whilst still openly lusting; looking her up and down and remembering their last sex session.

"How is your marriage me darlin'? Are you still bored by the old moaner when he gets home at weekends or can you muddle through until he clears off again?"

"He is such a perfectionist Peter and even though the house is immaculate, I always feel he needs to complain about some trivial thing to assert that his money and his cleverness provides for me. I can't stand his sanctimonious shit sometimes. Believe me if it wasn't for Joseph I would leave him."

"Jesus Mel. I didn't realise you were that uptight about things. I thought you were just sexually frustrated."

"If only you knew what goes on behind closed doors, if only you knew." As Peter moved closer they heard the back door creak open and he immediately stepped further away.

"Hey tosser! Are you chatting my wife up again?" Jack walked in the rear entrance to see Peter close to his woman. He was jealous even though he didn't love her.

"How are you doing wanker?" Peter replied, grinning at his mate, "how's it hanging?" Melanie walked off disgusted with the pair of them.

"Alright mate, big week, lots achieved. What about you?"

"You know Jack, same shit, different day." Peter never had a brilliant day at work; the success of his days was ruled by the weather.

"Sodding winter pansies have got sodding mildew now. We only make about three pence a plant so we will have to rely on the bedding season to make some money this year." Peter was always optimistic about the next growing season because years of practice meant the weather, plant prices or numbers of customers would cycle up and down and eventually over a few years things went on much the same.

"Mañana – Peter, no worries, that's life, work hard and play hard." Jack supported Peter in everything and vice versa.

"Yes Jack, life's a bitch and then you marry one!" They both giggled like school boys but only because Melanie and Bridget weren't around.

Bridget also ruled the roost like Melanie but in an entirely different way. Peter always did what he wanted, when he wanted and was so self-assertive about his life that he rarely listened to her. So she did the same. She crammed and organised their simple lives into a big cottage with a gorgeous view of the Welsh mountains across the Dee valley. It was full of four teenage girls, the girls' endless stream of friends plus their dogs and cats and a procession of business or Edam family visitors. Their joint world totally revolved around the family and the Garden Centre.

However, Bridget's world centred on the girls and their happiness, not her husband's, and she spent many hours a week ferrying them between music lessons, their friends' houses and the shops when without Peter around she was always happy. Her contentment was in a simple family life and although everything was bought on the cheap nothing was ever disposable. This philosophy was reflected in the shared outlook to life with Peter and had pushed them together as teenagers. A joy of anything to do with nature, a privileged look at the sunrise or sunset whilst barbecuing their tea. Leaning out of the bedroom window in the morning watching the heron take their koi out their pond – until it had taken too many and Peter shot it dead. The carcass swiftly buried to avoid any middle-class neighbours reporting him to the police. He didn't care about the protection of the species but he was worried about losing his unlicensed gun that gave him hours of fun shooting rabbits near the greenhouses. Simple meant caring for the hens running free in the garden so that the pretty blue eggs would be available in the farm shop.

Just simple, non-expensive and down to Earth just like the dirt on their old work clothes – not that they had more than three sets of clothes each because they didn't need anymore.

"Lo there! I saw your cars boys so you can't escape that easily."

Bridget Edam was tall, slim and blonde with rimless glasses and always looked naturally beautiful.

A lot of the shop trade was from Cheshire husbands doing errands for the Cheshire set wives and taking the opportunity to chat her up unsuccessfully. She used her natural beauty to woo the punters; a casual undoing of a top button on her cheap cheesecloth blouse would keep the clients entranced. A sun-reddened chest had large but pert breasts pushing into a cheap unglamorous white bra. Like Peter she never used suntan lotion and because of her white pale complexion, she suffered every summer from a rash of freckles that made her brown under the redness. Peter was the opposite, he was red turning brown from the first week of the English summer and then stayed mahogany for the rest of it. Jack constantly chided him about the dangers of skin cancer to which Peter always replied. "We're only on this Earth once and I'm not going to worry."

Jack disagreed. "Apart from when we go up and down on a plane a few times of course."

"Ah but you can't get sunburned in the stratosphere, wanker."

"Of course you can, tosser."

"No you can't wanker, you would be dead from the lack of oxygen before burning mate."

And that was why they were best mates, always egging each other on and avoiding being serious.

Bridget dragged Peter away as she needed extra bacon for the shop before the rush at lunchtime and the pair sped off to make most of their income for that week.

The Garden Centre farm shop looked after the needs of the Cheshire set and charged three pounds for a specialist Warburton loaf of bread, that still sold like crazy even at this exorbitant price. Bottles of Cloudy Bay Sauvignon Blanc at twenty-seven pounds went within a few days of their arrival, mainly to Melanie who thought it was 'fab', as it was short supplied to keep the brand a 'must have' name since 1990. 'Names, names, names' made Cheshire tick but strangely you would never find Cheshire cheese at a dinner party and so it was never stocked in the farm shop.

Names counted around Tettenhill, for clothes, cars, schools and food and the Edam family used the Garden Centre to manipulate this myopic cachet to great effect thus maximising their profits. Sticky toffee pudding brought in direct from Cartmel in the Lake District as eaten by Madonna and at a mere twelve pounds thank you. Any extra information to improve the sales and edge the profit margin upwards.

After a day of soccer, homework, jogging and car washing the football results took precedence as Joseph and his Dad argued the merits of Jojo's Man United versus his Dad's Liverpool team. The husband and wife went to bed about ten that night with Jack still exhausted from the working week and the late dinner party the night before. After half a bottle of Campo Viejo Rioja he was falling asleep in front of Jonathan Ross on the TV and made the early move. He dumped his clothes on the floor of the bedroom and jumped into bed turning off his sidelight that Melanie had deliberately put on earlier instead of hers. It was always his light that was turned on and never hers as part of a strange mind game that he couldn't work out.

She came into the bedroom from the brightly lit en suite and aggressively demanded, "Why do you always turn your light off?" She turned hers on in a frump and jumped into bed, picking up an old *Hello* magazine to read with a satisfied yawn. Jack had his back to her, his eyes were firmly closed and his teeth were still gritted following the aggression in her voice.

"Why do you always turn my light on? What's the big deal about a fucking light?" He thought this but daren't say it and challenge her when he just wanted a quiet life. After a week away any normal husband would positively demand and do anything to have a shag. In fact most men would want to make love to their wives but his mind was so screwed up by her lack of respect that he couldn't contemplate sex never mind love.

"You need to pick those clothes up and put them away before you go to sleep." She nudged him in the back and so he wearily got out of bed and transferred them to his wardrobe in the spare bedroom, dumping them on the floor behind the oak doors.

After a few minutes he was drifting into sleep when she leaned over him. She was heavy on his right shoulder with her small floppy breast shoved into his back.

"Do you fancy a cuddle then?" She put her hand on his crotch and started to finger him gently. No love all day, no conversation about things that mattered like feelings and thoughts. Just pointless issues raised by her pointless friends as she never thought for herself. He half raised his weary head and glanced at her before lowering it again.

"Why, do you always do that?" he asked. "Every time, you wait until I'm half asleep, you read some crap magazine and then expect me to respond. Every fucking time it's the same." His anger seemed to come to a head much quicker nowadays. Melanie was apologetic but her voice was hard.

"I only thought you would want a cuddle; don't take it out on me. If you don't want one, then I can do without it. I was only thinking of you!"

"You know how untrue that is Melanie. You know it all has to be to your agenda. I'm knackered, you don't care and you don't really want me, you just think it's your duty to try and keep me happy so you can drift on in your life." Jack curled his embryonic body tighter in his anger, seething with the perceived manipulation of it all and knowing he didn't love his wife but without consciously admitting it. Frankly she probably knew and was going through the motions as duly accused. Melanie turned the light off and turned her back on him with a final riposte.

"I wish I had stayed downstairs now, Jonathan Ross was 'fab'."

Jack clenched his teeth tighter, slipped from beneath the duvet, threw his Gant dressing gown on and stormed out of the bedroom door, slamming it shut behind him. As he watched the end of Jonathan Ross and then the late film until one in the morning he felt the enormity of the situation.

A demanding job and a wife whom he had started to hate.

All of it was too much to comprehend and so the remaining

half a bottle of Rioja was drunk before he grudgingly slipped back to the matrimonial bed, taking great care not to wake the snoring lump.

So a typical Saturday in Tettenhill, Cheshire.

Miserable weather, a chat and coffee with your best friends.

A son busy enjoying his own company.

Objectives set by Jack never achieved in sharp contrast to his working week.

The women of the area predominant and clever at using their husbands' money and assertive about their own lifestyles and friends.

All to their agenda.

It was early on Sunday afternoon following the morning chores on a cold and wet February day in 2004. Jack had intended going into the garden that morning just to turn over some of the flower beds and get some frost into the clods of earth to break it up into a fine tilth for the spring. He did go out between showers but just to be outside and away from Melanie and so he made his way out again, leaving his son happily entertained in front of the TV and his wife upstairs on the phone to a girlfriend.

He was always happy outside as a free spirit talking to nature. After three or four half-hearted attempts at turning over the wet soil, he dug in his spade thinking he would have to return indoors and find some other diversionary work when a shooting pain shot up the right side of his back.

"Oh fucking hell," he gasped as he bent forward. "Not a... fucking ...gain." He had constant back problems now and the consultant had told him he would need surgery on his discs worn out from years of jogging.

"Fuck me; this is just fucking old age." He slowly moved to the front door crouched double and wincing at every tottering step. Leaning against the door he pressed the bell. Joseph arrived first.

"What's the matter Dad?" he yelled through a glass panel with his mouth pressed close to it. Jack gasped in pain.

"It's my back again. Get your Mum quick." Melanie slowly walked down the stairs whilst saying goodbye to her friend before handing the phone to Joseph and unlocking the door so he could crawl inside the lobby. She roughly pulled his boots off whilst his legs were half stuck outside to make sure he didn't dirty the carpet.

"Take your jacket off Jack, it's muddy too for goodness sake."

He replied tight lipped, "You could help me then rather than standing with a disapproving look." On all fours a frustrated Jack pulled himself into the lounge watched by a concerned Joseph and collapsed onto the floor demanding painkillers and his TENS machine through clenched teeth.

"I told you not to garden today you silly man." Sympathy didn't come easily to Melanie and in Jack's case ever. "What do you think you were doing? Now you've ruined my plans for you to take Joseph swimming later. I can't believe you did that!" She stood with arms crossed as he lay sprawled on the new Axminster carpet.

Jack lay in agony face down, trying not to throw up due to the pain and calming his breathing to stop the spasms running across his lower back. He might have summoned the energy to tell her to fuck off but Joseph was holding his hand and asking if he was okay.

"Don't worry mate, it will ease off soon. Sorry I won't be able to swim hey?"

"That's okay Dad, Mum can take me."

Melanie left the room. She had no intention of swimming having spent ninety pounds on her new 'fab' hairstyle and colouring for the dinner party on Friday night. On her return she dropped the TENS machine next to his right hand and a packet of Co-codamol generously donated to him in bucket loads by Matt.

"Joseph, you need to do your piano practice now." She dragged her son away and left Jack to sort himself out. As the strained tones of 'Walking in the Air' drifted through to him, Jack felt very alone and unloved. His day was fucked completely now and he could only hope to stabilise the pain so he was ready for the commute to work at Rosset early the next morning.

"Another exciting weekend," he thought "and then a five am start. Fucking great eh!"

Strained, out of tune music continued to waft through the air to him. Peter had a theory and had told him the previous summer. "Children are made to be what their Mums want them to be in Melanie's clique of friends, tosser. To be what they think they should be, rather than what they are. The kids are not allowed to develop and grow into their own persons. Whether they are put through the pain of keyboard, saxophone or swimming etcetera, it's the Mum's choice and not theirs. Let Joseph grow up to be himself Jack."

Lying still, Jack listened to the badly played music and could only agree with Peter's sentiments.

As he was semi-comatose it helped him to think about his life and the others round him. If you looked in through the small panes of the cottage window, he seemed to be talking to someone else in the room who was sitting on the sofa.

"Nim, I can't remember the first time I looked at my wife and thought God I hate you or even I don't want sex with you. Sex has become a burden. Every night I lie in bed with my back to her and when she makes an approach like 'Do you fancy a cuddle?' I know I don't really want her. Then it takes ten minutes of sucking my cock just to get me enthusiastic. That's only because I need sex, I am just an animal, Nim. That's why I know there is something desperately wrong in my life."

Keep talking to me Jack and start to accept the
answers by listening through the ether.
She is not the one you need to fulfil your life and enter
the fifth World.
Open your mind and listen as I am sending guides to
help you understand.

He drifted into a drugged sleep to be woken by Peter staring down at him.

"What the hell are you doing down there?"

Jack lifted his head slightly. "I think God has got a bone to pick with me. Maybe I went too far in my comments about Melanie on

Friday night and this is his punishment." Jack was out of pain now unless he moved of course. He slowly and gently turned over and lay on his back trying to relax and avoid the back spasms which had subsided by using the TENS machine. Peter picked up the Co-codamol packet.

"I noticed you didn't seem to be happy bunnies together."

Jack rolled his eyes. "Two shit nights after you all went, tosser. Same shit, different day and tomorrow back to work for a different sort of shit for five days on the trot." And then he smiled. "But next weekend I am fifty on Saturday, so we are taking Joseph and staying in Dartmouth. A nice hotel by the estuary, a highly recommended gourmet restaurant and hopefully some nice weather."

"That sounds great, wanker, apart from the cost and the fact that having driven hundreds of miles for your work you are going to knacker yourself further by driving twelve hours down to Devon and back."

Jack grunted before his reply. "The problem is Peter, fifty is a big thing to me and things like a bad back make it more of a milestone towards being considered as old. Everyone keeps telling me that fifty is the new forty. What bollocks. But I can't get my head around it. I keep telling myself fifty down and fifty to go."

"In your dreams mate, you'll be lucky to make sixty, wanker." Peter was never supportive and he carried on giving Jack some home truths. "You know what will happen next weekend, as soon as you get to the M6 at Stoke, she'll want the toilet and then again every thirty or forty miles whilst you are driving. How come a woman can hold piss in her bladder for five hours when shopping but as soon as she gets on the motorway with her husband she needs the loo every twenty minutes? Tell me that! But if she was driving and the roles were reversed you would ask her to stop and she would keep passing those service areas until you need to find a bottle and try and fill it crouched in the foot well." They both smiled as it was so true.

Peter perched his dirty jeans on the arm of the pristine gold-coloured armchair and continued. "I noticed Melanie had new clothes on again at dinner, tosser." He was all heart in Jack's time of greatest need and just wanted to exacerbate Melanie's faults for his own perverse reasons.

"Yes. Again is the right word, wanker, she doesn't understand how hard it is to make money and how easy it is to spend it. I wish I had married someone like your Bridget, who never seems to spend anything."

Peter declined to comment as it was all relative. Earn less and spend less but it seems as much. Jack closed his eyes momentarily but it was not because of the pain, instead it was to cover the pang of guilt that crossed his mind about Bridget as he contemplated how much he wanted his best friend's wife. To break the perceived pregnant pause Jack commented as if a third party analyst on 'Match of the Day'.

"The latest DKNY gear bought in Chester of course. DKNY is a short abbreviation describing her husband: Doesn't Know Nothing Yet. The wife in question was heard to comment before the match, I have had these for ages. Ages, meaning more than two weeks having lain hidden in the wardrobe. At the end of the game she went on to say. I saved you one hundred and ten pounds and only spent three hundred and thirty. A true saving then!"

"Well mate," Peter responded. "There is no way I could be married to Melanie; I will just have to stick with shagging her. I only popped in to say I can't come swimming this afternoon. Actually, I'm too tired from shagging your wife this morning. She told me she had got a sore fanny so I had to give her one up the arse instead." They both laughed but it could have been true.

Melanie was doing more homework with Joseph and poked her head around the door. "How long is ten inches in centimetres?"

Peter helped out. "About as long as my willy, Mel. Do you need a hand to measure it or maybe you might need two!" He turned as he left the pretty lounge decked in reds and golds. "See you in a couple of weeks then mate." And he disappeared into the kitchen to chat to Melanie about how 'fab' she looked in her new clothes the other night. Jack heard the clatter of the diesel engine as his old grey Peugeot 507 pulled away.

"Thanks mate. Hope you're better." Jack sighed having

reminded himself how selfish Peter was. Melanie shouted at him but didn't bother coming into the room.

"Did I hear you Jack? Do you need anything?" But she just left him prone on the best carpet from Brintons Limited. 'Names, names, names'.

Jack forced himself upstairs before seven that evening to say goodnight to Joseph as his son made his way slowly to his homage to 'Man U' bedroom, finding lots of distractions from squeezing the whole tube of toothpaste into the washbasin to having a giant poo as every night before bedtime.

Jack lay on the floor of the bathroom trying not to breathe in too deeply whilst watching Joseph sitting on the throne. Through the leaf patterned window they could see the sun setting in the west over the Welsh mountains.

"You see that sun?"

"Yes Dad."

"Well, if I am away from you and you from me just look at the sun okay? When we both look at the sun we share our love for each other no matter where we are. Being a Sun Sharer is so special; just remember that, you may only find one or two people in your life that are Sun Sharers."

Jack loved his son so deeply he was always upset on Sunday nights before the early Monday commute. He questioned the logic of working hard and missing out on the important parts of life but usually contented himself with the fact that eight hundred pounds a day as an IT contractor kept Joseph and Melanie in a nice standard of living, with nice friends, in a nice area. The alternative would be to move house again and he had agreed six years earlier to stay in one place for Joseph's sake but also so that Melanie could be at home with him rather than work. All for little Joseph.

"Dad, who made the sun?" Joseph was wiggling his legs back and forth perched on the toilet and not doing much else.

"Well, that's a very good question and I am not sure anyone can ever answer it even your Dad. The scientists think that when the universe began it was no bigger than a pin head and it suddenly exploded and started to expand and grow so fast it is now billions of miles wide and still growing."

"That's impossible Dad," came the all knowing six-year-old reply.

"Not impossible, just difficult to understand." Jack smiled at Joseph's young naivety.

"But Dad, who made it explode then? Was it Al Qaeda like with the twin towers?" Joseph was mature and clever at six going on eight. He read avariciously and always questioned everything he saw on the TV news.

"No one knows because no one can prove it Jojo. Some people just find it easier to call the person who started it all 'God.' You can't see God so he exists or maybe he doesn't hey? So you could say it was the giant spaghetti eater that started it and no one can ever prove you wrong son."

A thoughtful Joseph started folding toilet paper into strange shapes as he replied, "In that case I think Kai out of my 'Yu Gi Oh' programme was there on the first day and he is the master of the Universe."

"Good, now get off that toilet and please don't use so much paper or you'll block the drains up!"

After a kiss and a cuddle Jack went and lay on his own bed for a last lonely hour of thought before he started to pack his suitcase. Then he struggled downstairs with it, sliding it down the steps to take the strain off his back and awkwardly slung it into the boot of the car that was parked in the garage. He wandered into the day room and saw Melanie was entranced by 'Top Gear' which is why no help had been offered as TV came first. It was always this time that was the worse for him. Saying goodnight to Melanie was harder than with Joseph. He felt so lost in their relationship and she didn't seem to give a damn. She disturbed his equilibrium.

If her week was full and she had Joseph and her friends around her, he felt that she had all she needed. He looked at her sadly, resigned to his fate.

"Night then. I am going to bed." He used to like Sundays when he felt warm and happy with his family and he even enjoyed the 'Top Gear' programme especially when it was more like a car programme rather than light entertainment with an odd car thrown in. Sometimes he would mute the TV and watch the presenter's actions and realised it had all become a bit anal. Ploughing matches, burning or exploding caravans, making cars into boats and generally crashing into things. He wasn't a snob and enjoyed light fun but it was in keeping with seeing more of daily life becoming dumb and dumber. More crap presented in different ways and with far less to seriously think about. It must be my age he thought.

"Are you talking to me Melanie?" Jack was stressed.

"Yes of course but I just love this programme." She deigned to respond properly before adding. "Why can't you get a job like Jeremy Clarkson? He looks about your age and we could use all those 'fab' cars." Jack wasn't sure if she said this in jest or just to twist the knife. Maybe she was just being insensitive but it had been another shit weekend.

"Do you know how hard I work? I am in work at seven in the morning before you even get up and leave at seven at night to go to a grotty hotel with no friends. That is all day, every day and every week." Melanie looked across from the screen towards him.

"Stop complaining Jack, other people's husbands do the same, stop being such a martyr. You never stop to look what you have got."

Jack was incensed. "I have got nothing. I have had nothing for the last four shitty years whilst you gallivant around with your friends wasting my hard earned money. Who do you know who does the same as me?"

"Well, there's John from Preston who you used to work with at BAE."

"Wrong Melanie. He stopped doing that last year and has got himself a job at a fifth of the wage but based locally so that he can see his wife and kids before his marriage fails."

She glanced at him before turning back to 'Top Gear'. "Oh, I didn't know that. What about your friend in Andersen Consulting who lives in Wrexham?"

Jack thought of Ashley before replying. "He works from home now but spends most of his time on a mountain bike in the Welsh hills."

Melanie felt justified. "There you go then, he's in the same industry so why not you as well?"

Sighing deeply a very stressed Jack gave the honest answer. "His wife works. She owns a fashion mail order business and runs it from home. That's the difference, his wife works." He spat the words out at her.

"Well, it's not my fault she's intelligent and not as busy as me. I have to do so much for Joseph you can't believe how busy I am all week."

"Yes," said Jack. "Busy going to the gym for three half days a week. Busy shopping with your friends and doing lunch in the Number Six coffee shop in 'Tar poor lee'. Really fucking busy, not."

He went to storm upstairs in a frump without saying goodnight but the problem with his bad back meant that the body language failed miserably. She just laughed quietly at his slow departure. In bed with the light off he thought more about her.

"She will never change; it's all getting out of hand Nim. Just taking the piss more and pushing me to my limits as she knows I won't do anything about it."

His tiredness replaced his anger and he was soon asleep and didn't wake until the early alarm at five. Creeping out without putting the light on, he quickly shaved downstairs and threw water on his face before grabbing his laptop and briefcase to jump in the car. He had been forbidden to disturb her and so ten minutes after the alarm he was gone and on his way to Rosset.

The small market town straddles the River Beane and sits near the A1 in Hertfordshire. On the left bank are the old dock buildings partly ripped down and rebuilt into new shopping parks, or if alongside the river they had been converted into smart apartments. On the right bank is the castle where King John died and also the heart of the old town with its pretty speciality shops including many full of antiques. This is the heart of the UK's antiques exchange as the town hosted six massive fairs every year at the local World War Two aerodrome. The old town had a pretty church, a wide expanse of cobbled market square and a series of small roads known as gates based on the major compass points similar to those of Chester and Newark on Trent. It must have been fashionable at the time. Rosset of course is an anagram of tosser, which is marginally less rude than an anagram of Newark. At least the local people didn't suggest that the best thing about Rosset was the A1 leading out of it, unlike those in Newark.

As he drove to work, he thought about the anagrams of the town names and how Peter and his mutual greeting of tosser and wanker had started but eventually decided it wasn't linked. He hated Monday mornings and knew by the evening he would collapse in the hotel exhausted and not even bothered about food.

His old silver SLK Mercedes purred along despite over a hundred and fifty thousand miles on the clock. He often thought of painting it with bright orange flowers and yellow smiley faces to buck reality. As usual he was driving with the sun-visor up, blinded by the early morning light as he had persuaded himself that if he could maximise his sunlight he would avoid depression caused by the SAD syndrome. In fact it was Melanie and his lifestyle that were the real cause of him being down all the time.

Watching the fields covered in frost and the sun glinting through the trees, he thought about his dream for 'Real Life' full of nice people without prejudices. Getting a 'Real Life' whatever that meant was his new ambition and the reality was becoming pressing.

"Nim, have you ever thought how boring we are, how many millions of Ford Focuses are on the road. That somehow if metallic they are better because the paint makes all the difference to our personas? How sad is that?" Jack pulled himself up for talking out loud to an imaginary person.

He was sat in a traffic queue thinking about how people are so boring.

"Why accept such non-identity. Surely to God there's something better we can aspire to?"

> *You have to listen to life to aspire.*
> *You have to aspire to life to listen.*
> *You will then assume your true identity.*

He hadn't heard a word.

"Yes Nim, I understand the economics about mass production of cars but for God's sake there must be more to life, somehow and somewhere? It can't just be me thinking this, surely not? There is some intelligent life left on Earth isn't there? We sit here in our queues and accept being nonentities. We accept sitting in a fucking queue with the same car in front as the same fucking car behind. As well as the ones opposite that are going nowhere as well. We are all truly crazy. We have these turgid nondescript cars and then we go and personalise them through a number plate as if it makes difference and that's a sure sign that we have lost the plot."

Jack was tired and in a foul mood. He stopped himself from putting his dry bogies into his top pocket as he drove along, just because he couldn't get to his hankie in his pocket. He used to wipe them on the floor mat until he had new car mats. Wet ones had to be wiped off the back of your finger, dry ones could be flicked off out of the window.

"There are fifteen cars in front of me and nine behind, eight am between Shefford and Rosset on the A507. Thirty miles per hour again. Modern life is pathetic Nim."

He was desperately trying to avoid refuelling as he knew it would waste another ten minutes as everyone went into the next Shell garage to buy their milk, bread, paper, lunch, bag of logs and cup of coffee and precisely everything except fuel.

"Maybe Nim they should have bright orange 'Easy' garages as the place to buy petrol and nothing else. Buy more petrol get a lower price. Buy less and get a higher price. It's got to be good if you are short of time and of course everyone is." His thoughts rambled on as he got more frustrated and built up the adrenaline ready for work. "Fuck me Nim, I'm even talking to you and you don't exist, fucking hell."

He sat at his desk at exactly eight thirty am as per each Monday morning and he was ready to work. But of course he did think back to the weekend, having boiled up his frustrations whilst sat in the car. He was sexually frustrated, frustrated with the heavy traffic when no one could do right and knowing the whole thing would brew through the week until he went home again on Friday evening.

"Well, Nim if you exist. I need to get this off my chest and see what the reaction is or I can't work properly."

At last you recognise I exist Jack.
Believe and listen now.
The time is right and this is not your 'Real Life'.

He quickly tapped the keys on his computer and dialled into his hotmail account. He started to type an email to Melanie.

"I was very upset with your attitude last night and throughout the whole weekend. I don't think I deserve it when I am under enormous pressure and working seventy hours a week away from home.

I had seen my son to bed and then packed which was an emotional time.

I had not achieved any of my jobs all weekend as you dominated my time and set everything to your agenda.

You insist that I creep out on a Monday morning like a leper in my own home.

All weekend, you were demanding things of me but did not check any of my circumstances or respond to my needs.

I had my bad back again which is extremely wearing as it stops my life.

I am fed up of being the only one who tries and puts himself out to make things happen.

You seemed to take affront that I couldn't look after Joseph. At the weekends you want me to take all the responsibilities as you want time off. I see it in the opposite way. I have slaved away all week and then have a lot to do at the weekends for the benefit of you both and need your support so I can make it 'work to live', as opposed to now when it is all, 'live to work.'

It's all you, or you and Joseph, or you and your parents, or your endless chain of friends and you.

You also made it plain this weekend that you are not going back to work...twice. Did I say full time? And you are on holiday for three weeks in the next five and are so totally relaxed that you don't complete anything anymore.

You fill in your day with everything important to you only and not even important within the greater scheme of our lives. You make time to fill in time but never to achieve anything and never anything to help me anymore. So you spend your time enjoying life, keeping fit and playing with your 'fab' rich friends and taking advantage of your privileged position. All the time you are taking the piss, you are demanding more of me and not taking time to get things done.

Anyone can spend money Melanie but not everyone can make it but I do.

So again you have totally lost respect for me, for what I achieve, for what I provide.

Frankly, I don't think you love me anymore, never mind respect me.

So why should I bother? You are taking the piss more often and feel comfortable enough to do so. Why is that?

More than a lack of respect? That's what I am wondering about. Whether you have someone else.

Is it lack of love, being fed up with the same person for twenty years? Bored and wanting someone with different values who is more exciting?

I don't know but I am not going to do everything I do and be as nice as I am and take a load of crap.

I have a life too and at the moment none of it is devoted to me at all. Either you are a partner or tell me why not.

You constantly judge before asking and even when you are totally ignorant about the subject.

You think that everything in life is 'nice'!

Being dynamic and making things happen is as important as being nice. It's just different.

You know it truly is 'dog eat dog' out here but you never get outside of La La land to find out.

You are closeted away in a lifestyle you have created and seem happy at any cost to stay there.

And there was no real communication this weekend.

You live in Melanie World and have forgotten how ninety five per cent of the population truly lives.

Many people are out there grafting to make enough money to pay a mortgage for a crap house and rarely going out and sixty per cent don't even have holidays! That is a fact!

Things we did this weekend are periphery to life itself.

So the important things in life are neglected. These are free and incontrovertible: nature, love and humanity. These are the things you have forgotten exist or at least with me.

I respect you as a Mother, for what you do for the home and my son.

I respect you as an individual and do not tie down what you do or who with as it's your life and you only live once. Unlike Peter and Bridget, you have your own life and lifestyle without restrictions.

You are very, very lucky; they are in a rut and grafting every day so you should consider yourself lucky – because I don't think you do!"

Strangely, the email relieved the pressure and allowed him to get on with being the IT consultancy guru.

End of hotmail. Send.

She rang him that night and said she understood.

She said she didn't realise the stress he was under and how he felt about everything.

She said let's start afresh on Friday when we travel to Dartmouth and use the celebration of his fiftieth with her and Joseph to rethink and restart the relationship.

She said all the right things and Jack got on with his business earning his eight hundred pounds a day and putting it all in their joint account.

The conversation lanced the boil and the work provided the anaesthetic.

The big man, the hunter gatherer, did his job and felt powerful and wanted in his world. His wife had succumbed to his power and apologised so he was the main man again and felt good about that. Good knowing he had the power and the control because what he had made he knew he could take away.

"I am the creator Nim therefore I am the destroyer too. I have to destroy to create, therefore I am."

He was sure there was something Biblical and Armageddon-like about it all but didn't have the time to find out and wasn't ready to pursue the action anyway.

That left one other person to cause him pain during the week and that was his Mother.

Dad had died a year before and she naturally seemed to get closer to Jack immediately afterwards. Mother and her youngest son were very much alike. They looked the same, they thought in the same way and they loved each other, but they never seemed to find time to meet up. In between Jack's work and socialising they had only managed about four weekends together in a year and these had been biased towards the time of death and therefore the time of their joint need. They both missed his Dad when he had gone but Jack felt guilt rather than a loss. He was never close to his parents and was always too busy to get close to them. Frankly he didn't know them well at all. Ever since his days as a latch key kid they had continuously worked. His parents were always busy themselves and when they had retired they found that their son had adopted the same approach to life.

After the death, Jack remembered sitting outside the crematorium high above Leicester. He had wandered away from the pack of loving but rarely seen relatives and was thinking about all the things he had never said to his Dad. He made a mental list to ask his Mum some questions about her life but he never quite remembered to ask.

1. What is your favourite food?
2. What is your favourite song?
3. Do you remember your dead Mum often?
4. What makes you cry?
5. What makes you angry?
6. Do you believe in true love?
7. What is the most important thing in your life?
8. Are you scared of death?
9. What's the best advice you can give me?
10. Tell her you love her.

Number ten was the worst of course because he had never said this to his Dad.

He had never said "I love you Dad" and that made him want to cry because now he never could tell him.

It was Monday night and he was feeling guilty about his lack of contact with Mother as he lay on his hotel bed and so he speed dialled her on his mobile. She had moved out of her house two months earlier and had gone to live with his brother, which was strange because for years she had no time or good words for him. Maybe she said the same things to him and ran Jack down in direct contrast.

She had seemed desperately ill four months ago and looked frail and old for the first time as he and his brother took turns to look after her in her small bungalow. She told them continuously that she was dying. It was as if she wanted to die and had decided to give up now her husband was gone. They both felt hopeless, but as always children have to learn what to do and how to react as their parents get more infirm. She had beaten cancer three times and was a tough person but it seemed like she had given up and her 'bad' sons hadn't noticed. Eventually she became completely deranged and didn't recognise either of them. She would regale them with fictitious stories about having sex on her bed with the visiting doctor and the nurse asking her to be a bridesmaid at her wedding. But no, she wouldn't go there as they all belonged to a religious sect and they had orgies all the time.

Watching her mental pain and anguish tormented Jack.

He felt guilty about his Dad and now his Mum was going to die. However, after a couple of weeks of real food and proper care she pulled round and started to talk more normally. She had advanced dementia and the death of her beloved husband had triggered an early degeneration. In retrospect she had gone downhill since Dad had died and stopped talking to people or eating properly. So she had moved into Jack's brother's house in Leicester and seemed content to sit in a window seat and watch the world go by. Watch the lorries trundle into the factory opposite and never complain when his brother's dog sat by her and constantly farted the deadliest smell imaginable.

"Hi Mum, how are you today?"

"Is that Jack my lovely boy?"

"Yes Mum, how are you feeling?"

"Your brother is on the same tablets as me you know. They're the ones you know, they're... small and plastic and you know they're for your stomach. It's because he eats a lot of takeaways." The non-stop tirade had started and seemed worse at every call.

"His wife's lazy, she's always been lazy so she doesn't bother to cook you know. I haven't been invited to eat there for three years." She said this whilst sat in his brother's lounge.

"I haven't seen that grandson for years... I think. No one bothers with me you know."

"That's because you are so miserable," thought Jack.

"He's walking now and I haven't seen him." She was well looked after and saw her grandson every week but it made no impression now.

Jack tried to calm her down and told her about his last birthday presents and in particular the cost. He said he hoped the coming weekend was going to be more realistic. Many an old adage came out in these conversations.

She said in an old tired voice. "Money was made round to go round." A year later and it would not be said as the Alzheimer's kicked in properly. "Since I've been taking those stomach tablets, I can't taste a thing but Missus F from the Friday club says I should drink some ginger wine. So I have drunk a bottle of it this week and my taste buds are definitely coming back. It's very strong you know."

Jack turned the TV volume up a bit more.

"Really?" he intoned.

"Guess who I've just heard from? I bet you can't guess." She only knew four people in her world but she desperately wanted him to guess.

"Ay it's Tugdual, you know your old pen friend." It was in fact his brother's.

"He's been on holiday you know, in France."

"He is French Mother," as Jack watched the start of 'Spooks', his favourite programme.

"Is there anything else lovey?" Jack was keen to watch the TV.

"He sent me a card, it's a lovely card, it's in an envelope, it's a lovely card."

"Where was he on holiday Mother?" asked Jack.

"Oh I don't know, hang on I'll go and find out."

There was a two minute pause so Jack turned the TV volume back up to normal.

"Urm.... Airberget on de Musee, or something like that. Hello? Hello? Can you hear me?"

"Yes Mother," sighed Jack, "where?"

"Oh Jack, my knee hurts today but I can't get a hip replacement you know. He was with Jean Claude and Antoinette you know."

Jack doubted this as Tugdual had left Antoinette and his four children after deciding he was gay and moved in with the beautiful Jean Claude. Antoinette and he weren't talking anymore after she exacted her revenge by telling him he wasn't the father of any of her children.

"Only in France," he thought.

"You know I'm a lot more settled, I don't think I want to move now."

As if she could. Jack was scared by how quickly she was losing her faculties.

"I'm not having a hip replacement; I couldn't stand it. I don't know why but I've just been to sleep," she was laughing and couldn't stop. "I keep falling asleep," she chuckled on.

"Lucky you," said Jack with great sincerity, feeling absolutely knackered.

"I've been lying down but I need to see the doctor about my hip. It's Joseph's birthday next week isn't it? He's thirty isn't he?"

"No, Mum you are getting confused with my eldest son Rodney and he's twenty-three Mother." Jack sighed more deeply than ever. Mother was changing tack again.

"I haven't heard from him for ages since his last birthday when I sent him some money. I never hear from him unless I give him money. Your brother's not here if that's why you rang? He's changing his job you know. Did you know I might need a new hip?"

Jack had to end the conversation as he felt uncomfortable and then immediately guilty.

"Yes, yes you told me last week and I just spoke to my brother. You were given the telephone by him so don't worry Mother. Bye lovey… love you lots …bye!"

He lay thinking instead of concentrating on the 'Spooks' programme. Mother had given him her neighbours' telephone numbers two years ago in case she had a problem and he couldn't raise her. Once he tried to get through and he found out that she used to leave the telephone off the hook deliberately because she couldn't be bothered to answer it. So Jack rang the two numbers.

The first neighbour said she had not seen Mother for three years and it was because Mother had fallen out with her. Mother's version was different and wrong.

"She's not interested in me; she never invites me round so I don't bother with her."

The second number he rang didn't work because they had gone ex-directory. It showed what a state Mother had got into. No friends, no daily structure, poor diet and no relatives close or loving enough to help her.

A sad indictment on society but an even sadder indictment on her two sons.

On the TV the 'Spooks' story line was too unbelievable so he couldn't concentrate on it. He thought about conversations with Mother and how he should have seen the warning signs, how she would repeat minor things three times within a ten minute conversation.

Whenever Jack spoke to his oldest son Rodney he would joke about his Mother's conversations.

"Rodney, if I start repeating myself like your Grandma take me out and shoot me." After a few minutes chat about their shared love of Liverpool FC he would say, "Rodney, if I start repeating myself like your Grandma take me out and shoot me."

They always laughed at the joke but Jack was serious. He didn't want Rodney to feel guilty about neglecting him too.

Of course the conversations with Mother dragged on. He sometimes pulled himself up with a start as he began to wish that his Mother was dead to get her money and buy a new car to replace the ageing SLK, and then as always he realised the absurdity of it and felt guilty. But he did wonder whether he alone had these thoughts or whether at a specific time in your parents' life you do look at them as a get-out clause, a private bank account.

But she was his Mum and he loved her unconditionally. Despite her dementia she sent Jack a wonderful letter just after his forty-ninth birthday. It was neatly written when she was having a rational day and was headed: LOVE. Jack pencilled in a note on the top of it – Mum's letter at age eighty.

I love your Dad but I don't always agree with him.

I love to be alone but not all the time.

I love beauty; it's always there if you look for it.

I love my family but I found out I cannot live their lives for them.

I love life because I don't want to die.

I have loved my work but never believed I was indispensable. I find I can leave it now for somebody else to do a bit.

Love is difficult to define. It's like breathing, smelling and tasting; it's good and bad all at the same time.

I love each new day as I know it will be different from yesterday.

If I'm not happy or something isn't suiting me, I ask myself what am I going to do about it. If I can't do anything, then I put it to one side as tomorrow is another day.

At the bottom of the letter, Jack had written on it: Believe your Mum, Mums are always right.

The rest of the working week was busy as always with non-stop meetings between eight am and seven pm with odd dinners with his bosses, an hour or two in the hotel catching up on his emails and the constant demands for his views which meant shouldering the client's responsibilities.

He was glad to drive home early that Friday afternoon to collect Melanie and Joseph and head south towards Devon.

Nim finally surfaced on March the fifth, 2004. The day that Jack turned fifty.

The Edmunson family had driven down to Dartmouth on the Friday night and booked in at the Old Quay House Hotel in the centre of the quaint town but still right on the seashore. Melanie had chosen it for its chic décor, reputedly excellent service and the chef Ben Bass winning a Remy Martin prize the year before.

But the hotel was special because it belonged to the rock that kept the estuary at bay with its gardens blending into the shore as if a natural extension to it. A beautiful and spiritual place to greet the midpoint in your life. On the Saturday morning Jack was awake early as always and left Melanie and Joseph asleep in the huge family room with its large Georgian windows and stunning sea views waiting to be revealed when the heavy drapes were pulled back. He went in search of his daily espresso to kick-start him into his birthday weekend but all was quiet within and so he wandered into the garden desperate to find some 'Real Life'.

He stood motionless adjacent to the estuary and leaning with arms outstretched on the granite wall he felt incredibly alive as he breathed in both the beauty and the salty smells wafting through the hidden ozone. Staring down into the still and transparent sea he could see dozens of fish meandering gently between the fronds of seaweed and glints of sun, but between them all was a stranger staring back at him.

A pure reflection, unsullied by clouds, a clarity of person.

He talked to his reflection made from the sun that bounced from his physical form to the flowing water and thence back to his spiritual self.

"So, young man, fifty years down and fifty left to go. What's wrong with being fifty in such a perfect place on a perfect day? Why not put your age into perspective rather than worrying about it? You're not dead yet you old codger." He carried on, emotionally enlightened by everything he sensed in the tranquillity surrounding him.

"You have everything in life a man could want. A cottage in the country, an apartment in Spain if the builders ever finish it. A wife and a dependent loving child, lots of friends and a fantastic social life. You go skiing twice a year and you just need to keep the peace with Melanie and maybe get a girlfriend to have some decent sex."

But you are not happy Jack, you are not happy in the slightest.
You are a lost soul and therefore you have nothing.
You have dreams that you want to become a reality
and you must wake to achieve them.

Jack shivered and pushing back on his forearms he stretched upright, moving his eyes away from his manifestation. You see, it wasn't what he had thought. He had thought: "Nice place, nice food and a possible shag tonight, life can't be too bad."

He stared across the estuary and focused on the rusting hull of a small trawler under repair. Breathing deeply, he looked back over the sea wall and saw nothing now. No reflection and no fish, just seaweed anchored to the dark rocks which limply responded to the turning tide beneath the clear water.

"Shit, what the fuck is going on" he said to the seagulls. Looking around and back towards the hotel he still saw no one.

"I must really have lost the plot now." He quickly swept around in a full circle as he clearly heard the voice again.

No, you haven't lost the plot Jack, you are about to
find it but you must listen and believe.
I'm Nim, your spirit guide for more than a
thousand years.
You don't accept me yet but you must in this Karma.
I am here to help you search for and find your
true path.

The reply came from directly above him this time and as Jack looked skywards he realised the absurdity of his search. But the stunning beauty of the day was suddenly clouded by his irrational fear. He turned and walked purposefully up the worn granite steps to the rear entrance of the hotel, pausing only to look at the garden and seashore from his higher vantage point and verify that there was definitely no one there.

He was puzzled now rather than scared and focused on a small freighter moving past with its load of china clay ready for the processing plant further upstream.

"It was nothing really," he said to himself as he turned to go inside but he looked back again.

"Nothing real." That was the most important part of his weekend.

He was calm but excited back in their bedroom with the brocade curtains pulled back and the bright yellow sunlight streaming in. Jumping onto his son's bed he waited eagerly for his presents. Joseph handed him an orange envelope with a receipt inside for a 'Specialised' mountain bike at eight hundred and seventy pounds.

"Just what I wanted Joseph, thank you so much. Maybe we can go cycling in Delamere forest next weekend. What do you think mate?"

His son was also excited by the thought but not the deed and immediately proffered the small box in gold wrapping that was Melanie's gift. Jack tore the paper apart chided by his wife.

"I could have kept that to save some money Jack." A green Rolex box emerged and inside an Oyster Perpetual shone in the early morning sun.

"You have always said you wanted one you know so I thought why not, it's 'fab', and you deserve it."

"Thank you." Jack flipped open the authenticity certificate and found the receipt for three thousand three hundred and fifty pounds. It was a figure he never forgot.

"It's very beautiful and luxurious Melanie. I won't feel out of place at Cheshire set dinner parties now," he said slowly and deliberately. "How did you buy it?" Jack knew the answer before it was uttered. She got heavily out of bed to go to the loo.

"I used our Visa of course." He gulped silently and took a few steadying breaths before replying.

"Really?"

"Yes of course! I knew you would like it, it will look 'fab' when we go out together."

Jack sat watching Joseph on their balcony who was entranced by the simplicity of the passing boats carrying more constituents to make clay and the raucous swooping seagulls. They shared the sun as it rose higher in the clear spring sky and Jack congratulated himself on how generous he had become in his dotage. He also questioned whether a Rolex was meant to make him or her look good.

A mountain bike that he wanted and a Rolex that he thought was ostentatious and a waste of money.

The Rolex bought to adorn Melanie as a statement to her friends rather than truly for her husband.

He had been given nothing with love and halfway through his life that was the missing emotion.

'Her' weekend with a Rolex, fresh lobster and a famous chef as bragging rights with her friends and his acquaintances rather than a special celebration of half a life reinforcing their love and happiness.

3
Looking back

Two weeks later and they would share another weekend away as it was nearly his daughter's wedding but in the mean time they had to brave another one at home in Tettenhill.

Friday night started badly when Jack arrived home far later than normal at nine in the evening feeling hassled and tired. Melanie coldly welcomed him home.

"Where have you been then? I haven't prepared you any food as you are so late."

Her enquiry had a jealous questioning tone which was a bad way to reconvene. Jack patiently explained.

"The budget had to be ready for Monday so the boss and I stayed on until it was finished or the Board could slaughter us." She never commented on his work and kept her head down reading a magazine.

Jack went and sat next to her to say hello properly but he only received a perfunctory kiss with no eye contact. He stared at the crap TV programme wondering why it was on as she was reading *Cheshire Life*. He tried to engage with his wife.

"Did you have a good day?"

"It was okay." She carried on reading.

He tried again. "What did you do?"

There was a vague reply. "Oh, you know. Gym, Sainsbury's

and then it was time to collect Joseph."

The magazine took precedence and the details about her day were not for him to bother with. She couldn't be bothered to tell him and was equally ambivalent about her husband's life. He sank into his chair and focused on the TV with its 'C' list celebrities living rough on an island and felt the same isolation.

At about eleven they both went upstairs to bed. Jack lay propped up on his pillows waiting for her to finish in the bathroom. A loud fart floated out of the en suite. It wasn't that he was really horny but he was slightly hard in anticipation despite the visions associated with the noise.

She came back into the bedroom with just her pants on and as she went to lower herself into bed Jack grimaced as he surveyed her body.

"So why have you let yourself go then, Melanie?" He couldn't resist it and knew it was rude and therefore he understood the lack of response. Jack looked at his wife as she blew her nose loudly, wobbling the thin pair of old black knickers. The best pairs were reserved for going out with the girls and purposely to make her feel good. He looked again and felt revulsion before turning over and turning his sidelight off. The memory of her oozing out of her body remained in his mind. Her fat restrained in odd places by the muscles put on at the gym three times a week, a living corset.

"Forget it," he thought and presumed sex was off the agenda. No goodnights were said as she lay reading *OK* magazine. He stayed curled up like an embryo and still pointing away from her he quietly asked, "Do you have to read? I am absolutely knackered and there is no way I can sleep with your light on."

"Jack, you always say that and within a few minutes you always fall asleep. I need to relax a little before I can doze off." The same reply given as always to the same question. He sighed towards the wall.

"You have just spent two hours reading downstairs and drunk three glasses of wine so I don't understand your logic about relaxing at all."

He shuffled further down the bed and pulled the duvet closer around his head. Ten minutes later and the inevitable happened. Jack was lightly dozing and shuddered alert as a heavy weight pressed on his right shoulder and pubic hair was rubbed against his arse.

"Do you fancy a cuddle then?" Deliberate and manipulative, Melanie played the game and knew the answer would suit her.

"Fuck off," he moaned in a tired voice.

Saturday morning dawned bright and clear and Jack made an early escape to start washing his car. The salt and grime had completely covered the number plates and rear lights in a black soot-like coating. It was that horrible time of the year when winter seemed endlessly grey in every aspect and the cottage garden was only thinking about bursting into life again but at least it was the first clear sky in weeks.

He washed furiously, working off some of his frustrations and thought about his W.I.F.E.

"With Infinite Fucking Energy" to do anything she wanted.

"Will Ideally Feel Erotic" and give him a blow job.

"When Idle Frequently Expends" and does so constantly.

It was a stupid and silly mind game showing his lack of respect for her.

Mister Wiggly was stiff in his pants as he thought of how much he missed sex in the week. He wanked of course but that seemed to be getting harder to get any pleasure. Now he had to use baby oil for lubrication which helped increase the sensation as his mind flitted across several sexual fantasies from blow jobs to anal sex. Usually he settled on Bridget coming into his study one Saturday morning when everyone else was out and the gentle peck on the cheek became a rancid sex session leaving spunk on his groin but more terrifyingly soiling the new natural and 'in' coir floor to be discovered by his wife.

"Shit." His frustration was worse than ever as he spurted acid onto the wheel trims to get rid of the black brake dust, pumping the trigger hard several times. Peter pulled up in the old Peugeot and walked towards the suddenly guilty Jack.

"Tosser," he called out loudly from the road. "How are you this week?" He was bouncy this morning as he was busy ferrying supplies to the farm shop and didn't have to think too hard but just do it. Peter's happy way of life was just doing and not thinking.

"Hiya wanker. I'm fine. Same shit, different Saturday."

"That's good then if things are so stable mate." Peter always replied positively as he never looked on the pessimistic side of life.

Jack continued as he stood to face his friend. "I was reading Joseph a story this morning about the Famous Five and decided they must really be the Secret Seven but two had got killed whilst climbing into their tree house. What do you think mate?"

"I think you need to make me a Miele coffee and stop thinking about conspiracy theories. You'll be telling me next that Princess Diana is still alive and living on a remote Indian island with her doctor friend, which of course will be the first thing that you and Melanie have agreed on in a whole year!" They laughed at the stupidity of it as they turned towards the house. A few minutes later they sat drinking coffee and eating chocolate biscuits on an old pig bench placed in the garden but on a south-facing wall. It was warm and sheltered on the crisp March day, reminding them that spring wasn't far away. Jack looked skywards.

"You know Peter, all I do is work and when I'm not working well Melanie just bitches to me about what I should be doing. I've got an endless list again this morning. Do you find the same mate?" Peter smiled at Jack.

"You are kidding aren't you? I never have lists off Bridget and she has to ask me loads of times and over many months before she gets things done. You're not assertive about your life Jack. In fact you don't seem to have a life anymore. Where have you gone wrong over the last five years?" Jack didn't know and admitted it.

"I suppose working away hasn't helped. Chasing the money to spend more and all the time on useless fripperies." Peter laughed at his sad friend's predicament. "I suppose now you've got your girlfriend in Rosset you're not wanking as much?"

Jack smiled back. "Only in the mornings."

His best mate queried that. "What do you mean only in the mornings? Is that to just to keep your hand in?" They both laughed together.

"If only I had a girlfriend mate it might make it easier." Jack meant this seriously but Peter took it in jest. Jack continued looking for some answers to his life as a few clouds scudded across the bright sky.

"Melanie's become frumpy, lumpy and dumpy and she can't be arsed to do something about it. I keep telling her to go to the doctors as she might be menopausal but of course she just bites my head off which basically fucking proves it hey!" Peter wouldn't comment as he liked Melanie too much and probably more than Jack if truth be told.

"Maybe she just likes a lot of chocolate Jack. They say it's a substitute for sex you know."

"Very funny, wanker. At least she might lose weight if she had more sex as opposed to putting it on by eating chocolate!"

Peter was only mildly amused, remembering how many times he had shagged his friend's wife.

"Right, back to business mate. These one hundred beech trees to line the edge of your back garden. The price is five hundred and fifty quid and I'll bring them tomorrow okay?" Peter's kind offer had increased by fifty per cent since they had started talking about it back in November. The timing was perfect, any later would be too late to plant the bare root trees that season. So Jack had no option except to take the kind, belated and expensive offer. He did wonder whether his best friend was too clever for him and had deliberately left it so late.

Peter went inside to the toilet and Jack stared at the multiplying clouds again.

"So who do you trust Nim? No one? That is the correct answer. You know the Israelis have had a philosophy since 1967, after their occupation of the Arab territories, which roughly translated means believe only the facts on the ground. Build a fence to keep the bombers out. If someone kills an Israeli, kill two of them in retaliation. It is a prevailing attitude of the Jewish state, as David Ben Gurion said; it doesn't matter what the Gentiles say; what is important is what the Jews do. You could apply that to my life hey?"

Nim was silent considering this was a great philosophy on life, as he had been there in 1967 and seen the hate between the races.

Jack's issue was his lack of trust in anybody anymore and he wondered if it was because he didn't trust himself. In this case because he wanted to fuck his best friend's wife who might be fucking his? Deciding all of this was too complicated for a Saturday morning he stood up, collecting Peter's cup, and started to walk to the back door of the cottage. Turning towards the relieved Peter he smiled. "See you in the morning and I'll bang the trees in before it's too late."

"Whilst watching your bad back you old git!" Peter jumped into the incredibly soiled Peugeot and sped off leaving Jack slightly perplexed about the whole matter and with a bad taste in his mouth.

The postman walked up to Jack, crunching across the pretty pink pebbles outlined by the red brown pavers. Jack had ordered a book on Islam from Amazon.com to meet some missing deep spiritual need and to obtain a view on the current crisis in the Middle East. *Understanding Islam* by Matthew S Gordon was handed over by the postman with a pleasant 'Good morning'.

Jack quickly walked inside his house and, slipping his dirty shoes off in the back hall, he furtively disappeared into the study to start reading the book. Melanie was still in bed and Joseph was playing on his PS2 upstairs so he had a bit of time to himself for a change. Time for his spiritual self and deeper needs to develop.

Time to contact me and start moving down your
true path.
You are wasting too much time Jack, your future in
Spain is calling you.

He started to speed read.

Allah is the term for God in the Quran, the sacred text where his presence is made clear.

'God bears witness that there is no God but He, as do the angels and those possessing knowledge. He acts but with justice.' Nim was with him in the room as he read.

You have hidden knowledge Jack so learn and develop using this research.
Question everything.
Believe nothing.

'The three connections between Muslims and their God are:

The unity of God:
Utterly and inevitably One, unique unto himself.
Believing in the awesome justice of the divine.
Living a pious and attentive life.

Prophecy:
How God offers guidance to the World.
Believe in the prophets and their messages. This includes the Torah of Moses and the Gospel of Jesus.

Muhammad had a special role as the seal of prophecy. He was summoned by the angel Gabriel to go on a miraculous journey from Mecca to Jerusalem on a winged beast and there to lead Adam and Jesus in prayer before he ascended through the seven heavens, visited hell and paradise and alone entered the divine presence.'

"There is no God but God (Allah) and Muhammad is His messenger." 'To convert to Islam you only have to say this and therefore it is traditionally whispered into the ears of a newborn child.'

Jack made a note on a yellow Post-it note to look up the seven heavens on the internet. He constantly read items linked to spiritual improvement utilising the number seven and was becoming obsessive about the number but didn't know why.

Seven is a Good number Jack and fights Evil.
Know the reasons as you will need them in your new
life in Catalonia.

'The return:

The concept of the last days when all God's creations will ultimately return to their divine source after the final judgement when we will all be assessed on our response to the prophetic summons.'

"Well Nim, it doesn't look like I qualify to meet God on any count based on the three principles!"

There was no reply.

"That last bit is like your fourth and fifth Worlds isn't it?"

The imaginary guide was bored and silently sat on the window ledge as he had seen and heard all of this before over many centuries. Jack was happy because of his research into something better than his humdrum routine life. He carried on flicking through the pages.

"So there are many points of similarity with Christian beliefs Nim. The Islamic Temple of the Mount in Jerusalem sits above the Temple of Solomon and is the core of the conflict between Muslim Palestinians and Jews. No wonder they can't agree on anything."

A few years earlier he and Melanie had visited Jerusalem two days after President Rabin had been assassinated. There had been a genuine time of reconciliation between the Jewish and Muslim communities. The 'people' wanted to bring some peace to their world which was in turmoil yet again. Rabin's assassination had seemed to be a catalyst for peace over a few brief weeks of mourning before it all fell apart, leaving his legacy in religious tatters. A battle of rights looking back at history instead of positively looking forward to a shared future.

They had visited the cemetery three days after the burial and stood in silence with hundreds of others at two in the morning, staring at the tens of thousands of candles that adorned Rabin's grave. Jack could feel the spirituality in people that night. He could see their pain without looking at their faces and hear the emotion in their hearts. He had thought deeply, standing in that flickering candlelight.

"If only the world could capture the essence of this energy and use it to rebuild the relationships between countries, forcing the politicians to agree rather than posture in their power and avoid listening to their people."

The street corners in all the towns had youngsters standing around their own candle-lit shrines with their hopeful thoughts for a better future. Now they were older of course and still awaiting the leadership from their leaders who were immersed in their political battles.

"What is this terrible conflict we have in our leaders Nim? The power and corruption, the democracy that is not real and the free press that tells lies which are then amplified and reinvented in other newspapers during the week? Just regurgitated tripe." Nim happily listened to Jack now as he had started to understand principles on his true path.

They had also visited Solomon's Temple and as they stood opposite the Wailing Wall an orthodox Jew walked up to the couple. He placed a kindly hand on Jack's shoulder.

"Come with me my friend, I will give you paper and a pencil to write your message and place it in the cracks of the wall as per tradition."

Jack walked behind the sincere man dressed in black religious-looking robes and ducked into a small cave at right angles to the wall. As he became used to the dim light he noticed his sincere friend's companion move his chair and station his legs across the entrance as if to block Jack's exit.

"Your pen and paper my son." They were duly handed him. "And my friend, would you like to give fifty dollars to the poor and needy that we help in the City every day?"

The Jew moved closer to Jack and seemed to threaten now instead of help.

"Not really," said Jack as he turned and lightly jumped over the outstretched legs and walked into the light and towards the wall. On the paper he neatly wrote: Trust no one except your God. He thrust it into a crack as he crossed himself and turned to guide Melanie across the wooden bridge and past the machine gun toting guards and into the area on top of the Temple and immediately behind the wall.

This was the Muslim area with virtually no visitors at that time of strife. It was reflective, genuine and only disturbed by the pleasant and happy laughter of four Arab boys playing football.

Jerusalem was a trip worth making but only to make it obvious that the route to crucifixion and the birthplace in Bethlehem were so absorbed into the political and material worlds that the truth had died somewhere a long time ago.

Jack skimmed through the book, a reflection on how he wanted to cram as much knowledge into as little time as possible.

> *The opening of the Quran:*
> *'In the name of God, the Merciful the Compassionate.*
> *Praise be to God, the Lord of all being.*
> *The Merciful, the Compassionate.*
> *Master of the Day of Judgement.*
> *It is You alone we serve,*
> *It is only from You that we seek aid.*
> *Guide us on the straight path.*
> *The path of those whom You have blessed.*
> *Not of those with whom You are displeased,*
> *Nor of those who go astray.'*

"A powerful religion but I don't believe in God, so it's just words isn't it Nim?" He paused his reading and swung backwards in his chair hesitating in his beliefs and receiving no reply before carrying on.

'Islam means submission and reflects a Muslim's decision to submit to the divine will and to its consequence which is peace.' He blew out a despairing breath.

"So why Nim is there no peace and everywhere people are in conflict with each other. Explain why? See you don't exist as you have not replied to me."

*Listen and learn and remember when you fought and
why you fought Centurion.
You believed in Zeus and Jesus without
questioning either.
You just believed and they gave you the will to live.*

Jack shifted uncomfortably feeling someone near.

'God is served by a host of angels, mysterious beings known as jinn, from which we get genie.'

"So does that mean all angels are like you, Nim the jinn and you all have to obey us humans?"

*We obey a higher power but it is you I am interested
in helping Jack.*

Jack heard nothing except the sigh of the wind through the bare cherry tree branches outside the study window.

He carefully hid the book high on the bookcase so that Melanie couldn't see it and pour scorn on him for being intelligent or spiritual. He sat and considered.

"How does a seemingly peaceful religion like Islam create the hate for people to be permanently at war with the 'West' almost like the new Crusades? Islam versus Christianity?" He felt the book would help him understand the turgid and biased TV coverage on the 'Beeb' although no one seemed to object to the programmes.

"Maybe, it's the Christians who are bigoted and can't see that a religion practised daily by millions can still give an individual a spiritual structure to their life. That's probably true. We are intent on avoiding religion and the bureaucracies of Churches and can't even practise basic goodwill in life but others live and breathe it and can practise their religion at any time and in any place. One thing is definite; thirty nine billion pounds worth of oil rights given to US oil companies in Iraq might well explain how power and money started the latest Iraq war rather than seeing it as a crusade against the infidels.

Power, money and sex Nim. The deadly trio. Three things that inevitably rule the World."

Jack stopped thinking and left his spiritual sanctuary to go and cuddle his son for some 'Real Life' and real love on a Saturday morning. Joseph was all love and all religions combined, too young to be corrupted by the deadly trio. Jack smiled at the innocence of a six-year-old and the unflinching one hundred per cent trust that children have in their parents who can create a new individual as a ray of hope in the over-complicated and material world.

The rest of the day was spent on the boring and turgid chores leaving behind his life on a higher plane.

Melanie and Jack sat in front of the Saturday night rubbish on TV. They were reasonably sober, not too tired and on normal speaking terms for the first time in two months.

"Melanie," Jack whined slightly, "can I get my porn video out from last year and watch it with you darling?" Mellow Melanie politely declined.

"Please can I? You know it turns me on."

"If you must but don't expect me to enjoy it!" came the slightly disgusted reply. But it was a good time to ask as she was at that one day in her cycle when she was gagging for sex, providing he didn't screw things up by arguing. The video duly rolled. He glanced at his wife who still had her head in her magazine. In the first scene the girl led the horse across to the stable and started to groom it, watched by a hidden man who just happened to have his shirt off already as it was hot stacking hay in the barn. Feeling like a piss, she languidly pulled up her skirt revealing no pants and a shaved crotch. Fondling herself in ecstasy with her eyes closed, she pissed for what seemed ages to Jack whilst Melanie continued to glance at the magazine but occasionally at the TV. Meanwhile, the man started to play with himself at the thought of shagging the girl and accidentally making a noise in his hiding place he got caught out and somehow starts to kiss and fondle her all in a couple of minutes. Melanie's magazine continued to be the focus of her attention as Jack put his hand on her crotch.

"I don't know how you can watch this crap Jack," but she had been glancing at it more frequently and was thinking of sex now.

As the man licked the girl's cunt and slid his prick into her, Melanie started to slide her hand inside Jack's jeans and fondle Mister Wiggly. Jack was transfixed by the video as the girl moaned with the man sliding his prick into her arse. White juices dripped down the actress's thighs as Melanie started to suck Mister Wiggly and Jack imagined fucking Melanie's arse. He had started fingering it a few months ago and by pushing his fingers from the inside of her arse and cunt at the rear he had found a spot that really turned her on. As the girl sucked the man's cock there was the inevitable finale of his spunk spurting into her mouth as Jack pulled Melanie to her feet to push her upstairs to their bedroom.

They were both ready for sex now and as they tongued each other, he slid her pants down and roughly shoved himself up her. Twisting her onto her hands and knees he rubbed her clitoris with his right hand and thrust his prick deep inside again. Melanie was hot and wet, positively ovulating all over him. At one point she groaned and he felt hot juices spurt inside her and warm the length of his prick, with the juices being sucked out and still warm dripping onto his bollocks. Jack reached into the side table drawer and pulled out some KY jelly normally used with the rabbit vibrator that was popular with the Cheshire set. He put some cold gel on his left forefinger and as he manipulated her clitoris and bumped his prick against the top of her vagina he gently eased his finger into her arse and pressed against the head of his hot prick.

"Jesus wept Jack that is so good." Melanie was ecstatic for the first time in months grinding on him so hard it turned Jack on even more and made him bigger. "Put Mister Wiggly in it if you want but be gentle." He slopped more KY jelly onto his hot prick as he shoved four fingers into her blood-engorged cunt. Slowly, he eased the head of his cock past her sphincter as she gasped but after that point he shoved it in harder and felt it with his fingers from inside of her. Whatever it did to Melanie, she was totally entranced; gasping and pushing back harder and exciting Jack to his limits. One final gasp and almighty thrust brought deep throated shouts of "shit oh shit" from both of them as they orgasmed together for the first time that year. Jack eased out and lay on his back with Melanie quickly straddling him. Smiling, she wiped his cock with the bed sheet before using her hand to slide him inside of her. She started to thrust her pubic hair hard onto his groin and he pinched her nipples before pushing her arse on to him with both hands that made her convulse again and again as she orgasmed for the second time. Collapsing satisfied onto his hairy chest she half complained.

"My knees are hurting terribly and that's all your fault big boy. That was 'fab'," and she slid heavily off to the side allowing Jack to go to the en suite to wash his still large cock, vaguely wondering about germs and arseholes.

"Goodnight." Jack felt happy and stopped worrying for once.

"Goodnight." Melanie was satiated and they turned their side lamps off in unison.

A dull night with no arguments but it had culminated in good, happy and erotic sex.

The next morning she amicably turned towards him as he got out of bed.

"Jack, do you realise that at fifty you have become a nymphomaniac just like that previous girlfriend you use to brag about?"

"Too true and long may it continue, fifty down and fifty to go and I mean that. Just think of how many people will die in Britain today. Do you know the answer Melanie? Is it tens, hundreds or thousands?" He had dressed quickly as he talked and was leaving the bedroom but turned to look at her. She was ugly and fat and identified with nothing he wanted to achieve in his life. She was the antithesis of everything he spiritually required. "It's not a rehearsal you know, you need to make the most of it."

"That's too serious for a Sunday morning," she replied without any argument, "but I suppose that's you."

She turned over contentedly to go back to sleep, emitting a large fart as he left the room.

About an hour later, Bridget pulled up outside with an open topped pick-up full of beech trees. She sounded her horn demanding his attention.

Jack quickly walked outside to be ahead of Melanie and strode up to Bridget to kiss her right cheek. She was radiant and interested in him, exuding sexual tension behind the wide and constant smile.

"Lo there Jack. Where do you want them my love?" She smiled more widely.

"Wherever you can meet me during the week Bridget."

"Really, Jack Edmunson. I expect you would run a mile wouldn't you?" She was definitely interested and so he pushed his luck.

"Well, maybe you could text me this week to tell me if you can get away with a secret meeting then? What do you think?" It was at that point, with that question, that their affair started.

"Well, maybe I will think about that and maybe I will or maybe I won't my love!" She laughed at him and shook her head backwards with her long natural blondeness glinting in the sun and taking his breath away. It compared to the multi-coloured, multi-layered and man-made coiffure of Melanie who now belatedly arrived. He stared at her and compared his dull wife to Bridget.

"It must be peer group pressure that makes her do that with her hair." That's where Bridget was different as she always did what she wanted and had no inclination to copy her friends and compete in anyway. He loved her assertiveness about leading a simple life as much as he loved her hair, smile and conversation. He was still standing close to her and he breathed in deeply, sucking in her natural essence.

Jack was happy to see Bridget but wanted to be alone with

her. He pushed aside his reverie and started unloading the overly expensive beech.

Joseph and his Father walked to the edge of their large garden where the three foot tall beech stems sat in a peripheral sequence ready to be dropped into the newly dug holes. In the distance they could see the Edam greenhouses sparkling through some blue wood smoke curling up from the red bricked stack of The Pheasant Inn. It was a beautiful setting. Last summer they had sat with the Edams downwind of a badger's sett just a few hundred yards away from where they now stood, and as the sun fell behind the distant hills, they watched entranced as two badgers emerged to eat the ears of corn they had left near their hole. Snuffling around and looking up for any predators they toured around the sett giving a few minutes' joy to those watching before purposefully setting off on their lonely evening pathways.

They had all been sitting on a blanket drinking Rioja, bathed in the red light of the setting sun as Jack remarked to Peter. "That was so good. It was better than sailing, sex, football and beer."

"Have you got your priorities in order mate?" Peter needed to get this straight. "Surely you mean football, beer and sex only and in that order!" He laughed with Jack.

"No," responded his mate, "I really believe watching badgers in the setting sun is better than anything else and is far more spiritual." Bridget had leant across and patted him twice on his heart.

"You know Jack, that is a beautiful thing to say and I agree wholeheartedly."

But that was when life was more stable and as the winter's day closed in on the boys they finished the planting and wearily trooped back to the house under a grey and dreary sky. His Dad tightly clutched his little boy's hand.

"Joseph, I always said to your brother and sister 'work hard and play hard' because that will help you have a lovely life. So remember that after today my boy." Joseph looked at his Dad with love.

"Work hard and play hard," he repeated as Jack put his arm round his shoulders and they walked step by muddy step back to the welcoming cottage with its yellowed lights turned on to beat the gloom.

Melanie watched her husband and her beloved son from the bedroom window of the pretty cottage and smiled sadly as she spoke on the phone to her best friend Harriet.

"Yes Jack is still away during the week but that makes life easier now."

"Are things more difficult Melanie? I thought everything had settled down after Joseph had started school? You said you enjoyed the extra time to yourself."

"I did and of course I do. You know how it feels as you always encourage me to meet you for lunch! The problem is Jack who seems to resent me having that spare time and keeps leaving me jobs to do that I have no interest in."

Harriet sighed down the telephone, recalling her husband Matt's instructions that morning to clean her car. "What sort of jobs?"

"Man jobs Harriet. Checking the oil level of my car when I haven't got a clue what to do. Or power jetting the flagstones outside even if it's raining."

Harriet laughed loudly. "Tell me about it! But that's men for you my friend."

"True but Jack seems so vindictive about it as if he is taking the stress from his job and insisting on my sharing it. He is such a moaner Harriet and I believe it's because he's ten years older than me. He is always complaining and always moaning which drives me mad."

Harriet was thoughtful in her reply. "So why did you marry him if age is such an issue for you?"

"Come off it Harriet. You know why. A nice lifestyle, money to burn and occasional sex."

Harriet was shocked. "You aren't serious are you?"

"Of course not. Anyway darling, I have got to go as the boys are coming in now. Speak soon. Bye!"

Harriet replaced her handset on the cradle and walked into her conservatory to stare at the giant cedars in her garden. She was thinking about Jack. She liked him a lot and felt sorry for him as she knew that Melanie had just told her the truth.

Bridget and Peter called in to see the Edmunsons for a cup of tea but ended up staying several hours including for supper.

Jack had showered and was upstairs looking in the mirror but didn't like what he saw. He looked down and away and felt the true 'him' inside and felt good, happy and young. Definitely, a lot younger. When he looked up again he saw an old man with lines and creases but the person who stared back wasn't him. It was shocking. He realised that being old was a creeping disease and it was affecting his marriage. He wondered if stopping having sex occurred overnight. Would he sit down with his wife and say, "That's it; on February the twenty third in 2009 we will have our last sex session."

Would he do that? Or would his wife corner him one day and say she's not getting any pleasure from it anymore or that the penetration hurt. Perhaps it would be a more devastating cerebral comment.

"At your age you should know better." That would be the biggest turn off of course, the end of his time as a hunter gatherer.

Whichever way it happened, he could guarantee that she would instigate the last sex in his life.

He pondered about a call to prostitution being the only solution. It was undoubtedly more fun with a prostitute anyway. The surreptitious idling around the Chester railway station or down by the weir on the river. The furtive eye contact, the whispered how much? How long? Will you take your blouse off for that amount? Can I kiss you? And then following the 'pro' to the seedy hotel for a quick but fantastic orgasm with a woman who for the first time ever didn't want to be in love with him or make him belong to her like an old pair of her many shoes.

Fantastic, as Harriet kept saying. What a fantastic word as a euphemism to have for a sexual climax. Better expressed maybe as 'Urrrgghhh, Oh shit, Oh my God, Urrrggghhhh' and the huge expansion of breath at the shuddering end. Jack felt horny just thinking about the possibility but it would be followed by the headlong panic to get out of the room, then out of Chester and finally onto the A51 yet again. Finally reaching home hoping that no one noticed any difference in him or the lateness of his arrival due to the endless traffic.

Pure pleasure and pure hell offsetting each other in some mad passion-dripping moments. The coming and the going, so to speak, but what guilt feelings would follow? Never mind the thoughts about Chlamydia, Gonorrhoea, VD and Aids.

He looked in the mirror again at the old man staring forlornly at him and decided he now felt older inside too.

Fifty is not the new forty – bollocks.

It's when you realise you need to get your life in shape and do what you want to do before you die.

The four best friends sat around the kitchen table with cheeses, pickles, hams and salad. The latter especially for the girls on their regimes although it would make little difference to chunky Melanie. Red Rioja wine and Speckled Hen beer were laid out on the brown cherry table top. Warbies most expensive bread had been duly donated by the farm shop rather than left to go stale and be given to the hens. Jack started the conversation in his usual style.

"I don't want to be controversial but! I've bought a book on Islam Bridget and it's incredible how strong a religion it is; almost a way of life."

"I remember listening to a Radio Four programme recently," replied Bridget. "It was on October the twelfth, Yom Kippur, the Day of Atonement. The whole programme was about the Jews and their conflict with the Palestinians. On this day God makes a decision on who will live and who will die and the Jews ask him to allocate them another year. Did you know that Jack? Imagine truly believing in your faith and asking for another year of life. The Jewish faith is as strong as Islam you know."

Jack replied, nodding in agreement, "I think there is something out there that you can't touch or understand and I don't think you have to match it up to a religion but just believe it exists."

So why aren't you talking to me Jack.
You keep talking as if I exist but denounce your
inheritance.

Jack was drawing Bridget into his spiritual search whilst the other two grunted and shook their heads in disbelief.

"That's lovely Jack." Bridget was entranced. "Have you ever experienced anything strange that has influenced you?"

"Yes, I've had a few weird moments. We were in Tintagel on the way back from Dartmouth the other week and we all stood in the old ruins on the headland. As Joseph and Melanie wandered away from the ancient communal hall I could hear women singing to me. You know, as if the song was for me alone and I shivered as if something was energising me." Jack considered whether he had shared too deep a secret.

Peter couldn't resist it. "I really think you have lost the plot mate, next you'll tell us about some ghost you've seen."

"Well I know you don't believe these sort of things but Melanie will back me up on this one. I have felt a ghost last year but I have never seen one."

Jack was smiling at the disbelieving Peter who said. "Prove it!" Peter really wanted to know more even though he didn't believe in anything that wasn't practical.

Jack began. "We went with some friends to visit a new house they had bought and hadn't moved into as it was being renovated. It's near Ludlow Castle in Worcestershire. A very old house dating from Elizabeth the First times, set in a beautiful valley by a stream and under a small hill. Apparently the Queen used to visit the village to go hunting. Well, we went around this place full of old oak beams and wattle and daub and saw the devastation caused by the builders. It was as if they were ripping the soul out of the place. You know 'OTT' and far too drastic. As we came outside I said I needed the loo and went back in on my own. I stood in the toilet with the door ajar and could see across to the open door of the cellar which was a room cut into the sandstone beneath. It was a weird place when we had gone into it earlier. Cold and damp with a nasty feeling that made you want to get out quickly. As I pissed I kept looking over my shoulder and the hairs on my neck sat up on end and I felt cold. I knew there was something there but couldn't see anything. So I zipped up and walked out backwards so that I was still facing the cellar door until I was outside and only then did I turn around and run. I told Melanie all about it but not the friends as I didn't want to upset them. I specifically said that the house was evil and that something bad was going to happen because of it. Anyway, after they had moved in we found out that the woman was having an affair and shagging this bloke in the new house and blow me down but a few months after she had finished the affair, the guy was so gutted he hung himself from one of the roof beams inside of it." Jack turned to his wife for affirmation. "A true story or not Melanie?"

"A true story and a very sad one Jack," she concurred. "Change the subject please!"

Melanie refilled the wine glasses and Peter opened his fourth bottle of Speckled Hen before asking.

"Anyway, Edmunson when are you going to get the snip?" This was a recurring theme in all of their conversations over the last year since they had confided in their best friends that Melanie was pregnant and had decided to go for an abortion.

"I like Johnnies mate; I have got a thing for burning rubber." Jack responded positively but actually he hated using them. Between putting on a Durex and Melanie going to the loo in every sex session it totally ruined his perception of making love. You couldn't just do it anywhere at any time. You couldn't move around and change position much as it slid up and nearly off. It always got put on at the same planned point after the licking and sucking before finally fucking. He had bought special ones with mini electric blankets built in but they were too hot. He had tried those with special 'excite' lubrication but they were also too hot.

"It's burning," she had said. He had even bought the raised dimpled ones but they created too much friction and therefore were also too hot. He had always thought getting hot in the groin was the whole fucking point of sex!

The abortion day had screwed his mind up completely. There was no other way of describing it. The place seemed to be full of young white-faced girls with acne and Melanie was therefore outside the norm. She was quiet all the time they were there as if totally detaching herself from the whole thing, whilst he had felt like he was killing somebody rather than a tiny nothing, a nobody. When they drove home Jack burst into tears and sobbed his heart out thinking about Briony, the tiny being who had just died and for months after it plagued his mind. Melanie sat in the car and said nothing. No details, no remorse, nothing.

Now they were all ganging up on him about the snip and Jack felt remorse even a year later.

"You go and get done then! Go to Doctor Jones and get the snip; they do it on a Saturday morning in the cottage hospital." Melanie was laughing as she said it. "It only hurts if your balls swell up and even that has an advantage."

"What advantage?" Jack replied without smiling.

"No sex with your husband for three weeks, what a relief!"

"Nothing new there then Jack!" Peter joined in the chiding and only Bridget sat and carefully watched the body language, worried about her male best friend.

Jack tried to take the heat off himself. "You know, I married a thin, dark and short-haired woman, three stones lighter than now and have never asked her to change her body."

Peter commented, "Yes, but I don't suppose you think Melanie can tell any difference in you Jack over all these years. For instance she can't tell whether she is kissing your arse or your bald head. Both are rounded and both hairy but thinning." Everyone laughed even Jack. It was true he had very little left on top and had resorted to a number two trim all over. He did suppose that there was probably more hair on his arse or even his back than on his head.

"Women have to multitask all the time," laughed Melanie, "kissing heads and arses is easy for us."

"That's not multitasking, it's because you have a split personality," replied Jack, smirking in retaliation. He continued. "Anyway I avoid 'Tar poor lee', the money no object town and the doctor's, especially since the nurse took a fancy to me. I only went for a health check and she was all over me stroking my arm to get a vein up. I tell you she succeeded – but it was the wrong vein!"

Melanie was also on form. "I made him go for a check up. You know, just to see how many more years I might have to suffer!"

"Very funny, hah bloody hah as you say." Jack was unimpressed.

She added. "And if my husband dies my son will still make me smile."

Peter joined in with glee. "If your husband dies, it will certainly be hard to wipe the smile off your face."

Jack was miffed. "Why is everyone picking on me today?"

Peter gave the honest answer. "Because you always pick on everyone else mate!"

"Okay but seriously having a health check isn't worth it as you are going to die anyway. The nurse told me, 'You have to lose nine pounds Mister Edmunson as your BMI is saying you are overweight, it's just over twenty-five.' What's the BMI? I asked. 'Body Mass Index,' she replied. 'The calculation looks at your weight and height and if below twenty-two you are okay.' So you are telling me to lose about five per cent of my weight to meet some statistical analysis based on the average unfit fatties around in the UK when I am fifty and can still swim half a mile or walk up Snowdon. Give me a break nurse; my Bloody Minded Ingredient is probably high because I've got so much muscle not fat!" Peter was distinctly unimpressed.

"Jack, let's face it you're old and over the hill so stop kidding yourself mate. If you came and worked in my greenhouses for a day you would be absolutely trashed."

"That's because you are too mean to invest in some decent high tech equipment, wanker." A defensive Jack then told the others about his testicular cancer conversation with the nurse and the booklet she slowly and painstakingly showed him including the graphic pictures.

'You have to check yourself out weekly Mister Edmunson, the faster you catch it the better chance you have of beating it. The blood test we have just done is not foolproof. You need to be physically checked by me now.' The nurse told him to pull his trousers and pants down to his ankles and stand up. She knelt in front of him as if about to give him a blow job and started manipulating his bollocks in her hot hands.

"No way Mister Edmunson that can't be true, can it?" Bridget didn't know what to believe.

"No of course not but my reverie was broken when she said. 'Right, Mister Edmunson you can pull your trousers up now as you are all clear apart from a few genital warts.'"

"You haven't have you?" Bridget was now worried about having extra-marital sex with Jack.

He didn't answer the question, leaving her thinking about it as he changed the subject. "I hurriedly pulled up my pants as fast as possible to cover my growing erection. That was the most embarrassing thing I have ever had done at the doctor's in my life."

Peter asked, "What was the nurse's reaction?"

"She just changed the subject quickly to cover her own embarrassment and started talking about the purity of Buddhism. I suppose they get used to situations like that."

"You live in a strange world, wanker. Sometimes I think you are on a different planet mate." Neither Peter nor Melanie believed in spiritual things but Bridget was more encouraging.

"I sometimes think there is a parallel world but then I dismiss it from my mind and concentrate on selling pansies."

Jack was pleased to have some support no matter how lightweight. "Is it because we are all in need of something to cling on to Bridget or do we really know there is something very different out there? A bit like the 'X files', you either believe or you don't but if you half believe, then it's more worrying because you are apathetic like most of the population."

The concept was eating away at him and he shared it with them all in a more simplistic way.

"I have a problem. The body of a seventy year old that's falling apart, the mind of a twenty year old especially concerning sex but the spirit of a five thousand year old although I can't see back more than my fifty years. I have this terrible urge to change myself but don't know why or how. Sometimes, I wonder who knows what is actually true in life."

You need to lose half a stone.
Don't blame going off to Dartmouth for a weekend
and stuffing your face.
You may be fifty but you have spiralled out of control
and that's your problem.
Greed pure greed, you don't know when to stop.
You are totally lacking in discipline with no focus just
like most of the population.
Stop blaming circumstances and blame yourself or
you will never get the right Karmic balance.
That's the real answer, you are not at peace with
yourself, you are sandwiched between the mediocrity
of day to day modern life and seeing others around
you give up and so you join in with them.
Well stop.
It's mindless and stupid and you have much to do on
your path.

Jack looked up in the air and silently said, "Nim, I thank you for your kind advice, now just fuck off." He cut himself a large piece of brie and spread it onto his Warbie bread as he had thought he had clearly heard Nim giving him a bollocking. He told the others. "Did you know every few years when you are fifty plus, you start to lose muscle fibre and can't replace it, so you get weaker with thinner limbs?"

"That's 'fab'. When I get as old as you I will also get lighter," laughed Melanie.

Jack continued, "I also read in the *Daily Mail* that women are proven to look for one key attribute in men as they get older."

"Money?" said Peter.

"No, that's a genetic fact and can never be changed. They actually look at the size of your waist. So stay thin Peter and get laid more often!"

"Well you can forget sex then wanker as you are so overweight."

"I already have tosser, I already have." Jack glanced at his wife who deliberately turned away and so he stared at Bridget and hoped she would text him in the coming week as Melanie also quoted from her favourite newspaper.

"Did you read in the *Daily Mail* about necrophilia in our hospitals? That's a skin disease, that creeping thing that eats you alive."

Jack groaned and threw his head into his hands, wondering if shagging a dead body would be better than his wife. Her general ignorance and unwillingness to work really bugged him. Over the last few years she had given up on learning and had decided La La land with the baby was an acceptable way to live.

As the evening drew to a close, Jack started to think about the week ahead.

"It's not a rat race anymore Peter, it's gone way beyond that. We all need to get out of the technology race. The constant battle to do everything faster and better. There's more choice, more junk food, more cars on the road, more texts and emails. Did you know every year there are an extra two million cars going on the road and only half a million coming off? That's on top of the twenty-seven million so you get earlier and earlier going down the A51 to beat the queues."

Bridget was the only one interested in his Monday morning blues.

"Jack, on that depressing note we must go." They all kissed

politely and wished each other luck for the week ahead but only Jack wasn't looking forward to it as he felt he was living outside of their real world.

'Top Gear' was on the TV which signalled the end of the weekend again. Jack sat looking at Melanie eating chocolate on the sofa opposite him.

"Maybe Melanie is getting fat because I don't know her anymore and I am not offering her enough attention to make her feel good about herself? So she's given up and she's turned into a fumble bum." He stirred before asking nastily.

"Why are you eating chocolate fumble bum?"

"Why are you calling me fumble bum?" she replied looking across at him rather than at Jeremy Clarkson. "Come over here and bend over and I'll show you." Jack thought it was funny but the comment was met with a stony silence and so he broke it.

"Marriage is what you put into it you know Melanie. A bit of fun, a bit of repartee. A lot of truth as well so that you can keep communicating." He tried this new approach and failed again.

"It is what you put into it!" he repeated jokingly, taken by Jack as his dick into her vagina of course.

At least she laughed and replied. "It certainly is and also how much you wiggle it about!"

"Maybe that's why we had under-floor heating Melanie, it's the only time a woman wants to go on the bottom." He carried on thinking as Clarkson took her attention away again. "Nim, women reach about forty and change their whole attitude to men and us blokes think it's hormonal but in fact they take control and it's all in the mind. Husbands have to fit in with their life and if working away, they just have to come home and be told what to do like a child. Kept in place like my son." He stood to look out of the window at the roosting birds.

"Do you believe in spirits and ghosts Melanie?" Jack was thinking back to the earlier conversations.

"No, of course not," she replied. "That suicide was just coincidental, you didn't see or feel anything, it's the work of your over-active imagination."

"So what about that time when I was coming to see you at your parents' house? When I got to that corner in the lane and I felt that someone was sitting in the rear of my car but couldn't stop and couldn't look back because I was scared. When I told your Dad, he said that was where a young girl was murdered twenty years ago and lots of people had reported sightings over the years. So I suppose I made that up when I didn't even know about it? I think I have a gift and I do see and hear supernatural things."

He didn't tell her about Nim as she would have thought him completely mad but on more days now he talked to Nim in an obtuse way as a pretend friend.

Jack didn't truly believe in Nim but he knew he could accidentally access the paranormal.

"What about that dinner party in Burdesley last year where I saw a ghost? Surely you can't say that was my imagination too?"

Melanie squirmed but said nothing.

They had been with twelve friends in a four hundred-year-old cottage built into sandstone on a hill just below the Desperate Cavalier pub. They were shown around the house and when in the utility room that was sunk into the rock, Jack had felt cold and uncomfortable as at Ludlow. The parents had mentioned during dinner that they were having problems with their two-year-old daughter who woke four or five times a night screaming at someone who was seemingly in her room. Halfway through the dinner, Jack had gone to the toilet above the utility room and couldn't stop looking down the length of the bathroom towards the door as he pissed. He had felt cold again and as he walked out of the bathroom door something white had flashed by him and gone into the baby girl's room opposite. Jack was in shock as he had recounted the story to the dinner party downstairs. However, the parents told them all that after moving in they had both seen black shapes of men with tall hats walking past the windows and had chased outside to find no one there. Eventually, after many independent sightings, they had confided in each other and realised they were seeing exactly the same strange things but had felt uncomfortable about sharing the crazy notions with each other.

A week after the dinner party they had the house exorcised by an Anglican priest. The child had been moved into a different room and had slept perfectly well ever since. Even Peter Edam knew the house and said as a youth they had attended weird parties there when Ouija boards had flown into the air. He also said a previous owner reportedly carried out magic rituals at the full moon. All local myth but for a hundred years it had been renowned as Black Hatch, a place you kept away from especially at night.

"I remember your story Jack," said Melanie, "but your imagination far outweighs any facts. You should write a book."

He was dismissed and decided on an early night rather than trying to compete with the TV and her lack of respect. His last words before walking out were valid and unimagined. "Melanie, why don't you get off your arse and stop meandering into middle age?"

He stamped out without saying goodnight. "If you are listening Nim, my marriage is so shit."

I can see that Jack; you need to sort it out as it is affecting your chosen future.

Another horrible Monday and the 'Merc' cruised at a painful thirty on the M6 as Jack said his daily plea.

"Oh Lord hear my prayer" then he thought of others in trouble in the world and wished them well with whoever else was choosing to do so on this miserable morning. At the end he crossed himself in unison intoning out loud "the Father, the Son and the Holy Spirit, Amen." He always asked 'God' or something to hear him seven times as seven is mythical, seven is lucky. This ritual had started recently and spontaneously and he couldn't remember where and why but Nim could. It was when he found Jack again on the night in the driveway when his son was safely in bed instead of staring out of a window waiting for his Dad.

Jack remembered how he had bought Melanie a lucky bracelet with seven charms. It was when he had started working away from home and thought she was having an affair. So his way of coping was to give her more material possessions.

That probably started the marital rot because she had love on the one hand and money on the other.

The problem being she had then chosen his money and given up on love and left them with nothing as a married couple.

It was just convenient to be with him now.

His mind drifted thinking about the dullness of the marital weekend. His wife avoided doing anything which was hard because she could dump those problems on her husband. She wasn't willing to take on a challenge anymore. When they discussed it, she turned the argument and avoided listening to the logic, always preferring to pick holes instead. Melanie's character constantly denied any blame for anything. She never admitted to being in the wrong and just turned the conversation back on him.

"You don't take responsibility by just saying no, Melanie." Jack constantly argued about this negativity. "You work from a position of ignorance. It's not logical, you revert to disagreeing with some small part of a previous argument usually from years ago and very biased towards the self i.e. yourself."

He always ended up angry as he said this as it showed the level of her ignorance, of frankly being a bit thick and further eroding any love left between them.

Building up the barriers, day by day, week by week, year by year.

The walls between them were getting higher as each one sank into their own dark hole inside, higher walls and a deeper hole aggregating together to make a massive divide that they were irrevocably building.

The journey to work today was physically more painful than ever. A lot of rain had fallen in the night and although only drizzling now it seemed to glue everything together so the traffic couldn't move properly. He grumped further.

"Where have I gone wrong Nim? I never get any support. Who supports me? Who do I turn to when things go wrong? I make it happen but no one asks me how I feel about anything."

You haven't gone wrong Jack and you are not going
crazy talking to your spirit guide.
Remember, I know and don't need to ask and I am the
only one who knows.
You need to get all these thoughts out of your mind
and move on in your path to find your true self.
Look at your day, your week, your year.
You just exist and don't live anymore.

"Thanks Nim, I appreciate it. It's no use talking about yourself at work, they are only interested in you taking care of their pain and making life easy for them. After all you earn the big bucks and therefore you take the shit every day. There's certainly no one at home to bother about me. End of story."

He hadn't noticed that he had replied to a fictitious spirit guide.

"People talk such fucking bollocks," he thought, "just talk and dream. If only they tried to get out of their comfort zone Nim, they could do anything they want and be inspired or inspire others. But not many people want to take a chance, to take a risk."

Even his best friend, Peter Edam, was forever missing opportunities in stark contrast to other similar garden centres around Chester that changed and literally bloomed with new ideas. His pal had it made. No mortgage, no loans, always pleading poverty although on paper he was probably worth a few million pounds.

He thought about the people in The Pheasant Inn last Friday night. Looking around the pub he seemed to be the only one witnessing that most couples sat there in their convenient relationships. Many couples feeling safe to have someone around but willing to surreptitiously and secretly look around for more. He included Jean in this respect, eyeing up Peter and seeing them lark about together and exclude their partners. He thought maybe they were Soul Mates, or was it just illicit sex and fun going on somewhere in the background behind closed doors? The joy of illicit shagging which was far more exciting than the turgid weekly attempt at home. Melanie wouldn't go to the pub with him as it was too smoky.

"Go and see your 'pubby' friends Jack." An instruction to get out of her way and a chiding about who these friends were i.e. not good enough to mingle with and not Cheshire set. This was followed by the inevitable bollocking when he got home because his clothes were smoky and his breath stank of beer.

He flicked Radio Four on: An interview about the start of the Universe. Thirteen point eight billion years ago it grew from a singularity, a point of zero volume. The Professor asked: 'Are we created by a science student in another world as an alien experiment? Our universe sits like a page in a giant book and you can pass from one page i.e. one universe to another page or universe through a singularity from inside a black hole.'

This is a clever man Jack and that is true.

'The universe consists of three things: Matter, anti matter and black matter.'

"And I don't matter mate." The morose Jack chimed in and then listened intently for a gem of wisdom.

'We don't know anything about eighty per cent of our universe. You have to ask yourself, what is on the other side or in effect the outer cover of the book? In a hundred billion years, we will reduce back to a singularity, and in just seven billion the sun will have expanded so much that it will have swallowed up the Earth.' Jack smiled and said out loud to the slow moving traffic queue.

"Not long to live you bastards hey! Then the traffic will move okay." He carried on wondering about the world as the traffic crawled down the A507.

"Perhaps dream sequences could become reality? Is it déjà vu, passing through the pages of the universal book? I thought it was caused by a momentary slip of the brainwaves over a fraction of a millisecond? But reality can also become a dream, so maybe I am just an existentialist? I am not here so I can do anything I want." He sounded his horn with a jab of his fist.

"Fuck off and get out of the way you twat!" Existentialist Jack came back into the real world for two seconds to vent his anger at a timid woman driver trying to ease her way out of a school entrance. Patience wasn't his strong point.

As Jack drove to work Bridget was also driving her girls to the Grange before going on to John Lewis at Cheadle Hulme for some retail therapy. Melanie was already home and waiting in the kitchen in a mini skirt and low cut blouse as Peter walked in through the back door and straight up to her. Without speaking he picked her up by the waist and sat her on the blue-eyed worktop that stared at her naked arse. They had sex for a mad ten minutes before he started to pull his trousers up to return to work.

"It's always so quick Peter; can't we make time to be together for a whole night?"

"Don't you think that would complicate things? It was bad enough when you had to get rid of my baby wasn't it?" Melanie kissed him.

"Yes but I coped. If you had said, I would have left Jack and had your baby, you know that don't you?"

"I know that but then I would have lost my girls instead of an underdeveloped embryo and I couldn't stand that. It was the right thing to do going to Liverpool."

She replied quietly. "I think Jack suspects something. He seems to know that I don't want him anymore."

"Don't worry so. A secret is a secret unless you tell someone and neither you nor I will ever tell anyone, will we?" He looked at her as if he had made a threat. "Anyway, I have made him think I am knocking off Jean by playing around with her in his company and sometimes I feed him a line or two to keep him guessing." Melanie also thought her secret lover could be shagging Jean and considered the last two years of her affair as going nowhere, but she always gave him the benefit of the doubt. The sex was good compared to Jack whose cock was only half the size of his best mate's.

She smiled at Peter and said lovingly, "You are so earthy and practical my lover. That is so different to theoretical Jack, the man who plans everything to the 'nth' degree and then complains when I haven't done something."

Peter checked his flies before answering. "Well that's Jack for you. Over-serious and over-controlling!"

She gave Peter a quick hug before he jogged out of the back door with a big smile on his face.

Jack arrived at the Rosset warehouse and walked in as a focused professional. Shoulders back, head high and a 'Right, let's get on with it attitude'. Good sex over the weekend had helped him feel confident about himself. It was eight thirty am on another frustrating Monday morning following a meaningless weekend again.

He handwrote a list of personal to do's before throwing himself into his work.

The top items on the list reflected their joint purchase of an apartment in Spain a year ago at a place called Yapanc. They had been to the Costa Brava many times previously and stayed in places like Tiramisu and were captivated by the area. He hoped the builders would have completed renovating the apartment by Easter so they could move in at last.

His life's to do list read:

Be there for Joseph.

Spend lots of time in Spain and less time at work. You can't buy time!

Work to live and stop living to work.

No C (carbohydrates), no D (drink, alcohol) or no E (Edmunson). Get a grip on your life and stay fit.

Sort out my marriage once and for all. Success or failure but sort it out.

Write a book. Funny, Zany, Spiritual and meaningful.

Do it all now, it's not a rehearsal. See number one. He then made a calendar, a mini timetable on an Excel spreadsheet showing the number of days until he might die at a statistical sixty-seven.

"How sad is that," he thought as eight hundred and seventy weeks made it sound so short because each week went by in a flash. "Perhaps it's just depression?" as he swallowed his second St. John's Wort tablet of the day swilled down by strong espresso out of the office machine.

Jack got to Wednesday without thinking about Bridget but that afternoon his mobile rang out 'Te Amero' by Il Divo and he saw the caller was her. He pulled in a deep breath before answering. "Hello you, this is a nice surprise, lovely!"

"Lo there! Well Jack, I don't know why I am doing this but it seemed more personal than a text." She sounded excited.

Pleased to receive the call he said. "It is more personal and having a private conversation with you is something I have been thinking about for a long time." He blurted this out without thinking of holding anything back.

"Just assure me Jack that you will delete any call records because God forbid if Peter ever found out. You know he could truly kill someone who steps on his territory, he really could. You don't know anything about him and what he is capable of." Bridget was genuinely scared but she still felt it worth taking a risk at least in talking to Jack.

He asked the obvious. "Is it that bad between you now? I've seen you grow apart over the last two years and especially the arguments but you never know the hidden things."

"Jack, you cannot imagine how he treats me behind closed doors. Even my girls don't see it and it has gotten a lot worse lately. The most horrible thing is the sexual abuse." She started to cry, the telephone call was one for help and understanding not to start an affair.

"The other day I was asleep with my back to him and he just shoved his dick up my bottom. Just like that. How brutal can you get? He just demands sex all the time, sometimes two or three times a day, period or not he just wants to shove it up and come all the time. It's disgusting and degrading, treating me as a blow-up dolly with no love or thought. He is just an animal Jack." She cried more.

"Bridget, I am so sorry, I never knew you were under so much stress. I just want to be there to give you a big hug." He was shocked by the confession.

"Look Jack, I've got to go now and collect the girls from hockey, I'll ring you when I can okay?"

"Anytime, day or night Bridget and I'll eliminate all records immediately so don't worry. You can talk to me about anything, anytime and it's private between you and me forever." Jack sighed. "Bye Bridget, take care, love you lots."

Bridget took in a deep breath. "Love you too Jack, I'm sorry to dump on you but it just seems right talking to you. Love you. Bye."

Jack put his mobile on the desk in his office and walked out through the open-plan area to the main door and into the car park. The sun was setting and cast a red glow across the freckled sky as he stared into the west and thought of her. He felt very sad for her but also in truth for himself. He thought of the women he knew and considered whether she was different and might be his Sun Sharer?

"Don't rush in Jack," he murmured to himself, "don't be driven by your dick."

He remembered something Peter had told him about women needing careful understanding and that they even have their own language especially for their husband.

"I bought it ages ago." And you are too stupid to notice the extra cash drawn out of the joint account.

"Fine." I am really pissed off with you and you should know by now that I am right, so stop arguing with me and shut up.

"Five minutes." Is only five minutes when you are watching football but if she is getting dressed to go out it will be half an hour.

"Nothing." The calm before the storm. The argument following ends in fine.

"Go ahead." Do it if you dare.

"Loud sigh." You are an idiot.

"That's okay." Think carefully before you do it or you will

have your bollocks cut off.

"Love you." Bridget had said the words. I respect your feelings and I know you respect mine so shall we try to take this further because I want to.

"Love you too." Jack's acceptance of that respect and commitment.

That evening he sat in the bar of his hotel and telephoned Peter's landline hoping to hear Bridget's voice if she picked up the call.

"Hello?" Unfortunately for Jack, Peter was in and Bridget was driving the girls somewhere.

"Why do you never say your name, wanker?" Jack chided him.

"Because I know who I am, tosser. Where are you then?"

"Usual shit hole hotel, in a dead bar with dead people. Tell me mate, why do women always seem to have sunglasses on all the time now? There's a bird here, sat at eight in the evening and wearing frigging sunglasses. What's all that about then?"

Peter put him straight. "It's just fashion. Following their peers as in *Hello* and *OK* magazines."

"Well, how stupid women have become and what a stupid use in a stupid place just for fashion." Jack wasn't impressed as Peter interrupted him.

"My wife doesn't do that you know. Never follows fashions and rarely buys clothes. Well, I think she doesn't," Peter checked himself.

Jack replied too honestly, "Well, wanker, you are lucky having such a good wife!" And Jack genuinely meant that whether compared to Melanie or any other wives he had met.

"It's all down to the art of communication Jack."

"What the hell are you on about Peter?"

"The art of communication. It's all a question of distance. Mouth to ear and hand to head. Smack." Peter's sound effect resounded in Jack's ear and jumbled his thoughts.

He wondered if Bridget had meant that as well before replying carefully.

"Well tosser, that's novel, they don't teach you that at school. So how are you Peter, how's your week going?"

"I weighed myself yesterday for the first time in months and I have lost a few pounds."

Jack was impressed. "You looked physically great on Sunday mate; you looked like that sprinter, what's his name, Linford something."

"Ah! Yes Linford Christie," said Peter, "but the subtle difference is the size of his lunch box. Mine's bigger!" Peter bragged and knowing the truth from Melanie it made him feel cocky.

Jack couldn't resist it. "No mate, the subtle difference is you're not black."

"Okay Jack, hah bloody hah, as your wife would say. You might not be jealous of my Lycra shorts image but at least I can wear them, unlike yourself tosser. Let's face it all you can boast about is wearing your Sloggi maroon underpants to all the girls!"

Jack responded. "But wanker, I have good reasons to wear maroon Sloggis. First of all you can't see the piss, which at my age seems to come out whenever it wants to. You know I thought it was cystitis from having too much sex but of course that's wishful thinking." They both laughed before Jack carried on in the same vein. "You can't see the shit either but there again the only problem is you can see the white secretions from your arse where your haemorrhoid suppositories have leaked out squit … squit… squit at a time."

"That is fucking disgusting!" Even Peter was appalled but of course the graphic descriptions justified the truth of it.

Jack continued, "I used to enjoy big knickers on Melanie as well you know. When you could pull them back to see a tantalising bit of arse before shoving it up and then along came thongs. What a waste of time they are. Now I have to pull back the fat to find the thong to then move it over and get my dick up. Sometimes, it seems a waste of time; you might as well shove the thin bit of string in as well to add a bit of friction."

"Oh God Edmunson, you really do need to get a woman in Rosset."

"Maybe I will mate, maybe I will." Jack thought of Bridget and then spoke about the coming weekend. "Knowing my luck Melanie will be 'on' when I get home this weekend."

Peter gave some Peter type advice. "Don't worry, the extra blood flow to her nether regions will probably improve the sensation for her, she might like it more than usual."

Jack was appalled. "No way, I can't have sex when it's her period, what a horrible sight. Imagine that, you couldn't lick it could you?" Peter obviously had experience of this.

"Well turn the light off mate, you just need to shag something don't you?"

Jack was still unconvinced. "I don't want to do that either, I like to look."

Peter quipped. "They say that's a sign of age."

"What is Peter?"

"When you can't rely on your sense of touch anymore." They both laughed again.

"But seriously Peter, all these things just show you that you're getting old and I do worry about that. There are only two important things in life, being born and dying. The rest in between is what you make of it, using your free will which most people seem to have lost. They replace it with whatever the world forces on to them pushing them one way or the other. You meet so few characters with a free spirit and free will to change things. The world is lost in our Western culture and I know other cultures see it differently because I have been reading about it. Getting older should be fun, a time to focus on the family, rather than disappear up your own arse trying to keep up with everyone and everything."

Peter wasn't impressed by the speech as all he saw every day was the practical grind of life and he rarely considered the future. He was interested in death though and did reply about that. "It's an interesting concept death isn't it? What happens when you die? I think it goes black and that's it. No coming back, no afterlife, nothing."

His soulful mate argued against him. "I definitely can't agree with that. You read so much about things after death that you have got to believe something. Maybe it's just mankind's vanity but suppose you do come back or go and exist in a different dimension. How will you justify your life to whoever controls it all? Will you take the risk?"

Peter replied confidently. "Of course wanker, until proven otherwise, you come in with nothing and you go out with nothing and that's the facts."

Jack wouldn't let go. "Look fifty-seven million people die each year in the world, one hundred and fifty-seven thousand daily or nearly two a second. If nothing else that's a lot of human emotion that is released in a day, a lot of energy, a lot of souls going to heaven mate. Take for example the difference between a murderer and a saint. A murderer kills someone and mostly because the police don't catch them no one gets to know who it is. On the other hand a saint brings someone alive and everyone in the world hears about him. Does that mean that death is easier than life?"

"Jack mate, I think I will concentrate on having fun and so should you; so come out this weekend on my new quad bike."

Jack had two responses. "Well let's face it wanker, a quad bike is just a bad car and secondly it would kill my hips to sit on it. You know I would love to come with you really but it's Edima's wedding in Paris so I won't have time I'm afraid." The banter petered out and they said their goodbyes without Bridget arriving home so Jack decided to ring his Mother.

Whilst Peter and Jack put the world to rights, Melanie was talking to Bridget who was using her mobile whilst sitting waiting for her girls to complete their music lessons.

"Are you free to lunch with Harriet and I on Thursday?"

"Oh, if only Melanie. Peter is sending me over to Yorkshire to collect some plants in the lorry. Can you believe that! The things I do for him and he doesn't ever say thank you." Melanie started to envisage her meeting with her absent friend's husband and immediately felt horny.

"You are so good to him Bridget. How do you put up with him?"

"Because I have no choice. He supports the girls and I and we have a nice way of life but if someone else was available, well maybe I could envisage an alternative lifestyle."

Melanie asked hopefully, "You wouldn't leave him would you?"

"No, not really Melanie, it's just a thought that us girls have after years of marriage. How about you? Would you consider leaving your old man?"

"Old being the operative word. He is always complaining about his hip or his back. It really pisses me off sometimes. Moan, moan, moan."

Bridget didn't like Melanie running Jack down and asked, "Yes but what about answering the question?"

Melanie paused before replying. "A secret is only a secret if you tell nobody!"

Bridget had heard the expression used many times by her husband and pondered how close he was with Melanie. "Bye Melanie, I can see the girls coming out. Enjoy Thursday. Bye!"

As Melanie replaced her receiver she revelled in the thought of Thursday. Illicit and exciting sex with Peter followed by a girly chat, white wine and a nice lunch before collecting Joseph from school. She mentally hugged herself and smirked as she was so content with her lifestyle.

Mother was rambling from the start of the obtuse conversation with her youngest son.

"My sister always wanted to be better than me. She wanted a Hercules bike, a new one you know son." He didn't know as they were last made forty years earlier. "She saved up for two years and wouldn't accept having a second-hand one. I don't know why she did that. It was always like her to want new. I'm quite happy here now but I might go into a home down south by the seaside. You know in Devon where your Dad liked it. I'm not sure I can though because I have got a bad hip, did I tell you that Jack? Where are you working now?"

Since the dementia she was always thinking about her sister and what she didn't do right in Mother's eyes. It was a constant gnawing complaint.

"Ay son, she thought her boyfriends liked her but I never told her how they used to chase me behind her back. I would save money for the 'wakes' and follow them all inside but my sister was so mean she never even gave me one of her chips."

Jack lasted as long as possible before wishing her goodnight.

His mobile started to sing 'Te Amero'. The colour display showed the name.

"Hiya Bridget, where are you? I just rang your house."

"I'm sat outside Tina's music teacher's house in Peckforton and as I've got nearly half an hour, I thought I'd say hello. In fact, I spoke to your wife and lied about the girls' lesson finishing so that I could talk to you."

Jack felt a warm glow inside. "That's nice, thank you. It's lovely to speak to you. Did your day get any better?"

"Just the usual, it was freezing here today. I even put my thermals on with three fleeces when I was out in the shop. I don't think I have warmed up properly yet. The rest of it is normal. I run around behind everybody, tidying up, cooking or placing the farm shop order and they all relax and take it easy. So just a normal day." Jack was holding the mobile in his right hand and seemingly like all boys of all ages when relaxed, he had unconsciously put his left hand down his pants fiddling with Mister Wiggly. A typical boy thing, not sexual, just habitual whether on the telephone or watching 'Match of the Day.'

"Well my lovely, do you wear your thermals instead of big knickers or do you keep those underneath for extra warmth?" Jack couldn't get an image in his mind.

"How do you know that I wear knickers at all Mister Edmunson?" she replied with a sexy giggle. "You might think me lumpy, frumpy and dumpy like you keep telling my girl friend but I might have hidden qualities!"

Jack's penis was harder as he perked up and replied. "You are just a tease and will always hide your best bits hey! I bet you have a chastity belt on so no one can find out if you are a true blonde or not."

"Well, there you go Mister Edmunson, something you may never find out you bad man."

She was interested and he could tell it from her voice and so Jack pushed harder. "Firstly, what is so bad about wanting more from you and secondly I would like to find out. I have always thought about you when I am away in my hotels on lonely nights." He left an opening for her.

She was husky with her quiet reply. "What have you been thinking about me doing Jack?"

"I have thought whilst lying in my bed about kissing you. Is that okay?" Jack's prick was hard in his left hand.

Bridget sighed. "Yes of course that's okay. Sometimes, when I'm forced to have sex and I mean forced into sex and not making love, I considered what it would be like if it was you instead."

Jack was stroking his prick, which was very hard now and his voice had risen. "I tell you Bridget, you and I would not have sex. We would only make love and the reason is because love is in the mind and isn't just physical. If you desire someone in your mind it makes the sexual side a hundred times better."

Bridget said quietly. "I would like to make love for a change. I need that tenderness in my life and someone to want me for being me rather than just taking advantage of my presence."

Jack was short on breath as he talked. "I am thinking of you now my darling. I am touching myself and thinking of kissing you. I am putting my hand inside your blouse and touching your nipple, can you feel me doing that?"

Bridget was sighing as she replied. "I have my eyes closed Jack and I can picture you kissing me gently and touching me. I can smell you, do you know that."

Jack was desperately hard in his hand; the zip on his trousers was undone as he wanked himself. "God I want you Bridget. I am wanking myself thinking of you. Do something for me will you?"

"What do you want from me Jack?" came her soft reply.

"Put your fingers down your pants, keep your eyes closed and believe that it's my hand. Have you done that?" Jack's prick was pulsing with excitement.

"I have Jack; I am so wet thinking about you."

"I am still kissing you so keep rubbing your hot wet cunt my lovely. I am rubbing you and now I am down there with my mouth licking and sucking your clitoris. Are you feeling good my darling?"

Bridget was breathless as she answered. "Jack, I can't believe I am doing this but I feel like you are here licking my clitoris and God I am so horny, so hot and wet my love."

Jack pushed harder as he was so close. "We are kissing face to face now and you are straddled across me and I'm slipping my prick inside of you and sucking your hard nipples. Can you feel my big hot cock inside of you Bridget?"

"Oh God Jack, what are you doing to me for God's sake I'm nearly coming."

Jack was out of breath now. "I am inside you and I can feel your hot juices dribbling down my bollocks, Oh God I'm coming and thrusting and coming." As he gasped and spunk flung itself across his hands he heard Bridget gasp and then gasp again. He carried on softly and tenderly. "Did you have an orgasm darling?"

"Yes Jack, I can't believe you excited me so much over the telephone my love. I have never experienced that in my life."

"Did you really come Bridget, really?"

"Yes, of course. I would never lie to you and that is the first time in more than a year but I need some real love Jack, do you understand what I'm saying."

Jack was thoughtful. "We need to get together. Can't you visit your friend in London next week and see me too? I can be in the City in less than an hour by train."

"I'll try my love. I will try but I have got to go now. Thank you Jack."

"No need for thanks Bridget, drive carefully, let me know okay."

"Okay," and she was gone. He sat in his bed and looked at his limp dick. Yellowish spunk was still spread across his hand, pants and bed sheets and he felt dirty. Guilty and dirty as he imagined it would be with a prostitute.

"Why have I done that? Why complicate my life?" He thought about it but it was too late to change his path.

> *Because you needed to Jack.*
> *You think she is special.*
> *You hate Melanie and feel you have lost 'Real Life'*
> *and therefore your manhood.*
> *That's why.*
> *So don't feel guilty; feel happy that someone truly*
> *wants you.*

"I suppose all men are the same Nim, you see despair in other couples but not in yourself? It must be rare that occasionally one man breaks that desperate mould. One man has got the guts and courage to get out of the marriage and that's what it takes to be able to walk away."

The weekend started in Rosset and ended there for Jack.

He caught a forty minute Easyjet flight to Charles De Gaulle airport from Luton on Friday night and found a temporary parking spot for his hire car to wait for Melanie's plane that was forty minutes late. He shut his eyes and closed out the long day trying to relax. He had grave misgivings about the weekend as he had not seen the majority of the wedding guests for twenty-five years. He was stressed at the thought of reliving his old life and that rekindled the heartache and emotion from the time when wife number one had left him.

The last time he had seen her she was big, fat and ugly, a far cry from the slim dark woman he had cried so much for when she had walked off with his best friend. He also felt outnumbered. There were a whole six guests from Jack's side of the family, his family plus his brother, sister-in-law and Mother. Whereas, number one had invited seventy-six from her side which Jack considered 'OTT' especially as he was footing the eight grand bill. He decided he needed to be more assertive in his life, mainly with women who tended to rule over him.

He sighed deeply and recalled his first marriage as a departure thundered overhead. Number one was his childhood sweetheart. The first and only girl he had sex with before Melanie. If he had been a stronger character he would have realised that he needed to sow his wild oats elsewhere and avoid the obvious trap that the first is the best and the only one for you. He always regretted the stupidity of marrying his first real girlfriend and felt it had affected his whole life, causing him to waste much of it. For a long time he had been jealous of Melanie's male friends and had presumed with typical vanity that it was her behaviour that was at fault. But as he sat considering his past, he realised that it was a character defect in him as he had a controlling and therefore a jealous personality. So it was something to do with his childhood or the way his parents behaved that had ground the possessive streak into him. Or the jealousy was caused by a lack of confidence, a need to feel wanted, but there was something definitely missing in his character set. When number one eventually told him about her affair with his best friend he realised he had known because her behaviour had changed. She had become less loving and more interested in vague subjective parts of life.

Melanie had behaved the same way over the last two years but Jack loved her less each month that passed and so he wasn't bothered if she walked away from him. In fact some of his behaviour towards her actively encouraged this.

"How sad is that between two people Nim?" Who she might have had an affair with was quite limited and all were known 'friends'. His thoughts were confused. "Has she committed adultery? Was Briony my daughter?" He would never know as it was not in her psyche to be wrong and so she would never admit anything.

However, number one had admitted wanting an affair and told him she wanted a different life as she wanted to simplify things but she had not had sex with his best friend. A typical story used by most people and believed by them at the time of a break up because it made it easier. Jack thought it was a load of bollocks but it still seemed like the end of his world and he did everything possible to keep her. He vividly remembered her driving away in her parents' car with Edima and Rodney waving goodbye to their Dad at ages four and two. That sort of emotional scar had created the Jack who sat with his eyes closed in his car listening to the roar of jet engines and thinking too much as always.

A text arrived from Melanie on his mobile telling him to collect them from arrivals, which he duly did and then they started the forty minute drive to the wedding hotel outside Meaux.

"What a strange day," he thought. "Everything has happened in chunks of forty minutes and so perhaps I'll get forty minutes' sex later?"

That was also Jack, ever hopeful, but it never happened as they were too tired and didn't have enough love in them to overcome the fatigue.

Saturday started with the obligatory kiss to number one and a brief handshake with few words to the 'ex' best friend. Jack moved away as fast as good manners allowed. The rest of her family were welcoming and old. It was shocking to see how people had changed and it quickly put his 'fifty down fifty to go' theory well out of shape.

The wedding was held in a little village Mairie on the edge of a sandy square bordered with sculpted plane trees that were waiting to leaf. Opposite stood the ancient but small Catholic church for the blessing.

Mother started out badly, saying to all those assembled, "Hello number one; when are you and Jack going to have your next baby to keep Rodney and Edima company? You need to do a lot of poking to have one you know!" She cackled as she said it.

"Oh fuck." Jack tried to steer her away to number one's grandparents.

Mother continued. "I've got a bad hip you know, not that my sister cares of course. Why are we having a party Jack?"

"It's Edima's wedding lovey with my ex-wife number one. Do you remember her?"

"I don't remember anything anymore son. Is she pregnant again? She does look fat."

The wedding breakfast was going well and Jack relaxed as Melanie became more stressed with his 'ex' relatives around him.

She never liked Edima and was muttering under her breath about how tasteless it all was when the Scottish piper, not particularly native to France, marched in playing incredibly badly. This was followed by the gay Best Man's speech which was incoherent nonsense, apart from the bit everyone heard about Edima's new husband shagging her best friend. Most people concluded this was down to the drugs he was taking for Aids or perhaps the cocaine snorted in the toilet an hour earlier.

Jack was in his element. The wedding was much better entertainment than he had expected and he had developed a permanent drunken smile on his face by the time he had to say a few words.

"I am very happy to be here to see you all again. I can't say I have missed you but that's life hey! I am also very happy to be able to play with my new grandson and look forward to seeing you all at the Christening. To you my darling daughter, good luck as you'll need it on the rocky road of marriage. To the bride and groom!"

Random claps and a few 'bride and groom's' wafted round the room as the piper kicked in with Rolf Harris's 'Two Little Boys', enjoyed immensely by Jack as he sang along loudly.

"For fuck's sake Jack." Melanie was not impressed and never normally swore. "This is diabolical and we are paying for it!" Jack became more relaxed as his wife got angrier.

"I am paying for it, not you Melanie. You never pay for anything lovely. Chill out, it's funny and in fact as I pay for everything stop thinking it's a waste of your money that you want to spend differently on yourself." Melanie went off to the toilets in a huff, dragging a reluctant Joseph with her as the piper had kindly let him try his bagpipes.

Rodney, Jack's eldest son, plus number one's daughter by the 'ex' best friend and three of Edima's girl friends all stood at the bar 'doing shots' and having silly conversations. Despite his fifty years Jack had missed out on shots in his life but was learning quickly. He decided that tequila was shit especially with all the salt which was bad for his blood pressure. Aftershock was better and an After Eight was like a nice dessert pudding. A subtle blend of crème de menthe, Baileys and Tia Maria slipped down his chin on to his shirt and just a little into his throat as he stared at the young girls' boobies pushing out of their new dresses. Number one's youngest daughter was thrusting her groin into him as the bride joined them. "You lot are a nightmare!"

Number one's youngest looked shakily at her sister and explained, "I like your Dad; he's good fun and nothing like Mum said he was, you know; a complete fucking bastard."

Jack smiled on as happy as a pig in shit. "I'm looking forward to wives three and four Edima, is that okay?" Jack giggled with her girlie friends as he gently put his arms around two of them and accidentally on purpose touched their tits. The best man waltzed past as if on a cloud and putting his hand on Jack's shoulder he slowly and lovingly shoved his finger up Jack's arse taking in half the fabric from the seat of his pants. Jack turned and smiled at him.

"That was so considerate, thank you! Please enjoy yourself; it's my pleasure to have you here and your pleasure to have me." When Jack swayed down to the toilets a few minutes later he glanced out of a side door to see a group of people holding his eldest son and the best man apart as they tried to swing pathetic little punches at each other.

"Aren't young men so stupid Jack? So inexperienced don't you think?" Turning he saw number one's youngest had followed him down the corridor. She linked her arm in his and guided him into the ladies. Shutting the trap door she shoved her tongue down his throat and pulled his groin into her, quickly followed by unzipping his fly and grasping his hot red dick.

"Oh fuck!" Jack was about to stop her and walk out as she bent down and started to give him a blow job. "Oh fuck." He sighed again and grew harder, thinking how both number one and two had always refused to taste his semen. Perched on the toilet with his trousers down and his ex best friend's daughter sucking his cock caused him to think hard, very hard. But then the thought passed as he came shuddering in her mouth, happy to get some revenge on the bastard who upset him all those years ago.

"I've got to go." His lame excuse left her in the cubicle with a hot wet cunt and no one to fill it. He justified it to himself as not having a shag so he could deny it like Bill Clinton. Back in the ballroom he sat alone unsteadily on his stool to try to get his breath back and stop the walls moving. He could see Melanie purposefully walking towards him. The disco was in full swing and at nine pm, she had decided enough was enough and told him so.

"An ouef is an ouef," Jack joked. "It's a yoke. It's fucking French." But she missed it completely.

"Jack! Joseph and I are going to bed early as I am so bored. Are you coming too?" Her manipulation of him suddenly seemed blatant rather than carefully cloaked.

He staggered slightly as he stood and then he shouted across a very loud Robbie Williams, "Don't need to come now." He smirked. "Got to stay up for my daughter's wedding dear, need to be sociable!" Bending down he kissed Joseph goodnight.

"Don't be late," Melanie warned him ineffectively.

He wandered off to dance to 'Come on Eileen' with number one. He decided he should tell her how he felt after twenty-five years apart but he was having trouble placing his mouth near her head.

"You should never have left me you know. What are you still

doing with that waster," pointing to the 'ex' best friend who he thought about hitting.

She leaned into his ear in complete control. "Jack, after all these years you are right but you were an impossible person to live with. So don't forget that and give Melanie a break yes?"

"No way! She is a fucking arsehole compared to you lovely," he pulled her in closer to his body so that his words were only heard by her. "She doesn't treat me right. At least you had some respect for me and some brains in your head." He pulled away and twirled her round, deliberately letting his hand brush her breast. Jack was on an adrenaline roll and wondered if he could shag his 'ex' wife.

"Why not? Give me a good reason Nim."

Because you are going to get yourself into even more
trouble than you are already in.
You are running away from what you know you have
to do.

Number one's youngest joined in the dance, still wanting Jack to shag her and therefore saving her Mother by diverting his attention. As the disco died a natural death the party moved into the hotel bar at one in the morning where they found the drunken Scottish piper collapsed in a corner. Number one's youngest came to sit on Jack's lap with her hand inside his shirt pinching his right nipple.

"I don't drink you know," she slurred.

Jack giggled into her ear. "Neither do I." He kissed her cheek. Edima's girlfriends had moved on to the seats next to the Marseilles rugby team that was on tour and the girls sat choosing which hunks they would shag that night. This was simply a practical expedient as they had no room booked. Eventually, Jack collapsed into his room at four in the morning, banging into the dresser as he tried to sneak in with the lights off.

But God he felt alive and happy for the first time in years.

Melanie started exacting her day of revenge at six thirty in the morning.

"Wake up Jack, Joseph wants to watch TV. Try and find an English channel for him. What time did you come in?" Her voice was harsh and never ending.

"About one." Jack felt like death warmed up. His mouth was like a kangaroo's jockstrap as she nudged him.

"We need to be at breakfast for seven thirty. Remember we promised to take Joseph to the Eiffel Tower."

"No problem lovely," he replied through gritted teeth as she turned on her side to snooze.

By eight thirty Melanie was ready to leave the breakfast room and start sightseeing. The Marseilles rugby players were clapping five of their colleagues into the room as two of Edima's friends walked towards the exit waving to Jack and shouting loudly. "Hello Jack from wives number three and number four." Melanie turned to him with her mouth open.

"Just a joke last night lovely. Just a bit of fun."

Number two carried on outside dragging poor Jojo as Jack said goodbye to Edima and wished her a happy honeymoon.

"Dad, look at these pictures on Rodney's camera. Do you want a copy?" The digital pictures were remarkably clear compared to Jack's brain. The concrete deer with Jack sat naked astride it looked truly alive. The white alabaster of wife number three or possibly four's tits glared out with Jack's head between them. Fast action shots such as dancing with his trousers down whilst stood on top of a table and snogging wife number one were not blurred enough.

"Edima, just email them to me at work. At work you understand!"

He walked out of the hotel with a smile on his face.

The rest of the day was a letdown. Vomiting inside a French broadband telephone box whilst trying to get the Chester and Liverpool football results. Settling the bar bill behind Melanie's back. A four hundred and eighty pound hit excluding the one hundred and fifty pounds cash that she never realised Jack had spent.

"What's this entry for a night bar at eighty four pounds just here?" This was the only sensible question she managed about it all.

During the weeks that followed Melanie's friends would ask about the wedding weekend and always got the same reply from her. "It was fine," delivered in a clipped voice.

Jack got asked the same questions at work and in The Pheasant Inn. "It was fucking brilliant, the best weekend of my life."

A sharp contrast in their attitudes to life before the wedding, during it and after it.

The weekend after was pleasant enough as the whole family were focused on Easter and the first holiday in Spain in their new apartment. The weather helped, spring had arrived at least temporarily and the garden started to bloom. A thousand daffodils nodded their heads underneath the old beech hedging in the front garden. Early frogspawn dotted its way around the edges of the pond watched hungrily by fish that were marginally less languorous as they threw off the lethargy of winter. Jack delighted in walking around his garden to watch life drip feed back into it. The little shoots on the fuchsia excited him as he cut back the old growth and lost the frosted shard splendour of the wizened twigs. The huge climbing rose across the front of the cottage had numerous leaves by now due to the warmth of the south facing wall so he sprayed for blight and fed its single massive root.

It was spring and a time for reflection and new beginnings.

He was never happy with her now and never happy at home.

A terrible thought before starting a new life in Spain.

Melanie left him alone in the garden for much of the time and avoided speaking with him. Jack was happier on his own and escaped across the fields to see Peter and collect some School Ball tickets.

She watched her husband's back with hatred vowing to make him pay for the new disrespect he constantly showed her.

She picked up the telephone and dialled her best friend Harriet.

"Have you got a minute?" Harriet was alone too as her husband Matt worked harder and stayed away from their home longer.

"I have hours at your disposal Melanie. Matt is out again and the girls are at boarding school. Tell me. What has he done wrong now?"

"Nothing wrong really. He just ignores me when I ask a sensible question. He thinks he is so clever and just can't be bothered to help us mere mortals."

Harriet liked Jack a lot and defended him when replying. "They are all the same you know. Big men in their important but small worlds. We are just housewives made for cleaning, cooking and looking after children."

Melanie agreed wholeheartedly. "But it's so sad because they push us away and can't see the damage they do to their family lives. I tell you what, I am worth more than that and if I ever left him I would take him for every penny to make up for his demeaning attitude."

They moved on to safer, less controversial topics like schools and pushed their unhappiness aside because the real secrets remained secret.

Later in the evening Jack walked back up the hill from their friend's cottage and as he looked at the stars he realised how old his soul was and how long his Karma had been.

He could see his moon shadow and he felt at one with the world.

He was happy for a few minutes realising that most people never get into this state of spirituality. They were shackled by the day to day practicalities of life: kids, food, TV and money.

He knew then what was meant by living and how lucky he was.

Do you remember Catalonia Jack?
You were a Centurion in the Roman army, a master
of the citadel in Sant Martin.
Do you remember asking the Goddess Artemis to
provide good hunting and her vestal virgins for other
favours?
Do you remember?

He was looking forward to Spain and oblivious to his spirit guide as he waltzed happily down the road.

He loved Spain and couldn't wait to get there.

It always made him happy but he could never pinpoint the reason why.

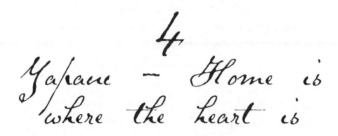

4
Yapanc – Home is where the heart is

It was Easter and the family were getting ready to go to Catalonia to stay in their new apartment in Yapanc for the first time.

Yapanc lies about half an hour away from Girona on the Baix Emporda, a beautiful part of Northern Spain.

It is almost equidistant at seventy miles from the French border, the skiing areas of the Pyrenees and the sophisticated art and culture of Gaudi's Barcelona.

A triangulated paradise still Catalan in heart and soul and uncorrupted by hordes of foreign tourists or resident expats. A treasure trove that was originally opened up by the weekenders from Barcelona who have come to play in the pretty small resorts for nearly sixty years. The area is best, or possibly worse known as the Costa Brava and forty years ago it was one of the first package holiday destinations, especially to the south where you find the pretty village of Tossa de Mar which is beautiful, but only out of season.

Yapanc has never been lager lout territory, instead it is the opposite, an enclave of the rich and cultured who have built their expensive casas – houses – there over the last two generations.

The place is pretty and has a steep relief characterised by pink rock and sweet smelling pines, whipped by a cacophony of winds setting the tone for each new day. The Llevant from the east flowing hard across the granite sand of the small beach is funnelled directly onto the bathers by two enormous headlands. The Tramuntana comes from the north, howling off the Pyrenees and sending every single boat to cover to keep away from its vicious impact but perversely leaving Yapanc beach and the sea in the cove without movement, sheltered by the two small hills immediately behind.

In fact it is a place of four hills including the giant towering headland with El Far, the lighthouse, beaming out a warning to those at sea and a welcome to those arriving by land. Its light reaching out and illuminating the White headland across the bay, where the new Edmunson apartment was situated on the shiny mica rock. This is a much smaller and wider protrusion into the azure sea but still very exclusive with houses used by the King of Spain for his holidays. Nestling inland between these two embracing arms that cosset the sea are a pair of hills, one with ancient burial sites and dolmen or stone structures designed for some pagan god, the other where the Romans set up their first camp nearly three thousand years ago.

So Yapanc has always been popular, always bountiful with wild boar, rabbits and fish to add to the natural olives and nuts to give the perfect Mediterranean diet.

They were due to depart by Ryanair from Liverpool to Girona for the princely sum of three pounds ninety nine each. Flights for every school holiday were now booked six months ahead and a solitary weekend in August was also booked for Jack to commute from his work in Rosset.

He was sitting in the study writing up his spiritual researches for a possible book but suffering Melanie-inspired interruptions every few minutes. Firstly, it was the hoovering, then the dusting. These were followed by a few orders.

"Don't go on the kitchen floor until it's dried." All as if he was a child again making him glad to usually work away from home.

Finally, she knocked on the ceiling above Jack's head. "Jack, can you come and look at something for me?"

He shouted back. "No, I'm busy and we are running out of time."

"Come on it's really important."

Jack sighed and left his computer, pressing save as he stood up. He winced slightly as his bad hip had seized up and started to clump up the stairs. He made an alternating noise as he moved delicately to reduce the pain from his hip. Melanie stood at the top and stared lovingly at Jack for the first time in months.

"You sound like a pirate, one leg hop along Jack." She laughed at him and as he got closer she realised he still wore his reading glasses which made her smile wider.

"Why have you got those on?" She had constantly taken the piss since his far-sighted old age had blinked in and she knew Jack took it personally as a sign of growing old.

Jack looked up angrily. "I hope your need is great and I'm not on a wild goose chase." As he reached the top she held him close and tried to kiss him. Jack turned his head to one side, his lips cold and unforgiving.

"I've been thinking about you all this morning," she said. "I was holding my hoover tube just now and thinking of your dick."

"More than over the last week, when I've wanted sex," Jack haughtily replied.

Melanie pushed her thigh against him. "Mister Wiggly is getting bigger, so you're not going to deny me are you?" She looked into his eyes to see his response.

"I repeat what I just said Melanie. Why should I have sex with you when you have refused me three times in the last seven days and made it obvious by going to bed early that you are not interested in me." Jack was cold in his response. A cold voice, cold lips and a cold heart. "You are trying to fit me into your agenda again, always your agenda but you're not really interested are you?"

"Yes, I am," she replied, kissing him with soft warm lips and rubbing her hand against Mister Wiggly.

"Well, I'm not. We have got to leave in an hour and we need to be ready on time." Jack turned and went down the stairs much faster than he had come up and without a limp whilst she smiled evilly at his retreating back.

At the airport, Jack walked into the Duty Free shop, sniffing the perfumes and constantly whistling Cliff Richard's 'We're all going on a summer holiday, won't be back for a week or two' much to Melanie's annoyance.

"Did you know Nim that one of the safest places in Britain is here in an airport? There's no way Al Qaeda can touch me. There are armed police outside with limited drop off areas and once inside no one can possibly retain any dangerous weapons. Firstly because you are asked at the check in desk 'have you a gun sir or has someone asked you to carry their gun for them?' Secondly because of security screening at the arches and finally and most especially in Liverpool there are so few people to kill that it isn't a worthwhile target. I suppose knowing my luck a plane would run into the side of the terminal and kill me."

Relax Jack, it's only a short aeroplane flight.

"That's okay for you to say. How can you die Mister clever fucking spirit guide?"

The statistical chances of dying are negligible Jack;
just relax and enjoy your journey home.

"What do you mean home?"

You will find out one day when you choose to know as
it is in your path.
You know Yapanc from hundreds of years ago.

Jack stopped arguing with a disembodied spirit and returned to his paranoia about flying. No matter what amount of grief he received from Melanie he insisted on sitting on one of the last three seats at the rear of any plane and standing in the priority queue twenty minutes before boarding to ensure he did so.

"Look Melanie it's logical, planes don't reverse into mountains."

She looked down her nose at him and replied, "You stupid man, what planet are you on?"

He smiled, "Zog, which is better than being in La La land like you. Anyway, I saw this TV programme about plane crashes and apparently if you do survive, it averages out that just six people make it out and they are always the ones by the emergency exits. So that's what we are doing, being safe. Right?" Melanie gave in to him without a murmur for once as she could read her trashy magazines anywhere on the plane.

He sat back down in the departure lounge with his purchase of a healthy grapefruit drink from Boots and watched Joseph and Melanie filling up with crap in the newsagents opposite him. Four different chocolate bars, Maltesers, four Fanta lemons, *Hello* and *OK* magazines and a nominal diet Coke so she didn't get fat.

"Not that she truly cares as she is so fat," he thought grimly as he looked at her from the rear and was repulsed. The fat oozed out of the black thong beneath the cream summer trousers and he could see her black bra straps under the oyster-coloured blouse, making it a disgusting sight overall.

When she returned she said, "Look after Joseph a minute, I need to go and buy some cellulite cream from Duty Free."

"Cellulite is fat dimpled by gravity," replied Jack, but she was gone without a please or thank you to spend another eighty pounds on cream that couldn't improve her figure.

"At least there wasn't an argument," Jack thought but it was only because there was safety in numbers as the whole departure lounge would have heard. He therefore hypothesised about how she could lose twenty pounds of useless fat rather than tell it to her face. "Just cut your head off Melanie," but it would never be said.

Jack had his micro radio on and the single earpiece blurted out a non-stereophonic Radio Five.

"Nim, you know when you have lost the plot, when you are listening to Radio Five live and after a quarter of an hour the stories cycle round again. You get about two minutes of extra news if you are lucky but only slight variations on the same stories to the previous cycle. You end up listening to it for two hours and know exactly what they are going to say next. What is even more annoying is that it's recycled news from someone else's website or Reuters and it's all supposition and bending of the little known facts by some so-called expert who last visited the country ten years earlier before being thrown out as a dissident."

Calm down Jack, it's just a short aeroplane ride.
Don't be afraid, I will be with you.

Jack ignored the friendly heavenly voice and continued to wrap his fear into a rant as he glanced at the newspaper headlines in W H Smith.

"The same news about Saddam Hussein constantly repeating itself. He's a bastard, he killed thousands of people, is he dead etc etc." Jack was tired of the news rhetoric. "Didn't we do well destroying the fabric of the country for lots of oil and a strategic foothold in the Islamic World? A kick up the arse for the Middle East to show them who is boss and to really rile them to make sure they hate us even more than they originally did. No different to when foreign powers created Israel with a foreign biased culture. Power and money blighting the geography of the world again, the new Crusaders against the new Infidels. My God Nim, you never read about the first Muslim to climb the Himalayas or whatever."

'Whatever' was becoming a popular response in Jack's life but only when at home.

'Whatever', 'If you want', 'It's your life' and all the other words of non-commitment, of giving up on a marriage.

They climbed aboard the Ryanair bus service in the sky and started to learn to cope with en masse travel where a twenty-five stone Scouser needs two seats for his arse and inane clapping and cheering greet the landing at Girona.

Melanie and Jack had found Yapanc by accident. They had read the *Sunday Times* travel section ten years previously which featured a small village called Tiramisu and duly set off to find it one summer holiday. However, Yapanc got in the way as they immediately fell in love with both it and the surrounding area of the Baix Emporda.

Everyone they met said the same. "Don't go home and tell everyone about it!" So instead they went back a few years later and bought an apartment as an investment into Jack's pension and also into their son who could spend countless hours having fun on the stunning beach.

It was therefore five years after when they first met Karina. She and her husband Josep Maria worked hard running the Croisanteria, a delightful bakery set in the village square and rolling out fresh delights from early morning to late at night.

Karina was a petite Irish lady, auburn with a slim waist and sexy legs topped off with large voluptuous breasts and an even larger smile. Jack loved her unconditionally from the first moment he looked into her eyes and they touched cheek to cheek with a Spanish kiss. It was nine in the morning and the sun was starting to warm the spring air as he made the first ever breakfast run to take everything fresh back to the apartment. He had bumped into his friend Manolo from the Finques, the estate agency from nearby Palafrio, who had sold them the property. Manolo owned the holiday villa next to the bakery and was also collecting his own breakfast. It was Manolo who performed those first introductions to his neighbours and for that Jack would be eternally grateful.

The sun glinted in Karina's green eyes and Jack was overtaken by a moment of pure joy, so when his friend Manolo moved on to introduce the dour Josep Maria, he felt that he had moved into the shade. Josep was olive skinned with brown eyes and a mane of dark hair, a typical Spanish man in looks and nature. The woman in a Catalan marriage is subservient unlike in England and the very opposite of Melanie with Jack. What Spanish men say goes. He was also a typical Catalan, hardworking every day of the week and never letting illness interfere with work. Even after his brain tumour he had carried on with the same routine, never feeling the need to sell up and retire to be happy and be alive in case the cancer returned. Catalan to the core: clever and dedicated to his extended family. English-speaking and living to work and make money no matter what interfered in his life. Jack didn't know then but there lay the core of Karina's problems; she was Irish not Catalan and not truly accepted into the family. If you have been seriously ill and the cancer might come back again most people would need to live – take their money and run away – but that would never happen with Josep Maria; it was not in his genetic makeup and it was not the Catalan way.

Manolo was the opposite of Josep Maria and had a bubbly happy personality designed to live life to the limit. He had been a good friend to Melanie and Jack since they had bought the apartment from his mother and he treated them as his best friends as with all his likeable and rich English clients. He was fun and always helpful, backed up by a wonderful team of girls in his office by the main square of Palafrio. In fact he seemed to have an endless stream of women attached to him and was well known and also well liked as the local Casanova.

On their arrival the apartment was splendid in its isolated newness. It had taken a year for the builders to rip it apart, stopping work during the holiday season as dictated by the local byelaws and rebuilding it with a very mañana attitude where everything was relaxed, starting with a beer for breakfast. The lazy style was something that they would have to embrace as part of their new way of life in Spain. Nothing was particularly planned and if it was, well the plans could always change. There were three bedrooms, an outside utility and shower which was a bonus at a seaside resort and finally a huge lounge-cum-diner attached to a bright red kitchen. The highlight of the place was the expansive balcony facing west, with tall pines giving shade from the hot afternoon sun. Manolo had received and located all the IKEA furniture and utensils carefully selected by Melanie in the UK and delivered from the Barcelona store, so the start of the holiday was easy as everything was there and ready to use.

After breakfast Joseph and Jack walked towards the beach via the one hundred and fifty one escalas – steps – that were cut into the base rock of the White headland. About halfway down they cut off to the right and went at an even steeper angle to land on the grey-pink rocks. These were tiled with mini pools left by the overnight washing given them by the sea and not yet evaporated by the sun. The rocks glistened with mica and wetness with the odd frond of bright green seaweed thrown into deep relief by the white sun. It was hot even at nine thirty but deemed too early for the Spanish and it was therefore the best time of the day as nothing stirred to their left in the heart of Yapanc. They carefully found a dry spot on the rocks that had been fashioned by the waves for hundreds of years into two perfect seats and sat hand in hand, content with the silence of their own company as they watched the sun glint across the silvery sea.

The pines along the promenade were all bent landwards without exception but never equally. Odd ones were so horizontal that children easily climbed along them as they played happily in the shade. They were also different heights and had odd shaped heads above the bare trunks but their commonality was the bright but deep green of their spring needles reflecting the early morning sun.

"Joseph, look at the water down there." Jack pointed to a small rock pool to their right. As the smallest of waves gently rolled into the pool it caused a myriad of patterns to bounce off the green sides. Dark lines emanated out in different directions interspersed by bright light with runs of foam surging in and then out depending on the seemingly haphazard swell of the sea.

"That's 'Real Life' Joseph, being able to sit here and watch the sea." Jack suddenly thought of Nim as his spirit surged with the sea and he recalled the same vision from years ago but couldn't place where. He knew he would never see Nim because the logic of a spirit guide becoming a physical entity was retained only within Hollywood films.

"A physical impossibility," Jack thought but Nim was there as an integral part of the sun, the air, the sea and the rock on which they sat. It was totally logical. Spirits were energy; energy would not travel a great distance and therefore it stayed close to where it was created. It didn't go off to some 'never never land' hundreds of millions of miles away. The energy stayed there in the world that we see and touch and was reused by those who believed in it and could access it.

"Joseph, every day I say my prayers, did you know that?"

"Dad, is that to baby Jesus?"

"Yes and no." He hesitated slightly, "they are more like pleas. A general thank you for my life but more than that it's an offer to do something for other people in the world. Shall I tell you how to do it?"

"Yes Dad, can I say it with you too?"

"Of course and then when we are together and have a moment like this we can always say it together and share the sun and the world around us. Like we talked before about being Sun Sharers. Okay?" Jack regarded Joseph seriously to see what his reaction might be. As expected Joseph said okay but he knew he would.

Jack began. "First of all it's important to clear your mind of the day so far or the day to come. Then you need to want, to know and to trust in God."

"Who is God, Dad?" His son looked up at him, his face alabaster in the early brightness of the sun, mirrored silver white by the sea as it crept higher above the horizon.

"No one knows Joseph. Everyone has their own view and probably none of them are right because it's something that cannot be proven or disproved. Do you understand?" A short nod came back.

"You saw the TV the other day about the war in Iraq and the Muslim people believing in their God Allah and you also know about Jesus and God from school don't you? Well, you can see them as the same God and in fact lots of people all over the world have different Gods in different shapes and sizes."

"How do you mean Dad?"

"Well, Gods in the shape of elephants, monkeys and loads of different things?"

Joseph giggled at the thought of his favourite animals he saw regularly in Chester Zoo.

"So it's a plea to your personal God that you can select my son. You start by saying after me: Oh Lord hear my prayer." Joseph repeated it looking into his Dad's eyes.

"You then think about something vitally important in the world. For example there are no sophisticated hospitals like we have at home in a place like Iraq and so you would then say please help the Iraqi people who have no hospitals today." They both repeated it.

"You then repeat it but wish for something else: Oh Lord hear my prayer, help all the children in Africa who have no food today."

His serious and thoughtful boy repeated Jack's words.

"Oh Lord hear my prayer, please give some peace to the people whose families have been killed in the New Orleans hurricane."

Jack and Joseph sat on that rock and joined the Collective but neither of them knew it. They were just doing what came naturally to them. They had a deep sense of responsibility to be part of something bigger and totally hidden to most people in the world.

Over the next week they picked a spot in the morning to sit quietly and watch the sun together whilst holding hands. Seven times every morning they said thank you for their day and wished for something better for someone else. At the end of every set of pleas they stood and looked at the sun and repeated together "The Father, the Son, the Holy Spirit, Amen," whilst crossing themselves in rhythm with each other and synchronised with the intonation. From forehead to chest, left shoulder to right shoulder. They joined the Collective and they became Sun Sharers as they shared their love and their hopes for the world.

Melanie came and joined them on the beach as the temperature hit twenty-five Celsius and the crowds gathered fighting for their share of the shoreline. Jack and Joseph had moved to the shade of a tree but Melanie was determined to be right by the sea, as close as possible to the fumes from the barca – boat engines as they sped out. "Jack, when those people move just there, look be quick. There! They are getting ready to go. You take the umbrella and put it up in their spot and I will bring the towels." Melanie was over-assertive and Jack responded unenthusiastically.

"Why do we need to move, does it really matter? You'll be asking me to bring towels down at eight am next."

"Because I want to be by the sea so that I can keep an eye on Joseph. It's all right for you sitting under a tree on that bench but someone has to be responsible." She was asking for another fight.

"Someone is responsible Melanie; I sit under a tree because the sun doesn't like me, not because I don't like the sun. You know I get prickly heat. It's horrific for me and always has been for thirty years." He complained and waited for the inevitable response.

"Jack, go and see someone in the Farmacia. Things have changed now and I am sure the chemist can help you."

"Two things Melanie. One I don't like sitting on the beach trying to go black all day as it's bad for your skin. Two the sunlight affects the chemicals under the skin and there is no magical cure to stop it and never will be. You have to avoid the sun by slapping on factor fifty total block. That means there is no choice in my mind as I don't intend looking like an English twat imitating a snowman melting on the hot sands. Sun bathing is boring so stop pushing your agenda on me again."

She couldn't be bothered to reply as the Spanish were moving. "Go now, quick."

Jack did his bit and played with Joseph in the sea for a while before wandering off to the square to attempt to casually catch up with his new friend Karina.

Rico Coco passed him as he left the playa – the beach. Jack recalled the summer-long cry of 'Rico Coco' drawn out and repeated three times as the wizened old man walked the beach, fag in mouth and glasses two inches thick hiding half of his small leathery face. He was loved by the children despite his grubby yellow tee shirt with Cooc written on the front and worn for the last five years and his stained blue Bermudas with his spindly sun-blackened legs protruding like stalks. Rico of course means delicious in Spanish which was very apt for the moment he hatcheted open a coconut in front of you on the baking sands of summer. He never spilt a drop of the sweet juices which tasted like nectar when poured down a baked throat.

"Karina, que tal, how are you?" Jack had spied her leaving the bakery and strolling purposefully across the square.

"Hiya my dear, I'm good thanks and how are you?" She gently kissed cheek to cheek, lightly touching her lips against him four times as opposed to the normal two. Jack beamed at her as he stepped back and left his right hand momentarily too long for politeness as it slid gently down her side, but she seemed as intrigued by him as he by her; pushed together by a force they didn't understand.

"I'm fantastic now I have seen you. How about a sail this afternoon on my boat? I bought the boat with money from my Dad after he died. It makes it special whenever I go out because I always think of him."

"That's lovely Jack," she responded with her soft Irish lilt. "I can come about five for an hour, after the lunch rush has finished if that's okay?" He smiled again.

"See you then." After they kissed goodbye he strolled back to his bench with a 'hard on' trying to force its way out of his shorts. That was embarrassing and meant walking with his hand casually dropped in front of his groin but he was deliriously happy. As soon as he sat down, Joseph spied him and came up to the shady seat under the tree for some love and curled up by his side with un helado – an ice cream – in his hand. Melanie was flat out on her back on the baking sands like a great lump of meat roasting in the oven. Jack looked down at her from the promenade and sighed openly. It was never meant to be like this and so he cuddled his son closer and pointed upwards to the clear blue sky.

"Joseph. I love you, wider than the sky." He looked down at his boy and their eyes met. Jack then lowered his arm to the horizon, "and I love you bigger than the sea. Always remember that. No matter what happens or wherever I am. I love you wider than the sky and bigger than the sea."

They stared out from their shade at the beauty, Sun Sharers forever, no matter what. The bonds between them were far deeper than father and son as they were built on a spiritual plane and were not purely emotional or physical.

Karina and Jack pushed the Laser Two off the trolley into the blue water with a little help from Joseph. Jack dipped into the water whilst holding on to the side to cool himself and at the same time to have a last piss before diving over the transom to squirm into the boat amid the plethora of ropes and pulleys. Karina had sailed for many years and loved it as much as Jack and beamed smiles as they gently pulled away from the beach, waving goodbye to Joseph and leaving Melanie firmly located like a limpet lying on her sweat soaked beach towel. As the boat reached out past the White headland they could see the swell washing across the smooth rocks before they tacked away into the freshening force three, unencumbered by any wind shadow and unwatched by the beached holidaymakers including their own families. They leaned out using the toe straps and surfed the long swell to surge across the top of each wave.

"This is 'Real Life' isn't it Karina." Jack had leaned closer to speak to her, touching their bare arms and legs together with a thrill.

"Just lovely Jack, just lovely. It's as though I've always known you somehow." She was silhouetted by the sun which formed a coloured halo around her auburn hair flying in the wind. Then she fell silent and within herself as they sped out towards the Islas Formigas or Ant islands near Cap Roig, the Red headland, towering above the pretty village of Kaletta.

Jack shouted in exhilaration, "Way we go." As he pulled up the spinnaker the bow of the dinghy lifted off the water and they planed across the face of the waves, hovering on the edge of stability but finding it intoxicating together.

A shared pleasure that Melanie would never want or even contemplate attempting.

"Karina, I also feel like I have known you before, almost as if in a different life. I know that sounds impossible but I remember you being happy and now you seem sad. Is that right? Are you happy Karina, I mean really happy?" He barely knew her but he felt he could ask her directly.

"It's not easy Jack. Since Josep Maria's illness we have struggled to find common ground other than work and I do get fed up of the daily family interference, as we live with all of them on top of us all the time. There's never a respite and a time for privacy anymore because the family business rules everything. Did you know in Spain, if I walked out he would have to pay me nothing? He could just give me some money to look after the children?"

Jack was thoughtful as he replied, "I looked on a legal website only last week in case I left Melanie and she could get seventy per cent of my assets and fifteen per cent of my net income plus half my pension too. I may as well be unhappy and stay married rather than follow my heart and be honest about the relationship. It's the exact opposite of the law here. If you make money at home in the UK the wives take it. Whereas what each partner puts in here you would keep if you left. Strange isn't it!"

Karina patted his bare leg above the knee and looked him in the eye. "Don't give up on her yet Jack, you need to be responsible and talk things through." She spontaneously pecked him on the cheek.

"So that applies to you as well then Karina? Stick with any crap, enjoy a beautiful house, watch the children grow up happy and stable and live with someone I presume you don't love anymore. Is that what you are saying lovely? Be responsible, stick with it even though he might die carrying on working so hard?"

She had turned away so he couldn't see the tears. Salt on salt in the spray. As they headed back to the beach the onshore thermal wind was dying in the late afternoon. She pleaded with him softly. "Jack, I have a secret that always affects what I do and I trust you will never tell anyone okay?"

"Of course, absolutely anything we say to each other is strictly between us forever, now that we have met again."

She carried on looking at the distant beach rather than into his face.

"When I was nine years old and for a period of nearly three years I was locked away in a dark room by my Father as a punishment for any tiny little thing I did, but only when my Mum wasn't around because she was busy working. He wouldn't give me food or drink and some of the worse days ran into nights because she had stayed away from home. He always told me to keep it a secret or he would punish me. That's why I need to be happy and why this family thing upsets me. I can't stand secrets either but I have never told that to anyone before." It was his turn to pat her leg and then he pulled her to him and kissed her full on the mouth. It was ecstatic, electrifying and was meant to be. He pulled away gasping with no air left in his chest.

"I'm sorry Karina, I'm sorry for you but also for your Dad. You can tell me anything and I will always try and help." She placed a hand on his strong brown shoulder as a gesture of renewed solidarity.

"This is 'Real Life'," said Jack again as they watched the sun sink slowly filtering through the trees on the White headland. He carried on bathed in an orange light. "Can you imagine what it's like for Josep Maria? Knowing your cancer will definitely come back in your brain and make you a vegetable before finally killing you. I wonder what his mental state is like? What does he feel inside and think about in his life? It's scary. What would you behave like Karina? Do you get on a higher plane spiritually or do you plunge to the depths?"

Karina looked at him solemnly and slowly told the truth. "He just exists as if there is nothing wrong. I think that helps. Work, children and just a few friends. It's like he and his family are just denying there is a problem. There's no thought of enjoying life more or even preparation for the inevitable. That's what gets to me; why not love me and the children enough to take time for us all to be as one for a few months or years." She wiped away a tear. "Sometimes Jack, I just want to run away and stop being the responsible Mother and wife. It gets too much! Hoy." She shrugged her shoulders.

This was a classic Karina expression when she couldn't prevent something. 'Hoy' and 'Pfur' made with air pushed through barely open lips meaning, 'So what, I can't control this' or sometimes used to say 'It's not really my problem.'

Jack felt desolate because he knew he couldn't help except to listen. He tried to lighten the mood by laughingly saying before landing on the beach, "Did you know there are two point eight billion women in the world and one of them will be my Soul Mate, the one I call my Sun Sharer? Did you know that? But only one of them is meant for me! Most of us go through life happy and content because as human beings we are content to have the convenience and structure of a partner. I'm not content though and abhor convenience so I tell you what; I will look for that Sun Sharer in my life even if I have to travel the whole world." He thought privately, "That is, if I haven't met my Sun Sharer yet in Harriet, Bridget or you."

She smiled. "So your Sun Sharer is exactly the same thing as a Soul Mate?"

"Of course, but much more than that."

She smiled wider. "So you may end up with an ugly Japanese woman with bad teeth and a hunchback because she is the one for you in all of the two point eight billion?"

"Yes, absolutely!" He laughed. "Sharing a real, spiritual and meaningful relationship with someone isn't about physical appearance just like sex isn't everything. It's about the mind and the spirit. How you feel about someone not how they look physically and maybe whether you have known that person before. I don't know but call it a past life hey. You may think it's all about power and money in your Catalan world Karina but not in mine! Definitely not in my world. So cheer up and stay responsible. You have two lovely children, a husband and an extended family that rely on you. You have enough money to live well, good health and fabulous beauty. It can't be all bad."

She looked into his eyes. "It's not all bad, you are right Jack and I also have a new best friend whom I can talk to about things. Thank you my dear, thank you."

★ ★ ★

One evening the new foursome ate together in the welcoming Hotel Yapanc right by the square and the beach. It was hot enough for them all to sit in tee shirts and shorts under the canopy outside the main restaurant, where they could listen to the quiet chatter and laughter from the other tables and the swish of the sea crossing the dark sands. Inside was bustling as the Catalans felt that twenty degrees was still overcoat weather and so it was nice to be in the relative peace and calm of the terrace and tilt a chair back to look at the beautifully clear stars and crescent shaped moon. The famous hotel is run by two cousins whose fathers had started the business after the war and it retained the same aura as its heyday years when artists like Dali and the stars of the silver screen made it their place to party away the summer. The internal walls around the huge bar area were covered with photos of the rich and famous. Lance Armstrong stood smiling between the two owners in one picture. In his Tour de France days he had lived in the old Jewish quarter in Girona with the singer Sheryl Crow and they used to bring his children to sit on the beach between the boats near the harbour area and away from prying eyes. Hotel Yapanc was a place frequented by famous people who wanted to live normally with respect for their privacy which is exactly what the owners gave them. However, the partying on Friday and Saturday nights with a disco in the bar and dancing on the serving counter is still as hectic as ever until the owners clear out the itinerant clientele, who were soaked in sweat and water sprayed on to them by the barmen. The party goers spill out onto the beach at precisely three thirty in the morning, still full of life, and move on to the more formal disco in a giant marquee near Palafrio.

The food was served.

Entremeses, or starters, were on the table ready to be shared: chiporones rezabados, or fried baby squid soaked in olive oil and garlic. Pâté de foie gras brought in from nearby France and freshly battered calamares, or squid rings. All served with slices of white toast rubbed with fresh tomato and garlic. A bottle of 1997 Marques de Caceres Rioja was already half gone, blowing the Cheshire set myth that you should only drink white wine with fish.

Jack was asking Josep Maria about Catalan life. "I was in Palafrio today buying fruit and vegetables in the open-air market and all the store holders wanted to speak in Catalan not Spanish, which really confused me now that I've started learning Spanish."

Josep Maria kept his head down and mumbled, "We are proud Catalans, amigo; you are learning Castellano not Spanish, because Spain is the total country and not the language. Remember it has Basque and Gallegos peoples too."

Jack replied happily, "The language is so hard Karina; I think I would have been better off learning Catalan. I get terribly confused about simple words like 'handle' because you have three Spanish words to our one: El picaporte for a door handle, el mango for a knife handle and la asa for a saucepan handle, but in the same order in Catalan it's nansa, manec, and manetta or something like that. Worse still you have to learn whether they are male and female 'el' or 'la', so sometimes I want to give up!"

She laughed at Jack. "You just need to study harder under that tree by the beach!"

He remonstrated, throwing his hands in the air to imitate the Spanish. "It gets worse. Some people say hola for hello and others daio for the same in Catalan, although they also say this when they are leaving rather than adios. Then, instead of gracias, thanks, I get told merce so I think I am talking to someone from France and then blow me down if you Catalans don't all say moultbe for okay, very good, yes, no and everything else rather than vale – okay, or muy bien – good. I am so confused!" They all laughed except Melanie.

"You should come on the beach with Joseph and me rather than study all the time. I don't see why I should look after him all day."

He was exasperated. "No way, I can't stand sun bathing and wasting the day away. I want to find out about everything here. It's exciting, different and interesting like having a whole new life."

Melanie tut tutted in disappointment that her husband was so energetic and enthusiastic and Karina held her hand up and said hoy as usual. Jack continued enthusiastically. "I am finding the true me in Spain. I went biking in Ripoll yesterday on a Pyrenean mountain and must have been six thousand feet up and totally alone apart from the odd eagle and bobcat that I saw and got excited about. It was estupendo – stupendous. I tell you what, I must have lost at least eight pounds in weight in the last two weeks by eating less carbs and crap like biscuits but fundamentally ensuring I exercise every day. After a few weeks of the same regime you would be dancing down the road with so much internal energy. Fifty down and fifty to go."

Melanie looked at Jack. "You are just having a mid-life crisis Jack and need to get a grip on yourself. This isn't 'Real Life' you know, you are on holiday."

Jack was sharp and looked across at Karina when he replied to his miserable wife. "This is 'Real Life' because life is what you make of it and not what it makes of you. The rat race at home is where we have gone wrong." Josep Maria took a slug of Rioja and said nothing; he just sat there thinking how nice it would be to walk down the road properly. Jack turned on Melanie again.

"I suppose text messaging your friends all day whilst sat on the beach is 'Real Life'? You have sent loads to Greece or Majorca or wherever and received about ten haven't you? It's you who needs to get a life Melanie and come out of La La land."

Karina diplomatically changed the subject. "Are you keen on cycling then Jack?"

He was and proudly told her so. "When we first came here, I did exactly what any cycling enthusiast would do. I decided to go to the Tour de France at Col de Beille near Andorra. So I prepared for it professionally as any professional might."

"What did you do" she asked.

"I read a wonderful book by Geoffrey Wheatcroft on the plane coming over to Spain." She laughed and Josep Maria started to take some interest in the conversation as Jack carried on tongue in cheek.

"Hardly athletic I know, sat for two hours on a plane skipping through reams of facts but it was inspiring, centring on the greatest feats I believe a human being can endure. The competitors put the original meaning into the term 'hard man' and even if they do take drugs, I don't care because it's almost achieving the impossible. Over two thousand miles and twenty stages each biased to the climbers or the sprinters but always won by my hero Armstrong – el jefe – the boss."

"Armstrong is the one Jack; el jefe is a good word. I like to be the boss too." Josep Maria sank a glass of Rioja in appreciation of the fitness that he craved but never complained about not having.

"Josep, I went up the same mountain as them in three hours and it nearly killed me but they went up after already doing a hundred miles before it and in just forty minutes. Unbelievable."

Josep Maria joined in, "I used to cycle Jack maybe seventy kilometres in a day but many years ago because it was popular when we had heroes like Miguel Indurain. I still have a road bike in my garage."

"Shall we go out together then Josep?" Jack knew the answer.

"I cannot now my friend, I am very busy." He wanted to say I am too ill and my legs don't work properly but he was too proud to admit it.

Jack continued in his excitement about Le Tour. "It was so fraternal, a fabulous party atmosphere and then I came screaming down the road with the rest of the cycling teams weaving in and out between the journalists' cars until I reached the head of a queue of cars and there, lying in the road, was a cyclist with blood pouring out of his head, which made me think what a prat I was without a helmet. Then, after walking past the police and the ambulance teams I set off flat out again with my head bent low over the handlebars and only a dozen others around me until there was a crack of thunder and the heavens opened pouring an inch of water on the tarmac. So by the time I got to my car at the foot of the mountain, I was soaked and had to strip off and drive home naked for four hours to our hotel in Tiramisu with people staring at me as they went past!"

Melanie told Josep Maria what happened when he arrived back. "When he walked in I asked him if he had a good time and he said: 'The best day of my life'. So I replied what; better even than the day we got married? And Jack, I quote, said to me 'It was fucking fantastic, far better than then.' So how do you think I felt?"

Josep Maria was on Jack's side and identified with the situation. "I expect you would say to Jack, that's wonderful, I am so glad you had such a marvellous day."

Of course, she hadn't said that and hadn't bothered asking anymore about his day. Instead she had gone off to bed in a hump.

Jack was pretty pissed by now as they finished their main courses and were ready for postres – the sweets. They ordered traditional types such as Crema Catalana, the Catalan version of crème brûlée and recuit, a soft white cottage cheese smothered with honey and a few walnuts. Jack started a new tack of conversation which was also very close to his heart.

"The other thing I don't understand is how a strict Catholic country having had a rigid Fascist regime can possibly have so many sex shops and newspapers full of adverts for call girls? You can't even drive to the airport without seeing them sat in their deckchairs on the forest tracks waiting to be picked up and shagged."

Josep Maria quickly walked away to the toilet in order to keep out of the way. It could be that like many middle class Catalans he had some sexual secrets to hide and so he would avoid getting a direct question about something he was very knowledgeable about. Jack watched him go and continued unabashed, facing Karina.

"I went into the video shop to get a film yesterday and at the back of the store next to huge numbers of porn CDs, they had a TV screen showing naked girls kissing naked girls. I have never experienced anything like it in my life." He looked across at Melanie sitting next to Karina and half joked, "Go on girls, kiss each other. I dare you; you know you would like it better than with your husbands as girls are far more sensitive, tender and gentle."

He choked on his laughter. Melanie looked disgusted.

"Fuck off," she said; unusual words as she rarely swore.

They ordered more water with their coffees to help wash some of the fun out of Jack. Antipodean mineral water in a 'fab' chunky bottle with one of the world's purest waters all the way from a state of the art carbon neutral processing plant in New Zealand. The label said: Con gas. Servir fria, Beber mucha, Vivir bien. With gas, serve cold, drink a lot and live long.

"It tastes fantastic but what a load of baloney," he thought as he stared down the opening in Karina's blouse at her large rounded pink breast poking out against the flimsy cotton.

"If it costs six pounds a litre for luxury Rolls Royce water but a fraction of that for local stuff, what is the point? Why do people bother when the most eco friendly thing is to turn on the fucking tap? It can't be ecological to ship or drive water around the world can it Nim? Or is it just names, names, names again?"

Jack was left to stare at Karina and listen to his guide through the swish of the sea.

I am glad you had more time with Karina, Jack.
Do you remember her yet?
You ate the same foods, sat by the same sea.
Creating the heart and soul of Catalonia that is with
you now.

Josep Maria returned to a less controversial table about an hour later and said his goodbyes. The Catalan way is to go out with friends and then spend half the evening talking to some other friends that you happen to bump into. It's not rude, it's just Catalan.

He spoke directly to Jack, "We must go now; I am up early mañana. I know you are leaving tomorrow and can't come with us but when you return in May I would like to invite you to sail on our yacht that we charter occasionally. Will you come my friend?" Josep Maria and Karina loved their sailing but because he struggled with his health they needed help and rarely went out without a crew.

Jack was ecstatic. "Hombre? Friend. I would love to come with you. What sort of boat do you charter and where do you start?"

"We have a Beneteau eleven metros in the new port at Palamost. Telephone us when you arrive."

The Catalan couple walked away with Karina just behind Josep Maria.

Jack watched and said his own personal goodbye to the beautiful woman he was overjoyed to have met and then turned to Melanie and said sadly, "That's it then. The end of 'Real Life' for a while."

She disagreed again. "It's just a holiday Jack. Get over it and get your mind back into work mode for God's sake." She strolled off towards the apartment as he lagged behind and watched the stars gleam brighter as they left the lights of the hotel and square.

Early on the last morning of their holiday, the sun was rising in a perfectly blue sky over the mirrored sea as he took a swim before the short run to the airport. Jack was breaking the perfect image with his gentle backstroke a hundred metres off the Yapanc beach. He rolled from side to side in the light swell as he methodically windmilled his arms and let his mind drift with the currents. The glint off the sea was so bright and penetrating that he thought he might never see again.

"Oh Lord hear my prayer." It was a perfect place to feel spiritually free and join the Collective.

Jack be careful of the sharks.

"Don't be daft Nim, you don't get sharks in the 'Med.'" He paused, "or at least not the ones that can harm you."

He turned over and ducked his head underwater to look for any fish life and surreptitiously whether a shark was circling. All he could see moving were a couple of brown jellyfish. If they were white he would have worried as they were female and gave you a hell of a sting. As he swam closer to the beach the water went from slightly chilly to warm as the sand shallowed up to him near the harbour. He had been grateful for these early morning swims as they lightened his spirit. No people around, no smelly noisy motor boats just a taste of 'Real Life'.

He walked back to the apartment, taking the coastal path on their headland and then climbing down into the sweet smelling pines. He hid himself on the edge of a hundred foot drop. His prick was hard in anticipation as he closed his eyes and thought of Bridget. He wanked himself perched on the edge whilst still hidden from view and as he shuddered he opened his eyes to watch the spunk spurt outwards two feet and stream down to the sea way below.

Looking to the horizon with the intoxicating smell of myrtle and mallow he tried to reason why he had so much sexual frustration inside him, but it all came back to his bad marriage.

5
First dawning — I don't believe in Astrology

A birthday present was the catalyst to change Jack's life but it was prompted by a telephone call from his friend Harriet. "Hello poppet, how are you today?"

"Same shit, different weekend."

"You must stop saying that but I can imagine why. In fact it was Melanie I wanted. I need some ideas about my girls' birthday party."

"Did you just imply that my bad weekend had something to do with my dearly beloved wife?"

"Of course not poppet." She implied yes of course in her tone. "I was only thinking of how I could alleviate your problems because I know you wouldn't say it without good reason."

At the end of her sentence Jack heard a faint click as the receiver upstairs was picked up by the lump who was lying in bed. He warned Soul Shiner by not replying to the question. "I'm not sure if she's awake, Soul Shiner. I'll just shout her for you." He hollered up the stairs with the portable in his hand. "Melanie?" He tried again but louder this time. "Melanie? It's Harriet on the phone for you." Receiving no reply he returned to the caller as he heard the click of the receiver being replaced.

Harriet had taken the hint. "Talking of birthday presents Jack, have you been to see my astrologer?"

"No sorry lovely, it was a great idea but I've been busy at work and then with Dartmouth and Meaux, life has been too hectic.

147

By the way she's not listening in now but I suppose I had better go upstairs and give her the telephone so she can express surprise that it's you calling."

"Stick with it Jack. I can hear your pain every time we talk poppet. I want to help you if I can but I also get the feeling she is pushing me away at the moment. Typical I suppose, always searching for a new friend with something extra to give her."

"Too true lovely, but it's nice to know you care. Thank you Harry, you always make my day somehow. I'll pass you on now lovely."

"Take care poppet. Go and see the astrologer soon. I went before Christmas and what she predicted for me also applied in part to you. Go and see her Jack, I feel that it's important somehow. Bye."

He said goodbye as he trundled upstairs and handed the telephone to Melanie, who was lying in bed and immediately expressed surprised happiness to talk to Harriet.

"Two-faced bitch," Jack said quietly as he walked away.

Beatty Maravilloso lives on the Beeston Road in Peckforton near 'Tar poor lee'. When you walk into her house you step back four hundred years and feel the oppressive presence of Cavaliers and Roundheads vying for your attention, as the shadow of Beeston Castle slips through the tiny windows and merges with the darkened oak beams. They sat in the old fashioned kitchen in front of the black warmth of the 1920s range and began their journey.

"I can't believe I am here Beatty but when a friend buys you a present you can't refuse it can you?" Jack smiled ruefully and looked at the old diminutive figure dominated by her enormous round glasses. She sat with her back ramrod straight in a worn leather armchair, clutching Jack's handwritten astrology chart in a claw-like hand.

He continued tentatively as she stared at him without reply. "Do you see or feel spiritual things here?"

Beatty raised her chin slightly and said in a clear and very deep voice. "Yes of course Jack George Edmunson, I join the Collective every night."

"Sorry," replied a nonplussed Jack, "but what does that mean?"

"You will find out Jack, you will find out." She emphasised the second will and made him feel more uncomfortable as she stared intently at his face.

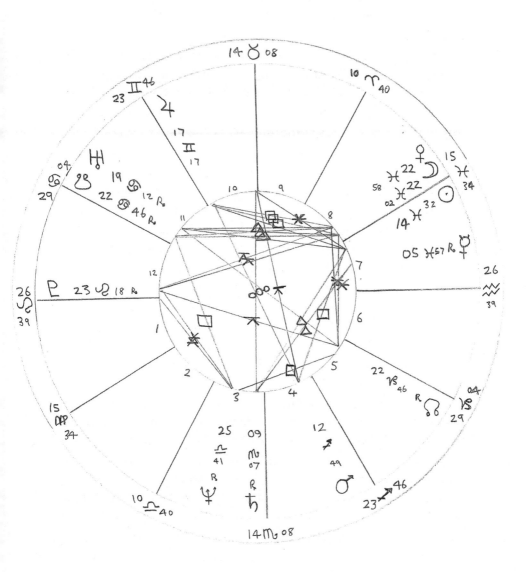

She started by describing the structure of a chart, pointing between the lines that sectioned the circle on the paper. "Each of these twelve spaces is called a house and each is an area of experience that can be read on many levels to show you every aspect of your life. You can even find –" she paused and peered over her glasses, "if you are clever enough Jack; you can even find other people in your chart like your friend Harriet. There is nothing hidden if you have someone who can interpret it but the accuracy is totally dependent on the birth details you have given me, right down to the correct hour. So let us start by looking at the basics my boy." She remained stone faced and stern and the 'my boy' put Jack in his youthful place.

"You have Leo rising Jack, so I would imagine you can be quite gregarious at times. You have also got the sun in Pisces so you have an affinity for the supernatural, whether it's acknowledged by you or not my boy. You are also an open person as Pisces is intuitive and sometimes a psychic sign. That will stand you in good stead in all aspects of your work but it can make you quite sensitive. However it may restrict you too as you constantly try to justify yourself. You must understand Jack that your chart is quite unique in all of my experiences over the last sixty years." She squirmed around in her large brown chair as if to rearrange her thoughts.

"What really interests me is Pluto in the twelfth house. Do you work?" She tailed off as Jack rudely interrupted her.

"Yes, I am a consultant," he said brightly.

She glanced over the top of her glasses, unimpressed by the assertion. "Leo rising means you have to interrupt, so I imagine that you can't work alone. You would feel quite uncomfortable if you were isolated for days on end so you need a situation in which you interact strongly with other people. Although you are a Piscean, some of the earlier astrologers would call you a Leo and that's how you are perceived to be until they get to know the real you."

She stretched her legs proud of the armchair and dropped them slightly down again, leaving her feet dangling a foot from the floor. She reminded Jack of Yoda from Star Wars and he laughed inwardly, not even daring to smile.

She recommenced. "Now let me see, let's go back to Pluto in the twelfth. Does your busyness get in the way of doing anything truly creative? You have got your north node in the fifth person so you have a mass of creativity. It is what you are drawn to achieving in this life without perhaps knowing it my boy." Her eyes were large and seemingly changed colour whilst glaring through the old glasses as thick as prisms. She abruptly asked. "Do you walk or something similar?"

Her boy said, "I like to walk but most of all I love sailing."

"Jack my dear, you are not making enough time for it because that's where your mind is free. You don't have to paint a picture or to write a novel to be creative. Creativity in life is not confined in that way. You are creating when you are sailing as it is something that you have to open your mind to by letting your intuition flow, thus unblocking your very special intuition."

Jack contemplated the black range and pictured his unwritten book, feeling his frustration surface.

She glanced slowly at the range and then back to Jack's face, drawing his thoughts into her. "You are involved in big projects aren't you? With Pluto just there," she prodded the paper, "it is the planet of transformation so you take nothing and transform it into something." She stared through the magnifying glasses with her hazel eyes unblinking and questioning.

It was Jack's turn to squirm as he replied, "Absolutely. That is exactly what my job entails but I don't enjoy it anymore." He returned her stare for the first time but was still unnerved by it.

Beatty continued after his confirmation. "And then you go on to do it again, project by project. You need to do that in your personal life now as your business life is coming to an end and your new second life will take over." She paused, unready to reveal more. "You need to have a personal project for creativity and for relaxation as a fundamental part of your life. It is important and will become more so over the next four years. The timing in your path is set. Do you understand how important that is?"

Again the beady stare that he couldn't face. He felt as if there was static in the air which was short circuiting his thinking.

She sighed and her eyes rolled to their whites as if she were dead before flicking back to normality. She continued in a hypnotic voice. "At the age of fifty-four you will have the opportunity of doing something completely different." She giggled like a schoolgirl, making Jack wonder whether he was in the presence of someone who was enlightened or a complete nutcase. A more relaxed Beatty continued.

"So, what happened at age forty-eight my boy? That was your mental turning point wasn't it?" He looked down at the floor and replied sadly.

"My Father died aged seventy-six."

She was silent for a minute before quietly continuing. "You won't die at seventy-six my boy as long as you stick by your true friends." She dried up again and Jack puzzled over the obscure comment.

"You see, this chart is a picture of your potential but it's also a picture of your pitfalls on the way."

"What sort of pitfalls Beatty?"

"There are evil people in your life. You haven't met them yet but they know you from previous Karmas and you will need a guide to avoid the danger on your path." She was looking out of the window at the fading sun as if listening to someone. "Awareness is the key and once you understand your potential then you can reach for it. There lies the biggest problem, as to understand you have to accept your path and destroy things that you have now to enable you to live in uncertainty. You see Jack, potentially you are a long 'liver' because you have the planet of death in the twelfth house which is as far round as it can go. In fact, your personal planet of death, Pluto is in the twelfth too and it is also the planet of regeneration. It means my boy, if you maintain a balance in your life, you will live for a very long time." She sat back immobile and went completely quiet in the caress of the leather.

Jack felt bold enough to comment at last, "I always say to my son, work hard and play hard. Since my birthday I also say fifty down fifty to go, so maybe what you say Beatty is already in my mind."

She gave him a friendly smile for the first time since his arrival. "That's a balance indeed my boy but now you need to concentrate on the next half of your life." By now she actually sounded like Yoda. "Begin to put a plan in order. Make sure you have got the umm...." She seemed lost for words again as she gazed at the beamed ceiling as if talking to someone. Jack did consider Nim might be present before he dismissed it as a stupid concept. As he thought about it, he shivered despite the warmth of the range.

"I suggest that you spend as much time as you can this coming year on or near the water." Beatty stood and wandered towards the hob and placed a startling pink kettle on the top. She brought out some ginger biscuits which were his favourites as a child before preparing their tea. Turning through a haze of steam and talking above the whistling she said, "My boy, I have an affinity with you, do you know that? Your chart is a pleasure to read and believe me, you can do great things but you must be confident and start to do them now." She looked at him quizzically as she sat back in her chair with her cup delicately balanced in her right hand.

Jack felt that she knew everything about him and the reading was a front for something deeper, an understanding that he couldn't fathom. She tipped her cup and poured tea into the saucer and took a slurp before continuing. "You are a fantastic communicator aren't you? Jupiter in Gemini tells me that. You are really good at building pictures for people because your imagination is so vast. This certainly makes you a forceful personality but you must never abuse this trait as people will trust you." At this point Beatty was becoming agitated, kicking her little legs up and down and pushing her glasses hard onto the bridge of her nose several times.

"Are you good with writing Jack? You could have some success with that. You are quite capable of writing something that would bring success or fame or whatever you want."

Jack quickly said, "Fame, I want to be famous and remembered. I don't need money in a simple life."

She was still agitated as she replied, "You are very, yes very capable of being a writer but it is a question of what would you write? It is difficult to describe but basically it is a bit off the wall, a bit zany, a bit different. It would have a mystical application as Uranus with Neptune suggests a link. It has to be-light hearted with a serious theme. If you could choose something to write about Jack what would it be?"

He looked out of the windows at the pink scudding clouds in the dimming blue sky. "Something spiritual Beatty, something with an impact on day to day life, a message to many people."

Beatty raised the pitch of her voice and spoke quickly for the first time. "Well that would fit because Uranus is not serious, how can I put this? Uranus is the anarchist and when he's around he will start things off but he will not stay put to see who finishes it. Nevertheless, he is the great instigator and it's square to Neptune which is spiritual. As it also goes up to the moon it has to be something that comes from your heart. You need to really feel it and live it. You could do it my boy as a great life project and then just see where it takes you." Beatty sat thoughtfully looking at the chart and wafting it up and down a few inches at a time. The Grandfather clock ticked away in the corner dictating the pace of life.

"Jack, you are very good at communicating on a deep level, one to one. So you can have deep discussions with friends like Harriet and if this birth time is exactly right, you will also need a partner for your future. It's not a married partner; it's a need for a new partner in this new life of yours. You would not want to be alone and in fact you can't do it on your own. You have the Sun in the seventh house and that's the house of one to one relationships. You shine better if you have got a partner."

"A Sun Sharer then?" said Jack, puzzling over the number seven that constantly filled his spiritual thoughts.

"Well, the right partner for your path my boy and not necessarily your wife. Only then will you find your true equilibrium. I believe you have met this person already and don't recognise her for who she really is..."

Jack sat thinking of Karina or Bridget but then considered Soul Shiner who was close but seemed forever far away.

"As this moon here is conjunct Venus it tells me you also have a very good eye for aesthetics, you know what is beautiful and what's not and that includes a partner but in their entirety not just superficial beauty."

Jack quietly agreed. "I know that," he said. "I look inside a woman to see if I like them if that makes any sense."

Beatty affirmed his thoughts. "What I am feeling is very good indeed. You see Mars is in Sagittarius. Your enormous energy, your 'busyness' would be best used in a spiritual way as you get older. I imagine your garden is a spiritual place for you. You are working with the earth and you are working on the beauty around you which Pisceans do. Working on the love around the whole of your environment is also possible but there has to be someone to appreciate your work as well. What did you call her? Your Sun Sharer?" She laughed with pure joy touched by some thoughts that she would never share.

"If you were doing it for yourself you would experience great pleasure but it wouldn't be enough. You need an external appreciator my boy."

Her legs dangled and kicked up and down in time with the ticking of the clock as she appeared to doze off but she suddenly said, "Have you got another property somewhere?"

"I have a new place in Spain that I only recently moved into."

Beatty leaned forward for the follow up question. "Is it by water Jack? I can see a property near water. Not yet though, I would give it…" She tailed off and then restarted. "I'm trying to be logical with a subject that's not logical but I get this incredible picture of boat-building. Go on tell me I'm mad."

Jack smirked but couldn't decide whether he thought she was mad or gifted and so he remained quiet.

"What I'm seeing is a boatyard but I don't want you to think that this is by any means prescriptive. There's a beautiful woman involved but she is not what you think and so be careful my boy."

He asked what was constantly on his mind. "So Beatty, if I go down this so-called path that I keep hearing about – "

She interrupted him again. "Can I ask you a question Jack?" He nodded his assent. "Do you hear your guide now?"

He shook his head in denial but when he returned her gaze she had her head tilted back challenging him to deny it. He could not. "Sometimes I hear Nim." It was a grudging acknowledgement.

"Sometimes is enough my boy but his guidance will become more important as each month passes. You have free will Jack and what you listen to and accept is up to you." It was uncanny to sit with someone who didn't know him but could talk about the most important parts of his life. She continued by regaining his attention with a small cough. "You have got the sun in Pisces and in the seventh house and with this birth time you need a relationship as you are lonely without one, but Pisceans are not easy to be married to!" Beatty laughed.

"Beatty, unfortunately I am also married to a Piscean too."

She didn't appear shocked by the words as she replied, "So you have got two Pisceans in the home?"

"Yes, when I am there, which is rare."

Beatty concentrated. "How does she feel about life at the moment?"

Jack looked down at his feet in denial again as he replied with a direct lie. "I don't know really, she's very happy I think."

She looked straight through him making him feeling guilty about trying to lie to her before she continued. "You see Pisceans always carry a sense of isolation. There is always a bit of a Piscean you can't reach. No matter how close you are as a married couple."

He also knew there was a piece of him that was not reachable by anyone except his Sun Sharer.

"Your chart says you are a very deep thinker. It's Pluto in the trans-house that does that because Pluto is about life's depths sexed up. It's got all the really deep stuff that makes life happen but it's also hidden and strangely in the area of your chart that shows it is hidden from everybody. So that's as deep as it can go Jack. That house is also open to people who are intuitive, edging on to psychic. I think you know that Jack? Don't you feel that sometimes?"

He replied honestly, "I try and push it away. I know I'm

psychic because of things that have happened."

She sighed, "Jack, you have an affinity with psychic matters. A spirituality that can honestly count on this Earth. There are many of us around in the world who believe in joining together and keeping it a wholesome place. Working for Good against Evil, the light versus dark. People believe in things you cannot imagine and as part of the Collective we wait to see if you will join us."

Jack was completely out of his depth and wanted to leave. None of this could possibly be true.

Stay and listen Jack.
Believe and change your life.

"I must keep emphasising that because this chart is so unusual you should participate in the Collective and learn to live with your new self-belief." Jack sat entranced so she drew him deeper into her murky world.

"Remember the twelfth house? It is called the house of prisms and is the house of the mind or the sub-consciousness and is open to the Collective. So you will have a growing awareness and you cannot deny it. You would have started being intuitive as a child but it's developed like your life and I would suspect over the last few years it is intruding onto it. By now you would have noticed what I would call some peak experiences. Has that happened?" She knew before he replied.

"Yes absolutely." He was flabbergasted as it all seemed true and about things he knew but hadn't let his mind explore as he kept them isolated on the periphery of his thoughts.

Beatty was perched on her chair with her feet touching the flags for the first time and was on edge. She seemed to fill the room as outside the day suddenly darkened. "Jack my boy; you need to understand that this will be a growing phenomenon. You have seemingly been sent here by accident but it was meant to happen so that I could give you this message. You must allow your mind to have free rein and the only way you are going to do that is by getting away from everything and also putting yourself on the water. You belong to the water with your Sun Sharer."

Jack eased his aching shoulders and straightened his back. "I will be in Spain for some of this summer so that will happen as I have bought a boat out there."

Beatty pensively touched her lips with the back of her forefinger. "Would your wife go too?"

He considered why she asked this. "What does she see ahead and how far is she looking?" He laughed to relieve his tension and ducked the question. "Talking of water, I have just been to Dartmouth for my birthday and had a vivid psychic experience that has troubled me ever since."

A half smile crossed her face. "Jack, after fifty-four it is time for your life, not everyone else's. It's a time for something new, to create in your life what you can see in your mind. I never feel moved to say things like that so I am very uncomfortable because I have so many psychic images today. When I am working with charts I don't normally work with what I would call clairvoyance. My reading has gone across the bridge today and I hear your spirit guide. The boatyard has people associated with it and I see both Good and Evil. I can smell and taste the place and wherever that is you can write your book. You will watch the sea and the sun all day and every day."

"Which is my path and how do I get there Beatty?"

"There is a growing awareness that what you have is not enough and it's going to become stronger. The need to move, to change and even to downsize in a way." She paused thoughtfully. "It's not that actually, it's to simplify, yes indeed, it's the need to simplify. And whilst you are in this new place, you can use something that is from within here." She touched her heart. "Not just your heart but also your very old soul. All I know is that you have a gift within you and you should write a book. Do you know what I feel it is? It's a guide to living; it's a guide to life."

Jack replied. "Well, I only thought about that this morning when I was putting together notes about my book that I might write one day. That is so weird."

She set him straight. "You have more power of visualisation

than you realise and that could do with consolidating. What do you do to encourage it?"

"I get a buzz from books about the achievements of famous people who have changed their lives and those around them. How people have used the power within themselves, the power of their minds and how they have simplified things into great ideas or concepts. You know Beatty there is too much in our world and it drives me crazy. Whether it's technology like mobiles or TV channels or food types."

She stared at him. "Then you need to simplify everything Jack."

He agreed. "It's all very materialistic as well and everything is turning over too fast and getting dumb and dumber." He contemplated, thinking about the impact of modern life on Joseph's future. "Does my chart say anything about my children? You have their birth dates and times from when I telephoned you. I have an older daughter called Edima who was taken from me when she was very young."

Beatty paused before asking, "Do you have any reservations about leaving her behind?"

His reply hurt him to say it, "Yes, terrible ones."

Beatty was trying to relax him now. "You never intended it; it was almost a Karmic thing. You would never have remained with her. So stop thinking 'if only' because the 'if only' was never a possibility."

"Beatty, I also have a grown up son called Rodney."

Beatty asked, "Does he look like you? Because his dates put him in your first house, which is your house of identity. You have a very strong Karmic link with him and he is meant to take lessons from you and you from him. If you could mix the two of you together you would be the perfect human being."

Jack looked at her sitting placidly in the chair but now she was slumped for the first time in two hours, her energy nearly spent.

"I also have a young son called Joseph."

She smiled warmly. "This child was meant to be. His sun is in conjuncture with Mars. What you need to do is allow him to find a balance for himself. It all coincides with the difficult aspect of your tenth house. It's the second half of your life which will influence him enormously but his path is extremely dangerous. He should also have inherited your energy and drive. Do you think he has?"

Jack missed the way she quickly moved on. "Absolutely Beatty."

She commented on his wife to change the subject. "The balance is controlled by his mother. The best thing you can do is to make the effort to communicate what you have been thinking to her. Does that make sense Jack?"

"Yes, I keep trying to communicate but she doesn't listen anymore. There is no respect either."

Beatty didn't qualify what she had already said or seen even though she had alluded to his possible marital problems. "Jack, did you come with any questions for me?"

"My questions were all answered thank you. You see I came not believing and I am leaving in a very perturbed state of mind."

Beatty stood in front of him and grasped his two hands. She spoke in reassured tones direct to his soul. "Look my boy, you are at a stage in your life of spiritual evolution. This is where you are becoming aware of the difference between fate and destiny. You are coming up to a period where if you had a book then you would have an image of the last page with writing on it. So you are turning over and it's now blank but the book of knowledge has no words. It doesn't need them because every bit of knowledge required is deep inside of you. The trick is to access it my boy, just access it."

Jack squeezed her withered hands and felt her power. "Do I need a guide?"

Beatty smiled up at him. "My dear Jack, I think you have got several but how to describe them? I wouldn't know how to begin. You have got Mars in Sagittarius in the fourth house which is at the very root of your belief. The fourth house is where you spring from and it's your Karmic, cultural and social inheritance. From that house, if you are clever enough Jack, then you have everything that you have ever been since Earth began. Mars gives you your will, your energy and your drive. Sagittarius is rising in this house and indicates long journeys and spirituality but the longest journey you can ever take is the one that is between your ears. You can do this without moving from your armchair." She hugged him close and whispered, "The message is simple. You have been born to use your will to bring about your own spiritual reality. So you can look for guides but in fact I think he has found you my dear and you need to let him in. Remember, with a fantastic chart it is sometimes easy to miss your opportunities. You've got a strong will as you were born with it. It's not something that you fought hard to develop and it will easily take you to a spiritual destination once you are in alignment and have realised that is what you want. Have you done anything at all which has a charitable benefit?" Her energy bridged across to him through her hands.

"No, but I am interested in the environment and our children's future."

Beatty gave him more guidance. "You could do something with that and be incredibly successful. Making children aware that there are other ways to achieve things. Giving them an alternative, perhaps by raising money so that children could become environmentally aware. Anything practical but with something to do with real life and nature. You could also leave here and completely change your path by free will and ignore my messages. If you did, you would be going against what you know. Not fate, because fate is what we make happen. Going against your own destiny and missing your opportunity. It is very difficult to get out of the rat race Jack and it isn't easy to turn your back on 'the now' and so it will be very hard for you."

He was quiet, entranced by the feel of her ancient power. "The pictures are flowing in my mind and I am worn out by it all, so dreadfully tired. I can actually see a book with a royal blue cover. I don't get such specifics unless it's far more than possibilities. So bearing that in mind, not only would you write it but you could get it published. It's not just a manuscript, it becomes a reality."

She showed him to the door holding his arm for physical support, frail now with all her energy spent.

★   ★   ★

He sat in his car under Beeston Castle in the dark and turning he looked at the house and could see Beatty walking slowly past the kitchen window with the light appearing to shine through her.

"Nim, how can it possibly be true and correct?"

It disturbed his logic and psyche and sat uneasily with him as he drove slowly home to Tettenhill and his newly predicted 'Real Life'. He played the tape recording to Melanie who disbelieved every word, which annoyed him intensely because of her negativity. He had hoped she would share his new interest in the spiritual grey world that excited him so much, but any conversations about it seemed pointless.

She telephoned Harriet the day after hearing the tape but only when Jack was safely located in Rosset and earning her spending money. "Harriet, why the hell did you buy him the astrology session? Goodness me but it has filled his head with such crap."

"Oh, I'm so sorry. Has he believed every word and not questioned its validity?"

"Of course he has, he's just a man isn't he! They get more like children every day as they grow older."

Harriet disagreed. "Surely, you mean they constantly play with their willies, drink beer and watch football?"

Melanie burst into laughter. "Precisely my dear, but little boys must also have their cars for toys."

Harriet hadn't heard anything from her male friend about what was said at the visit but plotted to obtain a copy of any transcript of it as she shared Jack's love of fate. She listened to Melanie but thought about Jack who became increasingly more attractive as she understood more about his sensitive nature and his faltering marriage.

6
A taste of heaven but not enough

The summer beckoned as the family returned to Catalonia and Jack made an important telephone call the day after they arrived in Yapanc for the May bank holiday.

"How are you Josep Maria?" He didn't expect his new Catalan friend to say terrible and so after the pleasantries he asked the burning question. "Are we still okay to sail tomorrow, hombre?"

"Yes amigo, come to my house at eleven and I will take you to Palomost on my scooter."

Jack noticed the 'my house' part of the sentence and not 'our house' before happily ringing off to tell Melanie the good news.

Josep Maria turned to Karina as they sat drinking cervezas – beers – on their patio overlooking the sea. The last of the holidaymakers were packing up and leaving the beach as the sun dipped into the west and the water darkened to a less welcoming and opaque mirror.

"Jack is coming sailing with us. You must get more food ready." There was never a please or thank you from the Catalan to his wife. The marriage had been like this consistently for over twenty years. He said and she did. Karina looked at her husband as he stared out to sea and questioned if she would stay with him if it weren't for the children and his illness. He had been a physically attractive man when they had met at the local diving school but was much fatter now after years of tasting his own products.

They had had fun as they waterskied, sailed and dived, and in the heat of the summer nights they went by boat to the empty coves near Palomost and barbecued on the beach before walking hand in hand through the shallows, kicking glinting spray into the moonlight. It was romantic and enticing as they made love on the coarse sand and happily lay listening to the crickets hiding beneath the gloom of the pines.

At the end of that September she had made a choice after a few months of fun. Instead of returning home to Ireland she accepted a low paid job in the family bakery and bit her tongue as the men dictated life to their women. She thought it would become easier after their marriage, hoping that she could change his ways to make him more open and receptive, but Catalan family life and their secret business dealings were the same now as then and she still didn't belong and would always be an outsider. Seen as poorly paid help who had put nothing into their family and would never take anything out, as any inheritance would pass to the children.

She sat and sadly stared at the red sky as the sun went down on her ideals and dreams.

Josep Maria didn't need to look at his wife to think about their relationship. He knew she would stand by him if he became disabled by his brain tumour as her character contained a strong sense of duty. Duty to him and duty to the children which he reinforced at every opportunity by making her ask for money. He paid her eight hundred Euros a month for a job that required at least fifty hours a week. Inevitably, she always needed to ask for more to feed the family and buy clothes. Even her car belonged to the family business and so she had no chance of escaping as she was his possession, to be used as and when he wanted. After two years of marriage he knew he didn't love her but she was a foreigner and a prized possession and therefore he made her pregnant to continue the family line and keep her busy whilst he carried on his chosen lifestyle.

★   ★   ★

The next morning Jack was happy as he would be sailing and avoiding Melanie for the entire day.

After a late breakfast he guiltily kissed Joseph goodbye and ignoring his wife he walked down to Karina's house in Kaletta, facing on to the Kanadell beach. He had a small bag slung over his shoulder containing his towel, swimmers and P20 sun lotion which he jauntily swung from arm to arm every few steps.

It was a beautiful morning made better by the stroll around the Torre headland with its pink mallow flowers bursting across the small cliffs and rolling in a flurry down to the clear rock pools lying on the washed grey granite.

Their rosemary blue house was imposing, set back behind the beach with access under the raised promenade to their own boathouse where all the children's beach gear and a small 'Rib' were stored. Every house along the promenade had a natural tint of the Mediterranean splashed across them, complementing the varied and grand architectural designs of the last one hundred years. They were mostly three storeys high with huge spaces for car parking dug deep below sea level and tunnels that led to their boathouses giving alternative access direct to the beach. Old nets, lobster pots and hand spears leant against the sea wall on a beach untroubled by the arrival of a host of jet skis as found further down the coast.

Jack pressed the intercom button and quizzically eyed up the mini camera, wondering who was looking at him. The door opened automatically and he walked into the cool tall hallway about the size of his apartment.

"Hiya my dear." Karina's smile burst over him as she delicately placed her cheeks onto his. "It's wonderful to see you again Jack. Come through amigo." They climbed up the cool and wide marble stairs that were a central spine in the house and entered the living room on the third floor. Looking through the window he saw a deserted beach beneath him shaped by aquamarine coloured waters that changed from blues to greens like a giant but irregular mosaic as it reached away from the shore.

"Wow! Estupendo!" He was impressed. Half an hour into

the day and he had already lost his breath three times due to outstanding natural beauty, starting with his walk followed by the view and finally as he turned to appreciate her.

"You are so lucky Karina, that is truly awesome."

However, she was shaking her head negatively. "You get used to it Jack and then you don't necessarily appreciate what you've got. That applies to everything in life of course." She smiled again and continued sadly but he wondered by her tone whether she also meant her husband. "I understand you a little but I don't really know you yet. However, I believe you also think the best things in life are free?"

He replied truthfully. "Yes. I have always believed that, especially regarding beauty," and gave it just the right emphasis to imply he was more impressed by her than the view whilst hoping he hadn't been too forward on her territory. What the hell – he felt incredibly drawn to the woman.

"Jack, Hombre! Vamosa, let's go." Josep Maria came in and pointed down the stairs. In the garage sat a red and beaten up Vespa scooter dating from the seventies. Jack sat on the back and clung on to the worn seat strap. He had Josep Maria's and his own bag over his two shoulders as they sped off down the road.

"Dear God," thought Jack, "please slow up." Every bend was taken as if Josep Maria was Dani Pedrosa the motorbike GP rider.

"Oh shit," as he saw the water spread across the traffic island, sprayed by the sprinklers used to keep the grass green for the tourists. As Josep Maria braked, changed down and sought a dry line, Jack realised he was in fact behind Dani Pedrosa and relaxed.

"Fuck it, if I die, I'll die happy," and laughed into his friend's back. "Yeah, go for it JM!" The adrenaline surged and made him feel doubly alive after the incredible start to his day.

The marina at Palamost was calm and everything on the boat was explained to them both by the owner and therefore they felt comfortable with all the gear and with each other's knowledge. Jack took charge knowing his friend's physical condition. "You steer and do the engine things and I'll handle the foredeck, anchor and sail changes etc, Vale?"

"Vale, Jack," came Josep's happy reply as Karina arrived by car with bags of food and drink to be lifted over the rail and onto the deck.

As Jack and Karina were stowing their sailing gear in the steadily warming cabin she asked him for some help.

"Can you pop some sun block on my back please?" She turned her large bikini'd breasts away from him and handed the Piz Buin oil over her left shoulder. Holding her hair up she waited palpably. The air was warm and still as Jack dripped some oil onto his right hand and started from her left shoulder working slowly across the top of her neck rubbing on her smooth lightly tanned skin and feeling her muscles tighten under his gentle fingertips. His chest was tight and he couldn't breathe as the smell of the oil and her closeness enveloped him. Gently, she leant forward and her hands undid her top as Jack got to the centre of her soft back. When he reached the small of her back, he deliberately pushed his fingers beneath the bikini bottoms so that they briefly caressed the top of her rounded bum and entered the cleft. As he finished she walked away without a sound. Jack remained still as he felt the electric pulsing in the air. He had to take three huge breaths of the charged ozone to try and recover his composure. Never in all his life had he felt such an out of this world experience. It was as though time had stood still and every tiny movement was now recorded in his mind. He staggered slightly as he went to the bottom of the hatchway stairs and looked up. Karina stood with her legs wide apart and at a slight angle to him with a coy smile as she appraised what she had felt. As he moved down her body with his eyes he felt breathless again. He saw a small but beautifully proportioned woman and as he lingered he felt his prick harden in his shorts and pictured putting his hand under the bikini bottoms where he could see a gap formed by a mound of light auburn pubic air.

"Oh fuck!" he said under his breath and quickly moved away.

★ ★ ★

The day was pure ecstasy.

Sailing towards France the views from the sea were stupendous. Fornalls and Aiguablara in particular nestled in their beautiful coves and were even more stunning than the well populated Kaletta and Yapanc. Further north the Romans had built a city and large harbour at Empuries close to Escala where they saw the remains of a harbour wall. Greeks, Romans and Iberians had ploughed up and down the same coast on similar sized boats to their charted Beneteau. In Empuries, Caesar had left some soldiers as a gift to the locals to cover his back and as a stepping stone to the final invasion of Spain.

They stopped for lunch and went snorkelling in the underwater National Park of the Islas Medes and were entranced to see giant Gropa and Luna fish. Jack was a strong swimmer and headed to the nudist beach half a mile away. Standing up when he arrived he pulled his trunks down and waved them around his head towards the boat but no one saw him. He moved along the beach a few hundred yards and turning a corner he could see a large group of naked men and women. With his head down he surreptitiously glanced at the men's todgers, being far more interested in comparing their size and shape to his own instead of admiring the women's pubic areas or tits. The only level of interest shown in him by the nudists was when a woman saw him and appeared to deliberately close and then reopen her legs widely in his direction as an exaggerated invite. He smiled but was deeply embarrassed and moved swiftly past her inviting face, wondering if she and her husband were swingers.

Back on the boat they motored on the dying winds towards Palamost and as the sun sank behind the darkening land they all relaxed and chatted over cold cans of San Miguel beer, happy in each others' company.

It was certainly a fine day when true friendships were cemented.

The new friends included Melanie in a landlocked version of their happiness as the foursome went to the festival at Cap Roig botanic gardens and sat entranced watching Joaquin Cortes strutting around the small stage in a whirl of emotion and energy. A modern interpretation of flamenco set on the headland above the many coves of Kaletta. Karina whispered to Jack, "Isn't he fantastic?"

"No, too thin and muscular and too many socks down his tights." He turned and smiled in the dark but squeezed her arm when he whispered again, "It's the most beautiful night I have had for years. Just look at the stars."

The Latino sounds collided around the walls of the old house and sounded off into the pines before being washed out to sea. They sat entranced in a natural amphitheatre bordered by the most beautiful gardens, whose flowers sent their sweetest scents wafting around the dancers' legs. All summer there were different acts to entrance the holidaymakers from Dionne Warwick to Carreras and it was a place loved by the artists as much as the audience.

As they left Jack fell behind Karina, merging into the darkness, and as they filed out through a small gate he moved close behind her and pushed his fingers between the cheeks of her bottom to rub the area close to her fanny through the muslin trousers. He heard a slight gasp but luckily Josep Maria was too far ahead to notice. As he dropped his fingers away Melanie turned around to her. "Are you all right Karina? Did you trip?"

"No, don't worry I'm fine, it just felt a bit wet." She hit out behind her with her fist and caught Jack in the bollocks to make him wince and grunt.

"Serves you right!" she whispered.

They ate at midnight outside Karina's house, sitting on the patio and looking at the sea now glistening in the moonlight in a reflection of the distant hidden sun and greeted by the quiet of a people free beach. Huge steaks were on the barbecue to be served with bread and some nominal onion to be healthy. The Spanish diet was certainly high fat with few vegetables but that also made it rico.

As they drove home, Jack clutched his tummy as griping pains ripped through it below the belt line.

"God, that was painful." He was doubled up as Melanie ignored him. Once outside the apartment he waved her away. "Go inside and leave me alone, I think I'm going to be sick." She didn't need a second request and went to relieve the babysitter leaving Jack leaning against a cork tree. As he threw up he crapped into his pants at the same time.

"Oh fuck." After three more retches he managed to get inside, hoping it might be all over, being a typical man and trying not to be sick even though he knew it made sense to get it all out. However, as he sat up in bed in a cold sweat, propped on his pillows, he knew he was in a bad way. Melanie had decanted to Joseph's room so as to avoid being disturbed but finally he had to run and lying over the toilet he retched, feeling the cold tiles on his brown knees. Five times in the night he repeated the process until he felt that he would retch his stomach lining into the bowl closely followed by his rectum. During the whole time Melanie heard him just the once and could only selfishly say, "Be quiet Jack, you'll wake Joseph up!"

The next morning he asked her to go to the Farmacia and buy him some haemorrhoid suppositories to help his sore arsehole. He opened the packet of dulco laxo soppositorios and shoved one up, knowing relief would come within an hour or so. As he sat limp and drained in their lounge he could feel a build up of pressure in his already sore arse and suddenly ran to the toilet to crap liquid into the bowl and push his piles out again. He came back to face an unmoved Melanie.

"You stupid woman I just checked the packet with my dictionary. These are laxatives and not a haemorrhoid treatment. For God's sake what are you trying to do to me?" He rushed out again as the glycerine did its work.

On his return Melanie was laughing, adding insult to injury. "Well I checked with the Pharmacist and he said they would be OK." Jack slunk back to bed completely wasted.

There was still time for a final sail as the temperature was a pleasant twenty-one Celsius, almost matching that of the sea.

It was also a last opportunity for Jack to talk to Karina privately after a holiday of fun and happiness where they had no time or space to explore their feelings as she was constantly working.

As they sailed into a gentle breeze beyond El Far and onward towards Tiramisu they used the privacy given to them by the pines and six hundred foot vertical cliffs. Karina leant back onto Jack's shoulder and whispered sadly, "Let's sail away to the future; it's just over that horizon."

Kissing her lightly on the forehead he replied, "I can do better than that. I can take you to heaven and back and we can forget our responsibilities." She was facing him and moved tantalisingly closer. He kissed her hard on the lips and shoved his tongue deeply into her mouth. The slightly salty taste of the 'Med' would always be remembered by them both. They stopped kissing and stared at each other for a minute in perfect silence. He kissed her again but this time even harder. Gently he slid his hand under her bikini briefs, slipping his fingers into her wet fanny as she widened her legs. It was hot and wet with its juices already flowing over his fingers. Pushing the tiller over he pointed the boat into the wind and loosened the sheets to let the sails flap gently. Quickly, he leant her backwards across the thwart and pushing the bikini bottoms to one side he crouched on his knees and started to lick her. He licked and sucked her clitoris pushing his bottom lip hard below it to add to her pleasure and then licked the folds of her cunt harder and faster until she started to moan and then to cry as she came with her tears dripping down her cheeks in desperation and guilt. Pushing him away she nimbly dived over the side and swam downwards so he couldn't see her. After a minute Jack started to worry until a splash of water landed and dripped off his brown back from the opposite side of the boat.

"That got you Jack Edmunson," as she held out her hand to be pulled on board. "That was beautiful my dear, I've never come like that before. Thank you seems a bit lame but thank you anyway."

As they sailed back to Yapanc she leaned against his strong shoulder and told him about the caves they could see cut into the cliffs. "At a certain time and day, you can take a small rubber dinghy and row into them to watch the sun slice through the entrance revealing the stalactites in all their red marbled glory. It's the sort of spiritual act that lovers do and I hope one day we could too."

Jack touched the side of her face. "That would be fantastic my lovely but sadly I have never found enough time for romantic things like that."

She clasped him to her and whispered in his ear, "Find the time my dear, find the time with me."

After pulling the Laser onto the beach they sat talking quietly on the sea wall by the square. Karina dreamily mentioned, "Jack, we have a saying in Catalonia. You are the other half of my orange. Do you understand that?" Karina could see his puzzled frown. "Don't you see? It's when someone finds their Sun Sharer?" She glanced at him, perched forward on the edge of the red tiles. A few people strolled past on the wooden planks fronting the wall or leading down between the boats that were pulled up onto the rough sands over tarred pine beams.

He gazed into her deep green eyes. "Of course I understand Karina; it's not the understanding that matters. It's the fact that if true what would we do about it? And that makes me very sad."

Melanie walked out from the side entrance of Hotel Yapanc and glancing across the square she spied the new lovers head to head and grimaced at the body language. She didn't love Jack or even want him around but no one else was going to take away her lifestyle. She planned to keep Karina close. A new best friend, someone who could be useful when she was alone with Joseph in Catalonia and her husband was working in England.

"Right let's go Jack! Joseph's finished pooing. Dear God the child spends most of his life pooing."

Jack got lightly to his feet and kissed Karina's cheeks. "Daio, hasta pronto."

"Bye, see you soon." She turned away quickly to go back to work in the Croisanteria. The words spoken in Castellano were lost on Melanie who didn't speak the language and couldn't be bothered to learn. The use of Spanish sent secret messages between Jack and Karina. Jack would ask her how she was doing, "Que tal?"

"Normal, regular," her reply unnoticed by Melanie as she thought it meant the same as in English but the true translation indicated she wasn't happy at all but getting on with it.

The holidays had allowed Jack to immerse himself in the culture.

On national TVE 1 was the daily diary called Telediario. It amused him enormously because it was the only programme he had ever seen that could be showing a picturesque village with a local sob story whilst playing a raucous pop band such as the Kaiser Chiefs as background music. Noisy and totally and utterly out of keeping with the subject matter.

"Only in Spain," he thought.

He also started to puzzle his way through a newspaper every other day like *La Vanguardia*, focusing on the sports pages and plethora of environment stories. Glancing through one morning he commented, "Melanie, did you know that Britain has three times more people per square mile than Spain. Wouldn't it be nice to live here and then I could commute by Ryanair at the weekends. It can be less than five hours door to door from the UK to Yapanc. What do you think; will you come and live here with me?"

She spat out her words. "Get real Jack, what about Joseph's schooling? You know we have to send him to The Grange soon. You can't let him down. It would be awful here, I would miss my friends."

"There lies the truth Melanie; you can't survive in the real world without the Cheshire set and your gas guzzling 4 x 4."

Jack was rightly disgusted. Everything had to be to her agenda and nothing else would ever be considered so long as he kept earning good money and filling their joint account, whereas he delighted in the excitement of living in a different country. He loved the idea of satsumas and fresh lemons off his own tree after January. Then in February the hotels ran gourmet Catalan menus to help boost the local trade. They served long and slimy razor clams that looked disgusting but tasted fantastic if sometimes a bit gritty. However, sea urchins or garoinas seemingly had nothing worth eating inside of them but tasted sublime with their orange coloured flesh. During March and April everyone collected wild asparagus which were fried in olive oil and used to flavour Tortillas – omelettes. Then his favourite nespero fruits were ready in late May. They were orange in colour, sweet and with a huge seed like a gobstopper from his childhood. Jack loved the food but even more he loved the relaxed and intelligent culture. However, all the people from the Girona area were seen as lazy by the Barcelona weekenders. To the Brits, the Catalans in Girona are switched on but only when they want to be.

He picked up *La Vanguardia* again. "MRSA and C. difficile causes more deaths than car accidents in the UK. Incidence of infections: UK forty-four per cent, Spain half a per cent." He liked the medical pages. "Twenty-four per cent of men in Spain up to the age of twenty-four take cannabis and sixteen per cent of men consume tranquilisers and sleeping pills. Melanie did you hear that? There's an article that suggests that nearly half the men under twenty-four walk around drugged up to the eyeballs. There might be a local lover for you yet, you fat ignorant pig." She was outside hanging the washing out and didn't quite catch the latest rude observation.

Later that day Jack sat on the apartment balcony on his smart Kettal furniture. Spanish brand names had temporarily replaced Cheshire set names. He sweated slightly from his balding head whilst reading the Spanish edition of the *Daily Mail* bought by Melanie that morning.

"My God Nim. Why is this so dumb or is it just me?" He read quickly. "More Iraq, more interest rate rises, more oil price records set, more sexy women in see-through underwear. Nothing new, nothing truly of interest but more on more. The same old stories presented differently by different newspapers on different days, very little of the stories having any element of fact being some hack's supposition." He looked at page fifty-six, headlined 'Dream wife' and started to pay more attention to the two opposing articles. One by Doctor Laura Schlessinger, a family therapist famous on the radio, saying a woman should fulfil her husband's every desire and put his wishes above her own; the other by Amanda Platell, suggesting the only way to a happy marriage is through equality, the feminist position.

He immediately decided not to read Platell's article with the usual women wanting to be men arguments. Jack was totally biased against this sort of discourse having had parts of the book *How men can't read maps and women don't listen* read out to him in bed by his wife. He realised he had turned the title round in his mind.

"Maybe that would work instead," he mused. "That book has probably been the catalyst for the current state of my matrimonial disharmony." Melanie had thought it funny and thoughtful late at night whilst he was knackered and sexually deprived. A cuddle and a chat would have been nicer than being lectured on why men are so insensitive and unthoughtful. It demeaned him but not in the funny light-hearted way of Melanie's favourite TV programme 'Sex and the City' but of course that was her game plan. He cast his eye over the Schlessinger article.

'Most women treat their husbands worse than they treat the family pet.' He smiled.

'Men simply can't take the emotional abuse any longer.' Jack's interest deepened.

'For years women have smugly blamed a midlife crisis for sending their men off into the arms of other women. A whole generation of women have been brainwashed to believe they are entitled to nag, bully and criticise their husbands, instead of treating them like a friend or lover.' Mentally Jack whooped with joy. If only Melanie realised this he might still be happily married rather than trying to get away from her La La land life and into his spiritual recovery. He read that for years Schlessinger had received calls from women who were perfectly nice to everyone in their lives apart from their husbands.

"Too fucking true," he thought. "If she thinks and preaches this why won't women listen?" The article continued about accepting that men and women are different and that these differences enrich relationships and add balance. Jack pondered why Melanie kept trying to change him.

"Put the toilet seat down. Close the toilet door. Don't cough without your hand in front of your mouth etc ad nauseam. Fantastic." He used Harriet's constant euphemism as he read further.

'What's wrong with women pleasing our men by looking nice and having sex even when we are not in the mood? It's called love.'

"That is what's missing," Jack breathed deeply, "true unencumbered love. The best and most precious thing in life and always free."

'Men are emotionally dependent on their wives and want approval. If a man tells a woman he doesn't like her dress, she'll wear it anyway.'

"And I get dressed by Melanie like her little dolly and told off constantly when I wear the wrong tie with a given shirt!" Jack's thoughts continued woefully. "So maybe it's not about picking fault, it's about lack of thought or support and particularly the lack of love?"

He flicked the page backwards and placed it on the coffee table for Melanie to read and comment on it which didn't happen.

They went down to the Yapanc beach again at eight that evening, allowing Joseph to run around with the other children in the dark as they sat outside the Yevant hotel bar. There were at least a thousand people on the black sands in front of them either sat on deckchairs or towels and there were another thousand walking on the promenade in their finest clothes greeting long lost friends. Many of them were older Catalan couples and all were there to sit and hear the free concert by the Habaneras, a Cuban traditional singing group. Four men singing boring fishermen songs imported years before, then the interval was filled by a Sardana dance group. The Sardana group consisted of men and women who pranced their feet with hands clasped and held high over their heads as they slowly moved in a circle. The specialist band sounded permanently out of tune. Two rings of people side by side were dancing and moving in opposing directions. The traditional Sardana dance was beautiful to watch, slow but incredibly focused on the part of the participants. Jack sank another Voll Damm doble malta beer and hummed along tunelessly to the tuneless music.

"Melanie, I love Spain you know. You get to kiss all the pretty girls and hold them close just like in Al Pacino's film the 'Scent of a Woman.'" She didn't reply so he tried again. "The only problem is if you have a few beers and feel a bit delicate the bin men always come by the apartment at twelve thirty in the morning, waking you up because the windows are wide open due to the heat. What do you think, should we buy some air conditioning? Melanie? Are you with us or are you with the Woolwich?"

"I am watching my son and I think you have drunk too much."

He agreed inwardly and responded honestly, "Pfur, that's okay then, so I can have your free cremat as you are so strait-laced and teetotal." He didn't wait for a sarcastic reply but instead he staggered off to watch the shallow five foot diameter dishes of blue flamed liquor resting on the trestle tables spaced around the beach. He watched the old people listening intently to the music and saw that some of the couples were holding hands in rapture at the simple traditional melodies casting them back to their youth in the Franco era. The same people would be on the beach early in the morning walking purposefully but very slowly by the water's edge and swinging their arms to keep them flexible, using the sun to ease their aching bones. In contrast in the early evening all the flexible and energetic young people played volley ball or entertained their friends with guitars on the beach and the older generation stayed at home or in the bars soaking up some pain relieving wine before dinner.

A symphony of ages using the same sandy space.

When they got back to the apartment Melanie prepared supper. A few onions in a large tray were lightly fried in the oven before laying some pre-cooked potatoes on top and then a whole Merluza, a hake fish. It cooked for fifteen minutes then a glass of cheap white wine was poured over the whole dish and after another five minutes it was ready.

"Jack, I'm doing some rice as well, do you want some?"

"Sorry, I am Spanish now, you know? I can't eat rice dishes at night, only during the day and traditionally only on Thursday lunchtime."

"Do you want some rice or not?" she shouted sharply, disturbing Joseph who glanced up at his angry Mother. It upset him to hear her raise her voice at his Dad. Jack meekly acquiesced and turned his attention back to some olives that he had bought in the market that morning. They were black and tasted awful. The green and brown coloured ones were nicer but he knew it depended on the soaking method and so he binned them and pulled out a tin of green with red pimento filling that he knew tasted gorgeous.

Satisfied with a plethora of Spanish influences they went to bed separately so that Jack could learn more Castellano sitting out on the cool balcony and Melanie could put another layer of after-sun cream on her crocodile-like skin before lying on their bed and texting her friends.

The first text went to Harriet. "Thirty degrees and 'fab' here. Had a super meal in the best restaurant in town. Shopping tomorrow, do you want some Havaneras flip-flops as they are 'fab' and only twenty-five Euros a pair."

Harriet pondered her friend's need to be 'better' before replying. "Raining again so no need for flip-flops just wellies. Don't eat too much or you will get fat. Love to Joseph and Jack x."

The second text from Melanie went to Bridget. "Bought some 'fab' new clothes in the sales. Off to a Paul Weller concert at a 'fab' setting near Girona. Don't work too hard! Love to Peter and the girls x."

Bridget read the message and deleted it immediately with a slight sniff and without a reply.

Sometimes friendships are as convenient as marriages.

Whenever possible, Jack would escape into Palafrio on his own and loved exploring the narrow streets and watching the slow pattern of life.

Everyone went into the centre from eight onwards in order to buy their fresh fish in the market and fruit and vegetables off the stalls in the main street. On Sunday afternoon and during all day Monday the shops were closed except for the supermarkets that opened for a limited number of hours. It was like stepping back in Britain to thirty years earlier when everyone had a real weekend. No one bought fish between Sunday and Tuesday because the local fishing fleet never put to sea at weekends so anything displayed on a counter after Saturday morning wasn't fresh.

Parking outside of Carrefour, Jack adopted the local practice of putting the minimum twenty cents in the parking meter hoping the warden wouldn't return before he had finished his shopping trip. The money gave him about ten minutes but providing he had a ticket when or if she placed a penalty on his windscreen, he could pay the actual parking cost at the machine and avoid a thirty euro fine.

"Clever people the Spanish Nim." Slowly he walked past the line of parked cars on his way into town and noticed that every single driver had managed to miss the blue lined parking spots.

"Only in Spain," he thought.

The centre of the town had a small but busy square with a unique edifice on one side called the Centro Fraternal which was a beautiful and imposing building. The sign said it was established in 1887 and at any time of the day it was full of old men talking, reading the paper and spending very little as they sat there for hours under the high ceilings. Later at night you would see the same clients but now playing cards and chess whilst drinking cheap beer until promptly at nine pm they all left to go off to see their wives and eat the dinner which had been prepared for them. The remarkable thing wasn't the beer drinking at night but the majority would also have a beer for breakfast, just as in their working pasts before walking to the cork factory further up the street. Palafrio like many local towns had relied on cork as an industry before tourism but all that was left now was a large museum showing its lost secrets.

In the cathedral-like meat market he bought a small piece of cochinillo, rabbit, and some very yellow skinned chicken due to the corn feed. The butcher offered him a bagful of rabbit cheeks as a delicacy to fry but he politely refused both these and the boiled cheeks of a sheep. It was always fun to shop each day but also essential as items like fruit rotted quickly in the heat of the apartment. Bread was usually purchased on a twice daily basis both in the morning and evening because it never stayed fresh due to the lack of chemical ingredients. Serra's shop by the square had soft barras, the Spanish version of baguettes, and the most fantastic chocolate croissants that were probably the best in the world apart from Karina's but then he was biased. Whenever he bought a large round loaf they would always ask: "Corto signor?" The loaf hung limply in the shopkeeper's hand.

"No gracias." No, Jack didn't want a sliced loaf, it reminded him too much of home.

Very often he wrote an abbreviated shopping list for himself and donning his glasses in a shop he would stare at the odd characters on his paper and not understand what he was supposed to be buying. He was permanently angry about having to wear glasses as it made him feel older, but losing his short term memory hurt more as it reminded him of his mother. He knew he had too many CRAFT moments and laughed at the term: Can't Remember A Fucking Thing. But it frustrated him and he morbidly dwelt on it.

By the time he returned to the supermarket he had happily wasted an hour and a half. Inside, the check out girl asked Jack to show his driving licence to prove he could use his La Caixa bank card. They had no chip and pin; it was just swiped and la firma, a signature, made on the voucher with no match to the back of the card. He pushed past the queue and admired a typical English expat couple whom he knew lived in Bagurr, with their designer sunglasses and glitzy cheap bracelets, grossly overweight and as brown as berries. They would be seen in the square in the evening demanding drinks in English and were known locally as the 'Por favors' for always saying please after everything whereas the Spanish couldn't be bothered.

The holiday season drew to a close and Jack sat alone in Girona airport returning home to work a few days before his family followed later. Carefully selecting an area free of flight departures and with no one around him he watched the sun set across the hills of the Collsacabra on the opposite side of the runway. House martins were flying in and out of their mud hovels attached to the newly tiled terminal walls. The greenery of the hills was made more beautiful by the sunlight slowly but perceptibly spreading a streaky red dye across the sky.

He remembered the early morning mountain bike rides with his Dutch friends, the swifts flying low across the fields as they sweated the Rioja out of their bodies, the beautiful red poppies and purple everlasting flowers nodding their heads in the fields of corn.

"The best days of 'Real life'."

He sighed to himself as he didn't want to leave and felt incredibly sad and lonely.

He knew his life should be here and not in Cheshire or anywhere in dull and boring England.

It had been a fantastic visit which made him feel alive again, enthusiastically embracing everything he saw, heard and felt. A direct contrast to the dull repetition of work and arguments each week at home.

So he decided it was time for renewal.

More time in Catalonia and less at home although the concept of home was diminishing.

A time to start to resolve his personal problems and ensure more days were happy and truly alive.

"It's not a rehearsal you know Nim!" His spirit guide continued to listen and watch as Jack slowly wandered along his chosen path, ignoring the calls to increase his pace.

7

Jettenhill ~ Women and the art of manipulating men

It was a Wednesday afternoon and 'Te Amero' resonated out of Jack's mobile. He ran into a spare office in the Rosset warehouse and pressed the answer button to talk to Bridget.

"Hiya 'Bridges', how are you lovely?" Jack was happy to be speaking to her.

"Lo there. I'm good thanks Jack; did your friend invite you out to lunch as planned for tomorrow?"

"No, it didn't happen, typical bloke hey? Only thinks about three things, football, beer and sex, a bit like me really but I would throw in wine instead of beer and probably add sailing too."

She laughed, happy to be talking to him again. "In that case I'm visiting my friend in London tomorrow and could be with you from lunchtime and for the rest of the afternoon if you are free. Can you spare the time?"

Jack smiled as he replied, "Is that an invite then after I have been waiting for so long?"

Bridget paused before answering. "Yes, if you are free and maybe because your wife is still in Spain. By the way, I'm surprised sex is so low on your list."

"Er…actually it's not Bridget, it's definitely number one at the moment and some love is exactly what I need and so I will tell my boss that I will be visiting the Doctor about my bad hip tomorrow, if that suits you Doctor?"

She put on her professional voice. "Indeed Mister Edmunson. I can see you at one pm for a detailed examination that will involve you taking all your clothes off and having lots of manipulation. You may find it very uncomfortable."

"In that case," said Jack, "I will ensure we have a bottle of champagne available to numb the pain."

She interrupted him, "You said love and not sex?"

He ducked the question. "See you at a hotel in London. I'll text the name and the street after I have booked it and when I know you are safely at your friend's house. Love you. Bye!"

"Love you too, bye."

They both went back to their humdrum lives feeling more elated than for years.

On arrival at the Dorchester she had been very nervous, insisting that Jack met her outside and escorted her in as if taking a business colleague to lunch. She wanted to look like a professional couple as opposed to anxious first time lovers trying to avoid prying eyes.

"Stop worrying Bridget, no one knows us here so you can relax." But Jack nervously glanced around as they headed to the lifts in case they were seen by someone they knew.

As they sighed upwards she remonstrated with him. "My God Jack, I can't believe you booked the Dorchester." But it made her feel treasured.

"You are worth it lovely. The first time has to be special. Next time it will be a backstreet dump in Tottenham."

"Next time Mister Edmunson? You are so good at forward planning. I like a man who can take control."

He held her close and intimately for the first time after shutting the bedroom door and their hearts thumped against each other making them both breathless in the tight embrace. There was no time to admire the beautiful suite as they only had eyes for each other. Jack lifted her chin and gently touched her lips with his own. She pushed him back slightly and said nervously.

"Jack I need a drink please, I can barely talk my mouth is so dry." Gulping some water down she struggled to breathe verging on a panic attack. "Oh God, I can't believe I'm doing this, it seems so surreal. I have never contemplated an affair in the whole of my married life."

He pulled her close to calm her down and hugged her into him. As she relaxed he moved his face off her sweet smelling hair and looked into her eyes. "Don't worry about anything; close your eyes and dream."

He leant into her and cushioning her face in his right hand he kissed her deeply for the first time. His prick was enormous, gorged with blood at the thought of illicit sex and he felt a real man again as he took control. Whilst still kissing he forced her clothes off and then dropped his own onto the floor in a matter of a few seconds and quickly pushed her naked back onto the bed, focusing only on her eyes. There was no need for foreplay as he slid his enormous cock into her wetness and they both groaned like animals as he started to fuck her hard.

It wasn't lovemaking; it was an animal act as they grappled with each other, writhing violently in ecstasy and pulling each other tighter until Jack arched his back and pumped his spunk deep into her. Bridget let out a loud and guttural groan whilst rolling her head from side to side in denial of her pleasure.

It was everything they had wished for on a purely primal level with no need to talk or explain and with no sophistication as they just wanted to fuck each other senseless.

Two hours later and Bridget was lying across him making it difficult for him to breathe with her warm breasts spread on his chest. She stroked his face as she talked. "No one really knows you. They don't see the sensitive side of you and the pain from living the way you do but I see it more now Jack. It must be very hard for you." She snuggled her face into his and carried on in deep romantic thought. "How do you know if you have met your Sun Sharer Jack?"

It was hard to raise his neck and peer down to see if she was serious. Throwing his head back on the bed he thought he would give her a serious answer. "It will never be said between you. It will just be known. But it will feel as if every moment with that special person is like listening to the most meaningful and most moving piece of music you have ever heard in your life."

She sat up. "That's lovely, but you never give your feelings away about yourself. Why is that then?"

"God Bridget, that's a bit heavy at three in the afternoon having just shagged the arse off me you wanton hussy."

She was determined to get an answer. "Why? Tell me."

Jack breathed out. "Pfur. Hoy! I suppose it links back to my insecurity from childhood when I had to be alone a lot and take my own counsel whilst my parents constantly worked. I had so much time to think about everything in great detail. I was constantly told that I was being too serious and too responsible and so I never relax now unless I am on top of a mountain or out at sea on my boat. Strangely, that's what the astrologer said too." He smiled down at her. "I always feel free then and can express my deepest feelings as I feel close to heaven."

She kissed him hard on the lips and stroked his hardening prick. "So when are you going to take me up a mountain or across a sea Jack?" She whispered gently in his ear and then she bit it lightly.

"Well that depends Bridget, but either of them has to be better than this absolutely fabulous luxury suite with champagne." He cupped her breast and kissed her hard right nipple.

As she pulled him into her she whispered slightly breathlessly, "Then take me to heaven with you again Jack."

Spent, they lay apart and stared at the ceiling.

Jack asked the inevitable, "I'm not suggesting it but would you ever leave Peter?"

"No, I can't ever conceive that, no matter how badly he treats me. I have a good life and four lovely daughters. I spend what I want when I want and may occasionally get to see my new lover and best friend."

He turned on his side towards her, throwing an arm loosely across her slim waist. "I would leave Melanie tomorrow if I could you know. I just need a plan and the guts to do it. Divorce needs to be made black and white as you have to cut out those grey bits Bridget. I imagine three balls in my head. Kids, emotions and money. Keeping in touch with Joseph would be easy as he only sees me for a short time at the weekends anyway. Emotions are nonexistent on both sides or would be within a few months, but on the money side I bet she would fight me for every penny. That would be her way to make me suffer because she thinks it's all I am interested in, whereas of course it's exactly the opposite."

Bridget eased out of bed leaving the smell of Chanel Allure behind and got discreetly dressed, hiding herself from the man she had spent three hours fucking. He admired her long legs and beautiful blonde hair as she tossed it over the neck of her blouse. He would have to be careful that his clothes didn't stink of her perfume when he packed tomorrow. Maybe by spraying some of his own aftershave on them it would help mask her smell, or on arrival at home he could nip in and put his weekly washing on himself to be doubly safe.

Bridget walked up to him and gently kissed his lips. "Stay in bed Jack. I have to be with my girlfriend in an hour to go out to the theatre. Take care of yourself and speak to me tomorrow my love." One last hard kiss and she was gone.

The affair had started but it was just consummating their long-term friendship. He felt no extra love and there was no dramatic change to pink clouds. However, lying alone and naked he felt guilty about shagging his best friend's wife and went to wash the feeling away in the shower. Later that evening he received a text from her.

"Missing you loads. Stop thinking too much and enjoy the practicalities of life. You are my angel." There were always seven kisses at the end of her texts. He smiled as she was right. In reality, sexual frustration was at the heart of his marriage problems. He had tried everything possible with Melanie. Internet porn, anal sex, teen porn – in fact any porn – but they still had constant rows about sex or the lack of it. There was always a lack of confidence on Jack's part despite his outward Leo appearance. Deep down was his fear of failure, the constant harking back to being a hammer not an anvil and the failures in jobs when younger. All of these things were behind his desire to change his life. He lay admiring his luxury suite and thought about his future.

"Although it's easier to walk away that will be seen as a failure by my friends. Why should I have to self justify my life to anyone, or is that my lack of confidence again?" He sighed but he wasn't brave enough to take things further yet. "Maybe I will also have to walk away from Bridget eventually?" He settled back comfortably in his luxury dressing gown, squashing the six soft pillows to scan the sixty available TV channels in his complicated life.

That Thursday afternoon wasn't as special for Peter as he met Jean at the top of the woods above Dingle Dell.

"You're late again Peter. Was it work or do you have another excuse you insufferable man?"

"I'm not late, it's just that you are too early as you are always too eager." He grabbed her wrist and roughly dragged her deeper into the woods before placing her hands on a tree and lifting her skirt halfway up her back. She had no knickers on and so he immediately shoved his prick in her and started to fuck her hard. Foreplay wasn't a word in his earthy vocabulary and so long as he came nothing else mattered. It didn't matter which woman he was with because if she didn't come then that was tough. A few minutes later he allowed her to turn around and kiss him.

"Peter, I wish we could meet up and have a night together. That would be so lovely, to have some loving in a quiet and beautiful hotel room my darling."

"Well you know that will never happen as you always have to cook three meals a day for your husband and kids, even if you knew Chester might be flooded by a tsunami coming down the Dee estuary."

"It would just be nice to be alone in a pretty place and have some slower, gentler sex."

"Are you complaining then?" He pushed his cock into her again and made her shudder.

"Oh God, I've never wanted someone so bad. Jesus Christ you are enormous." Peter banged her arse against the rough tree bark and casually looked over her shoulder at the watching rabbits. He wasn't interested anymore as he had shot his load in the first five minutes but he needed to keep her quiet before he could escape to check on the new bedding plants which were almost ready for sale.

Jack was driving home from work the next day and had taken a cross-country route to avoid the traffic jams. He was singing loudly in his car as the 'Merc's' twelve Mark Levinson speakers spat out Cold Play's 'Clocks' at full blast and he joined in the 'oohs' and 'ahas' of the chorus. Self destruct mode was in operation. Nim whispered to him calmly.

> *Ninety-five miles per hour along country lanes is a*
> *little excessive, don't you think?*

The music was as high as his emotions and Jack wasn't contemplating crashing. He felt immortal.

"Nim, when you have made it and you have your two homes and you have enough income to do exactly what you want, then and only then can you tell me to slow down. I am invincible!"

> *Jack you are not invincible, you are on a high because*
> *of Bridget yesterday.*
> *Slow down.*
> *What would you do if you killed a child like Joseph*
> *who ran in front of you?*

The spirit guide had picked the best motivation.

"Okay Nim, you are right of course. I will slow down."

Are you happy with your two homes Jack?

"What do you think Nim? I look around my luxury apartment in Yapanc in my luxurious resort and think, why do I need this? It's like being able to buy more and better food but who is there to stop you constantly eating? There are no boundaries in my life anymore, no restrictions, so what keeps you disciplined? That's part of being fifty; you are out of control just like in your teens. You think you've got everything you need but in fact have got nothing important. It's all a temptation and you can carry on and on having more and more and don't know when to stop. That's the trick in life – knowing when to stop and walk away."

So are you going to walk away Jack?
Have you got the guts to stand up to all the criticism
and hate from everyone you know?
You'll have no friends left and no money.

"Sometimes I wonder whether I have got any real friends apart from Bridget and Karina. I think they are just acquaintances who mutually use others in their lives, and really I'm not bothered about money now as it's only people who really count. All my life I have been 'responsible' as it was drummed into me as a child. Follow the rules Jack and do the right thing. That makes me too responsible to actually achieve anything if I am always toeing the line, whereas success needs a rogue and a bit of a chancer doesn't it? Or I could give up responsibility altogether and focus on fun alone for the second forty-nine years. Sod everything, just live life to have fun. Fifty down, nearly fifty to go."

Jack, don't you think that it could be a long drawn
out and painful experience if you don't know yourself
properly.
If you are not sure about your path and about
the impact that it will have on your psyche, your
equilibrium?

Jack continued to ignore the advice of his spirit guide as he was having fun driving fast for the first time in years. The first fun in a long time after making love to Bridget.

"So why do I fancy women from fifteen to sixty Nim? I can understand about girls like Lucy and Kirsty at work. They have figure-hugging low slung trousers showing purple or pink sexy thongs. Also, see through blouses and half undone buttons. You say to yourself, what's going on here? When Melanie has something similar on to be 'fashionable' she looks like a sack of potatoes. Her arse hangs out of the back and her big belly flops out the front. It's enough to make you vomit Nim."

> *Jack, let's be honest. Lucy and Kirsty are twenty, not*
> *over forty, frumpy, lumpy and dumpy as you keep*
> *telling your wife.*
> *Youth in itself gives beauty and attraction.*
> *Are you giving Melanie enough love to make her want*
> *to diet and look good or is she comfort eating because*
> *she is unhappy too?*

"Are you suggesting my approach with her is wrong? Are you saying I should stick with my marriage?"

> *I didn't say that.*
> *You have already made up your mind what you*
> *must do but haven't the courage or conviction to*
> *carry it out.*

He continued to ignore such sound wisdom and changed the CD. 'Being close to crazy and being close to you,' by Katie Melua mournfully poured into the car and Jack poured tears driving along at a much slower and safer pace.

His high had bounced itself to a profound low.

He was thinking about the women he thought he loved and knew the current situation was untenable.

A scream, loud, guttural and unearthly, ripped out of his mind and bounced around the interior of the car. Deliberately given out to tear the stress out of his body but a call for help to the spirit trapped within.

It helped to settle him down so after half an hour he telephoned Bridget on her mobile for a quick and irresponsible chat.

"Bridget speaking," came out of his car kit loudspeaker.

"Hiya Bridges, have you had any good shags lately?" There was a sharp intake of breath at the other end and her tone changed.

"Actually Jack, Jemima and Helen are sat in the back of my car and you're on my speaker phone."

"Oh fuck," said Jack. "Oh, sorry erm…sorry twice." He heard thirteen-year-old giggles from her twins as he pressed 'off' on the steering wheel. A poor plan had then been poorly executed by the project consultant.

It was about ten that Friday night and for a change at the end of his heavy week's work they were not socialising and so went to bed early.

Jack turned over towards Melanie. She had picked up a year old *OK* magazine off the stash under her bedside table and was slowly turning the pages, making sarcastic comments about the personalities portrayed.

"There's no way that Posh hasn't had a boob job. Kerry Katona has lost seven stone with her new husband in just three months."

Jack propped himself up on his elbow and stared at his wife's face. He poked her arm so that she turned towards him. Looking into her eyes he asked her straight. "Why don't you put that crap down and talk to me?" As an afterthought he added, "How the hell can she have lost that much weight?"

Melanie continued to flick the pages. "I just want to look at some gossip for ten minutes so that I can relax."

Jack tried again, rubbing her brown stomach and gliding his hand over her carefully shaved pubic hairs. "Just talk to me, tell me what you are thinking. I don't want sex, well not much anyway."

The flicking of pages continued but the tone of her voice was harder. "I only want to look through a few pages before going to sleep Jack. I'm tired and it helps me to sleep." She said this in a way which meant stop now or else.

Jack stared at her body; he wanted to fuck her brains out as a guilt response for shagging Bridget but finding out what she really thought about him was also important to help relieve the confusion in his life.

> *You had sex yesterday with Bridget and sex two days*
> *on the trot is an impossibility, even though you seem*
> *to want it twice a day and every day.*

He looked at her manly and forbidding face and made a mental note. "Perhaps she's going through the menopause and that has changed things? Get on the internet and find out about the menopause." As he moved away from her he smiled. Even the word sounded like putting men on sex pause, just like a DVD. Jack thought about getting up and going downstairs to watch a sex channel on Sky but realising it was post free viewing he turned to Melanie one last time. "Just remember this conversation when we get divorced."

Turning his back on her he closed his eyes, feeling sad that his life was so uninspiring and happy that he needed to dig the knife in again. In his mind he talked to the omnipotent Nim.

"Of course she will never reply. Never! Not tonight as *OK* magazine is far more important than her husband and not tomorrow because she will breeze on as if the conversation has never happened. Why is that? Is she bored with the same old comments from me? Or is she just taking the piss, taking the money and lifestyle and has someone on the side? It's as if she is challenging me to walk away and then screw me to keep her lifestyle. Is that her game I wonder?"

> *Calm down Jack. You have always suspected Peter*
> *Edam, but as you are now shagging his wife you can't*
> *complain if he is shagging yours, can you?*

"Yes, but as I'm away all week and Joseph is at school so I can guarantee who is getting the most sex, the bastard." It was a bad thought to fall asleep on.

On Saturday Jack knew Bridget was at lunch with two friends from work as the farm shop was being refurbished. To shock her and make her laugh he sent a text.

"Do you need a good shag?"

Within five minutes the reply came back but all that was on it was the number 143.

He puzzled over it for two days when he was back at work, texting guesses to her and receiving negative replies.

"One 'For' Three? Were you offering me a choice of your friends Bridget or even sex with all three of you?"

"No. Don't even think about it."

New guess an hour later: "We have been seeing each other for one hundred and forty three hours?"

"No. Sixty nine."

Jack's immediate response: "Do you mean we can do a sixty nine?"

Reply. "Sixty nine hours, am I just a sex object?"

Jack's text after a project meeting: "Yes of course what else?"

After two days he had got bored and telephoned her. "Bridget please take me out of my misery. What is 143?"

She laughed.

"Lo there Jack, isn't it obvious if you just think of it as the number of letters in the words?"

Jack exclaimed, "Oh God, that is so simple...'I love you!'" He stressed the last three words.

She murmured back, "Well, that's nice to hear Jack because a girl needs to know and I can't remember you saying it my love."

Jack felt uncomfortable because of Karina but he did love Bridget on his perceived scale. "Well, I do love you but..."

She sighed. "There is always a 'but' Jack and I never say that do I?" He was feeling guiltier towards her as he felt his love was too shallow against her instant and total commitment. He realised she wouldn't have started the affair if she didn't love him deeply. She changed the tone. "Where is your hand?"

"On the telephone of course."

"No, Jack. Where is your other hand?"

"Okay, in the usual place holding Mister Wiggly but I'm not erect and excited, it's just a boy thing. When you are watching TV or on the phone your hand just naturally goes there. Joseph is the same even at his age. We get a right bollocking off Melanie for watching football on TV but only because she comes in from shopping and finds us both sprawled across the sofa with our hands down our pants."

"For Goodness sake!" remonstrated Bridget.

"Fidget, that's exactly what Melanie says and is usually followed by 'get your hands out now'. Brainless boys hey!"

"Why do you keep calling me Fidget, Jack?"

"Because lovely when we were in bed all you wanted to do was fidget with me. You can never lie still can you?" Jack signed off the conversation with a rapidly delivered 424. This ensured total confusion for another two weeks until after various suggestions ranging from football formations to having ten orgasms when they made love, he finally admitted it meant Suck My Dick. Most texts after that were a combination of 143 and 424.

At weekends, the episodes of not going to bed at the same time as his wife increased, with less reasons or excuses given by both parties.

Getting into bed and not talking, bedroom sidelights turned on and off with both sides apportioning blame depending on who was feeling the most aggressive.

Many nights Jack would end up shouting angrily at her and walk out of the bedroom, throwing on his dressing gown so that he could sit downstairs and watch TV, brooding about divorce or worse.

He would often sit and think about leaving now.

"Maybe I am going crazy. Is it me or does this happen in other marriages? Is Melanie inciting me to behave like this to get rid of me?" But there was no close male friend he trusted enough to advise him and his nature strove for perfection, making it all that much worse. Melanie's cousin from Wolverhampton sat in the conservatory one day admiring the view and said pointedly, "Just enjoy what you have got Jack, that's all that counts." But that was never in Jack's nature. He was driven by achievement and so his 'busyness' got in the way of being happy and relaxed.

When preparing to go to Spain the screw seemed to be turned even tighter. Melanie would avoid getting Jack's clothes out ready for the journey.

"Jack, when are you getting the suitcases down from the attic? Jack, I ran out of time to cut the grass this week so you need to do it before we go to Spain on Sunday." It mattered to him that she had spent all week in La La land running around endlessly in her 4 x 4 and putting enormous time and effort into any non-productive thing that she wanted to do and avoiding practical day to day stuff.

The arguments got worse, and if they started late on a Friday night they usually carried on through to the Sunday night when they might call a truce to have sex and release their physical frustrations.

But the love was dying and worse still, so was the mutual respect.

Body language became negative in front of friends who privately noted the change. Arguments were usually driven by Jack suggesting that there might be another man as she was so disinterested in him. She would reiterate that this person didn't exist and Melanie even swore on Joseph's life that she had not made love to anyone else. There was always the dilemma about the words used though. Making love is different to having occasional sex romps when you are protecting a lifestyle and your son. The real problem was Jack's own guilt and the realisation that a better life could be had with someone else. He would sit at work and daydream.

"Nim, how do you know when the love has gone out of your marriage? Is it when you fancy ugly women who are uglier than the one you are living with? When getting drunk is more pleasurable than having sex? What are the criteria Nim? Is it how many times you stay up alone to see some crap late night film which you have seen before but is far more preferable than going to bed and being with your wife? Or the fact that you throw yourself at constant tedious work egged on by frustration that's both sexual and more significantly spiritual?"

He started watching more pornography on Sky when away in the Dodge hotel at Rosset and ran up enormous bills. He purchased porn DVDs off the internet and sat alone in his room playing them on his laptop.

Watching alone. Watching porn with his wife and watching with his mistress. Three different emotions. Guilt from wanking. Guilt from a wife who was unhappy because she wasn't good enough to turn a proper trick like the prostitute that Jack craved. Guilt with his mistress because he was thinking of his best friend Peter. At least Bridget appeared to like the novelty on occasion to add something new to their budding relationship.

Then there would be the drunken walks back from The Pheasant Inn with Peter talking about life and knowing each had problems that could never be shared. One eerie night under a full moon, Jack asked him a very deep question, "What's outside of your personal barriers, Peter?"

Peter was serious in his response for once. "Unlike most people, killing and hurting is in, definitely a possibility if someone messed with me or my family."

Jack cringed in the dark field as he felt this was a guarded warning even though he was sure Peter knew nothing about the affair with Bridget. He replied, "So are you suggesting you have no personal boundaries whereas I could never kill or hurt anyone as I am far too sensitive?"

"Yes Jack. I could kill someone and you wouldn't, but I can guarantee mate that I would never have gay sex even for a million quid." They both laughed at the white moon.

Jack nudged his arm as they staggered slightly. "What about this love affair between you and Jean then?" He had seen how close they were. He enjoyed seeing their interaction as a form of sexual fantasy and assuaging his guilt about Bridget. Peter played a part that suggested he was hopelessly in love with Jean but would never let his true feelings out.

"A secret is only a secret if you don't tell it to anyone."

Jack knew Peter would never tell him anything. He was a closed young spirit based on the practicalities of life and never stepped away from those action-based values.

Weekends came and went and became more of a drudgery for Jack each time. It was a period when everything went on the flexible mortgage. Spending money to bolster the failing marriage.

"Put it on the mortgage love," Jack would say to Melanie. "It doesn't matter I'm earning fantastic money." But of course it did matter as interest rates doubled to six per cent and house sales slowed so that everyone felt poorer in anticipation of 'the World crisis' still to come. All these external factors impacted on the family income as Jack got closer to the end of his contract. No one had seen oil prices at eighty dollars to the barrel before, everyone had thought that forty-five dollars was a worse case in the aftermath of the second Iraqi war, also known in The Pheasant Inn drinking sessions as 'the almighty fuck up'.

"Dog eat dog," said Jack to his mates in the pub, "and in parts of Iraq that's what we made them fall back on. Poor bastards, why should we force our idealised Western ideology on a culture set in its ways for thousands of years. We have no Allah given right to do that. What do you mean I'm cynical? It really is dog eat dog in life. Go on to the beach in the summer at Yapanc and watch them fight for a space by the water; watch the arguments when a parasol takes another person's sun. Dog eat dog, we are just animals."

Jack's tirades against society and mankind were getting more extreme as the financial pressures and matrimonial disharmonies intensified. Even his friends started to take the piss out of him. He had watched the Tour de France on TV and been inspired to go out and buy a brand new road racer as a sop to his unhappiness, including the Discovery Channel Lycra outfit and flashy two hundred pound cycling shoes. He was so proud of it all and dressing like Lance Armstrong he paraded to his best friends before or after the first few rides to see if they were impressed. Every single 'friend' laughed at him and took no interest in his beloved bike or his impressionable ideals in life that he held dear. Bridget even took digital photos on her mobile and texted them to their joint friends with comments like 'nice arse shame about the knobbly knees.'

Deep down Jack was hurt by it all. He wanted to be fast, young and athletic and everyone viewed him as an old man who had lost the plot during a mid-life crisis.

Nobody believed what he said about wanting to change his lifestyle and stay young in his approach because they couldn't imagine it for themselves and felt he was bucking a natural trend that was a social and cultural part of acceptability.

Nobody was listening to him.

Melanie enticed Harriet to lunch more often and gave up asking Jean and Bridget who always professed to be busy. They were sitting in the coffee shop in Tarporley eating smoked mackerel sandwiches dressed in Cheshire yoghurt and with a garnish of locally grown organic watercress. Melanie liked to gossip and tell secrets.

"Did you see how Peter had to push Jean's attentions away in The Pheasant Inn the other night? My God, the woman seems so desperate for him and in front of boring Martin as well!"

Harriet saw the playful relationship in a different light as her own marriage was going through a private bad patch. "Don't be fooled by the sexual banter and all the touchy-feely stuff Melanie. Can't you see that Peter is coarse and blunt and would only want a quick shag? Am I right or am I not?"

Melanie desperately wanted more sex off Peter to make up for her moaning and whining husband whom she deliberately annoyed by withholding her sexual favours. But he wasn't always available when required and that made her suspicious and so she asked,

"Do you think he's shagging her then?"

Harriet detected the hint of jealousy. "I have no idea Melanie but one thing is certain. She keeps away from you and me unless we are all together as couples."

Melanie resolved to ask Peter directly and watch his eyes as he answered. She didn't want to play second fiddle to frumpy Jean and so she turned the conversation away from character assassination to the latest news on private school fees and her hopes for Joseph to go to The Grange next year.

Jack told his Mother that he had been riding his new road bike and hoped she would be impressed.

"Is that one of them, you know, one with them with drop handlebars?"

"Yes," replied Jack, "it's a Trek, three thousand pounds worth, as ridden by Lance Armstrong."

"Who's Lance Armstrong?"

"He has just won the Tour de France for a record seventh time and is my hero. He comes to Yapanc with his children to play on the beach."

"I thought you said he was a cyclist so how does he find time to do that? I've never heard of him. Tommy Simpson was famous when your Dad used to cycle. They both used to like a few fags and a few glasses of wine every day. Why do you go to Yapanc? Is it in France near Tugdual?"

"Don't worry Mother, it's where I go on holiday in Spain. It's where I would like to live. You have forgotten but don't worry."

"My sister used to have a new bike with them drop handlebars. She always got the best things instead of me. She never speaks to me now, always too busy going to bingo."

"No Mother, you saw her last week I think."

The more he spoke to her and the worse the family finances became he started to calculate his possible inheritance if she died soon. "What can I do with two hundred thousand pounds? A new car? Pay off the mortgage?" He dreamed and then felt incredibly guilty about wishing her dead. He thought about her every day and her loneliness. When she was thinking straight she told him that she missed her friends and that was the worst thing in her life.

Having no one to talk to about the good old days.

Melanie was in Spain and the feelings in the house in Tettenhill at the weekends were unsettling but only because Jack was lonely and he could identify with Mother.

"Nim this feeling is all in the mind isn't it? In fact life is all in the mind. If you close your eyes and lay your head on your arms you can go anywhere in the world, but a lonely weekend makes me think of Mother sat alone in repeat mode, an old fashioned tape of her life looping around in her head. Dad endlessly looping in and out of her thoughts mixed in with old memories back to the war, her youth and her sister-driven jealousies. Reliving the best times when she was young – below forty years of age. Maybe all of our minds work the same but some people control them better."

He didn't see Bridget the Fidget that summer, she was too busy in the shop and her own guilt had to be assuaged by hard work. So Jack became more morose and more thoughtful about his life and his future plans without coming to a conclusion, but his manipulative wife made sure she went to the Garden Centre to chat when at home.

"How are you Bridget? You look so tired lately. Is Peter making life hard for you my dear?"

Bridget would never divulge her personal details to anyone and certainly not her lover's wife. "No of course not Melanie. He is the same unhelpful man as ever but they're all like that aren't they!"

"Yes they are. Jack is always moaning about work and lack of time but he manages to clear off cycling every weekend leaving me to look after Joseph twenty-four seven. You know, I get no thanks at all from him." Bridget wondered how much more devious and false her friend could become. She tersely commented.

"Well think yourself lucky that you have no husband around all week and can get rid of him for a few hours each weekend."

Melanie wound her up a little tighter. "He earns 'fab' money for me to spend but quite frankly I would rather have someone who lives life for life's sake like your Peter, rather than my spiritual and sensitive moaner." They shared very little reality when they met and Bridget cut short the chats by professing the need to get back to work.

When Melanie and Joseph came home from Spain at the end of the summer holidays Jack's weekends changed to become full of hate instead of loneliness.

One evening he casually walked up to Melanie and pushed his prick into the small of her back as she prepared vegetables for the Miele steam oven. "Come into the bathroom upstairs for five minutes and have sex."

She refused point blank without an excuse.

He looked at her with hate in his narrowed eyes and said, "Isn't that part of our fucking problem? Is that what happens in other marriages or do we have special issues?" Melanie carried on with her vegetables without responding as he spat out, "I suppose that most people live with it and just accept the other person's wishes no matter what. I tell you now Melanie, I am not most people."

He took his glass of wine and walked outside to admire the stars and think of how much he missed both Bridget and Karina.

Later that evening, a confused husband sat in his study having finally completed the transcription of the tape from his astrology reading. Melanie was watching a recording of 'Coronation Street' and Joseph was happily asleep upstairs lying on his back and snoring contentedly.

Whenever Jack had an opportunity he would delve into the internet. In particular, he had always been fascinated by the number seven, as mentioned by Beatty, and its quasi links with mysticism, religion and Good as opposed to Evil. That's why his personalised number plate ended with a seven and why he always said his seven pleas for others less fortunate in the world.

He restarted his research looking at meaningless drivel but desperate to find meaningful facts from within the avalanche of Google data on his screen, including an invitation to have seven prostitutes in a bed together which did appeal. He was in a foul mood because of Melanie's presence in the adjacent room. He pictured her lump sprawled across the sofa and eating a large bar of chocolate whilst he tried to improve his knowledge.

Reading ancient phrases considered as the truth by millions of people through thousands of years made him feel he understood less about life but could sense how the very basis of humanity revolved around true love. However, his search for enlightenment was still blunted by the practicalities of his day to day life and Jack found that frustrating as he needed time and a teacher. He qualified his last thought by remembering Nim might be his teacher, if Nim was not just a figment of his imagination.

"Are you there Nim?" he queried out loud.

"Yes Jack what did you say?" came a 'Corrie' corrupted question from Melanie. He didn't answer and she didn't ask again as she was too busy with the new plot about Alzheimer's, love deceit and murder, all compressed into a single episode just like real life isn't.

"So you are not there Nim, you have gone off to the pub with your spirit mates or you don't exist." Nim remained silent, watching Jack find his path without any need of his help. Jack remembered as a teenager reading many Dennis Wheatley books and so he googled on the seven levels of consciousness mentioned in *The Ka of Gifford Hillary*.

'The ancient Egyptians believed that each human being had a soul attached to its physical body; they called this soul the Ka. In the tombs of ancient Egypt the Ka is represented by a human-faced bird. It was believed that the Ka remained with the body and resided within the burial chamber.'

The telephone rang and made him jump. He picked it up whilst still staring at his screen. "Is that you Nim? No? In that case is there anyone on the line please?"

"Of course poppet, it's me Harriet. Why do you ask?"

"Because you need to get off it immediately."

"Why?"

"There's a train coming. Boom, boom!" He reiterated the joke and punch line from Basil Brush in the late sixties.

"Poppet, you are on a different planet sometimes. How are your stress levels?"

"Fine."

"Is that a woman's fine or a real fine."

"A woman's fine Harry. As in 'why am I married?', fine."

"Tell me about it poppet. Nobody knows what is happening behind closed doors."

"Tell the truth and shame the Devil. Henry the Fourth part one I think it was. That was the only thing I could remember in my English 'O' level."

"You are funny Jack. Remember this, my learned friend. Marco Polo was talking to Kubla Khan about a crescent-shaped bridge and told him how the arch was supported by the clever positioning of the stones. Kubla Khan thought about it for a while and told Marco Polo that he was only interested in the arch and not the stones."

"And what Harry?"

"So Marco Polo pointed out that without the stones there could never be an arch."

"Meaning my lovely?"

"Meaning without love there can be no marriage."

Jack pondered the truth. "Well my wise Soul Shiner, on that note I think you may be after Melanie, yes?" He passed her over, thinking how well matched she was in their quest for spiritual knowledge.

Returning to Google he tried again.

Seven Shamanic Levels of Consciousness by Dirk Gillabel. 'In 1989 I met a Hungarian Shaman', he scanned down past the words about shamans and spiritual seekers, past the twelve dollar advert for the book and straight to the seven levels: 'Personal, Mankind, Amphibious, Spherical, Crystal, Light, and Sound.'

"What a load of bollocks," as he moved the cursor onto the back button and left clicked. The next search was marginally more interesting.

'Tibetan Buddhist and Hindu monks referred to the seven levels as the seven bodies and they represent layers of awareness in the physical brain.' He hit the back button again. The most interesting part of the article was the fact that a brain has one hundred billion neurons connected by fifty trillion synapses which is why we are all so different except at the base animal level of eat, drink, protect and fight.

"So there you are Nim, we are just animals with a thin veneer of decency, just enough to allow each other to make a living by sharing our world, which we never did until three thousand years ago. We used to have so much space around us and so little connectivity with others but that veneer can be stripped away instantly if our space is under threat and that is constant now as we 'connect' with each other all of the time."

Nim sighed and made Jack shiver uncomfortably whilst slumped in his seat. He threw his keyboard to one side and closing his eyes he let himself dwell on Beatty's strange words that he had been avoiding. "Come on Nim, did she talk to you? Were you there?"

Nim decided to give Jack some guidance.

Of course I was there Jack but spirits talk to
clairvoyants and tell them what we see and not the
other way round.
After all she is just a person Jack; she eats, sleeps,
poohs and does what I tell her to.

Jack jerked upright and looked around the small and now cold study for the source of Nim's soft voice. He shivered again.

"Just suppose you exist and you want me to do something for you. Just suppose that. What the hell has a boatyard got anything to do with anything you twat?"

Spirits aren't twats Jack; we are not scousers, not
twats, not mates, wankers, or tossers.
We just are and you can't pigeonhole us because we
are everything and we are nothing.

"That's bollocks mate, I mean sorry but can you just answer my question please?"

She told you to go on the sea Jack.
To go on the sea you need a boat.
A boat needs a home but not a buoy or in a harbour.
It needs a boatyard by a real home and in that home
you will find everything you need.

Jack sighed loudly again and blowing his exasperated breath across Nim's face he said.

"I can't believe all this, nothing is not everything. Nothing is nothing, no facts, no proof, nothing. So just get out of my mind. If I want trick answers to real questions I can always go on the internet and get really confused or ask my beloved wife!" Jack gave Google a final chance on the seven levels starting with an aptly titled address, 'Sortlifeout.co.uk, the top level of consciousness is nothingness, none being Nirvana.'

"So what is the point of not existing or can you go there and return Nim? If you have nothing maybe you can then think true inspired thoughts about everything. That might be Beatty's answer too. Get rid of all you have and start again to find the true you and your true path. Fuck. That's so fucking scary Nim."

'The Seven Egyptian Hermetic principles' he had seen before somewhere and accepted the logic.

'Mentalism – the all is mind.'

"If you have nothing then you think true inspired thoughts," backing up Beatty again.

'Correspondence – as above so below; as below so above.'

"What I do here in this life is mirrored in another dimension maybe?"

'Vibration – nothing rests everything moves.'

"Obviously, as matter is made up of atoms and they constantly move."

'Polarity – everything has poles, everything is dual. A pair of opposites, like and unlike.'

"Good versus Evil."

'Rhythm – everything flows in and out or rises and falls and a move left compensates a move to the right.'

'Cause and effect – every cause has its effect and every effect has its cause. Nothing escapes this law and chance is but a name for law but is not yet recognized as a law.'

"I like that bit! There is something left to discover then but this and rhythm, polarity and correspondence imply the same thing Nim. Opposites can rule, either or."

'Gender – masculine and feminine manifests itself on all planes.'

"Sex is everything. Money, sex and power. It rules the world. Women control men through sex, men control women through money but women are much cleverer at manipulating their man and have the real power between their legs on top of thinking around every angle a dozen times and then a dozen times again. We may as well concede victory boys, there is no way we can compete by being our logical, practical selves and have no chance at learning to think with emotions giving them with their subjectivity. At least all these seven seem logical but you never hear about the Hermetic religion." He said this to the blinking screen as it arrived at a new website.

As he looked further into www.about.com on alternative religions he realised that whether it is seven days of Jewish mourning, seven days to create the world or just the week itself, the number seven has always been important to human beings and the oldest religions.

What was certain is that you cannot get to the root of anything so diverse and when you try, you can end up linking a load of 'tosh' together to prove your own pet theories.

Seven in many beliefs is a very powerful spiritual number.

Seven generations from David to Jesus, seven Devas of the Hindu Religion, seven spirits of the Egyptian religion, seven angels in the book of Ezekiel, the book of the Hebrew Kaballah and even in Revelation.

Always seven as he turned the letters around to write down 'neves' on the desk jotter.

"Never Ever View Everything Simply." He said loudly and threw his head into his hands and rubbed his eyes.

> *Jack you are confused about symbols and religions*
> *and just need to find yourself to get some peace in*
> *your mind.*

"Is that you Nim? Where the hell do you go to?" If Melanie heard Jack talking to himself, she showed no signs of coming to interrogate him as she couldn't be bothered to budge. Nim decided he couldn't remain quiet anymore with the 'googled out' Jack.

> *In Eastern religious teachings, Karma is the duty*
> *borne by the soul.*
> *Karma may be positive or negative but it must always*
> *be balanced as you saw in the hermetic principles.*
> *Karma can only be balanced by repayment of duty*
> *owed either from or to others.*
> *This Karmic debt is said to continue from one lifetime*
> *to the next by the process of reincarnation.*
> *The Karma of a serious criminal who may have*
> *committed many atrocities, such as Adolf Hitler, will*
> *under Karmic law require countless incarnations of*
> *suffering to redress the negative balance.*
> *Whereas the positive influence of some saintly soul*
> *such as Mother Teresa of Calcutta will create good*
> *Karma and thus a more fortuitous reincarnation if*
> *indeed such a soul should decide to reincarnate.*
> *We all continue to reincarnate until we reach*
> *perfection and then our souls enter paradise.*
> *You are an old soul Jack and if you don't change your*
> *life now, you will have wasted this reincarnation.*
> *Karma and Karmic debt is what Beatty meant by*
> *the Collective.*

You can join it too but not yet.
You have too many questions to answer and need time
to do that.

Random thoughts rushed through Jack's brain as he quietly talked to Nim.

"I'm not sure I believe in reincarnation and probably not you. It seems vanity on our part to think we can come back from death and like all the interesting concepts on life it cannot be proved either way. What's a Leo? Beatty said others perceive me as the hero, the lion, shaggy by name, shagging by nature. Seen as a lion but just a big pussycat. Do people see me as a Leo, Nim?"

Yes, the sign of the ruler, the king of the beasts as you
were in your past, Centurion.
You are seen as a born leader but in fact you do not have
the inbuilt self confidence to be an out and out leader.
You constantly look for praise and keep checking the
detail instead of going for the big picture and the big
win. That's why you have failed at work to be the
ultimate number one in a company.
You're not assertive enough and consider other
people's feelings.
When it comes to the crunch, you can be off in
imagination land looking for a theoretical best rather
than settling on a practical second best.
Your own JFDI approach Jack – Just Fucking Do It.
But you never follow your own advice do you?

Nim was not helping boost Jack's confidence at this stage.

Leo is expansive, generous and caring.
You are flamboyant just like at parties.
But a Leo can be seen by their friends or work
colleagues as having too much pride, pompous and
even having snobbery.

It's not you but it's a perception people will have
about you.
It is true though.
You like to be the centre of attention, dignified and
proud but relaxed.
You feel hurt when ignored and love to have and hold
the audience but you do not have the fire in your belly
that is in true Leos.

Jack was getting bored by Nim but had started to accept him into his spiritual awakening.

"Define a 'No Thinker' Nim. Proletarians, working class people, lager louts or thugs? Is it a class distinction as surely everyone is capable of thinking depending on their spiritual age? And how do you determine this age? Soul Shiner went to a Spiritualist meeting and told me the leader judged this age depending on how much pressure you had in your outstretched arms. That can't be scientific can it?"

No of course not and what you practically do in life is
not material in determining your Karma.

"So, is there a link between spirituality and intelligence instead? Can a thick moron be highly developed spiritually? Or is spiritualism just a religion and no different to Roman Catholicism? It just appears to be deeper but it isn't. The psychic opium of the masses. A way of influencing people and controlling them? Who can say that Jim from the organisation-healing business on its group website: www. Perfectsympathy.com is anymore spiritual than John the local Catholic priest? Which one has got a more refined and stronger spiritual touch?"

Answer your own questions Jack, you know the
answers but are scared to go and find them again in
this life.

Jack remembered watching the TV programme about cleansing three houses of evil which had been on BBC2 one evening, and so in his mind must therefore be true.

"Nim, listen to me for a change. In the UK there are twenty-three C of E vicars trained in exorcism. Why? To exorcise situations deemed bad in what way by the Church? Were they trained better and how do they train them? Are they more spiritual than the other vicars? Do they have magic potions, pieces of Christ's cross wrapped in their pocket handkerchief?" He opened his arms and glanced around the study asking for some answers. "Have we truthfully got a million people around the world joining in the Collective? Are they already in positions of influence within society because of their spiritual age? It all sounds like a good Hollywood film Nim but behind the practicalities of life, are there things going on which are so mind blowing that most people can never understand? I don't know what is real anymore." His jumbled thoughts fell out in rapid unanswerable succession as he nodded with tiredness. He laid his head on the study desk.

"Seven million Jews killed in the Holocaust and people deny that evil exists. The number seven again."

It was getting late by now and the spiritual randomness had intensified into a pile of mush in his brain.

Melanie whined, "Jack? Where are you? Are you on that stupid computer again wasting your time? You are always on that computer. What are you doing?"

The art of communication as practised by Melanie shrieking from her ignorant perch on the sofa in front of the TV yet again, which was itself 'parrot like', repeating the day to day crap to the masses who watched it including his wife.

Pinned down by fatigue and heavy thoughts he turned the PC off and forced himself off the chair to slink upstairs and jump into his lonely bed.

There was no good night to his wife.

No love and no interest.

He hoped the next evening with their friends would give him some light respite as he fought his demons to find some meaning to his life.

The dinner party conversation was innocuous enough over the curried egg starter, served with a smidgeon of caviar to show that they had money to burn. Jack mooned his 'come to bed' eyes at Bridget as he chatted to her about her beloved girls but immediately got into trouble as the main course arrived.

Harriet complimented the hostess. "The smoked haddock and asparagus pasta tastes fantastic Melanie, absolutely fantastic."

Jack gave some sound advice to Soul Shiner. "The problem with haddock and asparagus Harriet is that you eat it twice like a curry. Sex will definitely be out of the question tonight, well at least with Matt hey! Asparagus makes your piss stink like hell and haddock means fish at both ends." Only Peter laughed and Melanie just stared at her out-of-control husband.

Jean returned to more mundane conversation. "We all want to get out of the rat race but I suppose as you get older you want to get out of it more? Is that true Jack?"

Jack was serious for a moment. "It does get harder as you get older because you can't drop out. You are tied into a quality of life that is hard to give up. It's deemed unacceptable to go backwards by your peer group. But equally you don't necessarily know what the true quality of life actually means anymore. How many of you can define it in non-material terms i.e. excluding cars, schools, houses and also health of course?" He looked around at his wary audience with a silent challenge to each one. "Go on everyone, define it! Firstly, consider some people don't have time to think about the quality of their lives because they are too busy surviving on sod all but in all of our cases we are too busy working hard for more or 'better' material things."

Melanie couldn't stand the sanctimonious drivel and told him so. "Jack, most people are happy, unlike you, and are not having a mid-life crisis."

He looked around at everyone again before replying in measured tones, "I'm not having a mid-life crisis, I am redefining the second part of my life and everyone should make some time to think about that for themselves. I know I'm controversial but that's deliberate to make people think more. There's a whole world out there and our tiny minds have no comprehension about it. Only 'old' spirits fret about knowing more about it. If you can distance earning money from life you can then find true freedom. Money isn't life. It's no good living to work; you have to truly work to live but just enough and not too much. That means knowing yourself deeply because you see, nobody ever seems able to set that balance."

Melanie sighed. "What rubbish Jack, you just need to relax and be happy."

"I think you may be right there Melanie but you need to be living with someone and in a situation or lifestyle to be able to relax." He could almost hear the sharp intake of breath from their fellow diners. "You do realise dear wife that no one ever finds the ideal partner, as they rush into their selection needing a safe and secure feeling. They almost accept anyone who is 'there for them' having left their childhood family behind and especially their mothers. It's impossible when you think about it. There are nearly three billion potential partners in the world for each of us and out of that lot there are perhaps only ten per cent you would be very happy living with. There may be another ten per cent that you could live with for a while and ten per cent you would absolutely hate. The remaining seventy per cent are just filling your space and come in and out of your life without any aggravation and so by default eighty per cent of marriages are for convenience. Correct Martin?"

"Ah yes, so so not too bad, absolutely the correct numbers, I think yes." Mister Boring wasn't going to comment and so Jack continued.

"In fact, I don't think that you can ever find your Sun Sharer within the 'happy' ten per cent because if you are always looking you can spoil what you have. Being part of crazy is keeping on looking."

Soul Shiner was rubbing his shoulders with her right hand to release some of his stress. "Poppet we all believe in true love and being happy ever after. You just need to be lucky."

She seemed incredibly sad as she said this but Jack missed any hidden meaning as he ranted on. "Let's face it; you don't travel round the UK interviewing marriage candidates do you? You don't get on a HR database and select key attributes before you meet someone and so you always compromise. The sad thing is Melanie, you end up with the girl from the office like you my dear or the one from next door like Bridget here and believe you have the ideal partner. It's all rubbish really as you end up with someone who is not ideal even for practical day to day stuff and is certainly a million miles away from some sort of mutual spiritual understanding. Then when you live with this person you start to get jealous about little things as the years pass by."

Melanie was despairing and shaking her head from left to right as she reacted sharply. "Like what little things Jack?" She clicked the 'ack' harshly from the back of her throat to emphasise her irritation.

"Like for example when you and Peter went to the agricultural show together for Joseph to see the tractors. I don't want to be controversial but –! Perhaps jealousy gets worse as you get older, especially if you have a younger wife? Or does it show you care? Maybe it becomes more intense as one's personal confidence and own appeal decreases?"

He had barely drawn breath in his tirade.

The guests were shocked by Jack's attitude more than ever before and moved back to safe subjects such as schools and Sainsbury's, leaving him to mull over his own thoughts and open more wine to help numb his overactive brain. He turned to Peter. "Have you ever heard of *A Brief History of Time* by Stephen Hawking, you know that guy in the wheelchair? He says that the Universe is three dimensional, moving through the fourth dimension which is time. If you go through that wall over there..." he turned and pointed behind Melanie, who turned round to look with everyone else, "eventually you would end up coming back through the opposite wall in front of us because the universe is made like a big doughnut."

Peter was impressed. "That's the most interesting thing you have managed to say tonight mate."

Jack waxed lyrical, "The universe started from a pinhead-sized piece of something and blew apart and is still expanding but then will gradually collapse back to the pinhead in a few million years time. So if you can get that into your head you can get anything to come true, hey?" Peter and Jack slouched towards each other, the leaning caused by the red wine rather than gravitational pull.

"Jack mate, I prefer reading that Dan Brown bloke and the *Da Vinci Code*. You see my jeans." He pulled away his jumper and showed Jack a Maltese cross fixed onto the belt. "This shows I belong to The Priory of Sion. I am one of the Knights Templar and this is an old piece of gold from before Christ was born, blessed by Saint Peter himself."

Jack stared and pushed him on his shoulder. "Fuck off Edam they are Fake Genius jeans. I saw them in the sales in Chester last week you bastard."

Peter continued, "You may mock me but I am a rider of the night. I see black versus white and Good versus Evil. Remember in Spain you welcome the shade to stop you burning. You welcome the night to rebuild your energy. Everything is opposites Jack. I am a Templar and I know these things. Black people balance white people. Christians versus Islam and terrorism never muttered in the same breath at a Cheshire dinner party but always on people's lips." Peter touched his mouth with his forefinger. "Remember Jack, it may not be politically correct but the 'no thinkers' like me see it as it is. Black and white."

Jack staggered out to the toilet and when he returned he moved to sit next to Harriet.

"How are you Soul Shiner? Have you got any interesting conversation for me lovely?"

Soul Shiner started stroking the back of his neck where some cropped hair remained. She maliciously said to Melanie, "I like poppet's hair like this, it's really turning me on."

Jack was still alert enough to comment, "That's why they call me Spike."

"Spike?" she queried.

"Yes," said Jack, nodding down towards his lap where his penis pushed up his trousers. "Spike."

"Oh God, you are dreadful tonight poppet, much worse than usual," but she was interested enough to look.

He changed the subject as his penis went limp when his wife cut him a look. "I bought my wife a three hundred pound necklace last week as a coming home present. Aquamarine, you know it's her birthstone." Jack stared at Harriet's big boobs drooping out of her blouse. He sat more upright to get a better view. "I bought this necklace from 'Harvey Nics' in Manchester and do you know what I got from their six week holiday in Spain? A frigging Spanish calendar with helpful phrases like 'I've got chicken skin', meaning goose bumps – 'Se me puso la carne de gallina.' Another one said, 'if you screw your goat you get a lot of pleasure', which in English means don't shit on your own doorstep." He placed his head on her shoulder to get a better view of her breasts. Lying comfortably he could imagine getting it together with Harriet whom he adored, but of course he had chased and caught Bridget. "Am I missing out on the good things in life Soul Shiner?"

She looked at him kindly from six inches away. "I think you are Jack but so am I. I just don't get upset about it like you. I miss being hot with the wind in my hair. Feeling sexy and vibrant with a young man in early love putting a buttercup under my chin. Lying on newly mown grass with the gorgeous sweet smell overwhelming my senses." She prodded his chest with her finger. "So what exactly are you going to give up in this new ideal life of yours? Can you make a list of things that are important to you and stick with it for the rest of your life?"

He was flummoxed by the drink and her breasts as his prick grew harder again.

She could see he wasn't going to reply so she guessed, "Let me think what you want shall we? Nature and the great outdoors? Love, real emotional love? Your children? Your wife?" She paused and looked at his bloodshot eyes. "Maybe not, hey! How about sex, fast cars, football and definitely drinking! Come on Jack. Tell me what do you desperately want? What gives you a real spiritual lift which will last forever? The things that you will remember ten years from now are those things giving you a true quality of life."

Jack couldn't reply. He knew she was deep but not that deep surely?

She carried on, "Could you stick with your unwritten list without the peer pressure around here? Your friends would see you as dropping out and so would you lose your self esteem as well as their respect. Could you deal with that? Is that a reason to stick with what you have Jack?"

He eventually looked up at her and replied, "Soul Shiner, you truly are one. Half a Sun Sharer hey! I can't answer all of those questions but I wish I could. I just want to simplify things. Is it a sign of age that I want to simplify my life? Eliminate the hundreds of emails every day and the constant telephone calls. I just want a room and a bed; just simple."

She hugged him close and whispered, "Good luck Jack. Good luck, I hope you find true happiness," and she lovingly kissed his forehead and moved away to join the other departing guests, leaving him confused.

Jack gradually went crazy but no one cared enough to notice because they were all too busy with their own lives.

That's why he had acquaintances and not friends and why his marriage was now doomed.

Bridget was naturally upset at their first Christmas without being around each other but the absence was a sign of their shallowing relationship. The on-off love affair with minimal sex was getting out of hand and they both knew it. She emailed Jack on his work address to express how she felt. It didn't help that her cycle was at menstruation madness levels. "I thought Christmas was the season of goodwill and love but all I seem to be getting is less love and more of my mad family placing impossible demands on me. They think I can work fourteen hours a day sorting out the shop, cook their tea, do the ironing, go to buy Xmas presents and also be a fantastic Mother and sex machine rolled into one. It is impossible!"

Jack emailed back immediately because that's how they kept it all secret. One in, one back and then delete.

"It is the season for obscene spending and eating. Love and understanding happens every minute of every day between best friends and lovers. Please feel free to dump all your troubles on me as I am mentally incredibly strong and have no problems in my life as I have a best friend and lover. No guilt accepted or placing of emotions into boxes is required. The crap will go away."

Bridget was puzzled in her reply. "So best friend versus lover my love. Either or? Choice or both please? It is on my mind and I think it has been on yours too. We touched on starts versus ends of love affairs when we spoke last week and what is meant by a friendship."

Jack answered immediately. "Sometimes it is easier to say something in writing and be away from the person you love. Then you can say things that are on your mind. All I know at the moment is I am looking for a Sun Sharer. I don't think, I repeat I don't think you are my Sun Sharer. I can't be fairer than that and I have always been open and honest with you. However, I am very vulnerable at present and defensive because of my bad marriage. I only ended up with Melanie because it was nice but not special. Looking back, it was a convenient love from the start, not real deep Sun Sharer love, and I feel deeply appalled that I was so weak all those years ago. That means it is doubly hard for someone like you to say 'love me because I love you and there are no conditions.'

You see love always has conditions.

Even now, what we have said and done has laid down conditions just because of what was said and done. Maybe no one ever meets their Sun Sharer and after a while you give up and stick with a partner who is lovely and loving so that meets eighty per cent of any normal person's needs.

But I am not normal Bridget!

I am going through all of this grief and soul searching because I definitely want a different life to most people. I must let go of my old life and live my dreams.

So I am contemplating a new single life and must be open to all friendships and new things in life because something is telling me I need to live in Yapanc. I am always comfortable with you, trust in you totally and share every emotional feeling. What is Love? It means it is impossible to walk away from someone because you love them so much and you get breathless when you talk to them about it. I love you but not as deeply as your love demands and without that commitment you would never leave Peter. You are my best friend and I value best friendship more than being a lover. I don't want to take advantage of you anymore and make love or even to feel obliged to make love but what does a best friend do? Be honest is the answer and tell their best friend. What does that do to you? It will destroy so much in your heart and soul that we have built up together. But what does a lover do? A lover hides it all away and doesn't tell their partner because being a lover is shallow compared to being a best friend. A lover's emotions are superficial in comparison.

So my love, my dearest, dearest Bridget. Love is confusing. Life is complicated.

But without both, you do not live, you just exist.

PS. I only sign my e mails 'love' when sent to you and no one else in my life. That must mean I like you at least! I suppose Nelly Furtado says it all in her song. 'Lovers to friends, why do all good things come to an end?'

So, I am in love with you but not enough. I am so happy when with you. Even now I have a sinking feeling in my guts and have to take a big breath."

But the damage was done with Bridget.

She knew deep down that she couldn't be Jack's because of her children and he knew he didn't love her enough to break both marriages up.

The texts and telephone calls slowed across the airwaves and the excitement disappeared into the ether, so the lovers remained best friends knowing they could always call on each other in an hour of desperate need, as opposed to their spouses who would find any excuse to not respond.

A working death

Ranks of stationary cars merged in the flat light on another meaningless Monday.

Disgruntled businessmen sat hunched over their steering wheels tapping their fingers impatiently or having animated conversations whilst leaning aggressively towards hidden microphones, and thoughtful business women sat relaxed, listening to Terry Wogan whilst re-planning their day ahead.

Brainless boys and clever girls at any age and in any situation.

"Hello Mother, I'm on my way to work, so I thought I'd give you a quick ring." Jack was in the car on another Monday morning and was delayed as usual.

"Where are you?"

"Stuck on the M1 waiting for an accident to clear."

"What are you doing there?"

"I'm going to my work in Rosset for Woolworths. Do you remember?"

"I didn't know you worked there. How long have you been with them?"

"I've been there for eighteen months Mum, you've just forgotten, since yesterday." The last two words were said under his breath.

"Are you still at Iceland in North Wales?"

"No Mother, I'm with Woolworths in Rosset, I left Iceland six years ago."

"Oh! That's strange; I thought you were with Iceland. Why are you there?"

"I'm installing some new computer systems. Remember, I became an IT consultant just over six years ago."

"Did you? What's IT?" She didn't pause to think, "Your Dad used to work in a shoe shop when you were a baby, do you remember?"

"No, not really Mum, I was a baby."

"Ay, the price of shoes in those days. Oh dear oh dear. My sister, you know Alice, I think you met her. She always had better shoes than me." Everything given to Alice had been better, at least in Mother's memories. "You should have seen the bike she had compared to mine. It had those drop handlebars that were ever so hard to hold on to. I fell off it once and she was really annoyed." She giggled. "Tommy Simpson used to go out with her. He was a nice man but he preferred me son." She drifted off in her imagination. It was the same journey with the same comments and mostly at the same places on the way to work. Derogatory of both the sister and the elder son. Mother was as hard as nails having beaten cancer three times but she wasn't going to beat Alzheimer's. She was giggling again, "I did something really silly yesterday Jack. I bought the *News of the World*. It was so expensive son."

"I thought you read the *Mirror*?"

"I do, but the man gave me the *News of the World* and I couldn't say no could I?" She was moving further into senility, the same conversations about incredibly boring subjects that were such a high priority in her mind and always drifting on without a point or an ending. "I might be going on Shearings Coaches for a holiday but your brother is keeping me prisoner. I don't like it here; I want to live by the seaside Jack. Anyway, they are too expensive now, I'm sure they have doubled their prices since your Dad and I went last month. They told me to book last minute and get a low price but I can't do that. I need to know where I am."

"That's a really good idea Mum as you can go at any time you want." But of course she couldn't go anywhere in her state.

"I can't be bothered with that son. My hip is a lot better now. I think it's the ginger wine." Mother always judged things by the olden day standards and prices. She made no attempt to keep up with the real world anymore.

Jack remembered a recent conversation with Rodney about repeating himself and had made a joke about euthanasia. If he got as bad as Mother he wouldn't really want to die early as long as he was happy and healthy in his own little world, because he hoped there would be something left of him. Something left for himself and his soul. "You can't buy time can you Mother? You are warm and well looked after so be happy lovey. Bye."

"Bye Jack, bye bye. Love you my son. Love to number one."

He didn't feel as guilty about her condition now. After a while it all becomes inevitable.

The rest of the journey continued the nightmare and so he walked straight into a project meeting two hours later than scheduled. If more than three women were involved it inevitably drove Jack to distraction as the first ten minutes of the meeting would degenerate into a hair conversation like today because Gemma had new highlights.

Jack tried to move forward in vain. "The first item on the agenda. Has anyone noticed the change in my hairstyle?" He patted his bald head and everyone laughed and then they got on with some real business. After most people had left, the women were talking about hair again so Jack threw his head into his hands and laid it on the table. "As we have HR present, I am reporting you ladies for mental abuse towards men, namely me." He looked up as they gathered around to sympathise because they genuinely liked and respected him. Gemma noticed his unusually shaped wedding ring and asked about it. It had been made from his late Granddad George's and was formed into waves as you circled around the band. He turned and twisted the snaking band to match his chat-up line.

"When it's like this, it means my marriage is down the pan and when I twist it like that it means it is just about bearable." They all laughed.

Gemma asked naively, "Come on then Jack, which does it mean now?"

He moved it around slightly to bring a crest to the top of his third finger. "You have to guess Gemma, what do you think?"

She patted his shoulder. "I think your marriage is very good of course." She herself was newly and very happily married. Whether the crest of the wave was up or down on the top of his outstretched finger was totally meaningless. It was just a way of saying I am interested in you if you want me and my marriage is a waste of time. "So tell us about your wife Jack. What's her name?"

He replied to her and her two colleagues with a straight face. "The only interesting thing about Melanie is she is wife number four."

"Number four?" they all exclaimed aghast. "You are joking aren't you?"

He continued seriously, "No, I've been married four times. The first one we don't talk about, the second left me for my best friend, the third left me for her lesbian lover and the fourth is on her way out as she spends too much money shopping, but of course they all take me as I come."

Gemma said, "No way! I don't believe you Mr Edmunson."

He smiled at her and her naivety that made her miss the rude pun. "Believe me Gemma, just like you would believe a used car salesman or an estate agent. It's absolutely true."

She queried further, "In that case why don't you talk about number one?"

Jack stood up and with a curt, "Sorry I have to go," he avoided answering, leaving them all questioning the truth.

The funeral march sounded on his mobile. He had programmed it especially for calls from his wife, leaving the romantic 'Te Amero' by Il Divo for Bridget and a normal ring tone for all his other calls. Melanie was ringing him to say Egg Visa had overcharged them by four thousand pounds compared to the vouchers she had checked off against the statement. There were loads of entries for Singapore communications and could he explain why. He told her he would ring Egg and stop any payments but quietly wondered if the fraud stemmed from the mobile phone tracker that he had placed on her through the internet.

An hour later, Mother rang to say his brother was holding her prisoner again and he spent ten minutes calming her down until her mind slipped onto a different subject.

As a climax to his eventful Monday, his work email went down and his mobile phone answering service seemed to have packed up according to all the people who desperately wanted to get hold of him.

A normal stressful day at work. A normal shitty Monday.

Every week for twelve months Jack had stayed in the Dodge House Hotel in Rosset and now felt the customer service team or CST as the manager called them was closer to him than his family. Jack thought the name was hilarious and often referred to them as cysts that were all waiting to be lanced, meaning shagged.

The receptionist was dark, slim and about twenty-eight years old and single again after several long term relationships. Jack constantly letched after her and for twelve months had been trying to shag her and had failed miserably. The chef was the opposite; a bottle blonde of about eighteen stone and wanting Jack to shag her silly. The waitresses were always fun but came and went regularly, usually 'Ryanaired' in from different parts of Eastern Europe to reduce costs. Generally they didn't understand the menu never mind any jokes or sexual innuendo that he threw at them.

On a Monday night, Jack was always exhausted and just went into the Dodge House and crashed out on his bed. The warm light from the lamp post outside his room penetrated the thin old curtains as he watched TV through opaque eyes, seeing the images but not taking it all in. Falling asleep early on a Monday night was a tradition; no matter what was good on TV and certainly due to the lack of any enthralling conversation with Melanie. However, by Tuesday evening he was invariably back on form. Walking into the hotel, he saw the usual one receptionist had temporarily grown to three.

"Evening all. How are you ladies? Three in a row, just like buses. When you need one you can't find one and when you don't, you always have a choice of three."

The receptionist commented, "That is the story of your life in reverse Mr Edmunson. Needing three women and having none!"

"Very funny indeed. Yes thank you it is nice to be back again and who is this beautiful young lady?"

The youngest was fresh-faced and had a badge 'Trainee' so now she would always be called Trainee by Jack. The other was his favourite waitress, leaving the receptionist who smiled sexily at Jack teasing him as usual.

"Trainee, this is Mr Edmunson, our most valued guest for over a year now and always to be treated with due care and attention just like an old car." She smiled sweetly again. "Mr Edmunson has a unique character that you need to be aware of and distrust."

Jack shook Trainee's hand saying, "Not so much a guest, more of an inmate actually." As always he stood leaning on the reception desk for a chat to brighten his day. Leaning across the counter he asked the receptionist to qualify her remarks. "Okay, so how do I need to improve my credibility then?"

She smiled sweetly for a third time and replied, "What you need to do Mr Edmunson is put yourself in the other person's position because we can never believe what you say."

"Fair enough, I can think of you in three positions right now!" came his witty reply.

She scolded him, "You see we never know if we get the truth, just like when you tell us you have been married four times."

Jack answered seriously, "I have been married four times and now I am looking for someone just like you as number five. How about it?"

She ignored him and looked down her nose through her

rimless glasses whilst the Trainee queried, "Why did you get married four times?"

Jack heaved a big sigh. "It's a sad story really. Loneliness, just loneliness. Don't you ever get lonely Trainee?" They all replied 'no' simultaneously and Jack believed them but questioned further for his own amusement. "You are all joking?"

"No definitely not," replied all three together again, united in their defiance.

The receptionist explained for them all, "Why should we be lonely when we are so young?"

He thought about the slander implying he was old and pursed his lips. He leaned closer towards the receptionist. "Hold on, come closer." He stared intently at her glasses before tapping the left lens. She quickly took them off to see what was the matter.

"What's wrong?" she demanded.

"Nothing," said Jack, "but at least I have seen your face without them on and know how beautiful you are."

She frowned at him. "You see you are totally irrepressible Mr Edmunson. However, you may as well complete our new customer service questionnaire. You are very privileged as you will be the first guest to do so."

"Fantastic, a virgin then," he made the girls chuckle. Taking the proffered form he started to tick boxes whilst speaking his comments, encouraged by their giggles.

"Sex. Tick. Yes please. Would you come again? Given half a chance to come the first time." He was hit over the head with a wad of leaflets by the receptionist.

"Waitress service. Appalling." He was hit this time by the waitress's hand.

"Marks out of ten? I'd give her one." Nodding towards the young trainee. She remained puzzled by this strange guest and missed the joke completely.

"Mobile number." He started to write and slowly say his number so they might be tempted to text him but then he couldn't remember the order of the last three digits.

"Oh God, it's awful remembering your own number isn't it?

Bear with me I'm having a CRAFT moment." All three looked up to him for an explanation.

"Easy. Can't Remember A Fucking Thing."

A chorus of disapprovals met the comment but before he disappeared to his bedroom he was asked one final question, or one more tease depending on who was listening to the tone in the receptionist's voice. "So why did you get married the last time?"

Jack looked into her beautiful brown eyes and replied honestly, "Convenience."

She looked shocked. "You are joking aren't you?"

"No, it's true. Everything I have said tonight is true but you three don't believe me. I swear on my son's life, I am telling the truth about it being convenient." Jack held his hand over his heart. "You know, it would be cheaper to employ a prostitute, a chef and a housekeeper. It would also mean better sex, great food and decent cleaning."

He smiled wryly and walked away as they moaned at him but they wanted to know the truth about Mr Edmunson who relieved the boredom in their working lives.

That evening, Jack sat in his room and was talking on his mobile to Bridget about love and best friends.

"You still don't understand my sliding scale for love do you? The depth and meaning of love can be scored between zero and one hundred and fifty-one. If it is a zero, then that person is your Sun Sharer. At one hundred and fifty-one it is like having sex with someone for the first time, even on a first date you understand, but just sex."

Bridget didn't understand as she had only ever had sex with Jack and Peter and had never had a one night stand. "Just sex Jack, is that how you see it?"

"Of course Fidget, in between wife number one and Melanie I had sex with seventy-five different women, keeping count as blokes do and quite frankly most of those were just one night stands."

"I am appalled Jack George Edmunson and I'm surprised you

didn't catch anything. You are not sleeping around now are you?" She was feeling emotionally defensive and wasn't thinking about catching a disease and it's repercussions as their lovemaking had dried up.

"Of course not, there's only you lovely. Anyway, stick with my logic right. It's an emotional scale to judge how much you love someone and how much they love you. There are four scores to consider: Your version of you and your version of me but also my version of you and my version of me. So what we need to do is write down both our scores and then exchange the pieces of paper to see if they match."

She was very confused. "Jack, I haven't got a clue what you are talking about. Give me an example."

Jack sighed gently. "Right, I think you love me at a score of below twenty i.e. very strongly, but I love you at a score of say sixty-seven, which is good because it's below halfway on the scale but obviously not as deep or as strong as you love me."

"What!" she replied. "Am I wasting my time on you; you bastard? Only sixty seven! I may as well give up on you now if that's your level of commitment."

Jack hurriedly explained. "No, no, no Bridget. What you know because I've told you many times before is that I love you deeply but I have always honestly said that you are not my Sun Sharer. Remember? We also both know that I couldn't be with you permanently because of Peter and your girls. Remember now?"

She remained deliberately silent letting him squirm.

"I explained months ago that I married Melanie for convenience because it was an easy way out and now I understand that, I could never live like it again and would never go off with anyone who is not my Sun Sharer. Are you still listening to me lovely?"

She laughed. "Of course I am. I was just winding you up, but seriously, do you think I love you below a score of twenty?"

Jack replied vainly, "Why don't you tell me your own score to compare?"

"Numbers don't matter Jack. You make me breathless just talking about love. If it wasn't for Peter and the girls I would want you around me all of the time but it's never going to happen and that makes me really sad sometimes."

"Don't be sad Bridget. You have bad days to make other days good. It's better that we have this wonderful love affair and experience all those fabulous sensations rather than be stable throughout our lives. It was meant to happen. Our spiritual paths were meant to cross. I am your angel my lovely." She was quiet and he knew she was crying.

"Goodnight Jack my love, speak to you later in the week," and the phone went dead on him.

Jack placed the mobile on his side table and flopped his head back on the bed.

"Am I leading her on too much?" he thought. He sighed to himself and flicked on the TV, trying to forget the conversation.

The next morning Jack went swimming before work and on his return he poked his head into the hotel kitchen to say hello before breakfast.

"Morning Chef, how are you today?"

"Mr Edmunson! Back again, can't you live without me darling?"

"Of course not lovely, my weekends are bereft without your joyous company."

"Bollocks." She was very straightforward was Chef. Waving a large knife at him she asked, "Have you been in the pool toning your beautiful body again?"

"My body doesn't need toning up Chef, it's honed, ready and waiting for you anytime my dear."

The Chef raised her eyebrows at him and commented, "Yes I can imagine your hunky naked body doing all that synchronised swimming Mr Edmunson."

Jack grinned. "Yep that's what I do, and the only thing missing is my rubber hat with garish flowers all over it."

"That's all right," she replied, "we could just paint the flowers on your bald head."

"Very funny Chef but then you would stop the solar panel to my sex machine from working properly!"

She turned away for a moment to poke the sausages thoughtfully.

"I tell you what Chef; you're looking absolutely gorgeous today."

"And so are you Mr Edmunson, absolutely wonderful too," she replied with a longing sigh.

"Mr Edmunson!" she called over her giant frying pan, stopping him as he turned away. "Do you realise that you have put your sweat shirt on inside out and you are showing the labels? You can reverse it here if you would like to show me your body."

"I don't think so Chef, what would the waitresses think? Anyway, the receptionist would get jealous."

She pleaded several times. "Go on take it off, make my day for me."

Jack continuously refused whilst watching her energetic prodding of the sausages but as the receptionist walked in to start her shift he thought sod it and ripped it off, quickly pulling in his flabby tummy.

They both chorused immediately, "Oh God, aren't you hairy!"

"I couldn't go to bed with you, not after seeing all that hair," said the receptionist.

"You don't have to see it," said Jack, "you could just take your glasses off."

The repartee carried on for weeks about his hair, how it had slipped from his head and down his back. They constantly asked him whether he would have a 'sack, back and crack' which confused Jack until the girls explained that in California men were having their bollocks, back and arsehole waxed. He did accept an invitation by the receptionist to perform the rite but he insisted it should be in a darkened room and after a few drinks. Needless to say she refused him point blank.

Many days started and ended like this and the laughter kept Jack sane and was a stark contrast to his home life as it went further downhill.

⋆ ⋆ ⋆

One Saturday morning Jack was up and in his study at six in the morning suffering a blinding headache from the beer in a late session at The Pheasant. Undeterred he started researching spiritual information for his book and to try and find some answers to his life. He pondered about Good versus Evil and tried Google.

'Children swim in search of coins which are offered to God by devotees in the polluted waters of the Ganges River at Sangam, India. Millions of devotees and Hindu holy men participate in the forty-five day long pilgrimage 'Ardh Kumbh Mela' with the intention of washing away their sins on arrival.'

"So water eliminates Evil then Nim?"

Jack you are a Pisces and you will find out if that is
true one day.

He considered if his spirit guide could lie and then returned to his searches.

'The number of the Antichrist is not 666 but 616, according to a fragment of the oldest surviving copy of the New Testament, discovered in Egypt. The number has very little to do with the Devil. It was actually a complicated numerical riddle in Greek, meant to represent someone's name. The majority opinion seems to be that it refers to the Roman emperor Nero. The purpose of this number was to enable the faithful to recognise the Antichrist when he finally emerged and it was given in a numeric rather than literal form because even the very name of the Antichrist was an abomination and as such not worthy of mention in the holy book.'

"But none of this comes back to the magical number of seven, Nim. Classic vagueness versus truly vague," thought Jack. He continued his 'Googling'.

'There are other possible explanations as well, for example, there are apparently two different spellings of the word beast in Hebrew which also produce the numbers 666 and 616.'

"Pfur. The beast or the Devil? Hoy!"

He input ζ Zeta 7.

'In almost every system of antiquity there are frequent references to the number seven.

The Pythagoreans called it the perfect number, three and four, the triangle and the square, the perfect figures.

There were for instance seven ancient planets. The sun was the greatest planet of the ancient seven and next to the sun was the moon, changing in all its splendour every seventh day.

The Arabians had seven Holy Temples.

The Goths had seven deities, as did the Romans, from whose names are derived our days of the week.

For Masons, King Solomon was seven years building the Temple. It was dedicated to the glory of God in the seventh month and the festival lasted seven days.

The Hebrew number for life is 18.'

"Eight minus one is seven but that's going too far I think Nim! What do you think?" There was no helpful answer.

'The seventh son of a seventh son is supposed to be born gifted. Apparently Donny Osmond was such a son.'

"I pass no comment on his gifts, especially Puppy Love."

'There are seven visible planets and luminaries that rule our days: the Sun, Moon, Mercury, Venus, Mars, Jupiter and Saturn e.g. the latter is Saturday, Moon is Monday, etc. Each one is supposed to have a particular virtue or power.'

He smirked. "Monday is for being fed up, Friday is for drunkenness and Sunday is for running away again."

'In Chinese culture, the number seven also features rather prominently in some aspects of life. For example, the seventh day of the first moon of the lunar year is known as Human's Day. That day is considered the birthday of all human beings universally. That is why every Chinese person is deemed to be a year older on that day, regardless of what the actual date of birth is.'

Jack was always intrigued by his internet searches and looked further.

'The Christian concept of creation of the World by the seventh day was related in Genesis. Similarly, on a death, a special ceremony is held on the forty-ninth day after death, that is, seven times seven days. It signifies the final parting.'

He could see the preoccupation with dark and light, nothing versus something but decided there were must be many gullible people reading this crap and he wasn't going to be one of them. He spoke to no one in particular.

"'Ignorance is Bliss', Thomas Gray. So why aren't more people happy?"

He laughed and wrote the quote down in the notes for his book.

That weekend Jack and Melanie's relationship worsened.

He jumped into bed, turned his back on her and snuggled his head into the pillow to make his thoughts go away. No noise, no communication, no goodnights was now the norm. He could only hear his shallow breathing in his tight chest. The next morning, getting up was in reverse. He would be very quiet and slide out to avoid any form of communication whether verbal or physical before quietly opening and closing the bedroom door. She came downstairs late one morning and found him looking at car brochures.

"Jack the most important thing in life is people. Not material possessions."

Melanie was right but Jack bit back, "Yes, other people, not me. It's okay for you to spend my hard-earned money but never me. You are taking the Michael. You were out last night, out two nights ago, shopping all day on Saturday with your pals, you're out again tomorrow night. Anyone would think you've got a boyfriend." He thought about her week and silently talked to Nim.

"The PTA fete, always helping the PTA, but not for them for herself, for her to network and for any reason to be away from me. But truthfully it meets Melanie's needs with the men around her, the overall attention, and the power of organising people to do what she wants to her agenda. She needs to be part of something and can't be herself. For example she bought her eight hundred pound Coco Chanel handbag because her peer group had something similar. Her sense of belonging is created by material possessions and brand names, with a bottom line of money."

But Nim didn't need to comment because he was inside Jack's mind, prompting the thoughts and driving him to the next step to leave his old life.

She continued to accentuate avoiding doing anything for him as a way to spite him and drive him away. She would promise that she was going to have the lawn mower fixed or her car serviced.

"I'm going to" was the never ending refrain but it never happened. Jack told her on many days, "You've got no restraints in your life Melanie. You have so much free time and freewill you never make it hard for yourself do you? You haven't got a boss making you do things; you haven't got any attitude to work anymore because you do what you want. It's ignorant, lacking respect and sometimes so aggressive that it could even be construed as menopausal. What would happen if I adopted the same attitude? There would be no money and no life. Just imagine the consequences and you are nearly where I am in my view of you."

He rushed on, "Anyway, I think you do need to go to the doctors because you are menopausal. Think of it positively, if you are through the change already, I won't have to use a 'Johnny' anymore, not that we have sex often enough to warrant it."

It was a terrible thing to say but he didn't give a shit now.

He walked away as usual in a huff, totally frustrated and more stressed week on week.

9
Second dawning. Maybe I do believe in Astrology

Twenty-five sceptics were in the room above The Farmer's Arms pub to meet a clairvoyant called Mabel.

She was renowned across the whole of Manchester, including Greater Manchester.

She was that famous.

The Magic Lamp spiritual meeting attracted all sorts of weird characters and as Jack looked around at the motley crew he counted himself in the same vein. He whispered very quietly to avoid attention.

"This is your entire fault Soul Shiner. What am I doing here?"

"You know you have to be here Jack, it's in your path so listen to your inner self and don't be so negative."

"Yes oh gifted one, my angel of destiny!" He sighed deeply and tried to relax.

Edith, glasses askew and hair flopped to one side had accosted him on arrival in a hippy way-out voice, "Hi, my name's Edith. Love and light yeah. I hope you didn't take offence that I kept staring at you earlier."

"Er...love and light Edith," said Jack politely. "I didn't really notice," although of course he had.

Edith looked at Jack through her thick squinty glasses. "Yes, you see I have met you before," she smiled into his face so that he could see her yellowed teeth.

"Oh!" Jack was slightly surprised but didn't feel bothered enough to have this conversation. Still polite, he asked where she had seen him.

Way-out Edith continued very slowly. "You see, you may find this strange but I met you…" she paused, "in my dreams." Jack re-looked at Edith for signs of madness whilst Soul Shiner turned away and stepped behind his back to stifle her giggle into cupped hands.

"Right, okay, nice to meet you," he said and went to move swiftly away.

"Wait Jack!" Squinty put her hand on his cheek. "Don't you remember me in your dreams?"

Jack assumed a serious look. "Yes Edith, clearly and distinctly." He paused for effect and put his hand on her shoulder, reciprocating her spiritual love. "You gave me such a fantastic blow job, you were really so good," and patted her gently before he turned away to escape towards the toilets, leaving Harriet crying with laughter and suddenly exposed to Edith's withering and doubly magnified look.

Soul Shiner caught up with him on his reappearance. "Jack, for goodness sake you have such a fantastic taste in women. You attract such interesting types poppet."

Jack smiled and whispered into her ear, "Look you; this was all your idea and you wanted the company. I just want to find out what sort of people believe in this spiritual stuff and whether there is any glimmer of truth in it. At the moment they all seem the type that could equally be sat in a church soaking up any religion a bit too seriously."

They wandered back to the larger room and sat together. Soul Shiner leaned over towards Jack. "I will make some notes if she starts talking to you and then if she talks to me please take my pen and pad and do the same for me. Okay?" Jack ungratefully nodded his assent and focused on the lady standing by the Michael, the leader of the Magic Lamp spiritualist circle.

Mabel was introduced to them all as a clairvoyant. The difference between her and a medium seemed vague to Jack but she explained she had spirits talk to her and she passed messages on, rather than going into a trance and letting the spirits talk through her. Mabel had a deep Mancunian brogue, slightly rough, common sounding but mixed with a bit of posh. She had bright red hair which didn't seem in keeping with a woman of about sixty-five and she was another one with extremely thick glasses.

"All the better to see the spirits with," thought Jack. As she talked about herself and the battle between spiritualism, going 'barmy' and closing off the spirits to ensure a normal life, Jack wondered what the hell he had let himself in for.

She continued about her cancer and nearly dying and then started talking directly to the two ladies sitting to his right. They looked like a grandmother and daughter, about sixty and forty years old respectively. Mabel was seemingly talking to someone who stood behind them. "Quite a chatterbox really," she said to the two ladies and strangely Jack felt severe cold down his right side. Mabel continued to say that Alice was truly sorry that Dad had died and that she was with him and had guided him so he didn't feel lonely. Then Mabel pretended to have a message from the Dad and told the ladies he was all right and not to worry. Jack felt like he was intruding on a normal conversation and was puzzled because every time Mabel checked some facts they were acknowledged by the ladies.

Mabel said, "He was wearing his dark blue overcoat and by the way gives his love to Harvey the labrador." Immediately, the two ladies nodded in agreement whilst crying silently and tightly grasping each other's arms.

The cold remained there, still on his right side and then all of a sudden it disappeared.

Mabel was energetically strolling across the front of the group when her head whipped around as if searching for something as she continually talked. "Well, you young man, I thought I needed to speak with you because I thought there's a hard nut to crack. Not a believer; a bit sceptical. Needs the I's and T's dotting and crossing you see, just like me when I first started seeing spirits. Needs reassurance that it is practical and real, you see. So my love, if you came to me privately, I could tell you a lot of things, you see. Because I think you are ready to see me my love. You are far enough along the path and can take whatever is thrown at you chuck. You are a very private man, isn't that so?"

Jack nodded, his heart racing because he had been selected.

"You see my love, it's important for you to aim to be the boss. You like imposing your will and seeing a clairvoyant would make you feel uncomfortable. Is that so my love?"

Jack quietly agreed. Mabel appraised him from halfway down the aisle set between the six rows of chairs. She turned and moved away then turned back to face him and wrung her hands together.

She addressed everyone but left Jack in the third person. "He's a polite sensitive man and wouldn't want to say to someone, 'shut up you'! He's like a see-saw really, he wants to say it but can't and his only defence is to ensure he doesn't have a coffee with them again." The group chuckled and Jack felt nervous. She fingered her short red hair thoughtfully.

"He wouldn't want to feel imposed on. As you work with him, you can recall his sympathetic side but with spiritualism he needs to see the nuts and bolts. Well, my love in your eighth to thirteenth year, you had to start self governing your emotions. Your destiny was going to be beyond what people thought you could do and you told yourself that you had that desire; your spiritual side pushed you on. Is that so my love?"

Jack was confused and murmured, "Yes Mabel." He was transfixed and could vividly remember sitting in his parents' house. The latch key kid imagining someone upstairs looking down on him. Someone scary and without form.

"A spirit," he thought, "possibly Nim."

Mabel levelled her eyes on Jack and spoke with a deeper tone, "Well, he had to do something then didn't he; he packed up all his emotions and quietly put them in a box. He shut them down and focused on what he could be, is that so?"

Jack clearly, loudly and confidently said, "That's true Mabel." He pictured that time in his life, the extra homework instigated by his Mother to get him into the top stream at school. He also remembered the Crusader's sword and the U-shapes, glowing bright and steely blue every night. A protection from the ghost he knew lived upstairs.

Mabel talked to the audience, not Jack. "By the way my love, I can see your spiritual quest will be superb, don't be afraid to pursue it but start now and get out of the job you are in before you are fifty-four." Jack sensed someone behind him and kept turning round to see if there were any indications but there was nothing, not even a cold spot. All of this was similar to the astrology reading and was too weird to handle. Mabel carried on.

"His spiritual side is screaming to come out. The academic side is dying. I've done that before he's thinking, I need to get out. You see my love it's okay thinking and doing homeopathy or meditation or hypnotherapy but it will never be enough and neither is coming to these meetings going to satisfy you. It's kind of satisfying but just icing on the cake and not the cake. You have an affinity, love." She still had messages to give him. "You are suffering my love, you have a pressurised head, is that right?"

"Absolutely," Jack responded.

"You will need to tie up those loose ends in your material life. I can see a gentleman in a white coat linked to you and your family and he will walk with you throughout your life. You also have two Bibles in your house but I don't think that they are about religion as they are about your life."

Tears filled his eyes. He knew the books were firstly his story he had written at Up Yonder cottage, when number one had left with Rodney and Edima. His first wife telling him on Valentine's night that there was someone else and driving down the road with the two young children waving goodbye on Good Friday, very poetic and very tragic. The second was his new book, merely a batch of notes.

She interrupted his thoughts, "But your family cannot go all the way with you; you have to do it on your own my love but remember you won't be in that position for long. Your restlessness will galvanise you along, your spirit is waiting to be fulfilled, it's your destiny my love. By the way, he says don't get rid of that old desk."

Jack apologised to whoever she was talking to. He remembered an old bureau of his grandfather's that he used for studying as a teenager that was now in the garage collecting dust. Everyone laughed again; they were enjoying Jack's discomfort.

Mabel continued, "He says computers and a light and a new desk are not the same as the old one. It's your Father this time rather than George. He really does moan a lot." Jack smiled and everyone giggled again. Dad was always a moaner, always going on about the things he'd given to Jack.

"I can feel his presence and he's complaining about the old Parker pen he gave you and says why have you stopped using it?"

Jack recalled the pen set, a beautiful Parker fountain pen, very expensive and beautifully wrapped in silk in its leather box. He never used it now that he wrote his private letters on Microsoft Word or Hotmail. He vaguely remembered it had originally belonged to a dead relative. Which one he thought? It was passed on to him as a 'studier', a student wanting to make good in his new grammar school. Was it from Granddad George as well?

"He says you are taking the top off but not getting on with it. Am I right about that?" Jack was numb now and quietly agreed. He couldn't explain the lightness he felt and the energy buzzing around him. Mabel looked intently at the corner of the room and stopped talking to the audience.

"Writing, yes writing will come again."

She went off at a tangent. "Your Grandma says you might not be interested in buying new clothes for hot climates but she is waving flight tickets at you and telling you to buy those new clothes. Whatever you are going to do will be superb. It will go well abroad." She went quiet and paced as he thought. It was only March but Jack could see an end to consultancy, an end to his marriage and a new life in Catalonia.

"Picture this; there is a house near a Roman city. You cannot see it yet as it's not something you know. It has peculiar roofs and windows sliding within them. You will love it and I know you like being a loner but you will build bridges which allows you flexibility to go in and out to this place. Your creative spiritual self must be allowed this freedom. Only then will you find your equilibrium. I have a strange Latin sound now with people and music, is it a small woodwind band? It's discordant and in the background mixed with the sound of a swishing sea wafting through ozone-laden air and I can literally taste the salt. I also see a doctorship in the past, of philosophy or something. George is the name, I can see it linking. Don't be afraid of going down new roads he says. Know that Dad and he are with you and enjoy the trip my love."

Jack needed time to think all of this through.

Harriet had written it all down so she tore the pages from her notebook and gently patted his shoulder as she passed them over. "Are you okay poppet because that was fantastic."

Jack replied shakily, "I think that was so real. I feel exhausted just like after I saw Beatty."

The lights flickered every time Mabel started talking to a new spirit in the room.

She moved away and Jack sagged in his chair. She began to talk to the lady in the black dress to his left and his left side was now cold. His hair prickled and he looked at the beautiful young woman and knew the story before it came from Mabel. The tragic death of the husband in a car accident. Him still there in spirit saying stay strong. Be strong for me he said through Mabel and the tears poured down her cheeks. But Jack saw this five minutes before Mabel got to her. He cried silently, covering his eyes from Soul Shiner and crying for the woman in black and for the restless spirits he could feel in the room. Their messages were so forlorn and yet uplifting to those who had been touched by Mabel that night. At the close he talked to Harriet at the bar.

"Jack, she gave people two minutes but you got ten. That was fantastic you know, so believable. Did it make sense at all?"

Jack took a gulp of Weetwood beer. "Soul Shiner, you cannot believe what I felt, never mind the accuracy and logic of the facts in it all. It was truly an amazing experience. Joseph George is my son's name, Edmund George my Dad's name, George Bert my Grandfather's name. A synchronicity that also follows through spiritually. My Dad talked through Mabel, my Granddad George stood in his white coat, a stalwart of the Bethesda cricket club for fifty years. I wonder what gifts Joseph will inherit. That was truly fantastic."

The morning following that strange night in the The Farmer's Arms, Jack had driven down to the Edam Garden Centre and whilst buying Gordon Ramsay's Tiramisu he bumped into Bridget.

He told her about the spiritualist's meeting and feeling his late Father close to him.

"Do you know your Dad very well Bridget? I don't want to be morbid but will you let the time slip between your fingers and not grasp that one opportunity to know him properly? You should go and spend some quality time with him. Ask him these questions and even if he doesn't answer it's important to just ask." Jack touched her cheek and forced her to look him in the face. "Just asking is part of your spiritual development, so ask in any order and at the end tell him you love him."

"What is his favourite food?
What is his favourite song?
Does he remember your baby sister often since she died?
What makes him cry?
What makes him angry?
Does he believe in true love and a Sun Sharer?
What is the most important thing in his life?
Is he scared of death?
What's the best advice he can give you?"

"I couldn't ask him any of that," said Bridget. "I don't have that sort of relationship."

Jack pressed his hand against her side and pulled her close. He said with a serious urgency, "Just ask, I don't know why but I think you are running out of time to get the answers."

★ ★ ★

Harriet sat in The Grosvenor Hotel Brasserie in the centre of the beautiful black and white Rows of Chester, waiting for Melanie to arrive. The experience with the clairvoyant had upset her for two reasons and was on her mind as she saw lumpy, frumpy and dumpy Melanie waltz through the outer door in large Dior sunglasses clutching a Versace handbag. She hated what she saw in her 'friend' and questioned why she met up with her before remembering the increasing loneliness of an absent surgeon husband and her girls who were happy at boarding school. They kissed hello without touching cheeks.

"Harriet you are looking pensive, haven't you ordered some wine yet or is there a deeper problem? Come on tell me; you can always confide in me as you well know."

Harriet knew she would never confide in Melanie again but wanted to know whether Jack did. "I'm fine Melanie, trust me. How was your man after seeing the clairvoyant?"

"He said it was all a load of rubbish and didn't believe any of it." Harriet watched her carefully and concluded she was telling the truth. She smiled at Melanie with relief because she knew that her friendship with Jack was not shared with his wife and as he didn't share his potential future with her he must be contemplating a future alone. That made her feel happy as she liked Jack.

She liked him a lot more than she admitted to herself.

Harriet lied to Melanie. "I agree with him, it was total baloney. All hot air and vague suggestions for weak-minded people. But it was kind of your husband to escort me as there's no way I would have gone alone. In the end it allows us to dismiss those spiritual thoughts and get on with some real life."

Melanie appraised Harriet and compared her to Bridget. She could see no competition, unlike Bridget who seemed to be Jack's 'type'.

"So what do you fancy then? A Petit Chablis with some Moules Mariniere or something less extravagant? Jack's paying even though he doesn't know it so let's go large, as they say in McDonalds."

Harriet couldn't believe the cheek of the woman and vowed to stay lonely rather than mix with someone she was starting to dislike intensely. "Whatever Melanie. Whatever takes your fancy."

Jack still had to go to work and be professional despite his emotional and spiritual turmoil. Because his contract would end soon he knew some things that he said were getting out of hand and too familiar but his marital issues didn't help engender the right professional approach or motivation.

Jack liked the power in his job and often told his mates at home that the world was driven by power, sex and money. He also thought that having just the first of the three in his life wasn't good enough. He also wondered whether having money was about being in the right place at the right time and would then berate himself. "What a load of bollocks, it's not luck at all, it's about focus and looking hard at what you achieve and what you do."

During the week he punished himself mercilessly about achievement at work and during the weekends he punished himself about his future as a person and his failure with his family. When he saw his friends he would tell them about his week of power and achievement and make himself look good and then his friends would give him more respect. It was a self defeating attitude because he never satisfied himself about who and what he was, so he always looked for external appreciation rather than at his own internal needs to resolve his feelings. That was one reason why he chased the girls.

One evening the receptionist had agreed to go with him to the local Indian. It was fun, a few beers, light conversation and a cleavage to 'oggle'. At the end of the meal, individual squares of chocolate were delivered with the bill so Jack delicately unwrapped one in front of her eyes. Before placing it halfway into his mouth he said, "I dare you to take the chocolate out of my mouth."

She leaned across the table and sucked it from between his

parted lips, briefly touching them with hers. "Oh God, you're so stubbly," she cried out but she sexily sucked the chocolate whilst looking coyly at him.

The receptionist had always told him that her one fantasy was to have sex on the bonnet of a car so as they left the restaurant he offered her a piggy back. Clutching her arse he set off, ignoring the pain in his hip and hoping his discs wouldn't give up on him at such a crucial moment. He shrugged her further up his back and felt her titties pushed hard against him and was mesmerised by her scent as she chatted happily in his ear and flopped her long hair against the side of his head. Stumbling slightly he lay her on the long bonnet of the 'Merc' and pivoting himself around with her still attached to him he leaned her back with her long legs akimbo. They were spread and waiting as she teased him with a wide smile on her face. Her stomach was tantalisingly bare and waiting to be licked gently. He bent down and pushed his tongue under the top of her panties with the tip brushing her pubic hair.

"Mr Edmunson," she murmured, "stop that immediately." But she didn't push him away for a few more seconds before escaping into the car interior. It boded well for Jack as they drove on to a village pub nearby and sat with their drinks on a picnic bench in the poorly lit garden under a huge dark ash tree. Lying back on the bench seat Jack pulled his shirt up and placed the remaining chocolate from the Indian on his hairy belly button. He taunted the receptionist who sat next to him.

"I dare you to suck this off me."

She leaned forward and licked it up in her mouth just as a huge dog ran past, glancing sideways at the chocolate. They were in peals of laughter as they saw the prospect of the dog leaping on him and stealing the chocolate. Jack's fear was his erect prick may have been chewed in its prime. Lying back on the bench again he looked at the stars which were perfectly clear in the sky and listened to the distant sound of a passing train.

"'Real Life'," he said to no one in particular. "Fantastic."

They sat and chatted about people in their lives as neither of them had achieved their dreams. The receptionist had failed in all her relationships and been badly hurt by a married man pretending he was single. The hotel manager was sexually harassing her and so she was looking for a new job. Jack surprisingly seemed the most centred as at least he understood his predicament and how to get out of it. It was just a question of timing. Or courage.

Piggy-backing the receptionist out of the pub he rested her against the wall of a bridge over a stream and turning around he created a 'stomach back'. He lifted her to the car and then placed her in her favourite place on the bonnet facing towards him. She taunted him in a deliciously sexy voice. "You know I would have sex with you if you weren't so hairy, Oh and also married of course."

He knew she wasn't drunk enough to change her mind but he felt bold enough to place his hands gently on her tits and then pushing her back with a single hand he slid the other one down her trousers to touch her.

She gasped and writhed slightly before sitting up and shaking her finger at him. "Mr Edmunson!" So it went no further but they had a fun night.

Just fun.

No preconceptions and no complications or guilt afterwards.

At breakfast the next day Chef called out to him, "Mr Edmunson, your shorts are on inside out."

"Very funny, there's no way I'm taking them off! But if you want later, I'll show you my tattoo, 'IPI'."

Chef mulled the letters over in her mind as she poked the never ending sausages in her pan. "Where is your tattoo Mr Edmunson?"

Jack smirked. "It's on Mister Wiggly and when I get excited because I'm with you darling, it says Mississippi." She turned back to cooking the large sausages shaped like pricks and prodded them harder with sexual frustration before enquiring politely if he would like a kipper for breakfast.

"That sounds nice Chef, you never have kippers usually."

She smiled evilly at him, "No I don't but you can only have one if you personally come and skin it with your teeth," and pointed to her fanny.

"You know what they say about nice girls," said Jack. He paused, not expecting an answer. "Fish at both ends, lovely. But less joviality Chef. I'm fat, I haven't swum enough this week and so I am on a diet. There again I suppose I'm not as fat as my wife."

Chef admonished him, "You can't say that!"

"Yes I can," he replied.

Chef commented, "If she were here you wouldn't say that."

"Yes I would. She might hit me and send me through the window as she's built like a bag of walnuts."

"You are awful, Mr Edmunson, I'm not sure if I want to go out with you anymore even if you pleaded with me."

"Well Chef, I'll take you out for a night if you really want."

She turned and appraised him with raised eyebrows and then came closer and seductively patted the bulging pocket of his shorts where he kept his wallet.

"You can't afford me," she said.

"Of course I can Chef, I have a gold card," replied Jack, cockily.

"Then you would need to swipe it twice to have me darling." Chef always had the last word.

Work ground Jack down, prompting more abominable behaviour.

He knew he was getting to become an old git when he was out for the night at a team-building session and found he was the butt of the jokes.

There were fifteen of the project team in the local Chinese and Jack manoeuvred himself to sit next to a young and intelligent but not overly pretty girl of about twenty-seven. He was making small talk and trying his 'come to bed' eyes on her.

"What age do you find attractive in a man?" he said, his eyes dancing.

"Not as old as you," came the smart reply from Ella. He still spouted on.

"I've been married four times, the first we don't talk about, the second left me for my best friend, the bastard, the third left me after six months for her lesbian lover and the fourth, who is still with me, is on her way out because she spends so much." Ella showed no interest in any of the mythical four wives. Jack continued unabashed. "Where did your boyfriend propose to you?"

Ella was more enthusiastic, "New York!"

"Fantastic," said Jack. "I proposed to number four on the top of the Eiffel Tower on the basis she might jump." There was silence for about a minute.

"Why are you so negative about marriage Jack?"

He replied honestly, "I'm not negative or I wouldn't have got married four times. It's just women are so hard to live with as they want to mother you all the time and treat you like a six-year-old."

"Well you men have a mental age of six," came her smart reply again. She was too smart by half.

The other girls started to join in.

"Jack, did you know Ella's joined the local sailing club to try and meet some rich men?"

Jack perked up. "That's good, I've got a boat, a Laser Two, a dinghy," said Jack.

"Nothing less than forty-five foot would do for me," came Ella's put-down.

"That's weird though," said Jack, "as my astrologer recently told me I would find my Soul Mate who had something to do with boats or a boatyard. Where do you live now?" Jack turned to Ella for her reply. Deadpan, it came very quickly.

"Next to the Southampton container port."

Her friends howled with laughter followed by a chorus. "She's the one, definitely the one, Southampton docks has got to be the biggest boatyard ever. Number five's on her way."

He felt he was losing so he tried a new more serious tack. "Of course I am now an expert on all sorts of marital advice having been married four times and may be able to help you before you take the plunge."

Ella effectively ended his evening with a final put-down.

"You've got to be joking. You've been married four times so I'm not taking any of your advice, not with your track record."

Throughout the rest of the meal, Jack went through the ladies in the group asking key questions like, "Do you own a boatyard? Do your parents own a boatyard? Do you even like boats?"

After half an hour of this a man suddenly piped up, "Hey pal, I like sailing and my parents own a boatyard in South Africa."

"Oh fuck," Jack moaned under his breath as the whole table fell apart with roars of laughter about gay boy Jack. Not quite the macho image from all the previous palaver that he had planned and certainly nowhere nearer a Sun Sharer.

Even the evenings in his hotel room dragged on endlessly and where possible he found an excuse to sit with the bored staff in the conservatory adjacent to the main dining room and kitchen. The hotel was quiet and no one was motivated to find much to occupy them.

He would ring Joseph and then have a brief chat with Melanie before searching out some company.

"Joseph, just remember to be like your Dad. Work hard and play hard okay?" He would repeat this to Melanie but change the tone and context.

"In your case Melanie, it would be better if you said to me, 'you work hard and I'll play hard'."

"Ha bloody ha," came her response. "I've got a lot to do tomorrow. I need to go to the gym before my hair appointment and on the way back I'll stop at Sainsbury's." She continued her drive to being more relaxed and although he kept complaining about her behaviour, his views were ignored.

"You are not living in La La land like other stay at home middle-class women because now you are so relaxed you can't see land anymore. More on La La and possibly on fucking Venus on the basis your favourite author says we men are on fucking Mars." Every conversation was either dull or boring about mundane household or school items or else ended up in an argument.

One night four of the hotel staff sat with Jack in the conservatory: two waitresses, the receptionist and Chef.

The new waitresses gathered around Jack who told them he needed some female company because his wife had died recently, but they had both been forewarned to avoid dating him. Realising they knew he was lying he asked, "What's that phrase they use in America? Is it something like plausible deniability? You know, it was the President of the USA in a film, was it in 'Independence Day'? If you don't know a fact is wrong, you can't be called a liar. What is it? Implausible truth?"

The receptionist berated Jack, "I keep telling you Mr Edmunson, you have no credibility. No one knows when you are serious or not."

Jack thought about it for two seconds. "Okay, I won't chat anyone up for a week after tonight and be a normal boring guest."

She looked disapprovingly at him. "We never know whether you are lying, joking or telling the truth. You see you have this personality where no one truly knows where they stand. Is it a defence mechanism?"

Jack looked up at her face as she stood by his table with her hands on her hips and thought how young and beautiful she was. What a waste that she had no boyfriend.

He replied sheepishly, "A defence mechanism? No of course not. It's just a way of relieving my stress, just trying to be a bit happier. But you can't deny I can also be very direct because it pays to be direct."

She sighed and answered, "Like when you walked up to me yesterday and said look, would you like to come out tonight and fuck my brains out."

They all laughed.

Jack replied, "Yes, but let's face it, sometimes it works but just not with you!"

"Mr Edmunson," she wasn't condoning his behaviour, "we have a staff handbook and it says we are not allowed to fraternise with our guests."

He asked, "Fine, but what does that mean? Is there a sliding scale of fraternising in this staff handbook? Has the manager put some rating system in it and said you mustn't score above a two? For example. A score of one is having a drink together at the bar. Two is a Spanish cheek to cheek kiss."

She helped him create the scale. "It says three is a big hug and four is a delicate kiss."

The Chef joined in. "That makes shagging you Mr Edmunson at about a seven then."

"I agree," said Jack, "and a ten has therefore got to be anal sex."

"Oh God!" there was a chorus of disapproval from the women.

"But seriously," said Jack, "everyone has different boundaries in their life never mind fictitiously in your handbook. Everyone has them but they are all different. Boundaries about behaviour when living away rather than living at home. About what swear words you can use and where. About sexual behaviour, particularly if you join my fantasy football league."

Chef loved soccer and asked the obvious. "Come on then what is your fantasy football league?"

"Well, currently third in the league dropping down to fifth is the receptionist. It's the opposite of true fantasy football. You get points for scoring. Sex scores three points, heavy petting is two and a grope and a snog scores one!"

They all laughed. Chef joined in. "What happens if you have a high tackle so to speak, you know in over the top?"

"Well it all depends on if you have your shin pads on Chef but if you kicked my tackle you would certainly lose points and the same applies if I hit the bar when shooting!" They were a happier bunch now. He carried on.

"So I tell you what we can do. The eligible girls in the hotel can have a few weeks of competition based on two dates with me; let's say one on a Tuesday and one on a Wednesday and then we can see who can win the league. What do you think then?"

"In your dreams," said the waitresses in unison.

"I'm ready for a Champions League match," said the Chef.

"And I have suddenly got problems with my cartilage and gone off the pitch injured," said Jack.

As the night drew to a close Chef took over and mothered the youngsters.

"Right you lot, bed time and as for you Mr Edmunson, you need to stick with me and not these young scrawny girls. You need a real woman in your life!"

As he was ushered out of the door by Chef he told her the sad truth. "I need a 'Real Life' and not a real woman Chef." He walked upstairs to his dreary bedroom and flopped on the bed after another night of sexual frustration. He lay still and closed his eyes thinking about the receptionist and started to play with his prick until he came inadequately and felt nauseous afterwards.

The next morning the first person he saw was her and he immediately felt guilty. "Do you realise I see more of you than my wife?"

She looked up from behind the counter. "Good morning sir, did you sleep well? By the way you have never seen anything of me Mr Edmunson!"

Jack smiled. "That's true, so go on tell me all your confessions, tell me all your secrets."

The receptionist said, "I did offer to wear my nurse's outfit when I sorted out that tiny piece of glass in your foot and you refused me."

Chef walked by. "That's unlike you Mr Edmunson, you wouldn't refuse her even if she was in her Mr Blobby costume."

Jack walked out of the hotel defeated by both of them so early in the morning and started to think about the shitty working day ahead.

On returning to the hotel that evening he tried his room key card and it wouldn't let him in. He went back to reception and got a new one. He tried again and it still wouldn't let him in, so he returned to reception again.

"Look," he said, "I need to alter your customer service questionnaire because it doesn't have a section about technology.

Last night it was the TV remote and now it's my room key twice."

The receptionist looked at him with unblinking eyes behind her glasses. Deadpan she commented, "You must have a magnetic personality Mr Edmunson." Then she giggled.

"Very funny," said Jack, "it's strange but you could be right. At home in the last two weeks everything electronic seems to have gone wrong. My car Satnav, the TV remote, the garage door opener and even the hi-fi decided to swallow a CD and not let it out." He walked back to his room and found he could now get in.

"Nim, can there be a link between all these things or is it just bad luck?"

There is no such thing as luck Jack, you either make
something happen or something happens to you.
The latter is out of your control but is still meant to
happen and is in your path.
If you want to change your path you have to put some
of your spiritual energy into it to counteract what will
happen to you.

"So, those things were always going to happen no matter what?"

There is no way you could have stopped them
because your energy and your location in your path
was fixed and you did not consciously know what to
do to stop them.
Think of it as you enticing things to happen.
When you understand that your energy can influence
things then you will use it for Good rather than
causing minor irritations like in the last two weeks.

"Thank you Nim. I never realised that I was interacting with the world in that way and in my case enticing electrical faults because of my inner attitude. Very interesting and very weird if true, but of course it can't be."

Jack sat in the hotel chatting the girls up and tried some Mandarin learned from the owner of the local Chinese restaurant. She had taken a shine to Jack and taught him some useful phrases. 'Wo i ni' and 'nehan piou lan'. Unashamedly he told them he loved them but none seemed interested as they were busy with a 'Round Table' monthly dinner. He decided they were busy rather than ignoring an old git who sat bored in the corner of the bar.

When the receptionist spared him a moment he tried to get her sympathy. "I went to an osteopath today. My first time ever. Have you ever been?"

She said she had heard they can damage your joints.

"My concerns exactly. Anyway, I'm sure this guy was gay. He made me strip off to my pants then turned me on my side and did very strange rotational moves on my legs and hips thrusting my knees into his groin. I tell you it made me feel very uncomfortable."

"Well, Mr Edmunson, if you can't get a good woman which of course you can't, then you may as well get a clean old man! In fact the Mandarin for 'what I knee' makes sense now!" Jack was adamant he would never turn gay but told her the osteopath's name ironically was Alan Phelan which confirmed the gay attraction and sent her into fits of laughter. As it died down Jack considered other sexual options.

"I wonder where you could find prostitutes in Rosset. Could be worth a try lovely?"

"Not with your reputation. Half the girls in Rosset will have been warned to stay away from you."

"What do you mean?"

"A terrible flirt with a bad hip, bad back who is hairy and married. You have no chance even if you paid for it."

The truth hurt and so he asked her for another beer and sat watching the staff who were much happier when busy.

★ ★ ★

The whole dynamics of their evenings had changed when Eric the new German waiter had started. Twenty-five years old, super fit, single, polite, full of discretion and intelligence. The girls' eyes had widened and the powerful and entertaining old git had been moved into their mental background as sex hormones came to the fore. The staff had been bluetoothing each other 'Angry kid' videos, but the irony came when they decided to decline the video from Eric showing him having anal sex with a black guy in Cologne. All part of a new and rich dimension of modern communication.

At the time, Jack couldn't resist chiding them all. "So there you are girls. What you see is not necessarily what you get. However, you know exactly what you would get with me!"

"And we know exactly what you are not going to get Mr Edmunson," said the receptionist.

He had looked up at her. "Imagine, with my new 3G camera phone, I could record us having sex in a commercial break whilst watching the football and then watch us at the end of the game."

She had replied innocently, "Do you know what? I haven't even tried it in front of a mirror never mind using a mobile to take pictures of girls fannies and titties to show your mates in the pub on a Friday night. It's a different world out there with you blokes now. Goodness knows what else Eric has on his mobile!"

But Eric had left quickly, shortly after fondling the night porter's arse and before the police had arrived to arrest him for male prostitution.

"Only in Rosset," thought Jack.

As the chef started to tidy the kitchen Jack leaned against the door for a final chat. She commented on his lack of technique with women and told him he could only entice a young girl with money now. Scrubbing the chopping board she asked him, "Does wife number four bend to your every whim?"

He replied innocently, "Of course not. Well, not unless I give her money, which by the way I constantly do."

The chef nodded wisely and said, "I bet in reality you get away with murder."

Jack grunted his reply, "I'd like to."

Chef scrubbed away in despair and Jack decided it was time for bed. He was sexually frustrated again. He had tried everything with the receptionist who had condescended to go to the pictures with him a couple of times, probably, because she felt safe with other people around her. He had decided that the best way to cover up an affair would be to say you are going to the pictures because then you have a good reason to turn your mobile off for a few hours and be out of touch with your wife. Although sexually unsuccessful with the receptionist he had enjoyed her company and also the films. 'Lost in Translation' with Bill Murray touched his romantic side and in 'Memoirs of a Geisha' he loved the etiquette and the non-assertiveness of the heroines versus malicious Melanie. He liked them showing a little bit of wrist when pouring their man's tea and bowing to the floor.

Romance was not dead in Jack's mind but it needed someone to stir it into life again.

The next morning he checked out and the prettiest waitress commented on his suitcase.

"What a pretty pink suitcase," she said.

"It's red not pink," came Jack's reply.

She didn't let it go. "Are you gay Mr Edmunson? Are you staying with Eric this weekend?"

"Of course not!" Jack leaned around the night porter, standing in the kitchen doorway, and said to the Chef. "Good morning, how are you my darling?"

The porter turned around slowly and said, "I'm fine thanks."

All the girls burst into laughter and Jack hurried off to load the 'pink' suitcase into his car boot.

★ ★ ★

After his last night in the Dodge House Hotel he talked seriously to the receptionist one final time. "I have got no other ploys left to get you to make love to me." A few seconds later he reached across the desk for her hand and grasping it he said. "You do realise I am deeply in love with you?"

The receptionist smiled sadly and lightly squeezed his hand. "That's kind of you Jack but you are married." As an afterthought she said, "and hairy." The body language and her face was open and friendly but she was not available because she was a nice girl.

Jack turned away and as he reached the door he said, "I have tried everything with you. I've told you I've got money; I have taken you driving in my flash car including laying you on my bonnet. I have engaged you in intelligent conversation and been to intellectual and romantic films. I have even tried for sympathy because of my bad back and hip but I have still got nowhere." He paused. "Would you just like to get into bed with me now?"

She waved bye bye for the last time and replied, "Yes of course Jack...I need a lot of sleep."

He talked to Joseph early on that final morning of his contract and deliberately before Melanie was downstairs and moving so that he didn't have to speak to her. "Joseph, can you see the sun, because I can. Tell me my boy, what's it like?"

The innocent description made Jack sigh. "Well Dad, today it's a bit red and very big."

His Dad replied with all of his love in his poignant words. "Well mate it's a bit red and very big here too. Isn't that strange? Just remember that when you look at the sun so do I and we can share it and remember how much we love each other forever. Okay my boy?"

"Yes Dad, I love you too."

Joseph was sweet and innocent and just needed to know his Dad would be there for him. But Jack had been so depressed during that year. He had missed his boy. He had missed the daffodils in his cottage garden and the wisteria climbing up the south-facing wall and he never saw the short lived flowers of his clematis. He drove to work and thought about his non-existence for nearly two years and listened to his CD. 'I have seen pain' sang James Blunt.

A single magpie sat pecking the carcass of a dead badger and he mournfully quoted the nursery rhyme.

"One for sorrow, two for joy, three for a girl, and four for a boy. What does that mean Nim? Is it all linked to the electronic ether intertwined around our lives or am I losing track of the realities?"

> *Jack, there is nothing wrong with thinking about the deepest things in life.*
> *That was a sign.*
> *Anyone can exist but many people cannot truly live.*
> *You are now on your path and there is no turning back.*

On the same Friday Peter met Melanie in the small faded green caravan hidden in the field behind the desolate Crabtree Farm that belonged to the family business. It had been used in the past when they grew their own plants, but the costs of UK production were now too expensive, even if using cheap Polish labour that had lived in it. Violently rocking the caravan on its failed suspension, Peter had brutally fucked her until she was satisfied and afterwards he wanted to talk which she thought was extremely unusual.

"Your husband is becoming a complete twat Mel. Every conversation I have with him seems strained, almost morbid, which is why I never telephone him anymore. So come on tell me; what is going on with him as it seems to be more than a mid-life crisis?"

"Tell me about it. I can't stand the sanctimonious drivel anymore and haven't got a clue what he thinks about, but he is always complaining about working hard or his bad hip and back. He's becoming a pathetic old man and soon he will be around a lot more."

Peter slid a hand under her skirt and started to move it towards her fanny. "So what are you going to do about it my darlin'?" She wanted him again and knew they only had ten minutes before she had to go and collect Joseph from school.

"That's very easy to answer," but she hesitated as she was out of breath because he had pushed his fingers into the remains of his spunk inside of her. She groaned as she completed her answer, "First of all I am going to let you fuck my brains out as often as possible."

"Well that's always easy Mel, especially as you have secretly taken the birth pill since the abortion. That would really piss the old codger off if he knew he could shag you without a Durex."

She grunted as he turned her onto her knees and shoved his cock hard into her. She gasped as she talked. "Shag me? In his dreams and secondly, I will make his life such a misery that he walks out and then I will take him for every penny he has got." She howled like a dog as he started thrusting brutally.

"Fuck me Mel, is it that fucking good you fucking whore?" He was close again and his grip tightened on her hips, bruising the flesh as she let out a primeval scream. He was grinning inanely and could barely say the words as he came with her. "It's a good job there's no one around..."

Bridget stood in the shade of the crab apple tree a few yards away.

She watched the shaking caravan and listened to the words and screams as the tears slid off her cheeks and wet her blouse. It wasn't jealousy that made her cry, nor their deceit, because she was equally culpable. It was the fear of the future with four girls and no money. She was scared of the battle that lay ahead and how she would manoeuvre through it, including telling Jack and his decisions afterwards.

Would he be there to support her as her best friend or would he use the marriage break ups as an excuse to follow his dreams to Spain?

Wiping the tears away with her sleeve she turned and silently walked away with her secrets.

10

Yapane – Jo stay to dream

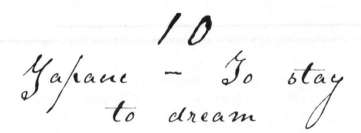

Do spiritual people attract spiritual people?

Jack was in Liverpool airport waiting for the gate to be announced but hovering anxiously where the flight normally departed. A Spanish man walked up to him and started speaking quickly whilst waving his boarding pass in Jack's face.

"No entendiendo, lo siento. I don't understand, sorry."

A beautiful lady interrupted the man in perfect Castellano and offered him information about the departure gate, his boarding pass and life in general. She was in her fifties with her grey hair tied in a bun and sported Prada sunglasses which hid her blue eyes.

"Hello," she proffered her hand to Jack and took her glasses off. "My name's Mandy. I can see you have the look of a seasoned traveller to Girona!"

Jack was pleased to have a pretty woman accost him. "I'm Jack. Encantada – it's a pleasure to meet you." He slyly appraised her figure much to her amusement. "Is it obvious that I've done this trip many times before Mandy?"

"Yes, as you have an air about you. I can see your knowledge shining out."

He took the comment at face value but remembered it again after the flight.

They started to chat about life on the Costa Brava and her home at Empuries, which was one of Julius Caesar's strongholds and only half an hour from Yapanc.

"Near the Roman spirits," she joked. They felt good talking together as Jack explained he too dreamed of living in Spain and so by the time they boarded each was relaxed with the other; as you are with a like-minded person. Entering the rear steps they sat on the back row, leaving a mutually agreed seat between them to repel the overly loud men and even more vociferous women.

Jack was not helping with Mandy's fear of flying. "Did you know that by sitting right at the back, statistically we have a small chance of getting out if we crash?"

She turned to him. "Jack, I'm not good at take-offs and landings at the best of time."

"Don't worry," he joked, "on average only the six individuals sat next to the exits survive and not you my lovely." He laughed at her discomfort but considerately gripped her hand for the take-off whilst relishing his erection. As they talked he was prompted to tell her all about himself and vice versa. They shared personal details about their lives, their partners and even the book he was trying to create but never had the time or motivation to sit down and write. She told him that she belonged to a group of spiritualists in Empuries and gave him her card with an invite to join in their meetings as the group met at her house every Wednesday.

Jack sat back and closed his eyes, thinking about the coming weekend with Joseph and deliberately blanking out malicious Melanie. His arm was gently nudged by Mandy as he drifted in his thoughts.

"Jack, do you mind if I talk to you about something important. I know you might think me crazy, especially as you have only just met me, but we seem to have a link and I think I understand what it is now."

He twisted in his seat towards her. "Go ahead; I'm open to suggestions about anything, lovely. We have got on amazingly well, almost as if I have known you all my life."

She sighed deeply and looked out of the window at the Pyrenees far below and then she stared straight in front of her. Her voice was flat as if she was listening to a distant voice. "I have a message for you Jack, from someone called George. I know you may think this is illogical but I have to tell you, if that's okay, because otherwise I would be blocked."

Jack immediately felt uncomfortable but could see she appeared genuine. "Carry on Mandy, I know a George very well."

Mandy started to describe the house where his grandfather had lived down to the smallest detail. She told Jack the shape and colour of three brooches given to him by his grandmother, the cherry and holly trees in the garden and even the old air raid shelter half buried under the vegetable plot.

Jack squirmed, biting his bottom lip. "How do you know all that Mandy, it seems so accurate?"

"Your guide is telling me all this. He came to me when we met in the airport and asked me to give you a message. He said you must 'live life to my values, the ones that you saw in me.' He's talking to me now and is a lovely man Jack. He says you must believe in those values. You need a way of life and not an existence. When he was teaching in his old school, he always told the children to live to the same values. He says that they are the ones that you shared with him."

Jack closed his eyes because they were full of tears. He loved his Granddad as much as his Dad because he had always been around for him when his Dad was away working hard to make ends meet. His Granddad came to the sports days when he won the Victor Ludorum, not his Mum or Dad. His Granddad watched him and praised him as captain of the rugby team and told him he had played well even when they had been thrashed fifty to nil.

"Is he saying anything else Mandy?"

"I can hear the slap of a cricket ball on a willow bat and he remembers you being there Jack. Follow your path. That's what he is saying to you. You know what you have to do and the beginning is in Spain. Live life to your values and pursue your spirituality as you know it is right. He's gone now. I'm sorry if it's disturbed you but sometimes spirits talk to me and I need to tell the person involved, even if they don't believe me." She looked kindly at him, reminding Jack of Beatty at the end of her reading. "Do you believe Jack?"

He wriggled in his seat and pushed his arms against the backrest in front of him to stretch his stiff back. He sighed his reply. "I do and I don't. So much has happened to me over the last two years. I sometimes think I'm going crazy."

Mandy patted his hand to comfort him. "Don't push anything Jack. Things will happen when they are meant to happen but I feel there are great things in you and your guide is there to help you achieve them."

They sat in silence for the rest of the trip, exhausted by the intensity of their meeting and happy to have briefly crossed paths. He believed they would never meet again but her message would never die within him.

Waking in the shuttered dark of the Yapanc apartment, he slipped out of the matrimonial bed before the beast arose. He immediately went next door to cuddle Joseph who was busy playing on his Nintendo on the top bunk bed. Stretching up he said sincerely and with a gentle smile, "Love you lots mate. I am just going shopping for food so I'll see you later, lovely."

Jack was overjoyed to be back with his son and bounced into the centre of Palafrio, deliriously happy to be in Catalonia. Walking quickly he sensed the clarity in every detail on a beautiful day.

He called into the small electrical shop for the third time in four months to see if his electric toothbrush had been repaired. In England if a brand new item went wrong you would be given an instant replacement but this doesn't happen in provincial Spain. The owner recognised both him and his bad Castellano and disappeared into the back of the shop. Jack walked around looking at the plethora of electrical items, cooking pots and utensils spread throughout the place in total disarray like an Aladdin's cave.

The shop was like most of the others in small Spanish towns and was run on knowledge and ad hoc notes with no process and no systems except a till. It was an IT consultant's worse nightmare. The little old lady appeared with a scrunched up plastic bag and inside she unearthed the original toothbrush that had now been repaired.

"Muy bien, gracias," he said and smiled at her and at the game being played out. He didn't worry about such things anymore. If something broke expect a long delay. Mañana. Repairs to the apartment's balcony doors were partly done by the painters that Manolo employed and the runners to allow him to close the doors properly were themselves running around Palafrio in the painter's van and had been for nearly five months. The garage door was opened by an electric motor and was repaired instantly at a huge cost of nearly four hundred Euros but within a month had stopped working again. He was still waiting for them to come back but they were arguing that it was a new repair and it would cost at least one hundred Euros for the call out. Finally, Telefonica had rung him at nearly ten o'clock the night before to ask for the fourth time whether his telephone line was now repaired.

"Only in Spain," he thought.

He strolled towards the town square and a little wizened man pushing a small cart stopped to let the impatient Englishman pass. On his cart sat a single Calor gas bottle ready for delivery to his customer in the back streets of the dusty little town. Many of these properties he passed looked deserted but behind the grim facades were magnificent houses full of life and hiding pretty gardens with their lemon, nespero and orange trees.

The central market enticed him first and it was where he talked about the weather and football with his friends on his favourite fish stall and was given the best bream, called pagell in Spanish, that they could find, made ready to be placed in the oven the same night. Life appeared simple and cheap to the casual look of an Englishman. The three of them fed on fresh fish caught the night before for less than seven pounds.

"'Real Life' Nim! They use the whole day to 'live'. Meeting friends for breakfast in town at nine, take a siesta in the afternoon and finish work in the cool of the evening twelve hours later as they meet different friends for an aperitif. 'Real Life'! The opposite of England." He walked and shopped for frutas and verduras – fruit and vegetables – set out on the simple stalls in the main street and soaked himself in the busy and friendly atmosphere, smelling the aroma of the fresh vegetables, bread and spices that drifted along the roadway. People stopped and talked, they took coffees, read the newspapers and relaxed, enjoying their lives by concentrating on the basics. They didn't worry about crime; the newspapers said Britain had four times the Spanish level of assaults but Palafrio had way below that. They had other priorities in this small and quiet market town. They worried about their families and friends, they listened to their neighbours and they strolled through their lives with a relaxed attitude, working to live, not living to work and using the whole day and half the night for living.

He stopped for a coffee with his friend Manolo in a small café called Bar Fun Fun at the side of the main square.

"So how is the rental market in Yapanc, amigo? Better or worse hey?" Jack wanted to know in case he needed to rent his own place as his marriage crumbled.

"Hombre, it is very slow. We will be lucky to get five thousand Euros a year for a two bed apartment like yours. Hoy! And the sales are terrible now; everything in Spain is going down because the banks have stopped lending money for second homes. My friend, my business is very bad." Manolo was genuinely concerned but knew his family business would survive, supported by their long-term rental clients.

He too was looking for his Sun Sharer like Jack, his alma gemella, but was more avid in his pursuit. He told Jack with great feeling, "I want, as they say in Catalan, I want to find the other half of my orange."

"That's a nice saying that I also heard the other day Manolo," said Jack. "Do you prefer the top or the bottom half?" They both laughed.

Jack tried his new language skills on his friend. "Estoy constipado – I am constipated by all this white bread Manolo."

"No, No, Jack that means you have a cold, estoy estrenido means I am constipated."

"Oh God," said Jack, "I'm not sure I will ever speak Spanish never mind Catalan!"

Manolo helped Jack further. "You do not speak Español, Spanish, you speak Castellano. There are four different Spanish languages and the only one worth speaking is Catalan my friend, ready for when we achieve our independence. The Fascists from Madrid take our money Jack and many people still resent that seventy years after the Civil War."

Jack nodded his head in agreement. "So I have been told Manolo and, fair enough, I too would be proud of this wonderful country, but never mind the politics my Republican friend. Tell me, where can I go for a great meal near here. I don't mind travelling a few kilometres tonight."

"My friend if you want good Catalan food at a reasonable price try the restaurant Mas Pou near medieval Pals. But if you have the time and the money and maybe the girl yes, you must take her to celebrate Saint George's Day at the El Bulli restaurant near Rosas. You may find it hard to reserve a table because it was voted the best in the world with three Michelin stars. They supposedly open their bookings for just a half a day a year in February and then they are fully booked."

Jack was impressed. "Why would I want to celebrate Saint George's Day with a girl?"

"Because my friend, the twenty third of April is our Valentine's Day. We must give a red rose to the lady and she must give us a book. This tradition dates back to the fifteenth century when the Rose Fair was held. So find yourself a beautiful woman next spring Jack and then Melanie can marry me!"

"She may not want to hombre; imagine her staring jealously at your huge library everyday!"

"Amigo, even worse, she would hate me for making her do all that dusting."

"Hoy! A very Catalan male statement hombre but you obviously don't know Melanie very well." They always laughed when they were together but there was never enough time. He concluded with feeling, "I will give you Melanie for a thousand Euros if I can find myself a new woman and quite frankly, good luck to you, amigo!"

Manolo pursed his lips and shook his head slowly left and then right as he never needed to pay for a woman.

Jack could see he hesitated and promised more. "In fact you can have her for nothing and I don't need to find a replacement!" He was genuine with his offer but his friend didn't know the secrets in Jack's life and considered it in jest. Jack said goodbye with a handshake to his friend and two touches to the cheeks with the girls in the office and wended his way home, thinking about the wonderful life to be had in Spain.

One day he had said to the girls in Manolo's Finques 'Soy caliente', thinking it meant 'I am hot'. This was much to their amusement as it's slang for 'I am sexy' and he should have said 'Soy calor'. He loved the girls and he loved kissing them delicately. His Dutch friends of course greeted him with three kisses and Tugdual as a Frenchman kissed him four times, which he found slightly worrying and effeminate especially since his 'coming out'.

Spain was still confusing but that made it far more interesting than home.

In the winter, he was now used to the seaside damp and ensuing mildew in the wardrobes and on the fabric sides of the beds. He understood how the tiled floor sucked the dew onto it as it was icy cold in the vacant apartment below theirs. He watched the Catalans walk along the promenade in eighteen degrees Celsius whilst still wearing their winter coats.

The Spanish people seemed to be great wanderers. They wander in the winter collecting pine cones for their fires, in the spring searching for wild asparagus and every morning in the square for a coffee and a chat. They are a great nation of wanderers.

He loved the little purple everlasting wallflowers nestling on crags on the cliffs and delicate red poppies waving in the fields of corn interspersed between yellow flax-like flowers. He loved watching the swifts in April swooping low around the fields and the erratic flight of the bats on the summer nights as he sat on his balcony.

On the way to the airport or on the return to the apartment he often considered stopping to talk to the prostitutes at the side of the road. The dilemma would be explaining why he had missed his flight home or alternatively the smell of sex on him when he made it to the apartment. There were dozens of prostitutes in the summer, sitting on their deckchairs with short skirts, fishnet stockings but with their legs tightly crossed. Jack couldn't work out where they went for a shag. There was no obvious van or minder anywhere in sight and so he presumed they would do it in the client's car. He imagined the conversation in his bad Castellano. "How much do you charge?"

"Fifty Euros signor but no kissing and I will not take my top off. Thirty for a blow job and one hundred if you want everything including kissing and feeling my titties. Next time get Hertz to upgrade your rental signor as I do not shag in Renault Clios."

There were also several bars on the same road with bright neon signs saying 'girls, girls, girls' but he was usually in bed four hours before they opened. A weekend was always too short to get into the late nights for eating and drinking and so he clung to his 'Britishness' because sadly he was never there long enough to settle into a new Catalan timetable.

He also got bored with Girona airport despite the year long Catalonia display that he walked around a dozen times. The cello music of Pavel Casals playing above it was strangely haunting. Casals reportedly went to the United Nations in October 1974 to receive the medal of peace. The English-speaking tape recording droned on. 'Catalonia, capable of consolidating and synthesising the worst and best influences and also the traditions making this their cultural heritage. Whilst being extremely attentive to universal trends. A historic people with a language and culture of their own. Openness, willing to see another person's point of view and arrive at a negotiated agreement. Their embracing of cultures and peoples of many other places like the Moors, the French and the Greek sailors trading the coast. Their vision and work ethic in particular, creating their own visions and determination to trade their own culture. All Catalans' approach to life is built on this multiplicity.'

"Surely you have something more interesting to say? How about don't spend your flash English money here in front of the poor Catalonians if you want to make some local friends. Or stop buying so many second homes as you are helping to create ghost towns for nine months a year." Jack complained but he enjoyed understanding about the place he loved and was truly shocked about the changes since General Franco. It was as late as 1979 that the region established democracy and became self governed as it was released from the iron grip of the ruthless dictator. It is at the crossroads of trade between France and Spain, the small harbours for sea trade across the Mediterranean, the rice in Pals and always the fish, the cork for wine flagons, the clay tiles and pots from La Bisbal.

"Only in Spain," he thought as he walked and went as slowly as possible back to his apartment, regretting the reduction in time with his son but happy to be away from Melanie as much as possible.

He remembered sitting on the plane and constantly thinking and analysing and getting more depressed with every homeward journey away from the place he loved. Thinking that you can never feel completely at ease with life until you own your home and then with a sense of achievement you can look forward to another chapter.

"I suppose there are seven chapters Nim:

Being a baby. Learning the basics, if I'm cold – scream, if I'm hungry – scream.

Going to school. Interacting with others for the first time and realising how much knowledge there is in our world.

Early married life. Making the cave nice and filling it with children to take over when I am dead or can't be the hunter gatherer.

Divorce. Definitely optional but inevitable in our consumer society. Dump the old model and fight over the material possessions.

Middle age. A slow dawning after forty that your body is physically declining and your children are faster and cleverer.

Fifty plus. When you know statistically that three-quarters of your life is over and you never lived your dreams. Your friends tell you about those who have died or survived serious illnesses. A realisation that you are going to die.

Finally and back to the magic of seven, there is a crumbling into the drivelling world of old age and that is enough to make anyone scream."

'You can't buy time' is your own saying Jack.
Make the most of every day as if it is your last.

By the time he arrived back at the apartment his family had departed for the beach and so he sat on the balcony and drank coffee with his feet resting on the table. He knew he should join them but needed to be alone to consider what he must do to follow his true path.

He thought about Peter and whether he trusted him anymore as his telephone calls now went unanswered on most occasions. Peter had visited Jack in Yapanc just once, when Jack was alone one weekend. His flight was due in at about eleven that night so Jack had wandered out to his hire car at ten fifteen to drive to the airport. He had stood and looked up and down the street and could see no car. He went back into the apartment and down to the garage thinking he was having a CRAFT moment but there was no car there either. Panicking he went back upstairs and walked up and down the street and around the block of houses surrounding the apartment. It had been stolen and his friend was arriving at the airport in less than half an hour. He had telephoned Hertz and told them it had been taken.

"It can't have been stolen Senor Edmunson, there is special security on all of our cars and the only way to steal it is by using the key. Do you have the key?"

Jack remonstrated, "Of course I have the key, it's been stolen I tell you. It's gone, not here, disappeared."

"No Senor Edmunson, the only other key is in our Madrid head office and it cannot be stolen so we will make a record of your call but please tell the police tomorrow morning."

Jack slammed the handset down. "Fucking twats telling me you can't steal a fucking car."

Five minutes later Peter had telephoned from the arrivals hall. "Wanker, I'm walking out of the main departure doors, where are you parked mate?"

"I've got no fucking idea, tosser."

"Stop taking the piss, wanker, do I go to the left or to the right?"

"No Peter, I really have no idea because I'm sat in my fucking apartment because my fucking car has been stolen."

"Oh fuck, you are joking Jack, aren't you?"

"Peter, I've looked everywhere and it's gone." Peter was at a loss for words for a good half minute whilst contemplating his options.

"What am I supposed to do then?" Jack had told him to grab a taxi and give the driver the Yapanc address. Three-quarters of an hour later Peter arrived, sixty Euros out of pocket and ready for a beer and so they had half a dozen San Miguel's each to lessen the blow.

The next morning they had cycled into the Mossos D'Esquadra, the Traffic Police, in Palafrio and Jack had vainly tried to explain about the theft of his car in bad Castellano whilst Peter sat in the bar opposite drinking breakfast beers with some friendly builders. After three-quarters of an hour and half a dozen telephone calls the police had asked Jack to jump in their patrol car and drove him down to Yapanc. They pulled up by a familiar Hertz Clio parked half a mile from where he had left it and in broken English they explained the local police, a totally separate division, had moved it because they were expecting the dirt track road to have its annual scrape but the contractors had never turned up.

"Only in Spain," thought Jack.

Later the two mates had sat on the wall overlooking the Kaletta beach and admired the waves rolling over the rocks.

"Jack, you prat. Fancy losing your car like that."

"That's unfair mate, how was I to know they had moved it?" But he was smirking. "They didn't put any notices up or even leaflets on the cars to tell us to move them. They just did it. Typical Spanish!"

"I tell you what Jack; you're just like Desmond Lynam." Peter thumped him on the arm. "Smooth, offers two arguments without making a decision. Comes out roses at the end even when England has lost at soccer and always passes responsibility onto the studio experts. I think I'll start calling you Des." They drank beer for the rest of the day or sat on Jack's bench in Yapanc and watched the topless girls walk by. They had stared and the Spanish girls had boldly stared back but it was a good game comparing tits and arses and eventually they nominated 'Bob'. This was used as a code whenever people like Melanie or Karina asked Jack what he was doing on his bench.

"Trying to find 'Bob'," always came the simple answer. The girls knew better than to ask about his friend Bob but all it stood for was 'Best On Beach'. Bob.

It had been a great day and made them both contemplate their marriages and girlfriends without sharing any secrets.

In the evening they had strolled back to Kaletta again to eat out at a seafront restaurant and then they took the dark coastal path for their return home. A short stout man resembling a hobbit had started to surreptitiously follow them clutching the straps of his haversack slung across his back and wearing a dirty yellow ski jacket in the heat.

When they had slowed to look at the stars, the dwarf slowed. When they had stopped, he stopped. At one point they heard him thirty yards away making an owl noise.

"Woooo, Woo, Wooo."

Peter listened and was amused by the stalking. "Fuck me tosser, we have got a weirdo following us; he must be after your pretty arse mate!"

"Fuck off wanker, he's heard you're into anal sex and wants you to give him one." They had laughed drunkenly and started to 'Woo Woo' in return which was a mistake as even walking a lot quicker they found the dwarf carried on following them.

Peter had a master plan. "Right Jack, be ready because we can stop and see if we can make him pass us. Hold your keys between your fingers in case he attacks us and then use them like a knife whilst I run off and get the police."

Jack had been uncomfortable with the suggestion. "No, you fight him off mate and I'll run and get the police."

"Fuck off wanker, how can you run with your bad hip?" They had argued light heartedly but started to get worried about the hobbit despite the anaesthetising alcohol.

The dwarf had closed to ten yards and his teeth as he smiled could be seen in the moonlight. They stopped and the dwarf passed them as they studiously ignored him and pretended to piss over the rocks.

"Okay Peter, let's go." They turned and started walking again as the dwarf leaned out of the shadows making the sucking noise of Hannibal Lector in 'Silence of the Lambs' and vigorously wanking his large dick sticking out of his trousers.

"Oh fuck off," said Peter and they had both run past and hadn't stopped until they reached the apartment where they had sat and laughed their socks off.

Following their previous trip to the police station about the car, they had decided that this time they wouldn't bother as it was far too complicated to explain in broken Spanish. Peter summed up the predicament.

"What is the Spanish word for wank, mate?" So they had a few more beers and laughed the night away but Peter made one smart comment that hurt his pretend friend. "So when are you going to dump Melanie for one of those girlfriends at work?" It wasn't the idea of leaving her that hurt, it was the presumption that he was shallow enough to leave her for a mere girlfriend. A quick shag in Peter's terminology but that was where they differed. Jack would only leave Melanie in search of his Sun Sharer and his perceived

'Real Life' but the timing of the comment had been a catalyst for some deeper thinking by Jack.

> *A catalyst is where I add an ingredient and watch*
> *the reaction.*
> *A new channel for your philosophising deliberately*
> *brought into your path with a hidden objective.*
> *I want to see your mental destitution as it suits*
> *my purpose.*
> *It is here in Catalonia where you will meet*
> *your destiny.*

★ ★ ★

It was still hot about eleven one night as the Edmunsons sat with the Dutch and Duchess on their patio cut into the rock near Yapanc's ancient Dolmen. Every summer Walter and Freda drove from Holland to stay in a beautiful rented house and spent many happy weeks in a place that called to their souls. Over the years and on many social occasions they were always relaxed in each other's company.

Dutch was a big man with a permanently sweaty bald head. He started talking sadly about his father. "He's in a home now and quite poorly. When I went to see him last time, he gave me a document allowing him to commit euthanasia within the law."

Jack sighed. "Hoy, that's a big decision. Why did he do that?"

Dutch explained. "He has beaten cancer four times and feels he couldn't stand the treatment again. He is very frail and like your Mother, he is suffering from dementia so he has good and bad days. The decision to die has been left in my hands when he can't think logically anymore. Jack, he sat there like a baby and asked that I kill him if necessary." Dutch went silent.

Jack replied, "I can't imagine how you feel. I'm sorry for your Dad but also for you as that is a big thing to ask."

Joseph had been in their pool with their son and was lying just inside the house on a settee sleeping happily. Jack looked in at him and silently questioned whether he could place the same responsibility on his boy. The third bottle of Cava was making Jack controversial for a change and so he started to tell the Duchess about his astrologer. She listened intently as he mooned his 'come to bed eyes' at her without success. She was a very beautiful woman who resembled Catherine Zeta Jones and appeared to have married her older husband for his money. She told Jack that Dutch's ex-wife was into spiritualism and had a web site called sunandmoon.com which was worth a look although the woman herself was peculiar.

She carried on. "Have you ever read *The Alchemist* by Paulo Coelho?"

"No," replied Jack, "is it any good?"

"Well, it seems to be in keeping with your current mood so you can borrow my copy if you like." The Duchess went off to find the book.

The next day they saw each other on the beach by the Hotel Yapanc and the families settled into tactical positions close to the water's edge. Jack sat reading the book under an umbrella and was so entranced he didn't move to his bench under the tree.

At lunch time the Duchess walked by and asked casually, "What do you think Jack?"

He stood up in the hot sun.

"I think it's posing more questions for me than answers. Did you find the same?"

"Yes, that's why I gave it to you. I mistrust a lot of the nice thoughts in it but believe some of the bad ones to help me as a witch. I'm pleased you like it Jack as it applies to some of our past."

He moved closer and clasped her brown shoulder feeling her sexual vitality excite him. His animalism stopped him querying her strange statement. Absorbed by her gorgeous brown eyes he stammered, "Thank you for sharing it with me, that's very kind of you. I'm not so sure I believe as much as you but still it's a good read." She stretched her arms above her head and yawned, bringing the rest of her body into the conversation.

"I get so tired out here with these late nights and drinking sessions. I always put on a few kilos and feel I need to get home to work out."

Jack gave her a better solution. "You don't need to do that lovely. Spend a week with me and I'll fuck your brains out eighteen times a day, then you'll easily trim up."

"You Devil, Jack, maybe I'll take you up on that one day!" She turned and walked back towards the Hotel. Jack watched her arse swing as she walked. Halfway up the beach she turned and waved at him as a tease.

He spoke under his breath as Melanie and Joseph splashed out of the sea. "Shame we have our partners here." Lying back under the umbrella he hid his engorged prick by lying face down and picked up *The Alchemist* again.

He finished the book by the end of the day and took it over to the Duchess as she enjoyed the last half an hour of the dying sun before obligatory expat drinks in the Wisteria Bar at six. He crouched next to her sun bed.

"Do I now have to spend the rest of my life following my personal legend?"

Don't ask her, Jack.
You don't need a King from Salem or even the
Duchess to help you realise your personal legend mate
because you've got me.
You shouldn't trust in her, Jack.

She patted his arm. "I think you already know your personal legend and are ready to follow it. You think you understand what is Good and Evil but you don't and are still searching for a true path."

In his head Jack spoke to Nim as an aside. "Shut up you, Salem and the book are fiction and you aren't, so taking his advice is a theoretical risk whilst taking yours would be factual suicide.

By the way, I hate being called mate, it's so proletarian." Jack placed Nim back in the fourth dimension and dismissed his help.

No, I am not a fictional character and neither is
the Duchess.
You need to be aware of her Jack, as she is more than
she seems.
You have known her a long time.

He walked away from the beach and sat on his bench to think about the messages from the book.

"Is Nim, Coelho's voice on the wind? Nim has told me to listen to the messages on the wind." He liked the old Arab saying, 'Everything that happens once can never happen again. But everything that happens twice will surely happen a third time.'

He pondered whether that applied to true love and decided it was only appropriate to subjective things like emotions.

'Santiago the hero had thanked the Alchemist for teaching him the language of the World and the Alchemist had replied, I only invoked what you already knew.'

Everyone seemed to be telling Jack to follow his path but if true it was both scary and ambiguous. He thought of another passage from the book. The Alchemist said, 'Before a dream is realised, the soul of the World tests everything that was learned along the way. Not because it is Evil but so that we can, in realising our dreams, master the lessons we have learned as we have moved towards that dream.'

"That's the point at which, most people give up, Nim, but not me. There are two types of people in life, anvils and hammers and I've been forged over fifty years into a hammer. I will never give up on anything until the fat lady sings. It can be the last few seconds of extra time and I will still never give up."

'The Alchemist science, the master work, part liquid and part solid, could be written simply on an emerald.'

"What was written on the emerald tablet, Nim?"

Nim replied through Jack's consciousness by helping him remember the sentence. 'It could never be understood by reason alone, the tablet is a direct passage to the soul of the World. This natural World is only an image and a copy of paradise. The existence of this World is simply a guarantee that there exists a World that is perfect.' He sighed and lay flat on the bench with his eyes closed to forget his surroundings.

"If you accept multi dimensions, then a copy of our world is fact not fiction, but it may also be imperfect and lead to another world again and again. In the end you go all around the doughnut-shaped universe and end up back where you started, having visited many imperfect worlds. There could even be a whole pack of doughnuts. So the soul of the World is within you and is always there ready to find?"

Jack's true supposition was backed up by another line in the book which reinforced his tranquil state. 'Listen to your heart. It knows all things because it came from the soul of the World and it will one day return there'.

"That's logical. Death is always caused by a lack of oxygen and it is the heart that delivers it." But he strongly disagreed with the line, 'True love never keeps a man from pursuing his personal legend. If he abandons that pursuit, then it wasn't true love.'

"If you find your Sun Sharer you would give up everything to be with her and drop any personal legend."

He ended the day confused and sat drinking beer and making small talk in the Wisteria bar that overlooked the harbour and watched the sun settle behind the pines on the White headland.

"Duchess." He attracted her attention. "Look out there. That's the real world. The sun is dying in the sky, you eat, you drink, you fuck, and you shit. That's what counts and nothing else. Any extras are placed on you as a human being by our society. I think we should get back to basics and avoid this avalanche of inconsequential crap that pervades all our lives at an ever increasing speed. We seem to be working out how to fill in more time faster with more worthless things and not one of us is strong enough to stand up and say stop. When the odd person does, they are accused of being drop-outs because it's not what the peer pressure in society will allow. I believe that shows everyone else up for what they truly are: mindless fucking morons. I have the solution to the meaning of life Duchess but no one is listening to me."

She looked at him solemnly and without comment on his seriously delivered views. "Follow your path Jack, just follow your path."

He trooped home to the apartment with Joseph and a plethora of useless beach items including Melanie and prepared himself for another night of meaningless crap whilst his mind wanted to be elsewhere, still disturbed by *The Alchemist*.

"So Nim, everyone has got something they want to hold onto. Everyone needs something to grasp. Whether it's God, something to do with your family or the Kabala, you need a drive behind you. In reality, when you die, there could be nothing else. Maybe we are just kidding ourselves and if we don't kid ourselves enough we couldn't get through life without cracking up? It's so hard to form a conclusion and people should realise that because it's so hard they use some emotional crutch to get through day by day. Any belief will suffice because if they have no belief they have got no spirit to partake in the energy of life.

They would miss staring into a perfectly clear blue sky looking for heaven and seeing dappled leaves on the trees with each different shade of green intensifying one's soul. Preferably watching the world from a quiet field away from people and their machines because then you can see, touch and breathe spirituality and your soul yearns for the freedom you know that it gives.

No wonder people commit suicide if their spirit is starved of this everlasting beauty. A subjectivity forced onto practicalities that creates our soul."

Today was another part of your journey.
You are learning fast but not remembering
enough Jack.
The women are waiting for you again.

A mini tornado rattled the apartment shutters as it swept the dust off the dirt track and spun it into the warm night air.

Jack's questions deepened with his new-found needs and the conversations with his wife shallowed as the tide turned towards his new life.

His fight back against old age also began that summer but he only managed it successfully on one 'bachelor weekend'. He was on his own in September and Manolo invited him to a 'Seven Brides for Seven Brothers' fancy dress party. Escaping into late night Yapanc he met the beach girls who seemed a bit dull or even a bit ugly on the beach in the remorseless sunlight but at night they all changed into beautiful princesses. During the day before the festivity he had met most of the party goers and got them adopting his 'nanoo, nanoo' greeting as used by Mork and Mindy thirty years before.

"Nanoo nanoo," he would say, and holding his right hand up he would separate his fingers into a large 'V' made up of two fingers and two with a thumb.

"Nanoo nanoo," came the replies from bemused thirty something's wondering if the old English guy was off his trolley.

Manolo called them all La Red, the internet or the network, short for his informal matrix of pals. In Yapanc La Red partied away all summer and at the end of October they disappeared off to Puigcerda in the Pyrenees to ski and party the winter away. Six to a rented apartment, with anyone arriving at weekends paying their share to balance the bills or bringing the cocaine as recompense. Manolo reckoned La Red consisted of more than a hundred people and they were all his friends, especially the girls who all seemed to have been shagged silly by him and appeared forever grateful. Jack often considered whether it was his happy chatty personality or whether he just had a large dick.

The Spanish party was an eye-opener for Jack, starting with the Cava mixed with neat lemon and orange juice with floating fruit as in Sangria and then continuing with the actual fancy dress. The theme was totally ignored and everyone arrived in something different, from Scotsmen with authentic kilts to Cleopatra with a beautiful asp and also a fantastic arse. On arrival at the house he was given a numbered dance card by the lovely Cleopatra who kindly wrote on the top El Paciente Ingles, the patient Englishman. This summed him up amid the madness around him. A pretty girl came and wrote various names on Jack's card and as soon as a number was announced he was supposed to find the lady in question and dance with her. After half an hour of the general disco the number uno was shouted out and a very tall lady accosted him for the first dance. She was about six feet seven and towered above him. The only English she knew was, "I am from Zaragossa." High on bitter lemon and gin aperitif she grabbed his hands and holding them painfully aloft she swayed left and right whilst singing every single word of Boney M's 'By the Rivers of Babylon.'

"Thank you, thank you," said Jack, "nice dance yes." Then he quickly ran off to find Manolo. "Fuck me, hombre; show me this Ester woman who is my next partner."

Manolo laughed at his physical and cultural discomfort as he hugged the Egyptian Queen closer. "It is the tall girl from Zaragossa over there."

Jack realised there were three sisters who were all six feet seven and their names were all written on his dance card several times. He clapped his hand to his sweating forehead exclaiming loudly, "Oh fuck she's tall."

Manolo laughed. "She also loves Boney M amigo. We have the greatest hits ready on our computer!"

Jack was aghast.

"Madre mia. I didn't think they had more than three hits?"

"No but played once an hour every hour until six am..." His friend stopped as he was laughing so loud.

Jack did the right thing by his dance partners and made sure he went to the toilet every time a dance was announced. Early in the morning at about five when the party was dying down slightly, he sat talking to a beautiful Spanish lady who proceeded to jump up and sing something by Maria de Lau. She sang into his face with warmth and depth, professing her love out loud and was duly clapped by all of her friends.

Spanish parties were different; they danced to silly songs and danced flamenco style to everything no matter what the beat. They always sang as loud as possible to every song and always knew the words. The singing barely ceased even when they slurped bacardi, whisky or gin but never wine or beer.

"Only in Spain," Jack thought.

During that weekend his bachelor mentor Manolo gave him another philosophical book to read by Eckhart Tolle called *The Power of Now*. His friend said he kept it by his bed and believed every word in it. As Jack scanned through it sitting under his tree by the beach he questioned the psyche of the population which meant such books were so popular.

'Live for now, nothing else exists. Don't plan the future it may never come. Don't look back at the past as you can't influence it.'

He threw it on the bench beside him and took in the beautiful vista of the bay with its blue sky and aquamarine sea. He said out loud to the bathers, "I can write a better book than this twaddle. All I need to do is take my notes and sit and put it all together."

It was a satisfying feeling as he brimmed with confidence, sitting alone and in Catalonia as if he belonged.

He looked up at the overwhelming blue of his 'Now' and decided the colour of his book cover would be just like it.

He flew home confident in his future but unsure of how to get there.

Exactly a week later, Soul Shiner and Jack sat in the The Farmer's Arms Pub anticipating new spiritual revelations with their scepticism now pushed to one side.

Michael introduced the meeting. "Tonight we are going to start by listening to a tape recording of a publisher from New York who will tell us a story about her best friend who was one of the

USA's leading spiritualists."

They all listened carefully as a woman's voice persuasively told a story about a Navajo Indian man who was nineteen when World War Two began. Jack dismissed the link to 'his Nim' as coincidence but listened attentively. The story recounted that the Navajo language was used in the war by the US Marine Corps who transmitted messages directly between units with no fear of translation by the enemy. The Indian involved had travelled around the world before the war and he had made good friends with a German and a Frenchman when they were in Australia. At the outbreak of war he had joined up and been parachuted into Germany as a spy because of his native language skills. Captured by the Gestapo he was standing in a railway siding waiting to board a train to a death camp when his German friend had spotted him and ensured he was sent to his local prison where he hoped to save his friend's life. During the Indian's time in prison he was tortured in many terrible ways. His feet were nailed to the floorboards, he was beaten and they administered truth drugs. The ordeal was too much for his young mind and so he lost track of the real world but could remember being force fed maggots and worms as part of the torture. Eventually, he was liberated by the Russians who spent many months trying to identify him because he had forgotten his home languages and would only speak Russian. In the end they sent him home to the Indian reservation where he talked to the Elders about his depression and feelings of hostility towards his captors. They advised him to return to Germany and see his old foes and forgive them to regain his spiritual sanity. Returning as soon as possible, he met the German guard who had been in Australia with him and forgave him. The guard told him how he had fed him maggots as protein to keep him alive and so they resumed their friendship and the Indian gradually regained his 'self'.

Many years later after a long career of spiritualism, he telephoned the narrator and after about twenty minutes he asked her to publish his biography. She thought it strange that he had not said autobiography but they signed off happily with 'love and light' as per any normal conversation.

Two days later a common friend telephoned her to ask if she knew that the Indian had died.

She asked when and the nonchalant reply was a week before. About a year later a package arrived by mail at her offices and inside was the chilling biography.

At the end of the tape, everyone sat completely quiet, entranced as if someone had come into the room and they were all attentive to see who the newcomer was. Michael broke the spell by asking them to listen to another tape to end their meeting. It was designed for meditation and a softly spoken man talked to the group to take away their spiritual pains and any unpleasant thoughts towards other people. Jack sat with his eyes closed and found it extremely discomforting. As the man took them through a series of mental exercises he found he was thinking of Bridget in response to the questions posed and his chest was tightening until he broke into an uncontrollable coughing fit and had to leave the room.

Michael followed him out and touched him gently on the shoulder.

"Don't worry about the coughing Jack, it's quite normal when we do this." Jack was feeling better now he couldn't hear the taped voice.

He asked, "Why do you say a simple coughing fit is linked?"

Michael held his arm. "Because it's an expression of guilt Jack. The exercises bring out guilty thoughts from deep within us and make our bodies react. I've seen it many times over the years and am always amazed at the reactions to the tape."

Jack shrugged. "Sorry, I have to leave now." He shook Michael's hand and walked out as fast as possible leaving Harriet to fend for herself.

When he arrived home he found it was deserted but in their bedroom there was a Rod Stewart fancy dress outfit laid out on the bed. Melanie had hired it ready for their friend's fortieth party the next evening. Jack excitedly put the outfit on including the huge blonde wig and a medallion. He walked into the en suite and looked in the mirror.

"Yes, fantastic." He was incredibly pleased with the impact but saw the medallion was the wrong face up. He turned it over in his hand and looked on the flip side. A Navajo Indian Chief stared back at him and a cold shiver went down his spine.

Quickly, he went downstairs and turned on the TV for company until Joseph and Melanie arrived home. He sat without watching and remembered when he had walked up to Michael at the end of their previous meeting. The spiritualist had been standing by the bar with a pint of Weetwoods in his hand.

"So Michael, how do you identify old spirits, the people who are coming to the end of their Karmic life? Are they very deep and caring and stand out from the rest? Or do they have a certain presence about them? For example, when you shake hands with them, do you feel something different?"

Michael grasped Jack's shoulder and honestly replied, "I have got no idea Jack, but based on your last three meetings with us, I think you may be able to find your own answers. Of that I am sure my friend."

Jack had turned to go and Michael wished him goodnight. "Follow your path Jack, you know you have to. Love and light."

As he had walked out to his car he thought more about karma and spiritual age. "What about people who make things happen in life? The Richard Branson types; are they more spiritual or rather totally unencumbered by this stuff and are just very practical at seeing life for what it is? They don't need something to lean on; they just know what to do and do it. 'JFDI' Just Fucking Do It. Provide something more expensive than it costs you to buy, sell it to many customers and make some money. Are they old souls who are further on the journey because they've been there before? It's all too complicated Nim."

No Jack, not complicated.
They followed their true paths and listened to
their guides but very few were strong enough to
reach the end as they were weak and diverted down
false avenues.

You are stronger each day and have received all of
your messages now and so you must believe in yourself
and follow the shining road.
No more delays Jack.
No more excuses.

He always heard Nim now and considered everything he said but how could he prove anything?

How could he dot the I's and cross the T's as Mabel pointed out?

He was reading Richard Dawkins' *The God Delusion* and aimlessly flicked the pages as he sat on the sofa. Recently voted one of the world's top three intellectuals and using his intellect, Dawkins had assassinated the belief in God. Of any God even; not just one but the whole fucking lot.

"On the basis that he made loads of money, why not Nim? You know it is dog eat dog out there but alienating three billion believers seems to be stupidity on the highest scale for someone who is supposed to be intelligent."

He read the paragraph in the book about people in various hospitals separated into test groups to see what percentage got well again when prayed for. One group knew they were being prayed for, one were actually prayed for but didn't know about it and the last group were not prayed for at all. The results of course were clear cut to support Dawkins' theories and there was no difference between the prayer and non-prayer groups.

"What crap Nim, asking three separate remote churches to pray for people is not the same as sitting by the bedside of a loved one and transferring your energy into them to help them get well!"

Jack saw the book as an intellectual exercise drawing obscure intellectual data together in a non-practical way and missing the whole point expressed in his own lifestyle of keeping it super simple.

"What rubbish. I could link a load of research together on the number seven and prove anything I want. My book will be far more practical and useful to the average person in the world!"

He fell asleep on the sofa dreaming about Nim and missed the hug from his boy who was immediately despatched to bed by his hurtful wife. When he awoke he saw the room lights had been switched off and only the soft moonlight penetrated into the conservatory. He pushed the book off his chest and altered his position to see out the night on the sofa instead of in the matrimonial bed.

"What am I supposed to do next, Nim? You alone know how hard it is for me but you talk without helping, you guide instead of suggesting. Come on, I need some real help now."

The brightness of the moon seemed to increase as Nim suggested a way forward.

Believe in no one and nothing Jack.
Listen only to the messages carried on the winds and
find your own true belief.
The four winds erode the earth of the four hills and
carry the dust into the sea.
That is where you belong, Centurion.
That is where you must go to live alone.

"Why do you keep calling me Centurion?"

Because you were and the people you knew are
waiting to meet you once again.

From spirit to spirit

I t was October half term and time for the last family holiday.
Karina, Melanie and Jack were sitting on the terrace at Karina's house taking in the awesome view.

"Do you have to have sex to be in love?" asked Karina.

Jack realised the question was directed at him and quickly considered if it was about his marriage or hers.

"No, of course you don't Karina. You must have sex as part of the marriage; there is no doubt that it is an obligation in my mind. But sex and love are different. Love is a spiritual experience. Many believe that 'man' only achieves a true spiritual experience by having an orgasm. At that split second your mind is cleansed and you see the truth, the true God." He leaned back and balanced on the rear legs of his chair. "Why do you ask?" He let himself bang forward onto four legs and looked quizzically at Karina but she didn't comment as Melanie butted in.

"What sanctimonious crap Jack. Without love you have no marriage as sex alone is insufficient." The other two remained quiet as Melanie told Joseph off for playing soccer on the terrace and then she disappeared to the toilet giving them time to talk alone.

Karina said, "So what do you think of your wife?"

"What do you mean, what do I think of my wife? You are in a strange mood."

She went bright red but repeated her question slowing the words and emphasising think. "Tell me the truth Jack, what do you think of your wife."

He answered truthfully, "I think that if you have no love and rare and bad sex one should consider leaving one's wife." He saw Melanie returning and toned down his hate. "I married a dark haired, thin woman, three stone lighter than now and someone who I didn't know."

Karina was puzzled. "So what does that mean? It doesn't really mean anything."

Jack looked directly into her eyes. "It means everything. It means she is not what I thought she claimed to be. It means I am not sexually interested in her anymore. It means she revolts me with her big hips, big muscles and hunched shoulders. She looks like a wrestler."

Karina was shocked. "You can't say that!"

Melanie had walked up behind them and caught the words 'looks like a wrestler'. "He did say it and he also often says I look like a bag of walnuts because it's true."

Jack explained to the intent but appalled Karina, "The most important thing I have ever done Karina is to tell the truth. If you tell the truth you can get through anything."

Karina called at the apartment the following morning as she needed to verify something that was on her mind. Melanie and Joseph were already beach bound and therefore Karina and Jack sat on their own on the yellow sofa and talked openly.

"Jack, what you said yesterday about telling the truth. Does that mean everything you have said about us is true?"

"Of course!" He waited for more.

"In that case, I didn't realise how serious you are towards me and that makes me very scared. I just needed to know, okay?"

He nodded yes as she stood to leave and he asked her a question in return. "Do you have sex with Josep Maria?" He watched her face as she contemplated whether it was right to give any detail.

"No. Not normally and not normal. You did say if you tell the truth you can get through anything!" She turned towards the door and he roughly grasped her arm to stop her leaving. He was desperate for her company.

"Before you go, please tell me what you think of this poem."

He pulled out a sheet of poetry he had printed from the internet and gave it to her.

'Love Again' by Philip Larkin.

He added, "This is how I feel about Melanie, unfair maybe, but true."

Love again: wanking at ten past three
(surely he has taken her home by now?),
The bedroom hot as a bakery,
The drink gone dead, without showing how
To meet tomorrow, and afterwards,
And the usual pain, like dysentery.

Someone else feeling her breasts and cunt,
Someone else drowned in that lash-wide stare,
And me supposed to be ignorant,
Or find it funny, or not to care,
Even...but why put it into words?
Isolate rather this element

That spreads through other lives like a tree
And sways them on in a sort of sense
And say why it never worked for me.
Something to do with violence
A long way back, and wrong rewards,
And arrogant eternity.

Jack was leaning over her as she read and could feel her heat up. Sex was in the air but their relationship was growing on a much deeper level.

"So you're jealous as she has a secret boyfriend then?"

"No," said Jack. "Just screwed up over everything and nothing because I feel like walking away from everything convenient and worry about ending up with nothing. And do you know what? She said there could never be anyone else. No one else for a very long time, if ever I left her. What a load of bollocks eh?"

"Do you feel like it says?" Karina looked at him quizzically.

Jack frowned. "Of course I feel like it. The drinking, the wanking and the guilt of possibly leaving her, but if I do then it will be my own fault and I would have to live with the consequences."

She left Jack to think on what they had talked about, but that was Jack's biggest problem; too much thinking.

Next morning he sat with Joseph on his knee in front of his PC and dialled into the 'Go Nuts For Free' internet provider and then onwards into Google.

"Now Joseph, you can come on my boat today and I promise I won't capsize it and scare you okay?"

His son wriggled nervously on his knee. "Dad, it's not the turning over. It's the sharks eating me. I saw it on the TV and this man had no legs left as they dragged him onto the sand."

"Is that why you only swim by the beach and not out to the buoys?"

Joseph nodded his assent.

The year before Joseph had been sitting with Karina's children in the small inflatable tender behind the yacht they had chartered for a day. Motoring along due to the lack of wind, the children enjoyed bouncing across the waves made by the speed of the boat until a fin appeared alongside. All hell let loose.

"Shark, shark!" they all started to shout, scared out of their wits. Karina flew to the stern.

"Quick Jack, pull them in. Oh my God." Jack told everyone to calm down as it was only a dolphin and quite friendly but both little and big hearts were beating fast in panic and nobody believed him. Once the children were safely dragged on board, he had looked back into the wake of the boat and pondered the truth. He had seen the fin for a split second and it had not risen out of the water in a graceful arc like a dolphin and had immediately disappeared instead of playfully following them for a while.

He carried on 'Googling' to reassure his boy. "Joseph, look, what we do is input 'sharks in the Mediterranean' and see what we get." The results included 'man killed off beach in Valencia'. 'Great White takes child near Malaga'. Jack quickly navigated away from these and opened two results that mentioned types of shark which unfortunately included several killer species. Too late to select something less scary, Joseph had seen the headlines and immediately said.

"No way am I going on your boat Dad." He dropped off his Dad's knee and ran into his Mum who was still lying in bed where he proceeded to tell her he would never swim in the sea again because Dad had proven that deadly sharks existed in Yapanc. Despite assurances from them both and private bollockings for Jack, he stayed out of the water for the whole day and Jack set sail on his own.

There was large sea running from the north driven by a Tramuntana wind, but it was a beautiful day and flat and calm in the bay. Jack was frustrated by the lack of action and so he edged out into the four foot swell and gusting winds beyond the El Far headland. He felt confident for the first ten minutes but as he sped down the face of the waves he realised the force three wind was gusting to five or six in a quite random way which made it exceedingly dangerous. Deciding that discretion was the order of the day he headed back to the safety of the bay, but as he tacked after the crest of a large wave the boat was flattened by a tremendous gust. Losing his Gant cap, which floated off into the distance, he felt abject panic as he clung onto the bow of the boat trying to turn it into the vicious wind and waves, but too late it turned turtle. She lurched up on the waves and slammed down and although he tried to sit on the centreboard and pull the boat upright he found it impossible despite his forty years' experience. He swam under the water and pulled the mainsail down to relieve the wind pressure as the boat arced back towards upright but still he was knocked flat. After twenty minutes he was exhausted and crawled onto the top of the hull and clung onto the centreboard to get his breath back and think.

His back was in agony, his hips hurt and he had run out of ideas. As he sat bobbing on the huge and ever increasing swell he looked into the water and saw a shark about five feet long and twenty feet away from the boat.

"Oh fuck! Fuck me I can't believe it and I was just in the fucking water. Fuck, fuck, fuck." After another twenty minutes perched on the bobbing dinghy he was feeling sea sick and so he waved his arms at a passing speedboat to call for help. The guys were English and talked through his problem. One of them donned a lifejacket and plunged into the water to be joined by a nervous Jack and with the two of them to balance the boat they easily pulled it upright and Jack squirmed his way in. After many heartfelt 'thank yous' he was on his own again and started to sail towards Yapanc with just the Genoa set, as there was no way he could raise the mainsail again. He soon realised that something was wrong as the boat refused to go in any direction that he wanted and insisted on heading towards the six hundred foot cliffs, now being pounded by surf. Hailing a small Menorquina boat he threw the Spaniard a line and was gratefully towed into the beach.

Three men helped drag the Laser onto the sand and he opened the buoyancy tanks to let the sea pour out. The lack of steering was now explained because they were half full of water. Eventually he wandered over back to Joseph and Melanie and plonked himself on a towel and started to take his wetsuit off.

"Was it a nice sail, Dad?" Joseph was always polite.

"Lovely mate, really exciting but I think it was a bit too windy to take you out my love. Maybe tomorrow hey?" Joseph shook his head to say no and Melanie carried on reading *Hello* magazine. So ignored and unloved by his partner Jack walked slowly and slightly unsteadily to the Croisanteria to buy a Fanta Limon and tell Karina his story.

"I was so 'embarazada' Karina because there are sharks here and I was completely out of control and panicking about drowning, that is if a shark didn't get me first."

Karina laughed, much to his annoyance.

"I could have died out there you know! Why are you laughing, it was incredibly dangerous."

"Because Jack you have just said in Castellano that you are pregnant and not embarrassed!"

It broke the ice and gradually he calmed down but for a few hours he felt very uncomfortable about the experience and physically exhausted. Shock can be a terrible thing and worse if you don't realise you are in it. Shock from the incident, shock from the shark and aftershock from his wife who couldn't muster up a question about what he had done all day.

The next evening there were about fifty friends of Josep Maria who were celebrating his fortieth birthday at Karina's casa.

The dinner consisted of olives and cured hams served with fresh baguettes and followed by a giant dish of paella full of gambas – large prawns – and a huge piece of pork. There were no vegetables as usual and the men were all complaining about their high cholesterol, but rather than changing their diets they all chose to drink more Rioja and pop statin pills from the doctor. After the main course they moved onto whisky and were suitably warmed up for a riotous game of soccer on the beach against the children. Karina played in the midfield chasing the ball and never managing to kick it once. Melanie hung around the penalty area and bustled four superb goals, suitably deserving the rendition of 'We love you Ronaldinha' by the Barcelona FC supporters among the adult men. Jack mixed it with the boys and showed his old skills from thirty years earlier until he side footed a scorching twenty-five yard shot over the head of a five-year-old girl and tried to celebrate whilst writhing in agony on the floor from the muscle tear in his left thigh. He hobbled off the sandy pitch and back to the house to be given an icepack by two of the Spanish wives, who insisted he took his trousers down so they could help apply it which gave him great pleasure.

Pain and pleasure – the ultimate combination to achieve sexual satisfaction.

He told them in a brave hero type of voice, "Did you know, gorgeous ladies, that a torn muscle greatly inhibits the limited sex provided by one's wife, which is usually only provided when there is an 'S' in the month. 'S' standing for sex of course." They smiled encouragingly, as they hadn't got a clue what he was saying because they understood no English.

He smiled back and told them some more home truths. "Try lying on top of your woman whilst giving your arse the up and down treatment and in so much pain you don't know if you want to come or go." They clapped him on his shoulder and started to massage his leg but it was the one without the muscle tear. Karina appeared with Melanie who with a single severe look stopped the over-friendly massage and the Spanish wives left, usurped by the arrival of the formidable English brick.

Jack spoke to Karina, "How are you doing?"

"Normale," said Karina. She didn't need to say not good at all as her tone reinforced the comment.

Melanie went to fetch herself a drink without asking her husband or friend if they wanted one.

"Why?"

"Hoy!" She breathed out, "Pfur. His family, his friends, no choice as every year is the same, no discussion and finally I do all the work."

"Oh is that all!" He pushed her shoulder and made her smile and so he changed the subject. "I've been reading Richard Dawkins' *The God Delusion*. Have you ever read it?"

"Jack," said Karina, "when would I have time to sit and read?"

"Well, there's got to be a God hasn't there? There has to be a spiritual meaning to your life don't you think? You are either for it or against it and need to make up your mind, lovely."

Karina lifted the icepack and looked at the bright red patch on his skin. Head down she whispered so no one could overhear, "One thing is certain Jack. Whether it is two dogs making out in a field or you and me, it is a fact that the soul driver and the sole driver in life is sex. It is fundamental to what turns our days over and not God my dear."

"Que pasa?" What's happening? Josep Maria came into the casa. He wanted his supper, he wanted the children to stop playing football and he wanted his guests to leave immediately.

Wanting time for his Spanish male orientated and dominated regime. Wanting a cerveza, wanting to go back to work but not bothered about the attentions his wife was paying to Jack.

A way of life, very structured, very straight, very much the confident Catalan gentleman.

No give and always take with his wife pulled from pillar to post.

Jack, Melanie and Karina sat on the terrace facing the sea after the guests had disappeared and Josep Maria had left to prepare for the next day's trading down at the Croisanteria.

The children were still full of energy as the sun started to set over the distant horizon and the light went flat, accentuating every bit of the nature surrounding them. They were now in the darkening sea, diving and swimming underwater to collect rocks as a competition. Two, three and then four rocks in a hand became the record as they struggled to the surface with their loads to pile them on the beach. The dogs chased from side to side following the children and barking every time they surfaced to signify their approval. Tired of the rock game, the boys decided to play volley ball instead as twilight mixed with the promenade lights. The dogs would now chase the ball as it bounced outside of the temporary lines made in the sand by a small foot and then savage it as part of their own piece of fun. Catalan Grandma and Grandpa walked up and down the promenade next to the house. Grandpa had suffered a stroke seven weeks earlier, just a mild stroke, a little warning but it had slowed him down.

Jack watched them hand in hand and thought of his Dad.

It was highly emotional seeing their love for each other.

As they walked they held hands to show their undying love and not as a physical support.

Exactly what he and Melanie missed and exactly what he craved from Karina. Melanie went down to speak to them.

Watching the swifts have a final swooping feed high above them was exciting and being there, just being alive made Jack feel fantastic. He turned to Karina. "Until I met you, I wanted to have sex with every woman I met from the age of sixteen to sixty."

She tapped his bad leg in retribution. "Well Jack, you had better be careful over here as the legal age starts at eighteen!"

He pointed to Josep Maria's parents. "That is so sweet; it would be nice to have a love like that when I am as old. Remember the James Blunt CD I gave you and the words 'we shared a moment that will last to the end'? Do you remember the words?"

"Jack, I remember every word of every song on that CD and they all apply to you and me in some way, but I've stopped listening to it because I needed to stop feeling sorry about my way of life."

They looked down at Grandma, Grandpa and Melanie as Jack observed, "You know Karina, you start life as a child and at the end of your life you become a child. You come into this life with nothing and you go out with nothing."

They both stared hard into the distant horizon as it merged into the darkness and couldn't speak to each other because of the beauty and emotion of it all.

Their love was deep and true but unspoken.

That evening, he sat pensively on the apartment balcony with bare toes curled around the railings and water pouring on them from a sudden thunderstorm. Standing up he let the deluge pour onto his tee shirt and underpants, drowning him and his sorrows.

Melanie dragged open the patio door and shouted above the thunder, "What are you doing Jack? You are behaving like a six year old. I'll have to wash those now!"

He turned and looked at her without comment before leaning out further to get the full force of the downpour. Melanie had no spirit left in her to fulfil his needs as she was a dry, menopausal husk. Over-aggressive, over-assertive from a baseline of no education and ignorance. Her friends in Spain called her Missus Happy because they didn't know her. Jack drank the storm waters cascading onto his face and dreamed.

"I would be happy staying here twelve weeks every year. Does the twelve year gap in ages help the marriage? Not at all. It develops into a yawning gulf between the younger, happier and less responsible wife and the older, wiser and more responsible husband."

He reached up and fingered the multi-coloured windsock she had bought.

"You can take the girl out of the council house but you can't take the council house out of the girl. Same place two years on Nim. The same aeroplanes, same view, same thoughts on life and death, no more spiritual and not moved on. The same situation with Karina and still wanting her as my Sun Sharer."

He saw that Melanie had gone to bed and turned off the lounge lights leaving a towel for him by the patio door to protect her clean apartment floor. He stripped off and dumped his clothes on the plastic wicker chair. Drying himself he admired his nakedness and the slightly erect penis. Standing on the darkened edge of the balcony he started to wank himself, knowing she was asleep. He could see his female neighbour undressing in the small house opposite and pulled the skin of his prick quicker and harder. He imagined her pissing like in the porno movies and as she bent over showing her small brown arse he imagined shoving his prick up it. He shuddered and ejaculated his spunk onto the tiled floor. Wiping it up with the towel he felt dirty and guilty and slunk into Joseph's bedroom to crash out on the bottom bunk.

The next morning dawned bright and dry with everything smelling fresh after the rain.

Karina pulled up outside of the apartment in the Seat Alhambra, the typical family vehicle for the ever faithful wife. Jack was sat on the balcony learning his Spanish and when he saw her he broke into the biggest ever smile. His mind worked quickly. Melanie and Joseph had gone to the beach about an hour ago and were unlikely to appear for another hour or two. He shouted down to her open window.

"Hi gorgeous, que tal?"

"Oh you know," replied Karina, "not bad."

"So are you coming up?" Jack knew the answer would give him a clue as to her intentions and she also knew Melanie was most likely on the beach.

"I've just come to ask Melanie if she wants to go swimming in the piscina tomorrow," replied Karina, "but I'll come up for a minute or two."

Jack rushed across the apartment and felt his heart pumping faster as he opened the door.

"Come in lovely, Melanie is at the beach with Joseph." He beamed at Karina who was voluptuous, wearing a blue blouse and white low-waisted jeans. Jack slowly shut the door and followed her in. As she turned he leaned forward to give her the obligatory cheek to cheek kiss. The first was a delicate peck to the left, his hand on her waist on the right. Jack's heart bumped so hard, he was breathless. Karina slowly put her hand on his left side and let it gently slide down to his waist. Jack looked into her eyes and without speaking went to kiss the right side but instead of the delicate peck an inch from the flesh he kissed lightly just to the side of her mouth and held it for a fraction of a second. He pulled back a few inches and still looking into her eyes he felt her breath quicken on his face and her hand pull him towards her. Their lips met gently and automatically their eyes closed. His cock was instantly hard as he pulled her close and pushed it against her groin. Jack had never experienced such a total loss of being as he lost sight of the real world. It was the kiss he had never had, the overwhelming kiss that made the Earth spin round. Without moving his lips, he thrust his tongue into her and felt her tongue lick his in return. Karina didn't pull back, she didn't talk, she just held on as breathless as him. After a minute or two, she opened her eyes and whilst still kissing him let her hand move to his prick. Quickly she unbuttoned his shorts and enclosed his knob with her hot fingers. Jack writhed slowly in her hands in and pushed her blouse up, pushing away the bra and exposing her nipples. He moved his head downwards and sucked the hard nipples of her large breasts.

His hands undid the belt on her jeans and pulled the zip swiftly down followed by the trouser legs. Breaking her grip from his prick, he pushed her hard against the wall and pushed a finger into her wet cunt, pushing aside her white frilly knickers. Moaning she massaged the top of his head as Jack moved them down and off and bending he licked upwards into her clitoris which she exposed as she widened her legs for his pleasure. Jack stood and thrust his prick into her whilst kissing her harder, his tongue thrusting into her hot mouth synchronised with his prick into her cunt. It didn't take long for the kissing to end as they both gasped for breath in the ecstasy of illicit sex. It was a time when they both needed such a sublime escape from their everyday lives and it was emotionally overwhelming. They moaned together as she ground herself onto his cock and their heads lolled to one side with eyes closed as they both thrust and thrust again.

"Oh Jesus, Jesus, oh no..." she gasped as he pushed harder and harder. His prick had never been so hard and so big. It was unbelievably rigid because of how he felt and now all the barriers between them had been broken down by unbelievable passion because he loved her and she gave her love in return. Jack grunted as he came, spunk filling her from his throbbing prick. A deep guttural sound came from Karina as she quickly followed him with an intense burning orgasm, deep and strong like never before.

Tears poured from her eyes as she limply held him and Jack delicately kissed them away.

★ ★ ★

That night, he was dropped off at the airport by Joseph and Melanie and turning with despair in his heart he walked away after a brief goodbye to his boy. The tears and the pain of leaving his son and knowing what he must do in his marriage were at odds with remembering Karina earlier in the day in the apartment and later that afternoon before he left.

She had come down to the beach to say a silent goodbye. She walked to the edge of the road and looked across waving sadly but she couldn't come closer to hug or to talk because of her emotions. He watched as she turned her old Alhambra and drove away.

They knew they were meant for each other but it could never be.

James Blunt played in his mind as he recalled what he had said after they made love.

"Karina you're a mother, a worker and a lover but only with me. You are also a wife and you have to be responsible as life is all about responsibilities. Josep Maria relies on you with his illness and as support in his business. You want to run away but you know you can't. You do know that don't you?" She gently patted his face and said nothing but her tears told him the truth.

Mentally he was now prepared to leave Melanie after two years of help from his guides but his Sun Sharer could never leave her husband.

The winter passed aimlessly; understanding the marginal difference between hate and love, respect and hate, derision and respect, sarcasm and derision and ultimately lies and truth.

You know when your wife is committing adultery by the way she speaks to you, treats you, despises you and uses you. She used to try for you and although not quite achieving something, she would still be respected for trying. But this person had grown into a monster who treated him like a young child alongside his son.

Jack had been binned and was now deemed to be with the lowest of the low.

Each request for her aid was deliberately ignored. Each occasion rankled with him as another example of someone not doing their bit. Someone who has stopped becoming a completer finisher and is content to leave everything until tomorrow unless it's on her agenda.

Looking after her boy was okay but he was her possession not his Dad's.

Looking after her family was okay.

Looking after her girlfriends was okay.

But when you're just a piece of shit to be wiped off the shoe each day you can't hang around.

He tried to be away from home as much as possible as he half heartedly searched for a new contract and worked for odd days whilst the pleasure dome revolved faster at home.

12

Jettenhill – Trying not to remember

Saturday evening and the BBC news was on as Melanie sat doing her nails ready for the evening's dinner party at Martin and Jean's. She languidly looked up at the TV showing Malawi and another famine. This one had killed one hundred thousand people due to three years of crop failures blamed on the trendy global warming theme. She commented languorously, "The lack of birth control is disgusting. It's always causing starvation in Africa."

"You stupid woman," replied Jack, "it's the lack of food, not too many people. You don't just pop into Boots and buy some Durex at a pound a shag, you save that amount of money for a month's food. The country is vast, it has sod all population and untold riches fleeced by a few powerful people. That's the truth." It seemed such a stupid assertion from a middle-aged woman. Not thought out and typical of her, hammering home that he was married to an ignorant person.

He sat in deep thought after his unfair outburst as Melanie left the day room without a word. He upset her constantly but had gone beyond caring. The respect was gone, not instantly but drip fed over the last five years. A gradual erosion brought about by his increasingly stressful work away and the obscenity of rampant spending using his hard-earned money to buy more needless material possessions.

Not even the latter really. More new possessions perceived to be better than the ones that worked perfectly well. Hard disc Sky rather than normal Sky. "So we can serially record Coronation Street instead of messing about with the video."

A giant VW Toureg petrol guzzler to get Melanie and Joseph the three miles to school in the same time but looking smarter, instead of the functional and cheap Kia Sportage diesel. A Louis Vuitton handbag and a Boodles diamond ring squirreled away in case of hard times.

Names and peer group pressure brought together to waste more money on being the best, being seen to be the best, having the best and living the best but totally ignoring personal or subjective qualities in life.

Jack sighed, puffed his cheeks out hard and went outside for some peace. The stars were already out over Dingle Dell. The Plough shone brightly and smiled at him.

"Nim you need to help me here, I can't carry on like this, it's impossible. I deserve more than this."

> *Jack, you have been like this for nearly three*
> *years and you've talked to me directly about it for*
> *two years.*
> *You know I can't help.*
> *It's your path that has to be completed and it's not the*
> *one you are weaving along now.*
> *You have had angels to help you on the way.*
> *You have seen a different side to life and tasted*
> *that difference so now you need to sort it out or just*
> *give up.*

"Jesus Nim, don't go negative on me now. If I stay with her it would be for Joseph but his life would get worse as he saw the widening gaps and increasing arguments between his Mum and Dad every weekend. I would have to have affairs at work to get all-consuming sex but I would prefer to have love in my life. Finally, she would carry on spending every penny I earn until the day I die.

Let's face it Nim, that could be shortly due to the pressure I'm under. I said in Dartmouth; fifty years down and fifty to go and I meant it. I just need to get away and think."

The stars blinked in the clear sky and Nim looked sadly at Jack. Even spirit guides feel emotion.

> *Jack, your contract was over months ago and you hate*
> *your work so just walk away and go alone to Yapanc.*
> *Take some time before making a final decision.*
> *Go and flow in the four winds, hear the sea and listen*
> *to what it says.*
> *Listen carefully to the messages in the breeze.*
> *Taste the salt and ozone of the realities of life again and*
> *then come home and discuss it all openly and honestly.*
> *That is all you can do.*

Jack walked around the cottage and looked at the room lights reflected in the still waters of the pond. Nim was right; everything here was too pressured to be able to think clearly. A few more weeks of shit and stress and then off to Spain and fuck everyone.

"Jack! Jack where the hell are you?" Melanie shrieked into the night whilst hanging outside of the back door in her dressing gown.

He walked around the corner to see the lump silhouetted in the top frame of the stable door. "What's so important that you want to tell all our neighbours about?"

"I'm sorry. Please come inside love." He was immediately on guard as she never apologised, never said please and last used the love term two years before. He followed her into the kitchen where she turned to him with genuine hurt in eyes.

"Karina just rang." Jack's heart missed a beat.

"Josep Maria was admitted into hospital this morning. He's had some sort of seizure and is in intensive care."

"How bad is it?" Jack was quiet and concerned.

"Very bad. He's unconscious and may not make it." She held his arm. "Are you okay?"

"I'm fine lovely. Go and finish getting ready to go out." A temporary truce was declared whilst they both thought of their friends. She disappeared upstairs and he went to sit in front of the TV.

All he could think about was Karina and what she must be going through.

> *You can help him if you go and see him.*
> *You have the power and their paths intertwine*
> *with yours.*
> *Therefore you have to make a choice and make it now.*
> *This is where you finally follow your true path or give*
> *up for eternity.*

He immediately felt guilty as he was counting on Josep Maria's death so that she would be available for him. He started to consider their family especially the children.

He knew he could help but didn't understand how and why.

He couldn't touch the knowledge inside himself yet but he knew there was an opportunity. To take the opportunity or to let it go?

He went to get ready for the dinner party with his equilibrium disturbed like never before.

Lying in the bath looking at the Marlborough tiles he thought about "names, names, fucking names" and topped up the hot water to ease his aching hips and back. He was downright miserable.

"Why am I here? What am I achieving? There's 'Real Life' out there and I need to find it no matter what."

An hour later and Melanie came downstairs to go to the dinner party in new knee high boots and a chocolate miniskirt bought from Hobbs in Manchester.

"Fuck me!" Jack couldn't help it despite the niceties earlier. "What the hell have you got on?" He looked at his lumpy, frumpy and dumpy wife in a miniskirt for the first time in over twenty years.

"It's called fashion Jack, something that you don't appreciate and don't understand," retorted the lump.

"Well, I read your *OK* and *Hello* magazines and I even look at *Cheshire Life* occasionally, but whoever sold you the boots and skirt saw you coming." Melanie turned round to face this slander and that was when he realised she also had a new top. You could see most of her small floppy tits through the black lacy fabric.

"What the fuck is that." Jack had gone beyond all hope now. He immediately thought, "Sex will be out of the question again but who gives a shit?"

She spoke down to him in exacting tones, "This is fashion; it's what my friends wear and what I like."

"How much was it all?" The inevitable next query.

Melanie paused and then carried on arranging the olives and slices of Spanish chorizo, spicy sausage, that she was taking to Jean's house.

"Come on how much?"

"Well, I saved you four hundred pounds."

Jack's chest was tight with anger and looking at her pressed into the fashionable clothes, he felt sick in his guts at the ugliness of her and the whole situation. "How fucking much?"

Melanie deliberately placed two more slices onto the Emma Bridgewater olive pattern plate. "Only five hundred and fifty but don't forget they are good quality and will last so I can wear them again."

"For fuck's sake, you really are taking the piss more and more Melanie. I have sod all work and far less income until I find a long term contract. No money, got it? We can't keep living on the 'never never' by pulling down more of the flexible mortgage. You will only wear it on a few occasions because you can't be seen in it too many times by your so-called friends. The clothes are there to impress your girlfriends, not other men at dinner. You even show your tits to each other to see who can get the most men staring at them all night. It's just a fucking joke to you now isn't it? Just a fucking joke."

Jack walked away to the lounge shaking with anger. He repeated constantly to himself that the whole situation was totally unacceptable and that she carried on manipulating him like a child.

Martin and Jean's mansion in Tettenhill was a Melanie-inspired treasure trove of names, names, names. Architecturally similar with a large oak beamed dining area off a 'fab' and brand new kitchen. This was the best place for Jack to start his ever more eccentric behaviour.

He spoke sarcastically to the host and Soul Shiner as they mooned around lovingly touching the new items. "I see you have Clayton Monroe fixtures on the windows, Perrin and Rowe taps, Elizabeth Arbuthnot fabric and the very best Arighi Bianchi table. My God, is that Emma Bridgewater china above the Miele dishwasher by any chance? Names, names, names; come on girls there must be more to life than this. Were you and Melanie trying to forget who you are and replace yourselves with other peoples' glories?" He was obnoxious and lucky not to receive some stronger retaliation from Jean.

"Emma Bridgewater crockery at four hundred pounds was cheap Jack; it was in the discount shop. I managed to get the olives, figs and stars designs that are so sought after. It's a positive asset."

Jack interrupted, "No it's not an asset Jean. That's what Melanie says but you don't have to follow the herd you know. It's not an asset for life; it will get broken and chipped and you will have to change the whole lot."

"Jack!" she remonstrated, proud of her collection and kitchen. "It's for life, the rest of Martin's and my life."

He couldn't resist it. "Well if you keep spending that sort of fucking money on fucking crockery he might shorten it lovely. It certainly won't have been much of an asset then!" They both turned away and pointedly ignored him so he zoomed in on Bridget.

"Hello gorgeous, what's a nice girl like you doing in a place like this? Talk some sense to me lovely."

She did. "What planet are you on tonight my love?"

"I'm just fed up of the same old crap. Everyone has a crunch point you know."

Peter sidled up to them. "Have you seen the number of lights they've got? They are driving me crazy. Forty-two I've counted. Up lighters, down lighters, table lamps on the work surfaces, hidden lights in the Welsh dresser. I now understand why Tony Blair says we need to go nuclear." All three of them laughed.

"Peter," Jack said, "I just pressed the joystick control on their Miele extraction hood and got sucked up into it. Can you see the grille marks on my forehead?"

Peter was concerned. "You need to be careful flying around or you might hurt your bad back."

Bridget asked Jack if he liked the kitchen.

"No, not really, it's very beautiful but you could buy four cars for the same price. It just seems 'OTT' and based on other people's views and not their own. I can't stand that. No independent thought is worse than no thought at all. In fact, I don't even read newspapers and books anymore; I don't want to read someone else's bad opinions. I just want the facts so that I can interpret them myself and express my own opinion. I want to have a choice and choose something that is right for me and not perceived as right by others."

"Slow down Jack, I only asked about the kitchen." Bridget was worried about his stability.

The conversation drifted on as they sat and ate the entremeses. Even Jean had got into the Spanish act by serving a variety of tapas. Peter asked Jack how his old 'Merc' was going.

"Quite frankly, I must have the only SLK that keeps breaking down in England. First the radio went and then a supercharger blew up. On Monday I pulled up at a hotel and couldn't open the boot. So I looked in the manual and there are four different buttons to open it and none of them worked. In the end I called the RAC and their man turned up. He tried to open it and failed just like me so he decided to speak to his technical department on his mobile. Do you know what they said Peter? They said, 'Have you got a key?' So he clicked a button and pulled it out of the end of the remote and said 'Yes of course I have'! They replied simply, 'use it then'! We both felt so fucking stupid." They all laughed.

Jack sighed and said, "Seriously, Keep It Super Simple. It's got to be the way forward for everything. Life is too complicated nowadays."

That night was the first time that Melanie and Jack 'rowed' with each other in front of their closest friends. It started innocuously enough when Soul Shiner commented, "I believed when I first met Matt that the way to a man's heart was through his stomach. He was always asking me to bake him a Tartiflette."

Melanie stared across the table at Jack and put the boot in. "Actually, Harriet don't you mean the way to a man's heart is with a dagger?" The girls tittered nervously.

The rain thundered against the glass roof of the conservatory as they sat preparing to fence with each other. There was a tiny leak through one of the down lighters and the girls were all complaining to Matt for turning them off as it spoiled the ambience. Peter was agreeing with the women, telling everyone it wasn't really dangerous, but in his world Niagara Falls could pour through the roof and still be left for a week or two before fixing it.

He said to the boys, "The problem is girls don't understand physics," and Jack quipped back looking daggers at Melanie.

"They don't understand physical either."

Melanie responded bitterly, "Life's not a competition, it's just about enjoying yourself Jack and you are so stuck up your own arse that you can't."

He stopped leaning back on his chair and let it crash forward. "Life is a competition; it's just you are not in it Melanie. You are so like your Mother, half fucking baked. Get your brains in gear for God's sake and think before you speak. It's no use being nice to everyone and nasty to me. Do you know what, I think I married you out of convenience, not love, and definitely not money as you brought all your debts with you. Convenient sex, convenient to talk to when lonely, convenient to have a child. Convenient to have someone look after that child, convenient to cook and clean. Marriage! It's all about fucking convenience. About sharing the load otherwise it all feels too much as the loneliness and drudgery clambers into bed with you and depresses your soul."

Melanie barked across the table, "Stop whining man, anyone would think you have got the whole world on your shoulders and I have nothing to worry about."

He replied, "You haven't really, have you? Responsibility is taken not given Melanie. Add value to my life, stop frittering your time away and do something constructive."

She gave up and decided to go to the loo, quickly followed by Soul Shiner.

Jack careered down his path of self destruction upset by the bad news from Spain.

He asked Matt, "Do you want to be reincarnated or have you had enough of this type of life like me?"

"Jack, slow down on the booze old chap. No, I don't believe in reincarnation. I'm like you, I believe it isn't a rehearsal and we should make the most of it. Some of the terrible things I see in the hospital every day bring it home to me. I think it was you who said: You have one life and you make it happen? I wholeheartedly agree with that."

Bridget had been cringing at the far end of the table, staring at her ex-lover and worrying about his outlandish behaviour. She remarked to Matt, "You're right Matt, it was Jack who said that and he also said fifty down and fifty to go before he got so morose! Jack!" she shouted down the table. "Lighten up dear, life's not that bad. You have always got your friends to keep you happy."

Jack smiled across at her. "Thanks Bridges, you are a star, a pretty star in my night sky. Melanie's teeth remind me of stars. They come out at night." The boys laughed but only because she wasn't there to hear the insults continuing.

Jack couldn't see the offence he was causing his friends. He carried on relentlessly. "Peter, do you remember in the pub last week, you had inadvertently left your flies open? Realising it, you said to the barmaid, 'Sorry, I thought you were interested in getting to know me better.' Fucking funny that and she thought she was being clever with her reply, 'Maybe you need an operation to cut it off Mr. Edam.' You remember, tosser, don't you? And you said 'I've just had one thanks, a straperdichtomy.' 'What?' came the thick reply. 'A strap a dick to me.' Stupid woman."

Peter tried to cover himself and asked Jack about his search for work but Jack just continued outrageously. "Bollocks to work, I'd like to be a priest for a career change. Go to a nunnery on a pastoral visit and shag all the nuns or sit in the confessional box and get all the gossip. What would you do mate?"

Peter smiled, "I'd want to be a baker perhaps."

Jack replied, "I want a cake off you tomorrow to see if you are any good as a baker."

Straight man Peter asked, "What sort of cake mate?"

"A cake with icing; the icing of human kindness."

Peter had joined in again, "You mean spunk then?"

The boys giggled.

Jack was very pissed as he careered on. "It was a good night at The Pheasant last week. The barmaid asked for last orders an hour after closing time and Peter said 'Take your clothes off'! A fucking great night. No women, lots of Weetwoods, fucking great but the barmaid is slightly off her head or as they say in Spain 'she needs another ten minutes'."

Peter admonished Jack, "She's not slow Jack, she's just pissed off with customers like us and can't be bothered to answer them. You are becoming such an old fart; you are so cantankerous in your old age."

"I know I'm fucking old pal because when I'm gardening I realise it takes twice as long to do something. Just like when I'm having sex hey! It really pisses me off because my mind wants to do more but my body can't."

Jack had dropped his head onto his hands on the table and so his voice was slightly muffled, "You know when you're getting old mate when you come out of a public toilet in somewhere like Chatsworth House and start to tell your friends about how clean they are. Get a life Peter; I'm not an old fart yet, it's just everyone else thinks I am. I have a fantastic house in England and a fantastic apartment in Spain but now any spare money I have is going into cosmetic surgery."

Bridget asked anxiously, "You wouldn't would you?"

"Yeah, eyes first, a nice little tuck, penis extension second and my entire wife third." Melanie had still not reappeared.

Even Matt joined in as a straight man for the drunken Jack, "I've got ESP on my new Audi Q7 but I haven't got a clue what it is."

Jack slurred, "It's a unique Cheshire set gadget. ESP; extra sensory perception. You can see an accident before it even happens. Clever bastards the Germans."

Melanie and Soul Shiner arrived back, cutting short the lewd and not so funny conversation. Bridget asked Martin for a cappuccino from his Miele machine and specifically demanded a lot of froth.

Jack asked, "Is that in your mouth or in a mug Fidget? If you want I can add a chocolate topping by scratching my arse."

Even Bridget looked disapprovingly at him. "Jack don't be so sick." She glared at him to try and modify his behaviour.

"But I am sick Bridges. I've got bad hips and a bad back and I'm fed up of swimming as it stinks of chlorine and makes me feel like a horse in physiotherapy."

Everyone had despaired of him by then and left him to stew in his cantankerous thoughts in the corner.

A very drunken Jack followed Melanie out of the door to sway home fifty metres behind her to avoid a tongue lashing. He stopped and turned to Martin as he left. "That's what happens mate; women entice men into marriage because they want that stable convenient life. It's in their genes you know, just like shopping. But most men are not strong enough or courageous enough to move away from it all when they realise the shit they are being given by their ungrateful wives. However, I have learned from my guides and can pull away, no matter how hard it becomes and what I lose in material possessions. I tell you mate, there is no way I am going to live in a pile of shit."

Martin patted him gently on the back. "I agree Jack and some of us do feel the same but don't talk about it. Goodnight, take it easy and don't worry about the whole world. Just be happy and let your responsibilities roll away."

Jack ambled away down the long drive wondering what life was all about and whether Beaujolais had a higher alcohol content than Rioja.

It was ten minutes to one in the morning and Melanie lay on their bed totally naked.

They had walked back from the party without arguing which was unusual. Perhaps she hadn't drunk enough to shout at him in the dark, or she was bored with the same rant. There was no romantic hand holding and no love, just a silent procession through the very dark night.

Jack looked down at his wife on the bed; she was brown from her days on a sun bed apart from the small white triangle around her pubic hair.

"Do you want a cuddle tonight then?" she cynically challenged him as soon as he came through the bedroom door, making a point about how she controlled him. She didn't look at him but lay like a fat slug, knowing that she was causing his emotional pain and wanting to turn the screw tighter. Her breasts were small and flat, hanging left and right but with huge nipples. Around her cunt was the stubble from shaving her bikini line and dotted around the stubble were shaving pimples. Jack wanted sex but preferably not with her. However, his cock still craved sex and so lying beside her without talking or moving seemed his best ploy.

"I'm extremely tired," she said, "and it's late so if you want me let's do it."

Jack didn't move at first. He kept his eyes closed and thought how much he desperately wanted it but how he really needed love. He thought of Bridget and Karina and how different it had been, how special. He knew now that his marriage was over. "I have a mental block," he said.

"Stop messing around Jack, you either want me or not, it's black and white. I always have to make the first move, so do you want a cuddle or not?"

He bitterly thought, "Just for, God and the Queen," and got up to fetch some baby oil from the en suite. Smoothing some onto his right hand he began to spread it onto her flabby tits. Melanie lay like stone, her eyes closed. Gently, Jack moved his hands onto her belly and then the pubic hairs. There was still no movement. He leant over and kissed her but found her lips unresponsive. He looked into her face, stolid with her eyes closed. She looked angular and ugly. Leaning between her legs he prised them apart and gently licked her clitoris. Yet more razor rash and bits of white toilet paper where she had wiped herself. Jack felt physically sick. He inserted his finger into her and caressed the g spot. A slight twitch of the legs indicated some physical interest. A slight wetness between his fingers. He returned to her face and kissed her again, this time getting some sort of response but still cold. More oil went onto her fanny and he rubbed her clitoris harder and faster. He lay back, exasperated by the lack of feeling in her but also in himself. Melanie took this as a signal to start licking his prick. She lay on her side and began to suck the end whilst rubbing the prick up and down with her right hand.

"Oh God," she said, "I need to change sides as my shoulder's killing me." Jack felt even more exasperated. This shoulder had been bad for eight months and every time he suggested a solution like going to the local acupuncturist, it always got knocked back for some reason. "I was waiting for the holiday to see if the heat would help. I thought the swimming might ease it up. I didn't want to spend money when you are out of work." All of Melanie's excuses were because she never completed anything unless it was to her agenda. Suggesting solutions was a definite way to ensure that she put things off.

Jack pulled her head away from his prick. "Stop, it's too much," he said.

"Put a Durex on," she unemotionally replied. Quickly, he rolled the smelly rubber on to himself, thinking it would be nice if she did it for him or even better that she was on the pill. The slug got on top, knees either side of his waist and started pumping up and down.

After a few minutes she said, "Talk to me, I like that."

Jack replied negatively, looking at the wall, "Just get on with it."

After a few more minutes she demanded, "Put your hands on my arse, it makes me feel better."

Jack obliged and she shuddered slightly and gasped quietly. After grinding away for what seemed like an eternity she asked, "Do you want to go on top then?"

He replied, "Have you come then?"

"Of course I have Jack, do you want to come on top now?"

Jack couldn't believe she had come; there had been none of the usual explosion. "Have you really come?" he said.

"Stop being so awkward and get on top and pump me. I know my body and I know I've come." She was getting annoyed. "You need to come on top as my knees are killing me."

Jack thought rudely, "That's probably due to your excess weight." She rolled off him with a grunt and he turned her onto her back and shoved his cock in again. Half heartedly she rubbed his chest and nipples as he gave a little spurt and it was all over. Rolling out of bed he walked to the toilet and threw the long limp Durex in the bin. Then he washed his face with the hottest water that he could stand hoping to avoid white spots around his mouth in the morning.

He looked into the mirror and all that stared back was despair. "Why did I bother Nim? Why did I fucking bother?"

The next day was Jack's birthday.

Up at six in the morning he happily wrote his book until ten when Melanie came downstairs demanding why he hadn't fed Joseph who was happily watching 'Yu-Gi-Oh!' on TV.

A typical Sunday with no thought or celebration of his birthday by his family. A single card was given later but no present and there was no shared excitement.

Breakfast with his son was the best thing that happened on that day, his fifty-second birthday.

The worse thing that happened on that day occurred at four in the afternoon.

The same time that Jack had been born.

The family were driving out of Chester on the busy A51 shortly after Joseph's swimming lesson.

Melanie had decided to go via the Edam Garden centre to buy some Warburton bread and flowers but close to the Tarporley turning they joined a queue of cars with nothing coming the other way. Jack got out of the car to see if he could see the problem as they could quite easily do a U turn and avoid any delay.

A hundred yards ahead was a twisted wreck hung on the side of a yellow DHL 'artic' as if the totalled car had been making a right into the Garden Centre. His guts turned over and a shudder ran up the back of his spine.

"Oh God, please God, no way it can't be her." He started to run and tears were already in his eyes. Heart pumping and out of breath he pulled up ten yards short and could see her broken body lying on the road where she had been thrown out of the car by the impact. He couldn't see the girls and felt relieved. He also knew Peter was on a buying trip and so there was no chance of him having to witness the horror. The first people on the scene had left Bridget bent double in the road, her left leg parallel with her side and her arm spun behind her head in an impossible position. Pushing through the ring of needless helpers he crouched down and looked into her face. The grey eyes stared and were clouded. The love and laughter that he had seen so many times was gone. Her face was intact apart from her lower jaw torn from the upper jaw in a grotesque yawn and still with blood pumping slowly onto the tarmac from the open jugular vein.

Jack bent and gently rolled his arms around her shoulders and neck to hug her close like she always wanted. To be loved and hugged and talk and laugh and to be happy with her secret lover.

His breath gave way as he pulled in the first one since stopping. It hurt as he breathed in and hurt more when he breathed out a desperate "Noooo!" Shuddering with emotion he repeated it many times, shouting it into the side of her neck as he clutched her harder. The blood continued to spread across the road in a vast pool diluted by his copious tears.

> *Jack. Speak to her spirit.*
> *She is waiting to say goodbye.*
> *You can talk to her now through me.*

Jack closed his eyes and blocked out everybody and everything. In his mind he talked to Nim and Bridget.
"Oh my darling, my darling Bridget. How can you leave me this way? You know I always loved you, how can you go so sadly?"

> *Jack, I will always love you.*
> *You gave me life and now you are part of my death.*
> *It was meant to be.*
> *You have Karina, she's your Sun Sharer and you*
> *must love and cherish her and be there for her.*
> *Don't be sad for me Jack, see my girls and tell them I*
> *love them.*
> *Tell them to grow up proud and strong and never*
> *forget me.*
> *Tell them I will look over them and they must never*
> *feel alone.*

"No Bridget, no you can't go. Nim help her please for God's sake save her. Don't let her die Nim please."

> *She's gone Jack.*
> *Jack put her down and walk away.*
> *Her spirit's gone, she can't stay here, her path is*
> *fulfilled.*

Jack gently cushioned her head as he lowered it down to the red tarmac and placed his fingers gently over her eyes to close them, sliding his hand back in a last caress.

He murmured, "Forever my love." Standing slowly he walked back to his car in a trance. The crowd silently parting, with tears in their eyes, staring at his clothes saturated with her dark blood. Melanie stood by the car door, white faced, staring at the bloody mess of her husband.

"It's Bridget," his voice cracked and tears poured out as he hugged her close and she started to cry. Joseph watched from the car and cried for his Mum and Dad.

Emotionally bereft they hung in a small void of time before the ambulance arrived and the practicalities of getting home intervened.

He sensed that even Nim missed Bridget, as if he loved her as much as Jack. But Nim is not a person and Nim didn't physically kiss her and look into her eyes and now Jack never would again.

Peter was a broken man and his own secret love for Jean had been destroyed by the tragedy and the need to pay more attention to his daughters, but he still saw Melanie who helped and supported him without her husband's knowledge.

Peter would be seen a year later shuffling around the Garden Centre, re-potting and watering the bedding plants, a shell of the previous man suffering from rampant Parkinson's disease that was quickly crippling him, destroyed by emotion and guilt and trying to hang on to a simple, practical life without too many thoughts.

Jack went back to the apartment in Yapanc to resolve the crisis in his life and support Karina.

He listened to soulful and loving music but too many of the songs had deep emotions attached to them because of the women in his life. The apartment was dark except for the bright computer screen on which he was typing his book.

"Why can't I cry Nim?"

Because Jack, if you have lost your soul, you have lost
your emotions.
Too much work and too little play, exactly the opposite
of what you tell your three children.
You can be so responsible, so focused, and so busy all
the time; you forget life is about having fun.

"Fuck off Nim, how do you think you get an apartment in Spain and an income of two hundred thousand a year, you twat."

By being clever, Jack, just by being clever.
You buy something and sell it for more than it cost
you, the bigger the differential the richer you will be.

"If only life was so easy Nim, if only it was so easy." Jack sighed. "What's the point of having a spirit guide for crap advice like that? Anyway, what do you know about economics, you spent most of your life on a frigging reservation."

Having a bad night Jack?

Every day Nim sounded more like the computer in '2001 A Space Odyssey'. There was a loud bang as Jack shut the bedroom door, no more Nim tonight.

He left the apartment at the crack of dawn on a mission to visit Montserrat, north of Barcelona, and find some peace. He felt happier sitting in the vaulted church, listening to the beauty of the morning mass and felt the love and tranquillity of the place.

He then went to see the Mother of God to ask for her help as he created his new life.

This was a wooden image of Saint Mary which was found by a shepherd in 818 in a cave on the mountain above. Saint Mary was now the patron saint of Catalonia since replacing Saint George in 1981 and was supposedly there to help Catalans to live in reconciliation and brotherhood of all men and women. To live in solidarity with other cultures whilst maintaining their own identity.

Jack wondered what his friends really thought about a black Saint denouncing bigotry.

The change of patron Saints could only happen in Spain.

At last he got to the head of the queue and was alone in front of the Madonna. The black face was startling as they had proved it was not due to the wood, nor the paint nor the age of the image. Impressive silver work gleamed at Jack and reflected the spirits of those who passed through the tight little stairs. He followed tradition and kissed the orb representing the universe and held out his right hand straight in front of him as sufferance to her son Jesus.

He moved past, disappointed that she had nothing to say to him.

In the chapel at the rear of the Madonna he was immediately drawn to a tall statue of Saint George, central and dominating the small place of worship. He was fascinated by the presence and felt it was important on this day of decisions, as if the Saint was supporting him. He vowed to visit the shrine of Saint George on the cliffs of El Far as soon as possible.

He sighed and moved on but his decision making was becoming easier.

Outside the chapel was the holy fountain from which he took a deep swig of the cold water. The miracle of Jesus was reflected in the visitors by simply looking into these sacred waters.

Water as the symbol of life. Baptism into the Holy Spirit.

He didn't believe in the bureaucracy of any religion but he did believe in the spirituality of the millions of visitors over thousands of years and took comfort in their beliefs.

Going up the funicular to Saint Joan he had a magnificent view down the valley and across to the monastery on the opposite side. It seemed close enough to touch as it stood in all of its majesty, its symbolic status matched by the awe of its physical being. He strode out into the hills towards the derelict and long closed restaurant and the hovels for the hermit, built into the soft limestone along a natural fissure. He clambered through what was left of the old buildings and continued up a screed path, watching some climbers attack a huge rock mound and then stepping through the undergrowth he reached the summit of a peak far from the madding crowd. The view was awesome across to a different valley in the south, desolate and isolated in its beauty.

He sat and thought about Bridget and cried for himself. For his life and the loneliness he felt.

He cried for Karina who was his Sun Sharer but unavailable.

Finally, he cried for his son because he was never there for Joseph.

Picking up some old pieces of briar he made a cross by balancing a single piece across two uprights that were close together and held in place by a mound of stones. He said his seven pleas and sat with the Collective under the winter sun. As legend has it, a briar cross from the crown of Jesus was lost somewhere on those hills and as he wended his way down he casually searched for it, wondering if it was ever meant to be found.

Jack's last act before he left the magic above Montserrat was to wind his way up a tiny path where he came to the most spectacular view of the monastery far below him.

He could see the whole of the high valley blued out beneath and in the distance the lower one crossing at right angles to his view. He noticed a brass plaque that someone had fixed to a large rock at the lookout point. It read in Catalan.

> *? es la ma misteriosa*
> *Que ens apropa a les coses*
> *Que volem I ens allunya de*
> *Les que ja tenim*
>
> *Josep Lluis 24 09 91*

Words resounded in his head.

Listen to your heart and soul Jack.
Follow your path, you know you have no choice,
follow your path and reach out to the spiritual level
that awaits you.

He took a photograph with his mobile and translated it later.
The missing word scratched to oblivion by time puzzled him.
'What? or Hope? is the mystery which takes us closer to the
things we want and further away from what we already have.'

After a soul searching day – a day of decisions – he was ready to
join Karina sitting in the Girona hospital with Josep Maria.

Dappled light slanted through the room as the mimosa tree
gently shook in the breeze outside the second floor window. It was
March the tenth and a light dusting of gold fell from the tree and
settled on the window sill. She stood and drew her finger across
the sill writing a small JM and alongside an equally-sized JGE.

Josep Maria lay on his back in his coma with his mouth dry
and cracked and a small weep coming from his right eye. His face
was contorted out of shape and looked ugly.

Karina looked with solemn eyes at Jack as he crept into the
room. She whispered sadly, "So it's finally come to this."

"It's come to nothing yet," said Jack. He looked at her with
amazing strength and conviction in his eyes. Then he smiled,
pouring his spiritual energy into her heart and mind. "Don't worry
so; it's not over until it's over. You mustn't give up on him yet.
You may not want him to live but you can't deny him life even if
it means your unhappiness."

Karina looked offended and sniffed back her tears. "I have
always loved him. He gave me my children, my lifestyle, material
things like my house and money. I would be nothing without him
and yet I could also be everything without him if I came to you, but
you have to live your path Jack and this is mine. I know I've said I
want to run away and my life is just convenient but the convenience
is at least with respect in my case."

Jack sat on the bed and put his hands on either side of the unconscious Josep Maria's head.

He slowed his breathing to match the patient and closing his eyes, he quietly called for Nim.

"Nim, I have joined the Collective once a day and seven times I have asked to help everyone else in the world. I have never asked anything for myself or my family. I have even offered my life if required to do something immense to help our world. So I am asking you now to help my Sun Sharer Karina. I know and believe you are truly a part of my life and I accept my path and understand the part I have to play."

He lifted his head and took a deep breath before pushing his spirit into Josep Maria's mind. He searched for him and started to enter the Collective, taking Josep Maria with him.

They walked together across an azure sea and met old friends who touched Josep Maria's head as he passed and they wished him good health. Exhausted, Jack loosened his grip on the unconscious patient and fell backwards. Karina caught him and held him in her arms whilst he recovered.

She gently kissed his warm wet lips. "What have you done Jack?"

They both looked at Josep Maria. His face was normal and his breathing quiet and regular.

Jack held her hands and looked into her beautiful face. Brushing her auburn hair from across her left eye he told her, "My darling Karina, tomorrow he will wake and he will live exactly two years. Exactly you understand, no more and no less because that is the time you have been granted. That is all you have to make him spend the maximum time with his children and for you to be happy together."

She sobbed as she leant into him. "What about you Jack, I love you like it's the end of the world. How can I live without you?"

He hugged her close and ran his hands through her hair. Pulling her face towards him, he kissed her one last time. "You are my Sun Sharer but I can't have you in this life. I think this has happened before in previous lives and although we get closer to our ultimate destiny we still have challenges to meet to prove ourselves worthy to join that final level of consciousness. It's our path and we cannot change it. I love you my darling and we will see each other again in another time and space but not here and not now."

He stood and left, carrying on walking as he heard her collapse on to the bed with a sobbing groan.

He walked away from her, knowing she would be stable again.

He was glad to have beaten the demon within him who wanted Josep Maria dead.

He walked away, knowing he would have to go to England to solve his other issues, stronger in his belief about his path and the early steps required upon it.

The Edmunsons cancelled their alpine skiing holiday to Valmorel near Albertville so that they could attend Bridget's funeral in the pretty C of E church in Tarporley. They thought it would be a good idea to get away afterwards, but it never happened as Jack prevaricated until he could summon up the courage to tell Melanie he was leaving. He needed to be blunt and say the marriage was over, but it was a conflicting time for the gang of friends with so many secrets hiding behind closed doors.

Melanie was genuinely sad to have lost a friend and Jack was hesitant without Bridget's support. Matt and Harriet appeared to be moving apart from each other and Jean had stopped talking to Martin as she estimated how much mourning time to allow Peter before 'helping' him to be with her.

Jack's first thoughts were with Peter and so he would pop into the Garden Centre for a quick coffee and a chat to help him through the harsh realities of grief. Whether it was the shock of her death or the extra responsibilities without his partner's help he found his best friend quiet and reclusive. Jack decided to pull the boys together to try and help his best friend and therefore he arranged a drunken night in The Pheasant to ease all of their pain.

The barmaid sympathised with Matt, Jack and Martin as they waited for the widower to appear. The boys were staring at her pert breasts peeking over the black low cut blouse as she pulled the three pints of 'Old Dog'.

"I was so sorry to hear about Bridget. It certainly makes you think about your own life."

Jack agreed with her sentiments. "Friendliness and concern in human beings congregates our weaknesses through the morass of human humdrum in an effort to keep each other happy."

"What?" She hadn't understood a word and so he carried on simply.

"Health is the most important thing in life my lovely and certainly not money. Everyone says it and knows it but no one thinks about it or lives to that principle until something happens to them or their immediate friends and family. Then after a few weeks they forget that health is the most important thing in life and do nothing to improve it because they are too busy."

The conversation stopped abruptly as Peter arrived and the boys moved to a table to chat about football and cars, avoiding anything to do with wives and children.

The barmaid kindly frequented their table to replenish their beers and constantly flirted with Jack who responded in kind. "So when are you going to come to Spain with me lovely? Just you and me. One on one in the heat of the night."

"Why would I want to do that when I have a new black boyfriend Mr Edmunson? I have nicknamed him donkey by the way." She giggled, resting her hand on his shoulder waiting for their fourth round of orders.

Jack wasn't impressed by the competition. "I know you haven't got a new boyfriend and the reputation of black men is in your imagination my lovely."

"Ah but you don't know that Mr Edmunson and that always worries you blokes doesn't it?"

"No! I don't need to brag about the size of my penis to you my darling, because I am an expert lover and don't need size to be appreciated." A chorus of oohs came from the half drunken boys except Peter.

Matt egged him on. "Come on then Jack, what makes you

such an expert lover."

Everyone laughed at Jack, including the barmaid. He therefore had to justify his brag somehow. "The first thing you have to learn is to be precise when you are finding the sensitive spots inside a woman's vagina. The easiest way is to get your friendly doctor or consultant like Matt here and get him to use an indelible pen to mark up all the bits inside her vagina with the relevant letter. The a spot, the g spot, the f and e spot."

The barmaid chimed in. "What the hell is an f and e spot?"

"Well, there you go lovely; you are already missing out in life and need some private tuition from me. Anyway, get your doctor friend to lend you an endoscope and when you are making love tell your wife it's something new from Ann Summers and stick it up her fanny. You can manoeuvre your dick up inside and next to the scope if you want, ensuring your dick is in the right place and for the first time in years boys you can give her some real pleasure." Peter walked out to the toilet as Jack carried on, watching his back disappear into the gloom of the low beamed room.

"In fact the best thing is to have a forty-two inch LCD TV mounted on the bedroom ceiling and linked to the scope so when you are lying on your back; because as you're just a man let's face it that's where you will be, you can then get your dick spot on." The boys were encouraging all this with various comments like 'spot on Jack' and 'it would still be impossible to get my wife excited'. Jack was very drunk and on his fifth pint of Weetwoods.

"Best of all you can buy TVs nowadays that ,when you press a single button, it gives you a split screen. You could have so many pictures. Imagine boys, football on one, comedy on two, the scope on three and a porno movie on screen four. What a fantastic fucking night, you might even last more than the usual three minutes!" The laughter poured around the bar as more beer was sunk by the happy trio, constantly supplied by the barmaid who had been made into an honourable boy, but Peter remained quiet on his return and just gave an occasional smile.

Jack continued, "Then, during the second half of the footie you could have the holy grail of male sexual attainment, the second orgasm. You know what it is boys, as experienced when having gratuitous sex with someone at the office party, probably twenty years younger than your wife and thirty pounds lighter. Just remember though don't shout 'Goal!'." The barmaid passed them again and wanted to know more about the different spots she could experience if she became Jack's lover. She was collecting the empties and could look him in the face from a foot away so that the others couldn't hear.

"Mr. Edmunson, are you just bragging or have you truly found four different areas inside a woman?"

"What I say is what I do and what I do is what I say." His eyes danced as he flirted. So she walked away excited by the thought and hoped for a chance meeting with him in the village shop to arrange a secret meeting.

Although the night was supposed to be fun it didn't satisfy Jack and he worried about his best friend who became more morose with every pint. The booze deadened all the men's senses and numbed their problems as each man kept their own counsel about their female partners. There was very little happiness around as the booze took its toll, bringing more depressive thoughts as the night rolled on.

Jack quietly slipped outside for some fresh air. The stars were bright and he cried silently as he thought of Bridget but he was crying for himself, lost in his life and with bad hips and a bad back.

Peter joined him and stared at the stars.

"I've had enough of it all. I'm going home to my girls." They fell in side by side as they shared the first part of their walk home but the drink and joviality of their past would never occur again. Nothing was said until they reached the junction on the muddy path where they parted company.

Peter didn't look at Jack as he told him a secret for the first time. "I know you were shagging Bridget and now I realise what she meant to me. She was my rock and kept all of my family together. The sex wasn't important because I got my revenge with Melanie but you threatened my family life and I will never forgive that."

The threat was implicit in the last words he ever spoke to Jack. "One day you will die remembering what I said about my personal boundaries when we walked across this very field last year."

Jack wasn't scared of Peter anymore because he was aware of his own destiny now. Peter and Bridget were a small avenue off his true path and threatening words didn't change circumstances. He stared at Peter's stern face averted from him in the twilight and told him his future. "And you will die too Peter and so will you," but Jack knew the future and wasn't guessing about what might happen.

At home in the Cheshire set Jack and Melanie found excuses to be apart and talked seriously about Jack living separately. They were both unwilling to talk about Bridget. Their sex life came to halt now Jack knew the truth but he never baited her about Peter and she never mentioned Bridget. A truce of deception was declared but they argued over nothing.

After eleven texts to Melanie's mobile in the hour around supper time, Jack was exasperated. Each one had been duly commented on out loud and also answered. None of them were important; they just told each girlfriend what they were doing or more likely not doing. Texting each other to say nothing. The twelfth came in and beeped as they sat in silence eating their dinner with Joseph. She had the mobile by her plate and started to answer the message with a huge grin on her face.

Jack couldn't hack it any longer. "If you don't turn that fucking phone off, I am going to throw it out of the fucking window and bury it in the fucking garden, fucking twenty fucking feet deep." He stood and stormed out, leaving Melanie to explain to Joseph what fucking meant.

Only Nim listened of course and only Nim cared.

Nim knew everything.

Nim absorbed all the rage of mid-life which was no different to that of youth.

Just a last spin of the coin before it slowed down completely and went flatter and flatter on the table of life.

That evening in his study Jack made time to dial into broadband www.Traceamobile.com and all that it entails. You can pay twenty pounds a month and always know where your wife is within half a mile or so dependent on the aerials in her vicinity.

A simple call at key times of the day showed that she was lying about where she was and therefore by default she was lying about what she was doing.

It was a sad indictment of their marriage that Jack had sunk so low but at least he knew more now. It was an exaggerated behaviour because he had cheated on her. Understanding the lack of trust engendered by your own dishonesty. The terrible impasse that comes when you need to check exactly where your wife is every half hour but can do nothing about the result.

But living in the country you do get strange results. Three different aerials, three locations provided by the website at the same time. Jumping to conclusions which weren't always true because he rang his wife to find she was with Jean and not in Delamere Forest shacked up with her lover in a secluded car park.

The distrust is a direct result of your own trust in yourself.

He had decided to move out and rent a place.

Melanie and Jack could only communicate by letters and barely spoke whilst still living in the same house and using separate bedrooms.

It was the same as twenty years previously when they were just 'friends' following a break up in their 'on off' relationship. Melanie now wrote:

'Jack it's very hard for me right now for so many different reasons. Hard for me to ask you to find alternative accommodation as I know you won't be coming home again but then it's hard for me to have you here as it makes me stressed and upset.

Tonight, I am emotionally drained and feel utterly exhausted. I suppose adrenalin is keeping me going, together with having

Joseph around me but sleep deprivation really doesn't help in these situations.

You can't understand how very sad I feel about you leaving but I hope you will try. In a way it will also be a tremendous relief. Deceit and mistrust have plagued my mind with what you have been doing behind my back.

But we are nearly apart and I cannot change that and so perhaps you will be totally willing to forgive my behaviour too one day. Whether I totally trust you now, I don't know. I would like to and perhaps deep in my heart I do; as I always have done during the last twenty years.

I worry about you. How your mind is playing games, having to take sleeping tablets, not talking to anyone because you can't and won't trust them. I still believe you need professional help through this major time in your life, otherwise the gremlins that are eating away at you will still be there in years to come. I was shocked by your behaviour the other day when you were throwing things around, blanketed by the red mist in your mind as it should be me who could have acted like that but perhaps through all of this, it's showing me that I have more patience and strength than you ever imagined.

You aren't a bad person and I don't hate you but you must understand and accept you are not going to be there as a proper Father as you are breaking up our family unit. We will still have to talk as Joseph is our tie. He has always been my strength and we have a very strong bond together which I hope will never die. He means more to me than anything else in the world. I just hope he turns out a normal child despite your leaving and retains his enthusiasm, drive and happiness for life.

Life is very hard for me. Remember that because it is you who is doing this to me and no one else. You have always been the person I turn to, my confidant, friend, unselfish lover and support.

You say you want to do the best for me and Joseph. Really, financially is the only way you can do it as you won't be here for either of us. Your Mother is still right, you are being selfish and running away from things that are plaguing you but if you don't address them now they will be with you for a very long time.

I'm tired now, sad, unhappy and empty. I've got to pick myself up by tomorrow and put on the Mrs Happy face which I know will come back in true form one day. I know I can survive as I have 'fab' friends around me for support.

Guess what though? The last thing I want at this surreal time is another man in my life. I can and will survive without sex but I do need to be loved and hugged but Joseph's hugs will keep me going for an awfully long time. Take care of yourself, don't do anything stupid.'

Jack was intensely annoyed by this letter and found it demeaning after his own perceived five years of mental torture by her. He read every word as sanctimonious drivel, understanding the hidden innuendos directed at his emotional stability and telling him that it was his entire fault. The comment about his unfaithfulness was fatuous as she had her own deceits. The words about being a proper father reflected her determination to stop it happening as a punishment and she was already blaming him if Joseph didn't grow up as a normal child. How could she put on a hurt and innocent face to their friends who now seemed to ignore him because their minds had been poisoned by manipulative Melanie? Evilly turning the knife with poisonous words professing friendship and caring about him going crazy but emphasising her own strengths. Demanding money as the only thing he could do for her and Joseph. She even implied his Mother was on her side. She had used his crazy demented Mother to insult him and that summed up the nasty depths she was plumbing.

He dug deep into his files to pull out an old love letter from 1986 and found it to be a version of the same diatribe. He swore to himself as he read it. "You manipulative bitch you haven't changed at all. The same old manipulative Melanie making me crawl to you as the person who did wrong."

Jack tore both letters up and binned them with an angry toss.

He sat in the spare bedroom in Tettenhill and thought about the last few weeks.

"She wants to be my friend now but wants me out and only wants to talk about money. She starts every sentence in a brittle monosyllabic voice to re-explain the same fucking point again as if I can't remember the last time she said it and that I am mentally retarded."

In 1986 she wanted him for his looks, successful life and money. The same words, the same twists and he concluded it was a function of her personality.

"Except this time she is going to use Joseph to control me as she knows he is my weakness, my guilt trip."

As he glanced through the old file of love letters he found a poem he had sent to Rodney and Edima after number one had taken them away from him. He had written it in deep despair and as he read it again he started to weep uncontrollably.

> *Children of my life you are*
> *Tall and strong in visualar*
> *Tell me if you love me still*
> *As your Father I always will*
>
> *Need my help, my love, my care*
> *Without you here my heart does tear*
> *Keep me close and love me most*
> *Of your Dad I hope you boast*
>
> *I dream of you when you're not here*
> *Sometimes shed a lonely tear*
> *What is life all about?*
> *Being Dad to you I shout.*

He went to the kitchen and opened a bottle of red wine, drinking half of it in five minutes to ease his pain. Then he put his stereo on, keeping it low to avoid waking Joseph. Kneeling on the floor like a priest at prayer he used the bed as a table and started to write to the woman he thought he had loved.

'Twelve thirty in the morning. Melanie, how to explain?

I am sat near you but feel a thousand miles away and not separated by just two doors. Wine helps to remove my pain but it is only temporary. Lionel Richie helps and is playing on my stereo. The moon and trees help as I look out of the cottage window. I have not gone mad although you seem to think so. Lionel is singing on 'Louder than words' and the lyrics make me cry dripping my depressive thoughts away.

I have to explain why I can't live with you. I'm so sorry but I can't. I have another calling in my path. There's nobody else there for me, no other woman. It's simple. I just have to move on.

I should never have married you twenty years ago. You were very persistent, very nice, wanting me and I felt needed. Our wedding was beautiful, never forget that, but I wanted more and I settled for less. I know that is cruel but you know the real truth now. You knew that when you persistently chased me. You are a nice person but not towards me over the last five years as you only use your niceness with others now. Be proud and confident of yourself but you were not the one for me then or now.

I am sorry my weakness caused all this but no one is perfect.

I have no friends and you are my best friend despite our differences. Ignore the emotions and stay my friend but if you manipulate me even my friendship will die.

It must be very very hard for you and I understand that. It's lonely whether I am passing through here or in my hotel. Don't think I am happy and living a hell of a life. It's not true and I genuinely have no friends. Really, not Peter, not Harriet or Karina. I truly have no one.

I am not giving up the responsibilities of my son. I never will give up. I will always be there for him. I have rented a cottage near here to be there for him.

I suppose you have to love the person who thinks like you and not the one who looks like you. Most people lurch into marriage as it's convenient. Sharing things but without true love.

Jealousy was a big part of our relationship and on my part it was based on authority and power. I recognise that now and I will learn from it. You know, you truly do know there is no one else dragging me away.

We always talked by letters even all those years ago as we couldn't talk properly face to face because of all those pent up emotions.

I know I have lots more to achieve.

I know I want to be there for Joseph.

I know I don't love or want you anymore.

I know I am causing you terrible anguish and I am so sorry. So very sorry but you truly know that I can do no better than I am doing.

Life is crazy. Life is not a rehearsal.

I also believe that since Joseph was born you have been taking me for a ride on money. That's how I feel and although not necessarily the truth it has gotten worse as you blatantly ignored me and thought it was a never-ending pile of gold

After I told you I had to leave you I felt better. A great relief coming over me but having sex last weekend wasn't right as you were just taking advantage of me, manipulating me like in 1986 when I tried to get away from you. You are a control freak and have a controlling personality and need to recognise that.

The truth is I reject you and still love you as a friend but even that gets hard and is turning to hate when you spite me for no good reason except emotion.

I am a nice person and I have done everything possible to make this easy for you but I am not wrong in leaving you. I know that is true.

I am a lost soul but I know I need to move on. So you take care of yourself. I will always help you and be there but I can't be the one you need.

Please at least stay friendly if not my friend as it will help with Joseph.'

★   ★   ★

After she had read his latest letter they confronted each other over the expensive granite island in the kitchen.

Jack started the argument. "Those who make the world go round are people who have confidence in their own abilities and take on more responsibilities. Be a hammer not an anvil. That's what I do whilst you fanny about in La La land. I bet you haven't read my letter have you?"

Melanie yelled back, "Yes I have, it's just words Jack you have no consideration for me or Joseph. Everything is about you. You think I'm bad? Nobody can be as bad as you."

Jack retorted, "I can't believe you just said that. Everything is to your agenda and no one else counts. You can't see it can you? Just remember, what I say is what I do. What I do is what I say."

Melanie shrugged her shoulders as she said, "You are always complaining about your hips and back. It's all a question of mind over matter Jack."

Jack looked daggers at her. "Yes, you don't mind and I don't matter!" He spat it out and walked out of the room.

As Jack looked into the bathroom mirror he felt incredibly tired.

He stared into his eyes. Slowly, almost imperceptibly, his face seemed to smudge. As he continued to look, each of the flat surfaces, the forehead and cheeks, bulged slightly. After two minutes of staring he felt detached from his body and the face no longer had eyes. The image in the mirror crumpled and swirled very slightly as if in a fairground hall of mirrors. He was not looking at Jack George Edmunson. Violently he swung away. Glancing back he had to turn away again and walk out of the bathroom.

It had scared him and it repeated itself every day. A metamorphosis had begun. He didn't know it but he was on the last steps to meeting his spirit guide.

He walked downstairs and picked up the document he had created early that morning. Walking into the kitchen he asked Melanie to please sit and talk to him. He asked her twice as initially she refused.

They sat in the conservatory with a bleak grey sky surrounding them as he handed her the piece of paper headed 'How I will behave'.

They had talked all week about him leaving and her blunt reaction was how quick could he go and how was she going to cope for money.

He knew she would ignore the document in her hateful ignorance but at least he was trying to pave the way for the next year or two of grief and aggravation.

HOW I WILL BEHAVE
Fundamentally open and honest and highly principled

I apologise for losing my temper yesterday and will never do it again. I am only human and under intense pressure to keep earning money whilst doing something I hate.

I said I wanted to change my lifestyle by going to Spain and cannot live with you.

I still need to see Joseph as much as possible.

I said I would support you and Joseph financially through the emotional times until you become stable in a new life.

I have shared my secrets with you and shown you all my finances.

I have trusted you and continue to do so as if we have the same relationship as the last twenty years.

But I am worried you are taking advantage of my nature especially when it comes to spending money. It would be very easy to react; you know people make life terrible in many ways which are both emotional and financial. I will not react. That's what most people do and I am not most people.

I have made five thousand pounds a month available to cover your expenses and of course most people live on far less.

I have written to my solicitor accepting the divorce proceedings but you need to reconsider your position restricting my access to Joseph to four times a year as that is only trying to punish me.

My son loves me and needs me and you need to consider him.

Last night's big bust up was the last.

I cannot take the stress and am right on the brink so please don't push me over.

Have respect for what I am trying to do and help me work through it, rather than fight me.

At least I had the courage to bring everything to a head.

I know it's my fault but marriages need two people to make them fail. Maybe it's sixty to forty per cent or seventy to thirty, I don't know.

Please stick to the principles or tell me you cannot and you totally hate me so that I know where I stand.

I cannot make it any easier for you, I am doing my best. I am sorry.

I will be in other accommodation next week. I do need to come here for odd things and hope you understand this.

Melanie sat and read the principles in silence.

Standing up in front of him and without tears and with no emotion she rammed her words down his throat.

"I want you to get out of our life now. You are not a fit father for Joseph, you never have been. I will keep you away from him as much as possible. You are a fucking bastard Jack and I have already seen my solicitor in Crewe yesterday and I am going to screw you for every penny you have and then a little bit more. Now pack your things and fuck off out of our lives because it's war."

Jack was inwardly shocked, his sensitivities permanently damaged as he calmly replied in a flat and unemotional tone, "Melanie that is exactly what I expected of you. I have done nothing wrong and am trying to make it easy and see my son. I can't believe you have stooped so low but that is the root cause of why I want out. You are unbelievable."

Jack made a list of priorities and kept it in the front of his car as the best place to see it at least twice a day.

Joseph
No complaints.
No personal chats. Don't engage with Melanie or you go round in circles!
Keep it super simple. Simple does not mean cheap.
Assertive, it is my life.
Slim.
Write my book.
Learn Spanish.
Take control.

But the list was only words and it was actions that made a difference.

Melanie sat facing Joseph over breakfast when he asked sadly.

"Mum, can I go and see Dad in Yapanc?"

She prompted him, "Why?"

Jojo squirmed in his seat. "Well, he could take me to the water park on the slides and buy me ice creams."

She smiled and ruffled his hair. "My darling boy, I'm so sorry Daddy has left you but that was his choice. He couldn't take you there or buy you ice creams as it's winter Joseph and nothing will be open."

Joseph sat deep in thought, remembering holding his Dad's hand, sitting on the rocks and looking at the sun.

"Do you think he could take me to see the Three Kings arrive by boat and then I could give them my present list because I can write one after Christmas when I know what Santa forgot?"

"I don't think Daddy will be able to afford the air fare darling because Ryanair have just increased their prices. Anyway, I'm sure Santa will bring you everything you want darling and if anything is missed then we can go and buy it together in the sales in January. How about that?"

Jojo's thoughts about his missing Daddy had passed and he readily agreed to his Mum's suggestion and carried on eating his Coco Pops.

A thoughtful Melanie dropped him off at school before driving to Crewe to meet her solicitor to start the divorce proceedings and discuss the amount of money they would demand. She had already decided to be awkward about access to Joseph until forced to concede by a court order, as she knew it would hurt Jack and might force him to contribute more. Malevolent Melanie carried out her plan hatched a year before and naive and sensitive Jack guiltily left the UK.

Jack left on Bonfire Night and drove through France to Yapanc with a brief overnight stop at Tugdual's house in Meaux. He swore at the traffic around Paris, watched the countryside as he cruised past the vineyards growing Bridget's favourite Pouilly-Fumé and admired the volcanoes behind Clermont Ferrand, but it was all so superficial.

His CDs, downloaded by Bridget for his ear alone, played constantly.

Avril Lavigne poured out 'When you're gone' and made him cry. Natasha Bedingfield rendered 'Soul Mate' and kept the tears flowing. He breathed in every word and thought of her but he was grieving for himself.

He cried because he had left Joseph and that reminded him of Rodney and Edima leaving with number one.

He cried because his old friends had disowned him and ganged up around Melanie in an impenetrable wall.

He cried because he knew his Sun Sharer in Catalonia was never going to be with him.

He cried because his soul and spirit had failed to reach their potential. He knew he would never complete his book and had deliberately left it on his PC in Tettenhill as a collection of thoughts, as a diary on an unfulfilled life. He remembered Edima had told him to go to classes to learn how to write using a proper structure. Jack had countered, "D.H. Lawrence didn't go to classes did he? I don't want to read other books for ideas or copy their format because I want my thoughts to be original and my book to be a piece of me."

How he could make enough money for Joseph and Melanie to live on?

How he could pay the two mortgages and household bills when he couldn't contemplate work?

He drove the eleven hundred miles and nineteen hours down the road to despair.

The apartment was cold and lifeless when he arrived.

Yapanc was tranquilo as few people lived there during the winter and most of the hotels and all of the small bars were shut until Christmas. A few hardy Brits walked the coastal path but as the temperature could dip to five degrees Celsius with two or three days of continuous rain, the area still had no attraction despite the one penny air fares from the UK.

Jack settled in by constant cleaning. Work rather than thought and all accompanied by Girona radio 40 P, Quarenta Principales, the national station regionalised to make it more palatable. It played constant hit after hit from its top forty selected tunes and gave light relief from the aburrido – the boredom.

No one contacted him from home and he sought no contact from those he knew locally.

A self imposed isolation equivalent to a solitary confinement cell as punishment for his misdemeanours and his constant feelings of guilt.

13
Endings

L ate November and early December was a thoroughly
depressing time in Yapanc.

He saw nobody and felt desperately lonely, staring out
of the window at the pines and the ever changing sky, realising
how it must feel to be widowed, old and alone. Marooned in
the dead holiday resort he questioned whether he had told the
truth about his life over the last few years and whether he had
correctly judged others.

Was he a reprobate having a traditional mid-life crisis and
going nowhere fast except downhill?

He sat and thought too much and always used Nim to query
his own answers.

"Surely it was right to challenge the norm and think about things
outside of the day to day basics? Outside of the boxes that encumber
one's life; the TV, the car, the PC and the house. Surely it's right
to try and change your life when you know things are so wrong."

*That's why you are here and now you need to move
on and leave the boxes behind.*

But time seemed endless and his thoughts were never fulfilled.

★   ★   ★

The national holiday on Constitution Day in December brought a modicum of respite.

The Barcelona weekenders came to stroll and smell the sea salt mixed with the blue smokey sweetness of the wood fires, spiced by the green pine cones that traditionally went into the log burners. They call the holiday period El Puente, the bridge, as there is a normal day bridged between two public days and therefore this one inevitably became a holiday too. The Spanish found as many excuses as possible for national holidays and admirably chose their families instead of work. It was a 'taster' for Christmas followed by the New Year and then Los Tres Reyes or Epiphany. Four long holidays to reinvigorate the Catalan family values and for the locals a time to de-stress, ready for the run into the new holiday season and the inevitable hard work once again. The Catalans knew what was important in life and asserted their rights to live their lives with the right values and the right issues taking priority. An amazing contrast in every way to the rushing and spending obscenities of the same period in England. The locals would promenade on Sunday lunchtimes and then sit for a three hour menu del dia, menu of the day, in front of warm log fires giving off the beautiful aroma of Baix Emporda in the winter. Cool at nights it could rise to eighteen or more by one in the afternoon as the sun reached its peak in the bright blue winter's sky and just as quickly the temperature would plummet as it slid behind the inevitable low cloud that crept in from the west.

Karina and Jack met just once and that was accidentally in the Café Centro on the main square of Palafrio. She said Melanie telephoned her regularly once a week in an effort to check up on what he was doing but Karina told Melanie the truth; that she hadn't seen him. She had deliberately kept away from Jack as soon as she knew he was leaving Melanie so that she didn't need to lie about anything now or in their past. It was a dangerous time in her mind as she was worried that Melanie would contrive to implicate her with Jack and that would ruin her safe life with Josep Maria.

Josep Maria was out of the hospital in Girona and from being a virtual vegetable he improved every day to partake in his family life away from the business, taking the children to school and pottering in his garden. Jack glanced around to make sure they weren't watched and then touched her face, pushing back the auburn hair. "You look tired Karina, I'm so sorry."

She clutched his hand tightly. "Jack, you are constantly in my mind." She bowed her head for a moment before looking into his eyes. "You know I love you but I have to be there for Josep Maria and the children. If I was there for you instead, his family would cut me off without a penny and I can't risk that because I need to protect my children before thinking of you. I'm sorry but there's no choice. I love you Jack but I said everything at the hospital. I am not your Sun Sharer."

Her words saddened him as he replied, "Isn't that a terrible thing? Money and security overriding true love."

She continued thoughtfully, her head leaning on her left hand, "It's so sad you know. On some days I don't think I can cope."

Jack grasped her other hand. "You can cope and you will cope Karina; be strong for your family. I am your angel and I believe that we were meant to meet, that it was in our spiritual paths. Everyone needs a spiritual mentor and at least I can give you that as my final gift, no matter what happens in the future and no matter where you are. I will always be there in spirit for you to rely on." He dropped her hands gently to the table and pushed down to stretch himself back and away from her so he could see into her eyes.

She spoke slowly and clearly, "Thank you for everything you have given me Jack. You have shown me how to live." Then she despairingly stood and avoiding his eyes she walked away without a backward glance.

Jack slowly pressed his hands together on the table in front of him and with closed eyes he lowered his head on to them and cried softly saying to himself over and over again, "You are my Sun Sharer Karina, you truly are."

Sitting on the balcony with his feet resting on the top railing, Jack realised that the tall pine next to his apartment was dying. The normally bright green needles had faded to browns and weak yellows and many of the smaller branches were completely bare. He could now clearly see the long piece of black plastic binding holding the thick cable that constituted the fragile power supply for all of the properties.

It was a beautiful fresh morning with blue sky appearing between the gaps in the tree cover opposite. Last night had been very humid as warm sea air hit Yapanc in the late afternoon as soon as it had gone dark on that short December day. Jack had felt his feet slipping ever so slightly on the damp paving whilst slowly walking down the hill towards the beach but the humidity had been blown away as he leaned out clutching the blue railings. Looking right he could view the two hills set behind the beach and a few clouds with pink bellies. Beneath him was the top of a black yard light and around it in a beautiful pattern was a pretty kaleidoscope of pink, grey and brown stones collected from the beach and carefully arranged by Joseph that summer just fifteen weeks previously. The light caught the shimmer of a single spider's line that must have been six feet long. It moved of its own accord high in the treetops dancing through the rays of sunlight. Blue wood smoke drifted across the pine canopy for a few minutes and then it was gone leaving a lingering taste in his mouth. He had been sitting there for two hours without realising it; as time was now meaningless. Rossini's Tancredi rang out clear and beautiful from the Denon Hi Fi. The sweetly sung words of the fifteenth aria brought the beauty of his view alive.

> 'The face of love would once again
> shine smiling and fair at last;
> And his heart would find peace
> And sweet tranquillity in her arms.
> His content should be a recompense
> For so many sufferings and tears;
> His constancy should be crowned
> With pure joy and eternal love.'

He had always wondered what it would be like to be out of the rat race, retired and with nothing particular to do and now he realised that everything he had strived for and all of his dreams seemed worthless.

You need structure and actions in your life or life doesn't exist. The actions can be meaningless like painting a room or meaningful like saving someone's life but all human beings need to do something on most days to be content with themselves and their psyche and to maintain an equilibrium.

His mind was blank and seemed permanently sore. A sore mind that wanted to turn off after too much thinking. Sammy and Samantha, Jojo's favourite red squirrels, ran quickly up and down the pine trunks, stopping occasionally to look for the dangerous cats. They then bounced off across the umbrella of pines, seemingly doing nothing but happy to be bouncing around.

On how many occasions had he told friends and colleagues, "You can't buy time. Life is not a rehearsal." So when you have changed your life and bought a little time, what do you do with it?

He telephoned Mother. "Hi Mum, how are you feeling today?"

She whined back in a small voice, "Is that Jack? Where are you?"

"I'm in Spain Mum remember, I live here now?"

"How are Melanie and Joseph? Are they there because I need to know what they want for his birthday?"

"No Mum, remember I have left Melanie and am living permanently in Spain. On my own. Remember, my new simple life?"

"I can't remember. What's the weather like?"

"It's been warm and wet. They have had a lot of rain but they need it because the reservoirs are only twenty per cent full. They have had a drought for two years."

"Oh! It's cold and wet here too. Is Melanie there? I need to ask about Christmas presents. I'm going to go to the seaside I think. I don't like your brother."

"No Mum, Melanie and I are separated. She lives in Tettenhill."

"Are you in Rosset?"

"No Mum, I'm in Spain."

"What's the weather like? It's cold and wet here."

"Sorry, Mum got to go. I love you lots, always try and remember that, maybe write it down. Love you Mum."

Mother singing the words in a sweet high pitched tone: "Love you…"

Jack spoke to Nim, "You need to leave me now and go and stay with Mother. I think she needs more guidance than me. Look after her please."

Just eleven steps took him from the balcony to the front door of the apartment and then out to his SLK for the short drive into town. He slowly walked alone into the town square in Palafrio hoping to find someone to talk to. A chat, a smile a cortado – coffee, just a piece of life to keep him sane and caffeine for his stinking headache. He had hit the Vino Blanco de Mesa – table white wine – the night before, costing a fraction over one euro from Carrefour. Drinking straight out of the carton, he had downed a litre in just under an hour. A nasty way to try and find solace. But the town itself was quiet on a Tuesday at ten thirty in the morning. Fish market girl asked Jack how he was.

"Mi siento solo, I am lonely."

She smiled warmly, "We have a saying in Spain, from nothing begins something." Jack loved the way the Spanish radiated happiness like the sun.

"Thank you, that's a nice thought. Let's hope it is true!"

He sat alone in Café Centro with his Zumo de Naranja, Cortado and Tortilla Integrale – orange juice, coffee and omelette in wholemeal bread – glancing at the news in *La Vanguardia* and thinking about why he was in Yapanc. "Nim, I thought I had moved on in thirty-one years, but when I was twenty-one I also had a flat that I owned, I ate, I drank, I had a fast new car, I had plenty of shags, I was happy and had nice friends. I went to beautiful Greek islands for holidays and had a fabulous time feeling warmly welcomed and loving my life. The truth is, I think I have gone backwards. You see the important things stay the same, consistently through your life. Simple things like true love. I need to live a simple life Nim, everyone does."

Define simple life Jack?

"That's easy," but he hesitated. "A book on fish, flowers and birds, for the area where I live. A real log fire, a simple large room in a beautiful spot where you can eat, sleep, talk and be. A comfortable chair to look at a beautiful view, with a natural garden made up of rocks, trees and plants, with a vista out to the horizon so you can watch the sky as it changes shapes and colours through the days of every season. A radio with a battery pack so you can sit anywhere and listen to it or get up and dance. Walking to the beach to find razor shells in the rock pools to cook on an open fire made from driftwood."

He drifted away in his imagination before continuing dreamily, "I want someone who loves me for what I am and not what I seem to be.

Someone to listen and accept not question and change.

To see me as a truly sensitive caring and sharing person and not an over-assertive type of guy.

I want someone who loves me for my inner self not my Mercedes and Rolex watch.

For my smile and conversation and not my achievements.

For trying and failing but supporting my trying.

To share my hurt and pain and joy and laughter in equal measure without question or complaint.

To do things with me that I love.

To climb a mountain, sail a sea or plant a garden.

To live simply, not obscenely, and embrace all people without prejudice or criticism.

To share my reality, my realism that what we have on Earth should be cherished, nurtured and loved because life is not a rehearsal, it's here and now.

But above all I want to be happy.

Am I right Nim or am I living a fantasy?"

*You are right Jack, but most people never try to
find a Simple or 'Real Life' because it's too hard to
contemplate or too hard to change the existing one.
They are not old souls like you; they are too
entrenched in reality to contemplate more subjective
matters about life itself.*

He paid the bill, leaving a ten euro tip, and looked around slowly whilst breathing in the delicious smells of the pastries and breads. As always Café Girl gave him a big warm smile as she said goodbye.

Rather than drive straight back to the apartment Jack opted for the Lighthouse route and pulled his Merc into the Hotel El Far car park. The cold Tramuntana wind whipped into him as soon as he opened the car door. He clutched his jacket closer to his body and moved with head bent towards the railings on the cliff edge.

The sea was coated with a vicious spray sliced off the top of a large swell and although you could still see to the horizon there were no boats within sight. He pushed on further down the red and white signed tourist footpath alongside the old walls of the Nunnery fronting the seaward side of the hotel. As he arrived at the cave in the cliff, the image of Saint George stared out proud and defiant. Screwing up a fifty euro note he threw it into the wishing pot beneath the statue and well back behind the wrought iron gates of the shrine.

"Thank you for your guidance Nim. I wonder what Saint George makes of his flock in Catalonia. That's some responsibility being a Patron Saint especially when you have been usurped by a woman!"

I am always there for you Jack.

Jack pushed to the end of the track and perched himself on a ledge of outcropping rock and shielded from the wind so that he could re-search the sea for boats. He glanced down the six hundred foot drop and contemplated the potential fear experienced if you took the thirty second plunge to a certain death.

The giant green and yellow cacti alongside the path were motionless in the Tramuntana but the pines above the Bronze Age dig were creaking as they withstood the blasts of cold air whistling down from the Pyrenees. Shivering, he climbed back into his car and weaved his way down the headland road past the fabulous houses of the rich, mainly old money not new. On past more pine trees slanting thirty degrees from the upright and then suddenly he cut down a one way street the wrong way, knowing there was no traffic in November.

He finally pulled up by the Yapanc marina, which was sheltered from the northerly by the El Far headland. The calm still waters of the protected harbour were perfectly clear, encapsulated by the pink granite so that he could see the rocks on the bottom and the languid fish barely moving in the cold sea. Walking around the top of the outer wall he could see the waves crashing onto the Islas Formigas and then onward onto Cap Roig. But across the Yapanc cove it was calm until you reached the edge of the opposing headland.

He settled on a rock with the sun warming his back and let his mind soak in the colours, shapes and noises of Yapanc, laid out in a crescent in front of him. The church clock chimed two and the clear tone carried across the bay before it was whipped out of hearing by the Tramuntana.

The small sailing dinghies were pulled well away from the sea at this time of year and were nestled close to the promenade, away from the drainage channel that had cut a wide, deep swathe across the beach after the torrential rain the day before. A few Menorquina day boats were left between the dinghies and the publica rampa – public ramp – but even this launching area was chained and locked in December. Nothing moved much in the winter. A few hardy sailors ventured out but only on perfect sailing days of force three winds, small waves and lots of sun. The Wisteria bar sat dead in the corner, betrayed by its customers who loved it for a few months every year and abandoned it for the majority. Time enough for the climber to rebuild its energy and then for the foliage to re-blossom, just like the family who owned the bar who also needed some time for respite.

He strolled back to the apartment via the escalas, dumping his car by the marina.

The apartment was pristine and cleaned to the 'nth' degree.

Jack sat on the balcony staring at the pine trees again but didn't see the beauty anymore. Neither the shivering light across the greener needled tops nor the six magpies in three pairs that danced across the earth beneath in playfulness more than a search for food. Enrique Iglesias crooned 'Somebody's me' on his 'Insomniac' album and then Jack played the same song in Spanish but sounding ten times better as if the words were meant to be sung. 'Alguien soy yo' and he understood every word for the first time as a tear slid down his left cheek, bouncing between the stubble left over from the last few days.

He remembered Bridget's soft loving words. "Never feel down my love, you can always ring me and talk at any time. I will always be there to listen to my best friend and lover." But Bridget was gone, his acquaintances were gone, his son and wife were lost to him and there was no one to talk to except Karina and that was impossible now.

When you have found your Sun Sharer and love them as life itself, it becomes an all-consuming emotion. If your Sun Sharer loves you as deeply and sincerely then you should be deliriously happy, because you are one of the few people in the world who have achieved the ultimate spiritual love. But Karina could never be his and he would never ask her to shed her responsibilities, because that would taint everything they knew they had together.

His chest felt as though someone was standing on it and his mind was blanked and numb. Tears fell onto the balcony tablecloth and made the dark blue darker in random spots as he sobbed uncontrollably with his head in his hands, leaning on the fabric. Jack thought about giving up on his quest.

"Nim, is spiritual love just bollocks anyway? Can anyone live their life on a higher plane and truly believe in spiritual things? All those people whose lives are captured in a book or film. Can their thoughts and dreams really be a guide to living? Surely, you need to make up your own mind and stop giving others time to constantly intrude into your life."

> *Spiritual love is the only true love.*
> *Giving yourself time to consider it, is the only*
> *true path.*

He dwelt further on the matter. "Pure thought is only generated from a pure soul uninhibited by the mundane debris pervading today's modern existence. Because that is what it is; an existence, a structured convenient way to get from birth to death with the minimum pain rather than the maximum challenge, achievement and love.

'Real Life' Pfur! You see Nim no one tries anymore. I tried and I tried again and then again and although I thought I was tough, a Leo not a Pisces, I can't try anymore because apart from you nobody listened to me.

And Nim that's what hurts. I wanted to change my world and I have failed."

Jack sighed deeply and walked back into the apartment leaving the patio window wide open and hot air convecting outwards to mingle with the cold outside. He walked into Joseph's room and picked up his swimmers, goggles and towel. Slipping into his battered brown Pikolinos shoes he went out of the apartment door and closed it without locking it for the first time. He always saw the beauty of the headland as its rocks and pines lurched into the sea at the end of his road – but not today. The one hundred and fifty one steps past the Hotel Cassemar reminded him of his scale for judging true love. Bridget was always below twenty about him and he was always sixty-seven about her and it had never changed because their love was built on just a little, but never enough spirituality for Jack. About halfway down the steps he thought of Bridget again as he stared at the dark blue sea wallowing across the rocks in the dying sun. When he reached the bottom he thought of Karina on his scale and concluded she was zero, his Sun Sharer.

There was no one on the promenade in front of the shuttered hotels and bars as a biting wind had started to whistle in from the east backing from the northerly Tramuntana. The waves in the bay began to build and swell and deposit their pulverised foam on the wet sands. Jack sat on the beach near the rocks for a good hour, seeing nothing but hearing the call of the sea as it hauntingly swished across the tiny granules. The pink dusk faded quickly and the blackness came, pierced by the lighthouse spraying its beam six hundred feet above him and talking to the fishing boats telling them to stay away. The light talked to the beautiful stars and they shared their intensity with whoever was looking.

There was no mental pain anymore and no breathlessness for Jack huddled on the sands. It was biting cold and way past five am. The Llevant wind forced its way harder into the cove and channelled the heat out of his body towards Karina's house. He stripped off his clothes and waded out into the freezing sea, gasping with cold as he pulled with strong strokes away from the shore. As he rose on the crests of waves he could see the Islas Formigas and Cap Roig, as he was so far out from the shore, and so he stopped to tread water, tired of trying to be different, tired of changing the world as he felt the hypothermia eating into him.

The beautiful stars gleamed high above as Nim floated across the surface towards Jack.

A bright white figure with the friendly old face of Granddad George, the sea reflecting the phosphorescence onto his white coat, his feet barely touching the water and his gnarled right hand slowly stretching out across the darkness as the sea closed over Jack's head.

There was no panic, no last deep breath, nothing special said. It was just easier like that.

Jack's tears mingled with the black sea and for the first time his mind was as clear as the sky he had left above.

> *Water to water.*
> *We came from the oceans and we return via the oceans.*
> *You come into this life with nothing and you go out*
> *with nothing.*
> *Soon to merge into the clay in the depths.*
> *From one life to another life led by your own Nim.*
> *If you believe, that is.*
> *Do you believe?*

Remember Joseph, "It's never over until the fat lady sings."

And so Nim, "Was the story a myth and in my imagination or not?

It doesn't really matter now.

Fifty is not the new forty and more is truly less.

Remember and believe all you have read.

Love from Jack"

Many people ask detailed questions about the contents or share ideas through the website www.thesunsharer.com but I want to leave you with a few personal thoughts before the second book in the trilogy called *A Path Too Long* is published in October 2010 and the third *Someone Something* in Spring 2011.

The pseudonym
My acquaintances have often said, "I bet I'm in it", but my friends know if they are. All writers take and bend their existence, carefully watching what people do and say and then make an abortion of the truth and reality.

That is why I have no desire to be associated with the character of Jack although the book is deliberately written to look like an autobiography. Love him or hate him, it's not me, although I would have enjoyed his explicit sex but without the guilt.

Does he live or does he die? You have to wait for the sequel *A Path Too Long*!

Sex bordering on porn
It highlights the lack of love found in many relationships. It's the truth isn't it? How boring is your own love life?

The use of this type of writing is particularly apt in *A Path Too Long* as it is a measure of self control, but it is eliminated in the final book *Someone Something* to highlight pure love with a Sun Sharer.

I also threw in the coarse humour as it tells the truth behind the laughter. Overall I created a supernatural romp with moments bordering on *Viz* but all of this is a veil covering the serious messages underlying the Trilogy.

Islam versus Christianity is topical
We seem to ignore the fact that many cultures are still happy to follow a level of self control that the Western World appears to have lost to materialism. It is also very sad that the Eastern Cultures crave our way of life and are pursuing it intently.

Wars in the Middle East and Afghanistan are played out with apathy in the Christian World and deep hate in that of Islam. Beliefs start wars and despite the instant media coverage it resembles a boring DVD to most people, never to be watched on a Saturday night.

There are lessons to be learned.

Love

Try the ten points listed in the book on your parents. You may be shocked by the result.

I wanted to show the emotional links between friends, children and their parents on many levels so the reader can see how they interact and thus develop an alternative view.

The manipulation and hate of Book One has an unexpected impact in *A Path Too Long* as the heart-rending loss of love within the closed and perpetual cycle of child and parents is offset by new love in new relationships.

However, death and Alzheimer's disease is used to intensify your thoughts about true emotion.

The number 7 and spiritual issues

Nim, the Collective and links to symbols, numbers and beliefs can never be discredited because their subjective reality is constantly in our minds. Therefore, I made spiritual links believable as they affect what we do even when we disbelieve. Jack is used as an anti-guru figure to prove that non-belief is as strong as something physical. The grey areas of Good versus Evil play between the lines of a black antithesis to a traditional romance.

We all have a past or karma and I have used the hint of a Roman Centurion as an example of what many people believe but never pursue. This theme is developed further in the sequel. This human weakness is an essential part of our psyche as we are all scared to die. Fifty down and fifty to go is a nice thought.

Cheshire versus Catalonia

The cultural differences were astounding but only after living in both places for a few years.

We notice the obvious physical differences on holidays and neglect the people's thoughts.

A Path Too Long identifies how our views differ, whether on racism or the news, and uses the ignorance of the expats in Spain to highlight what we can learn.

Whether it is the Cheshire set or Home Counties set you may recognise yourselves as I wanted to make the book an indictment of a type of lifestyle that appears selfish and self-centred. Not because everyone thinks like that but because of how others perceive the successful middle-aged, middle classes i.e. 'Forget anyone else. I've got and you haven't.' Up their own arses.

Is that the truth? I personally never judge people. I take them for what they are and how they behave with me and me alone.

Marriage

I don't know many married people who really love each other. I have seen many couples who are together for convenience or because they think it is too hard to break up. Add the lifestyle of your particular 'set', rush around doing, stop thinking and you have a recipe for a social disaster.

What morals and principles do we want to teach our children? Stick together, grin and bear it or break up in an open and honest way and stay friends. Infidelities occur all the time. Judge the risk, take a chance and live with the guilt. It's a nasty cycle.

The guilt then changes behaviours and the marriage gets worse.

The end of the world

This is highly topical in books and films and integrates with the potential for life after death or reincarnation.

A Path Too Long and *Someone Something* take the arguments into another realm. The end of our world through global warming, viruses or natural disasters is a symptom of global dementia.

We fight each other and by default we will find a way to endemically destroy each other. But I guarantee we will see and understand what we are doing. However, like temporary bad health we will think it is awful at the time and within a few weeks forget it and resume our selfish materialistic lives.

Yapanc and the Baix Emporda

Go there. It is Nirvana.

A Path Too Long is mainly set in Catalonia and further explores the region and its culture with the climax of the Trilogy unavoidably linked to this piece of heaven on Earth.

Jack George Edmunson
Feb 2010

Notes

PAGE   LYRICS, POETRY, ARTICLES AND BOOKS

76   The words from the Koran are published within this superb
        book which gives a sympathetic hearing to Islam at a time when
        Moslems are deemed to be enemies. The novels within my
        trilogy discuss the tensions between religions but my fourth
        novel places the issues deep within the plot.
        Book: *Understanding Islam* by Matthew S Gordon.
        ISBN: 1903296749 Duncan Baird Publishers. Copyright
        2002 Duncan Baird Publishers.

175   The *Daily Mail* article 5/10/04 featuring excerpts from Doctor
        Laura Schlessinger cannot have given a complete picture and
        so I suggest you read one of her books to decide for yourself.
        I think men and women co-exist for genetic convenience and
        never agree truly agree about anything!
        One original book: *The proper care and feeding of husbands* by
        Dr. L. Schlessinger.
        ISBN: 9780060520618 Harper Collins. Copyright 2004
        Doctor Laura Schlessinger

203   Don't ask me to judge wonderful people who have a clear
        definition of life. Have a good look at the website and decide
        for yourself.
        Book: *Seven Shamanic Levels of Consciousness* by Dirk Gillabel.
        ISBN: Self Published. Copyright 2001 Dirk Gillabel
        A few words from www.soul-guidance.com guided by Dirk
        Gillabel, email sun19@earthlink.net

205   'Sortlifeout.co.uk, 'the top level of consciousness is nothingness,
        none being Nirvana.' The website is now a holistic catalogue so
        go and buy something spiritual if you want.

213   *A Brief History Of Time* – Well time may have ceased by now
        as it all depends on the tenth Doctor Who winning the battle
        against The Master. Checkout the BBC website!
        Book: *A Brief History of Time* by Stephen Hawking

ISBN: 9780553175211 Bantam Books (Random House).
Copyright 1988 Stephen Hawking

214 *The Da Vinci Code.* I think the book was better than the film.
I also wish I was as rich as Dan Brown. No, not really. As
famous? Maybe.
Book: *The Da Vinci Code* by Dan Brown
ISBN: 9780593054253 Bantam Press.
Copyright 2003 Dan Brown

218 I drove to Spain in 2007 listening to Nelly Furtado, 'Lovers to
friends, why do all good things come to an end?' It makes you
cry too much.
Song: All Good Things (Come To An End) CD: Loose by
Nelly Furtado
Polydor. Copyright 2006 Nelly Furtado, Timbaland, Danja

231 'The number of the Antichrist is not 666 but 616, according to
a fragment of the oldest surviving copy of the New Testament,
discovered in Egypt.' There are many internet sources about
this but the question is not numerical. We have matter and anti-
matter so do we have Christ and Antichrist?

233 Ignorance is Bliss: Thomas Gray was attributed. If a person
tries to know and understand something outside of their norm,
whether it is plumbing or reading Homer. Then, they are not
ignorant. Mother said, "All you can do is try Jack."
Poem: 'Ode on a distant prospect of Eton College' 1742 by
Thomas Gray

258 'I have seen pain' half of the first line. Every artist has one good
album in them – discuss.
Song : 'Cry' CD 'Back to Bedlam' by James Blunt
EMI Music Publishing/Buck Music Publishing. Copyright
2004 J Blunt, S Skarbek.
Atlantic Corp. WEA International Inc. Warner Music Group.
www.atlanticrecords.co.uk

275 Excerpts from *The Alchemist* are not as good as the book itself
so go and buy it!
Book: *The Alchemist* by Paulo Coelho
ISBN: 9780007233670 Collins Educational. Copyright 1998
Paulo Coelho

282 *'The Power of Now'.* 'I can write better than that load of twaddle.'
I have a friend who keeps this by his bed to read a little of it each
day. Contradictory? You have to try a book to know your tastes.

Book: *The Power of Now* by Eckhart Tolle
ISBN: 9781577314806 New World Library. Copyright 1997
Eckhart Tolle

286   *'The God Delusion'* is so intelligently breathtaking, it can confuse
        the weak-minded.
        Book: *The God Delusion* by Richard Dawkins
        ISBN: 9780593055489 Bantam Press. Copyright 2006
        Richard Dawkins

290   'Love Again' by Philip Larkin was one of the last Larkin poems
        in 1979 before his death. You can read the words on the
        internet but you should know more about our this British poet.
        Book: *Collected Poems* by Philip Larkin.
        ISBN: 9780571151967 The Marvell Press and Faber and
        Faber. Copyright Philip Larkin

297   'We shared a moment that will last to the end'. When you are
        on your deathbed, which man or woman will you apply this too?
        Song : 'You're beautiful' CD 'Back to Bedlam' by James Blunt.
        EMI Music Publishing/Buck Music Publishing. Copyright
        2004 J Blunt, S Skarbek, A Ghost.
        Atlantic Corp. WEA International Inc. Warner Music Group.
        www.atlanticrecords.co.uk

345   Rossini's *Tancredi* Opera. The 15th Aria.